EAST OF THE SETTING SUN

EAST OF THE SETTING SUN

A TALE OF GRAUSTARK

BY

GEORGE BARR McCUTCHEON

AUTHOR OF
**GRAUSTARK, BEVERLY OF GRAUSTARK,
THE PRINCE OF GRAUSTARK, ETC.**

GROSSET & DUNLAP
PUBLISHERS   NEW YORK

Made in the United States of America

CONTENTS

EAST OF THE SETTING SUN

CHAPTER I

WHAT ABOUT GRAUSTARK?

THERE were several outsiders in the club on this
particular night. Not "outsiders" in the strictest sense of the term; merely members who did
not belong to the little coterie of old-timers who went
there night after night and assumed, by virtue of regular
and faithful attendance, the right to occupy the most
prominent and at the same time the most comfortable
couches and chairs in the lounge—that is to say, the
cushioned hollow-square fronting the massive fireplace,
and on this particular night, it may be added, a seat close
to the roaring fire was more to be coveted than usual, for
it was not only bitterly cold outside but inside as well.
Indeed there was something distinctly and unpleasantly
suggestive of an ice-house about the interior of the club
—except, of course, in and about that hallowed region
afore-designated as a hollow square.

There were fireplaces in other parts of the club, it is
true, but none of them seemed as warm, or as jolly, or as
clubby as the big one in the lounge. As the ex-Justice

of the Supreme Court held on this very evening, one might just as well be at home as to be sitting in front of any one of the others—a remark which somehow brought the group a little closer together and, by a quite sudden shifting of chairs, perceptibly nearer to the rosy heap of logs.

As for the so-called "outsiders," they were really quite excellent gentlemen, members in good standing and of long standing, and, as a matter of fact, rather distinguished and far from objectionable. Their only offense was that they had succeeded in getting through dinner a bit earlier than the autocrats of the "hollow-square" and had daringly usurped the choicest corners of the two big davenports flanking the fender. Or it may have been a sudden revolt on their part against the despotism of custom—an uprising, so to speak, of the casual against the established. In any event, three of these reckless "outsiders" were comfortably ensconced before the great fireplace when the first of the half-dozen or more "regulars" shuffled eagerly in from the chilly dining-room to take his customary corner.

This was the General. The publisher of a big New York daily was occupying his corner. Not only was he occupying it, but he had his feet on the fender and actually was having coffee off of the huge, upholstered arm of the couch. Opposite him, on the other couch, were disposed the persons of an editor of a well-known magazine and a doctor of considerable repute, likewise having coffee.

The General was staggered but not dismayed. He squared his shoulders, advanced with the firm and au-

thoritative tread befitting his station, effected a smart
"right-about" and halted directly in front of the fireplace, his sturdy back to the blaze, his heels well-spread,
his open palms exposed to the heat. Here he tilted himself three or four times on his well-polished shoe tips before remarking in a brusque, somewhat challenging, manner (to no one in particular):

"It's a most unpleasant evening."

"This club is like a barn," said the Publisher, casting
a full inch of cigar ash upon the hearth behind the
doughty general.

"The coldest snap we've had this winter," said the
Editor. "Lord, listen to that wind!"

The shriek of the wind through the cross-town canyon
rose above the blithe crackle of the fire; there was a
persistent rattle of sleet against the lofty windows of the
lounge.

"Most unpleasant," repeated the General, his eyes on
the waiter who was bringing his after-dinner pot of coffee.
"Put it here," he commanded, indicating a spot not far
removed from the Publisher's left knee. In grave silence
he waited until the man moved up a tabouret, containing
ash-tray and matches. The silence continued while the
waiter redeemed his tray from the top of a hissing radiator and placed its contents upon the little table. Four
pairs of eyes regarded with studied silence the simple
process of pouring coffee into the cup, the subsequent
addition of sugar loaves, and then the quite orderly withdrawal of the servant into the chill regions whence he
had so recently emerged. "It's an outrage," said the
General at last.

"Well, we've got to expect cold weather in February," began the Doctor.

"I mean the way the House Committee manages to bungle everything around this Club," interrupted the General, fiercely. "Why the devil didn't they have the boilers repaired last summer?"

"Better drink your coffee, General," admonished the Publisher, cheerily. "It's likely to freeze if you let it stand too long."

"By gad, sir, you're right. Iced coffee on a night like this! It makes me shiver to think of it. And it makes me shiver all the more to think that it may freeze after I get it inside of me."

He sat down sulkily beside the Publisher and proceeded to strain the hot liquid through his bristling white mustache.

"The coffee in this Club is atrocious," he growled, staring at each of the outsiders in turn. "What we need here is a general housecleaning."

"Will you try one of these, General?" asked the Doctor, proffering a well-filled cigar case.

The General hesitated—but not for long. The Doctor's cigars were well known. He was a very fashionable doctor and his cigars also were very fashionable, in fact they were almost exclusive. While the General would not have trusted him with the care of the most unfashionable street dog in New York, he was in no doubt at all as to the quality of his cigars—and said so whenever he had the opportunity. This was one of those rare opportunities. They were large, opulent-looking cigars. He took one.

"You can't get cigars like these in this Club," he announced.

At this juncture two more of the "hollow-square" autocrats entered the lounge. They were the Admiral and the Ex-Justice of the Supreme Court. The General, perceiving that they had stopped short just inside the door, paused in the act of striking a match.

"Pull up some chairs," he called out. "Make yourselves at home."

"It's a strange thing to me that they can't heat this Club," said the Admiral, without moving. "So that members could use all parts of it."

Despite the intensely passive onslaught of the "regulars" the "outsiders" held their ground. Retreat or surrender, therefore, was the only way out of it for the former. They chose the latter.

Presently they were seated well within the boundaries of the hollow-square, attendants having dragged up several huge and unwieldy chairs. The Banker, the Bibliophile and the Landscape Architect joined the group. They, like the others, were secretly oppressed by the conviction that things had come to a pretty pass, but they too made the best of it. After all, the Publisher and the Editor were decent fellows and no doubt were entitled to seats by the fireplace, custom notwithstanding. The radiant heat from the huge logs, the defiant crackle of the flames, the fumes of good tobacco, and a genial pity for all mortals who were out in that sleetstorm, had a mellowing effect upon the momentarily disgruntled company.

The departure of the Doctor shortly after eight o'clock

caused an immediate and general disturbance. Four gentlemen struggled to their feet and politely begged each other to take the desirable seat just vacated. The Admiral, being the nearest, succeeded in taking it.

The European situation came up for discussion; a trifle later than usual, however. As a rule, it came up about seven-forty and was pretty well settled by nine o'clock, at which hour it was the custom of everybody to agree that it *couldn't* be settled at all. On this occasion the debate was late in starting—fully eighteen minutes late—because the Doctor, having supplied the cigars, was entitled to the courtesy of the floor, and he chose to talk about golf. (He was leaving the next day for Southern California.) And so, at nine o'clock, the General was but halfway through his oft-repeated and inevitable tirade against the League of Nations.

This, however, did not alter the usual trend of events. Nine o'clock was the time when everybody yawned and began to show symptoms of going home. The big clock in the hall outside had started to strike the hour. This was the signal for a great stretching of arms and jaws, accompanied by gusty, whole-hearted sighs, the majority of which bore a singularly close relation to what is best described as a howl. The General did not cease speaking; nevertheless, he yawned throughout an entire sentence, translating his words into a prolonged succession of "ows" and "ahs." He was just starting to say Czechoslovakia when the epidemic reached him.

The Judge had been gazing pensively at the fire for the better part of ten minutes.

"My daughter was asking me about it only a day or two ago," said he, irrelevantly.

"Asking you about what?" demanded the General, abruptly brought up against the fact that he hadn't been holding his audience any better than usual.

"Oh, I beg your pardon, General. I fear my thoughts were wandering," apologized the Judge, blinking rather rapidly. "In fact, my wife was also asking me about it. Seems to have completely dropped out of existence. We heard a good deal about it twelve or fifteen years ago, but not a word since the war."

He seemed on the point of sinking back into the fit of abstraction from which the General's yawn roused him, when the Admiral, looking at his watch, exclaimed:

"That infernal clock is five minutes slow. What the devil's the matter with it? Last night it was six minutes fast. It's the way things are run in this Club lately. If the— Oh, I *beg* your pardon, Judge. You were saying?"

"And now," began the Judge, frowning thoughtfully, "I'm blessed if I can think of the name of it. Stupid of me. I know it as well as I know my own."

"Describe it," said the Architect, drily.

The Judge pondered deeply. He seemed to be in the agony of concentration. He fixed the newspaper Publisher with an accusing, almost threatening eye.

"You ought to know," he said, sternly. "It's your business to know all about such things."

"You flatter me, Judge, but I'm not a mind-reader."

"Hurry up," said the General, impolitely. "I ordered my taxi for nine-fifteen."

"Why, you know what I mean," said the Judge, irritably. "What's the name of that confounded little principality over there in the Balkans? The one with the queer name."

"Good Lord, sir," cried the Editor; "the Balkans are full of little principalities with queer names."

"Well, dammit," barked the Judge, "mention some of them."

"Why, my dear Judge, the Balkans—the rowdy old Balkans—were so mangled by the dogs of war that there isn't anything left of 'em to speak of," said the Publisher. "Jugo-Slavia swallowed a lot of those little states and Czechoslovakia gobbled up a lot more. I doubt very much if there are any of them left. I say!" he broke off abruptly, sitting up straight, a flash of interest in his eyes —the eager flash of the newspaper man who scents a "story." "You don't mean Graustark, do you?"

"That's it," cried the Judge. "Graustark! That's the very country I mean. What has become of Graustark? What did she do in the great war and what happened to her afterwards? My daughter was asking me about—"

"Graustark wasn't big enough to cut much of a figure in the war," remarked the General. "Had a fine little army, it's true, but it wouldn't have lasted ten minutes on either front. I met the Commander-in-Chief when he was over here some years ago. Can't recall his name. He came over with the Prince. Nice youngster, that Prince. Part American, you know."

"No navy at all," announced the Admiral, sitting comfortably back in his chair.

"Gad, I have no recollection of Graustark being mentioned at all in connection with the war," said the Publisher, thoughtfully. "I dare say she was in it—everybody was—but whether she was with the Allies on the Eastern front or with Austria and the Bulgars I swear I haven't the remotest idea."

"Well, it's about time you found out, isn't it?" suggested the Judge, pointedly. "If I ran a big newspaper, such as yours is, I'd— But every man to his trade, I suppose. I daresay you know what the public wants better than I do."

The Publisher stiffened. "My dear Judge, you must not condemn my newspaper because of the manifest incompetence of its publisher. I fancy if we were to go back over the files we'd find all we want to know about Graustark. She's probably been lost in the shuffle since the war but certainly she took part in it, and that being the case—well, I don't quite see how she could have kept out of print, do you?" He spoke in a kindly, tolerant manner, as one addressing a child in need of encouragement.

The Judge grunted, thus indicating that he was no child.

"More than likely the Bolsheviks have grabbed her," said the Banker. "Graustark was a prosperous, happy little country, just the sort of thing they'd grab and devour at one meal. The chances are the infernal beasts have ravaged the country, massacred the rulers and all the nobility, debased the women and—and all that sort of thing. Pauperized her, prostituted her, everlastingly ruined her."

"Spoken like a true capitalist," said the Bibliophile.

"That reminds me," mused the Magazine Editor. "Speaking of capital, didn't old man Blithers try to buy the Prince of Graustark for his daughter a few years ago? Great deal of talk about a romantic international marriage, more talk about the Blithers millions saving Graustark from bankruptcy, and then the whole thing going up in smoke because the Blithers girl up and married an American boy without a dollar to his name, or something of the sort."

"Will I ever forget it," groaned the Newspaper Publisher. "We sent a man clear across Europe to run down that story, kept him in Graustark for a month or two dogging old man Blithers. By the way, I haven't seen Blithers in the Club for months. Doesn't he ever come around any more?"

"He didn't get over the jar," said the Banker, "until he became a grandfather. He stays at home nowadays, amusing the kids, I understand. He's got four grandchildren and—"

The Judge broke in: "What surprises me is that you editors haven't realized the value of a news story concerning Graustark and the fate of her people. Thousands of people would be interested in—why, by George, just think of the people who would like to know whether that jolly young Prince and his Princess and all the Royal Family were slaughtered by the Bolsheviks, or wiped out by the War, or exiled, or turned into paupers begging for food in the streets through which they used to ride in pomp and splendor. Damme, I believe I could make a good story out of it myself."

The Publisher got up and started toward the door.

"Wait till I call up the office," he said crisply. There was an eager, aggressive note in his voice. "You've started something, Judge. You're right about there being a good news story in it." He stopped at the door. "As I said before, there must have been some mention in the press about Graustark's position and activities during the war, but if there was I've forgotten it and so have all the rest of you. I'll get Ratchett on the telephone. He's been over Europe from one end to the other, working on post-war conditions. He'll know if anybody does. I'll bet my head he knows more about the map of Europe to-day than the Europeans themselves. You know what a shark he is, Jim, in these international—"

"Don't stand there in the door!" boomed the General. "You'll freeze to death, man, and then the news will be delayed in transmission, as you newspaper fellows say."

The Publisher was gone ten minutes. On his return he found the cronies in a state of drowsy reflection. Indeed, some of them appeared to be dreaming, albeit their eyes were wide open and fixed on the replenished fire. It was easy to see that their thoughts were of that far-off, tidy little land in the turbulent East and of the good old days when the very name of Graustark stirred the imagination and played upon the fancy of young and old alike —Graustark, gray and strong and serene among its everlasting hills.

"Well?" demanded the Judge. "Was she blown off the map altogether?"

"I couldn't believe my ears at first," said the great Publisher, planting himself before the fire and sweeping the lounging group with a somewhat defensive gaze.

"Ratchett hasn't the slightest idea what has happened to Graustark. Admits he'd clean forgotten her existence."

"And you discharged him on the spot," said the Judge, more as an assertion than as a question. There could be no doubt as to what he would have done in the circumstances.

"Certainly not," replied the Publisher, smiling. "I merely instructed him to get busy and find out. It's just as I suspected. Graustark was like a speck of dust in a sandstorm. She has been completely lost sight of in the great upheaval. Ratchett is of the opinion that she has been absorbed by one of the new republics over there and has lost her identity. He is getting Washington on the 'phone at once. Some one at the Czecho-slovakian or the Jugo-Slavian embassies will no doubt give him the desired information."

"Have we got to stay here till this man Ratchett of yours gets in touch with Czechoslovakia?" growled the Judge. "Doesn't he know what time it is? Does he suppose the people in that Embassy have no office hours? Confound it, man, he may have to rout 'em out of bed— and we may be here till midnight, waiting to hear from him."

"I didn't ask him to call me back, Judge. I—"

"You didn't?" demanded the Judge, stonily.

"Well, I'll be jiggered!" cried the General, scowling ferociously. "Why did you call him up in the first place if you didn't intend to have him let us know the result of his inquiry? Seems to me you might have—"

The Publisher broke in upon him hastily. "Sorry! I'll get him again. Stupid of me. I'll have him call me here.

as soon as he gets an answer from Washington. But it may take him an hour or two, gentlemen. Do you feel like waiting on the chance that—"

"Ring that bell beside you, please," interrupted the Banker, briskly, addressing the Bibliophile. "I want to order some cigars."

"Good!" exclaimed the Architect. "I've been dreading the thought of going out in all this beastly storm."

The Admiral, weatherwise, spoke up. "Poke up the fire, boy, and put on a couple of logs. The worst of the storm will be over in an hour or so. I'm for staying in harbor till the gale subsides. Call your man Ratchett and tell him to get busy."

"He may need an interpreter," boomed the General after the vanishing Publisher.

"Now bring me some cigars, boy," ordered the Banker.

"Long ones," drawled the Architect.

They were all lighting long, black cigars when the Publisher rejoined them.

"He's got a call in for Washington. I've asked him to get in touch with me as soon as he hears anything," said he, rubbing his hands. "I say, Judge, you've started something, as they say in the City room. There's a darned good story to be had out of this Graustark mystery. Ratchett's as keen as the deuce about it. He says all America will be interested, and I believe he's right. If he finds there is a big story in it, I shall probably shoot him over there immediately."

"See here," broke in the Magazine Editor, a far-seeing, shrewd man of experience; "if I were you I wouldn't let Ratchett handle it. He's a cold-blooded intellectual, a methodical, analytical, old-fashioned journalist, accurate but as dry as dust. He'll make a hash of it. You'll get the dull, prosaic facts and your readers will be bored stiff. Ratchett has no vision, no imagination. Oh, I confess he's a shark on international affairs, military strategy and all that, but he's not the man for this job. As well send over your literary editor, who can tell you what a book looks like but who half the time doesn't know what's inside of it. You want some one on this job who can get inside of it and from that position look out at the rest of the world."

"I don't want any of your confounded novelists tackling it," grumbled the Publisher. "I wouldn't trust one of 'em around the corner. What I'm after is fact, not fiction."

"Lord bless you, I wouldn't dream of letting an author tackle it. I agree with you there, old man. You're right. You couldn't trust a novelist with this sort of thing. He'd muddle it. They always do, when you pin 'em down to facts. But what you do want is a trained, wide-awake feature writer—neither a novelist nor a journalist—just a live, keen, observing young fellow who can see without spectacles. It may even call for a daring, resourceful chap, perhaps a fool-hardy one. Ratchett isn't that sort. He'd sit around the Department of State, the War Office or the Museum of Natural History all day long, compiling statistics. A novelist—God bless 'em—would cook up a harebrained love story and paint word pictures of moonlight scenes in the Castle grounds and all that kind of rubbish. A clever young special writer would go slapbang at the heart of things and he'd turn out something that would be a darned sight more interesting than fiction and twice as authentic as fact. I know the very man for you—if you can get him. He's done three or four things for me and they've been corking."

"You don't mean Yorke," said the Publisher, pursing his lips and squinting doubtfully.

"That's the chap—Pendennis Yorke. Why, he poked his nose farther in Tut's Tomb than the excavators themselves and he saw more. Every bit of it verified, too, you'll remember. He did that story about the Czar of Russia and his family a year or two ago. Got as near to the bottom of that awful business as anybody ever can or will get. Then there was all that inside stuff he turned out concerning the Bela Kun régime in Hungary. Cleverest, most engaging chap I know. He isn't what you'd call a literary man, but he can write. He knows what to write about and how to write it. Take my advice and don't send old Ratchett over there on this job. Try for Denny Yorke. He's in London now. I asked him to go to Ireland and get the inside facts about conditions there. He wrote me he'd done a lot of fool things in his time but he'd be hanged if he would ever be fool enough to put his head in the lion's mouth, because—and this is rather quaint—he figured that if the angry lion were to close his jaws and begin to chew he would be utterly defenseless against the shillalahs with which the Irish would proceed to belabor him. This letter came only a day or two ago. He said he was planning to take a long rest. But I daresay if you were to make it worth his while, he'd tackle this job for you. After all he's been through, he might even regard it as a vacation."

"Where can I reach him?" demanded the Publisher, crisply.

"I will give you his address. Cable your London office to get in touch with him at once. For that matter, I think the story properly belongs in a magazine. It's certainly magazine material now, not stuff for the newspapers. I ought to go after it myself."

"The field is open, old man," said the Publisher, affably. He had his hands in his trouser pockets at the time. Whether it was intentional or merely an unconscious habit of his, he jingled some loose coins in one of these pockets.

"I can't buck against your bank account," lamented the Editor with a grimace. "Go ahead! I'm out of it. I only wish I'd thought of it first. Besides, it would be a sin and an outrage to bring the story out in a monthly magazine. The Judge here, for one, is entitled to some consideration. He'll want it hot off the press, in daily installments—for breakfast every morning—not carefully secreted once a month among our advertisements."

He spoke feelingly, for he was merely the editor of the magazine and not the head of its advertising department.

"How long do you suppose it will take that man Ratchett of yours to get in touch with the people in Washington?" broke in the General, impatiently.

"The storm may cause some delay in getting through, but I fancy he'll not be more than an hour or two."

"I hope you told him we can't stay here all night."

"By the way," said the Bibliophile, musingly; "didn't one of those Princes over there marry a Virginia girl some years ago? A Miss Calhoun, if I remember correctly."

"Yes; there was a Miss Beverly Calhoun who married the ruler of one of those petty kingdoms, a good many years ago—twenty-five or thirty, I should say," replied the Editor. "My wife used to know her in Washington. I think they went to the same school. Let me see, who was it she married?"

The Judge supplied the information. "She married the Prince of Dawsbergen. Thank God, my memory's coming to life. And that clears up another point. The young Prince of Graustark that Blithers tried to buy for his daughter married the Crown Princess of Dawsbergen, I forget her name. The daughter of the Calhoun girl, I mean. So now while you're about it," he hurried on, turning to the Publisher, "you might as well make a clean job of it. Find out what has become of Dawsbergen and its American Princess. There are a raft of people in this country who would like to know what has happened to Beverly Calhoun. She was— "

"Telephone, sir," announced an attendant, lifting his eyebrows slightly but respectfully for the benefit of the Publisher.

"That's Ratchett. Quick work," said that gentleman, weaving his way out through a gauntlet of outstretched legs and feet.

The February gale, instead of abating, appeared to have increased in ferocity during the last half hour. The clatter of sleet against the window panes came now in vicious gusts; the windows rattled in their sashes, the wind shrieked and yowled with pitiless fury as it scurried up the canyon toward the corner hard by. The General got up presently from his comfortable seat and went over to peer out of the window.   He came back, shaking his head.

"If this club had any gumption about it, it wouldn't pay a damned bit of attention to the Volstead Act. Especially on a night like this," he said, dejectedly.

"If it wasn't for the Volstead Act we wouldn't have to go home at nine o'clock," mumbled the Judge.   "We could stay here comfortably and—ahem!—advantageously until midnight or after."

"That's right," sighed the Admiral.   "And what's more, our wives wouldn't be uneasy about us if we were out after half-past nine or ten.   They'd know we were safe. But as it is now—why, by George, if I'm not home by ten my wife is absolutely certain that I've been waylaid and blackjacked.   It's an outrage to make the women of this country suffer that way.   Lying awake wondering *why* their husbands don't come home instead of merely wondering *when* they'll blow in.   My God, how things have changed.   I used to come in at three or four o'clock and my wife wouldn't even wake up, but now if I'm not in by ten she's so nervous and so uneasy that it takes her four or five hours to get to sleep after I do come in all safe and sound."

"And sober," drawled the Architect.

There is no telling what this might have led to but for the return of the Publisher.   He came in briskly, rubbing his hands.

"Well, what did he find out?" demanded several voices.

The Publisher opened his lips to reply.   Then suddenly his expression changed.   A slow, tantalizing smile stretched his lips, a mischievous yet triumphant gleam leaped into his eyes, and a chuckle broke in his throat. Instead of saying what he had first intended to say, he calmly substituted the following:

"I'm hanged if I'll tell you."

CHAPTER II

PENDENNIS YORKE was entertaining relatives in London. His mother, dear soul, had been unyieldingly persistent in the admonition: be nice to Uncle George and Aunt Belle. Ever since he was old enough to be aware of anything at all he was aware of the advisability of being nice to Uncle George and Aunt Belle. As a very small toddler in baggy jumpers he had learned to be nice and polite and respectful to them, although at that tender age he was not by way of knowing the reason why. And there were a great many times when he really didn't want to be nice to them, for he was a spunky youngster in whose tiny breast dwelt a heart that instinctively rebeled against avuncular discipline.

Uncle George was forever commanding him to be careful and not fall off of the chair, or to stop climbing up on the porch rail, or to watch out and not get too close to the horse's heels, or to let the matches alone, or to keep back from the fireplace, or to eat slowly, or to stop playing with the scissors, or to blow his nose, or to put down that paperknife, Penny, or you'll jab your eye out. It seemed to him that Uncle George never came to visit his mother that he didn't spend practically all of his time warning him that if he wasn't careful about something or other he'd be a cripple for life.

Auntie Belle was different. She wasn't a coward like

Uncle George. She wasn't afraid of anything. She'd let him climb all over the porch-rail, or stand up in his high-chair, or get his feet wet, or play with Fred, the coach-dog, or lean out of the window, or slide down the banisters, or almost anything. She was simply great. He often thought that she would make a much better Uncle than Uncle George. True, she had surreptitiously spanked him two or three times when he was naughty, but, even so, he loved and respected her.

As he grew older he found out the other of two reasons why he should be nice to Uncle George and Aunt Belle. The first reason—and he had known that from the beginning—was that little boys must always be polite and gentlemanly to their uncles and aunts because they were so much older and also because they were very good friends of old Santa Claus. The other reason—and the real one, it was revealed to him as he grew up—was that Uncle George was very rich and didn't have any children.

Uncle George was his mother's brother. He lived out West somewhere—out there where the gold mines are and the cattle ranches too—and mountains and bears and Indians. Pendennis couldn't understand why his uncle didn't have long hair and whiskers like Buffalo Bill and why he neglected to carry a pistol and a bowie knife. As a matter of fact, Uncle George was a thin, bald-headed man who wore spectacles, smoked cigars instead of a pipe, didn't even possess a pen-knife (at least, that was what he invariably told his nephew when that small person wanted to borrow it), never chewed tobacco, wore the same kind of clothes that mother's lawyer and the doctor and Mr. Simmons, the druggist, had on whenever he saw them—in short, Uncle George was a bitter disappointment to his nephew in his extreme youth, especially so when it came out that he had not been scalped by the Indians at all. That was not the way he lost his hair.

Denny's mother lived in Washington. He never knew his father. He had seen him, of course, but only in the most casual sort of way—that is to say, in the lofty, indifferent, unimpressed way that a babe only a few weeks old regards anything human or otherwise. Colonel Yorke died when his only son was seven weeks of age, leaving a very attractive widow, a modest estate, a fairly adequate life insurance, and a vast number of friends and acquaintances who were sincerely shocked by the passing away of so gallant a gentleman and so lovable a companion. And Denny's mother remained a widow to the end of her life, more than a score of years after the death of her husband, thus proving how much she cared for the Colonel.

She brought their boy up as she believed his father would have done had he been spared—and there were people who said, with conviction, that the Colonel could not have made so good a job of it as she did.

She cuddled him but she did not coddle him; she patted him but she did not pet him; she taught him how to walk in his own path, not hers; she saw to it that he understood the meaning of manhood long before he was out of knickers; she sympathized with him in his boyish misfortunes but she did not pamper him; and, more than all these, she made of herself the sort of mother that a boy doesn't have to lie to, no matter how shameful or how ignominious his misdeeds.

No doubt she had something besides allegiance to family in mind when she drilled her boy, with something like military severity, to be "nice" to Uncle George and Aunt Belle—but that is neither here nor there. We have no right to impute other than motives of affectionate esteem to her, and certainly no one will rise to contend that a youth should be anything but nice to his uncles and his aunts, no matter how much they may bore him or how severely they may try his patience. For when all is said and done, people cannot help being uncles and aunts.

So, at the advanced age of thirty-two, Mr. Pendennis Yorke, orphan, bachelor, gentleman vagabond, and one-time volunteer midshipman in the United States Navy, was behaving very nicely toward his Uncle George and his Aunt Belle, "showing them 'round the town," "taking them out to see the sights," "blowing them off to all there was," and helping them, in a generous sort of way, to decently and respectably obtain value received for the hard American dollars they were putting into circulation during a fortnight's stay in London. This does not mean that he allowed them to do all the spending. By no means. He spent his own hard-earned shillings and pounds with ungrudging lavishness; nothing was too good for the old folks from the land of his birth. It was their first trip abroad and they were both well along in the sixties. They had saved London for the last, because they wished to be there when their nephew was in England.

What odds if Uncle George had been shaking his head for the past eight or ten years over Pendennis and saying that he would never gather any moss? The fact remains

that he was proud of him, was secretly awed by him, and
on more than one occasion had confided to Aunt Belle
that he probably had been mistaken in prophesying that
Denny would never amount to much—although he ought
really to settle down.

And now they were at the very end of their stay in
London. They were sailing for America within twenty-
four hours after we find them dining with Pendennis
Yorke at the Savoy. Aunt Belle was dreading the voyage.
She had heard a great deal about the roughness of the
crossing in February.

"I was dreadfully ill coming over," she sighed; "and it
was as smooth as the mill pond they talk so much about.
What will it be like going back, with seas mountain high
and the ship shrouded in ice, as they say in the newspapers?"

"You'll be all right, Auntie Belle," said her nephew encouragingly. "You see, you're what is called a rough
weather sailor. People who get sick when the sea is
smooth never—*never*—feel the slightest discomfort when
it's rough."

"I wasn't sick a minute coming over," asserted Uncle
George, with a wry face. "So I guess I'll get it good and
plenty going back."

"All you have to do, Uncle George, is to drink plenty
of champagne every day," said Denny, grinning broadly
and nudging Aunt Belle.

"I'd sooner be seasick," said Uncle George, promptly.

"Now don't you go leading your Uncle George into bad
habits, Denny dear," cried Aunt Belle, her eyes twinkling. "You ought to be ashamed of yourself, advising a

young and inexperienced boy like George to break the Eighteenth Commandment."

"That's good, Auntie Belle. The Eighteenth Commandment! Thou shalt not drink."

Uncle George cleared his throat. "Penny," he began, solemnly and a trifle uncertainly, "I've been doing a good bit of thinking about you lately. I don't know just how well fixed you are financially, but I must say that I think you have been spending a great deal more money on your aunt and me than you ought." .

"Nonsense!" exclaimed the young man. "I've had a lot of fun out of it, sir, and I only wish I could have found ways of spending more money and more time on you. You see, I've never really had the chance to get even with you for all the jolly times you and Auntie Belle gave me when I was a kid."

"You've given us a wonderful time in London, Denny," broke in Aunt Belle, quickly. "You've been perfectly dear to us. If there's anything in London that you haven't shown us, I'd like to know what it is. You've tramped your legs off—"

"And I know we've kept you up long past your bed time a great many nights, Penny," put in Uncle George, drily.

(The reader of this narrative may have observed by now that young Mr. Yorke's Uncle called him Penny for short while his aunt called him Denny. This should not be the cause of confusion, nor should it be laid to faulty typography. Uncle George, a straight-forward, unoriginal person, apparently had deemed it unnecessary to go beyond the first syllable for a "nickname." Aunt Belle, more imaginative, more delicate, delved deeper into

the patronym for her pet diminutive. He was therefore
both Penny and Denny—and once in awhile, to his fond
mother, "Pennydenny.")

"And you've been so stubborn about letting us do our
share of paying, with all the money we've got," said the
old lady, frankness itself. "There is not the slightest
reason in the world why you should always be buying
the theater tickets and hiring the motor cars and paying
for meals in these expensive restaurants—and you know
it. We've been a terrible drain on you, Denny."

He squeezed her hand. "You're my people, Aunt
Belle—you and Uncle George. I've not been a very good
nephew, racketing about the world the way I do and
thinking of myself most of the time instead of being"—
he checked the word "nice" in time—"and neglecting
you. That is to say, in the matter of—"

"My dear boy," she cried, "you have not neglected us.
You have your own life to live, and you must live it as
you find it. Neglected us! I should say not. Think of
the dozens of long, wonderful letters you have written us
from all those out-of-the-way places—places your Uncle
George had never heard of until you—"

"See here!" interrupted Uncle George.

"Well, you hadn't, George. You said so yourself. Had
you ever heard of that native village in British East
Africa before Denny wrote that he'd been there and had
witnessed a royal marriage?—the time the king beheaded
all his old wives and took on a new lot of twenty or
thirty, all in a bunch? Had you?"

"Of course, I hadn't. Nobody else had ever heard of
it, either. Not even Penny."

"And just think, Denny," she went on, dismissing the subject that abruptly, "you are paid a certain amount for every word you write for the magazines. I suppose you must have wasted four or five thousand words on us. I don't know how much it would amount to if you figured it up at your regular rates, but quite a sum, I'm sure. You gave us all that for nothing—it was almost like money out of your own pocket—so—"

Her nephew interrupted her with a good, hearty laugh.

"You'll be the death of me, Auntie Belle," he cried. "You think of more ways to make me feel as if I were a spendthrift! Now, really, that *is* a good one—me wasting five thousand marketable words on you!"

She smiled up into his bronzed, handsome face. "They were priceless to us, Denny," she said. Then her eyes— as they had done no end of times during the fortnight— swept his tall, strong, clean-cut figure, and her mind went, as always, back to that long dead father of his, for he too was a fine figure of a man and handsome.

Here Uncle George suddenly and somewhat peremptorily cleared his throat again. It was quite evident that he had something on his mind.

"As I was saying, Pendennis, you have undoubtedly been living at a—er—I mean, in a rather extravagant manner. The—er—present high cost of everything— rent, food, clothing and all that—must make it—er—"

"Say it, George," commanded his wife, her eyes sparkling. "Don't hem and haw and—"

"Well, what I was about to say," blurted out Uncle George, as his hand shot quickly to the inside pocket of his dinner coat and drew forth a neatly folded slip of paper, "is this. We'd like to make you a little present, your aunt and I would. It's a—ah—it's an egg."

"An egg?" gasped his nephew.

"He means a nest-egg," explained Aunt Belle.

"Of course, I do. A small nest-egg."

With that he hastily tucked the bit of paper under the edge of Pendennis's coffee-cup, and gave vent to a sharp sigh of relief. They were having coffee now in a corner of the lounge. Self-consciously, he turned his head and proceeded to re-light his cigar, affecting an unconcern he did not feel.

The slip of paper was a check for five thousand pounds.
. . . Later on, Aunt Belle said to her protesting nephew:

"You've worked hard and you deserve a rest, Denny. Take a year off, dear. Stop working for a living for a little while. Don't pay any attention to what George says about putting it aside for a rainy day. You've already had your rainy days. Go out, my dear boy, and blow it in, as we say out in Montana."

"See something of the world," beamed Uncle George, fatuously.

"See something of the world?" cried Pendennis Yorke, with a groan. "Bless your heart, Uncle George, I've seen so much of the world already that I'm sick of it. What I want to do, and what I intend to do, is to settle down where I can't see any farther than across the street."

"Aha! I smell a rat! I suspect you are thinking of getting married," exclaimed his uncle. "That's just what all young fellows say when they contemplate matrimony."

"You ought not to put such notions into my head, sir.

Getting married is a great deal more dangerous than exploring Darkest Africa."

"It's time you were getting married, Denny," said Aunt Belle, shaking her head. "You are thirty-two, going on thirty-three."

"You forget, Auntie Belle, that I've already been married and divorced," he said, a whimsical twist to his lips and a soft chuckle in his throat.

"Oh, goodness gracious! That doesn't count," she cried. "It was just a nice, clever trick and nothing more."

"A gentlemanly trick," declared Uncle George.

"You did it to be obliging," said his aunt.

"And if I were you, Pendennis," said his uncle, pursing his lips, "I should destroy that snap-shot photograph. She was an extremely pretty young woman, and if I'm any judge of things, she's somebody else's wife by this time. You oughtn't to be carrying a snap-shot of somebody else's wife around in your pocketbook, my lad. It isn't proper. Suppose something happened to you—just suppose, for instance, you were killed or became very—"

"For heaven's sake, George, don't say such a thing," cried Aunt Belle, sharply.

"I'm only supposing," explained her husband. "And suppose they were to find her picture on your person—why, it might prove to be very embarrassing to a perfectly innocent and respectable young wife. Especially as the picture reveals you in the act of kissing her hand on a railway platform."

"And a perfectly strange young woman at that," said Aunt Belle, a lively thrill in her voice.

"Heigh-o!" sighed the young man. "That *was* a great

day. I've had a lot of adventures, Uncle George, but that was the strangest of them all, and the most unreal. I wonder if I have forgotten to explain that she knew nothing about the snap-shot that Higbee took. I have an idea that she doesn't know to this day that it is in existence. I didn't know it myself till Higbee sprung it on me a week afterward."

"You really and truly never saw her after that day?" inquired his aunt, in whose soul still dwelt the spirit of romance.

"More than that," said he, "I never saw her before that day."

"Well, it all goes to prove," said Uncle George, didactically, "what a dickens of a mess civilization would be in if the Bolsheviks had their way."

"The very idea of people being married without a clergyman, or a ring, or—or anything," said Aunt Belle. "It's indecent."

Pendennis absently flicked the ash from his cigar. A dreamy look had come into his deep gray eyes.

"She was an uncommonly pretty girl, my wife was," he said, musingly. "About the prettiest girl I've ever seen. And so frightened and nervous and apprehensive she could only whisper 'I take this man to be my husband,' or words to that effect. She was really pathetic, Aunt Belle. I wonder what has become of her. I daresay she's somewhere in this big old world—happy, I hope— and no doubt laughing over that quick little dive into matrimony. That's just what it was like—a dive. She plunged right in and popped right out again, just as one does when he dives into the water."

"And then being divorced in that way," went on old-fashioned Aunt Belle, fluttering her handkerchief before her scandalized nose. "Horrible!"

Her nephew laughed. "A perfect example of the end justifying the means," said he.

"You've never told us her name, Penny," remarked his uncle.

"As a matter of fact, I didn't pay much attention to it at the time. It wasn't necessary. Moreover, I wasn't interested. I daresay she's forgotten my name. Let me see—it was five years ago. That's a long time to remember the name of a man you were married to for less than seven hours. Come to think of it, Higbee confessed that she didn't even go to the trouble of using her own name when she took me as a temporarily convenient husband. I was obliged to use my right name, of course—so, you see, she had quite a decided advantage of me. In order for her to get the passport, it was necessary for her to be the wife of a bona-fide, properly credentialed American citizen. For a matter of six or seven hours she was an American subject.

"Yes, but she wasn't really married to you—not legally, I mean," protested his aunt.

"Oh, yes, she was. According to the social laws in force during Bela Kun's brief reign, she *was* married to me. Lord, how they simplified marriage over there in Hungary in those days! Wasn't even necessary to court a girl, or be engaged to her, or anything old-fashioned like that. You just saw a girl you felt like marrying and you put it up to her, either politely or arbitrarily. If you used the right sort of persuasion, she'd say yes.

If she seemed reluctant, you either grabbed her by the hair and said, 'Come along now' or you cast your eyes up and down the street until you saw some one else that looked promising. It didn't much matter if she was already married, you see, Auntie Belle. If she took a fancy to you she could divorce her husband in two shakes of a lamb's tail, and that was all there was to it."

"Well, anyhow, Denny, you were a gentleman about it," said the old lady, proudly. "That's more than a lot of those ruffians were, I'm sure."

Something like a spasm of pain flitted across the young man's face.

"Yes, it was hellish out there, Auntie," he said, after a moment. "Worse even than it was in Russia, I was told. Thank God, it didn't last long. They kicked Bela and his so-called government out in a couple of months. There were enough Hungarian gentlemen left to do that."

"What name did she give when she married you?" persisted Uncle George, who, once he had his mind set on a thing, was as nagging as a yellow-jacket.

Pendennis stretched his long legs out and, clasping his hands behind his head, leaned back in the chair. He blew a cloud of smoke toward the ceiling before speaking.

"Good thing we decided not to go to the theater to-night," he drawled. "This is a nice, warm, jolly place for you to spend your last evening in London. It's beastly outside. Coldest night of the year, they say. Of course, it wouldn't be called cold in New York—thirty-five above, I believe it is—but, somehow, it goes right to your bones and—"

"You don't feel as though you were taking cold, do you, Denny?" said his aunt, anxiously.

"I told you not to sit with your back to the open window in the taxi," said his uncle, reverting to form.

"There you go," cried the young man. "I must say I'm disappointed in you, Aunt Belle. You never used to worry about me when I was a kid. That was Uncle George's job—and, by jove, he's still on it. No, siree! I'm just happy and comfortable, and, I suppose, a trifle impressed with my own importance. I've never felt quite comfortable or at home in this part of the Savoy before. Never felt like just crossing my legs and glaring back at all these potentates"—he indicated a near-by captain of waiters and a couple of liveried flunkies—"when they give me the haughty, supercilious once-over, as much as to say 'What the devil are you doing 'ere, you himpecunious blighter, sitting on our chairs and using up our hatmosphere?' But with five thousand pounds in my jeans— Well, if the king were to walk through here now I'd probably stroll up to him and say, kind of careless-like: 'I say, George, old man, wot's the rush? Come over 'ere and meet the Emperor and Empress of Montana!' You don't feel anywhere near as comfortable and cozy here with twenty shillings in your pocket as you do with five thousand pounds."

"Guineas," corrected Uncle George. "It calls for guineas not pounds, my boy."

"Bless my soul! I'm richer than I thought I was. We'll have another glass of cognac, Uncle George—no, let's have a beaker or a flagon of it."

"Be sensible, Denny," scolded his aunt.

"Yes, and tell me the name of the girl," commanded his uncle.

The new plutocrat sighed resignedly. "No use, I see. Well, the name she gave—I've got it written on the back of that kodak print, with the date and everything—was Rosa Schmitz."

"Good gracious! A German?"

"No, Auntie. You see, it wasn't her real name. I guess I've been rather sketchy about the little affair over there in Buda Pesth. I suppose you'd like to hear the true story of how the pretty little white girl succeeded in getting away from the ugly Reds. Well, there isn't much to it. I met Higbee in Athens shortly after the war ended. He had been in our consular service. Man about thirty-five, I should say. Splendid chap. He was hanging around Athens waiting for instructions from Washington. We saw a lot of each other and I got to know him very well. I was on my way to Palestine, but was held up in Greece for six or eight weeks while the powers that be were trying to straighten out the boundary tangle. Well, I finally got off and spent a couple of tiresome months looking for that well-known biblical joke called the Garden of Eden. You probably noticed what I had to say about the former home of our forebears, Adam and Eve. It's not what it's cracked up to be.

"But that's another story. When I got back to Salonika, I heard of the revolution in Hungary and the overthrow of the government by Bela Kun and his Reds. So I made a bee-line for Vienna and subsequently managed to get down to Buda Pesth. Strange to say, Bela wasn't slamming the door in the face of any American who happened to knock for admittance. I daresay he figured on making Red Converts of us. Well, I ran across Higbee first thing. He was connected with some sort of Commission from the States, and he'd been through the whole blooming picnic. One day he came around to my lodgings and told me a seemingly incredible yarn about what he'd been doing to aid a no inconsiderable portion of feminine Hungary to get safely out of the Bolshevik infested country. But it wasn't incredible, at all, as I soon found out. He and two or three other Americans were doing what you might call a land office business in matrimony. As I explained the other day, all a man and a woman had to do under the Bolshevik system was to declare in the presence of a witness or two that they considered themselves man and wife and the ceremony was over. They were able to divorce each other with similar ease.

"Higbee calmly informed me that within the month he had been married fourteen times to fourteen different young women. By that bit of amiability on his part, fourteen young Hungarian women of the upper classes were transformed into American citizens and were therefore entitled to privileges and protection denied their unfortunate sisters. He did exactly what I did in the case of Rosa Schmitz. He escorted each of his wives straight to the proper officials and obtained a passport for Mrs. Ethelbert Higbee, American citizen. This permitted her to leave Hungary and—well, that was the game. Just as soon as the passport was signed and delivered to her, off she and Higbee went to be divorced. As I said before, divorce was as simple and as unconventional as marriage. All they had to do was to renounce each other and, zip! they were free. See how simple it was, Auntie Belle? Doesn't it make you sore to think that if we had laws like, that in the U. S. A. you could have sacked Uncle George the first time he gave you any back talk? Don't scowl, Uncle George. You could have done the same thing to her.

"Higbee came to see me on business—very urgent business, he said. There was a young lady of his acquaintance who just simply had to get out of Hungary. So he asked me to be a good fellow and marry her. He said he'd marry her himself if it weren't for the fact that the authorities were beginning to act as if they were a little suspicious of him. Fourteen Mrs. Higbee passports issued in a month! It *was* a bit thick. Fortunately the Bolsheviks were too busy shooting the bourgeoisie to notice anything else, so he got away with it for a month or so without being interfered with. Anything to comfort a lady in distress, said I to Higbee, carelessly, just like the debonair hero in the romantic novel. I even flicked the ash off my cigarette, and no doubt I yawned slightly.

"Well, to shorten the story, he told me to be at a certain place at a certain hour the next morning and he'd introduce me to my fiancée. I was there on the second—not because I was eager to meet the young lady, but because I had a lot of work piling up on me and I wanted to get the ceremony over with. It looked as if I were doomed to waste five or six hours getting married and divorced. The principal delay, of course, would be in securing the passport. I would have to take my wife to the state department, accompanied by some one from the consul's office to vouch for me, and then, if the officials weren't watching a procession of aristocrats going to jail, we'd have the passport in no time. They did such things as that in a hurry."

He paused to gaze abstractedly at the ceiling. The hand that held his freshly lighted cigarette was arrested in its progress and remained fixed some distance from his lips.

"Did she come?" inquired Aunt Belle, somewhat breathlessly. "I mean, was she on time?"

"I was a few minutes ahead of time," said he, coming back to earth. "We were to meet at the office of an advocate in a little side street not far from what used to be known as the Magnates Quarter, the fashionable part of the city. I had been there about ten minutes when she came in, accompanied by Higbee and an elderly couple who seemed to be servants or retainers of a rather high order. The four of us repaired to a small back room where I was introduced to my prospective spouse. I confess I was completely bowled over when I had my first glimpse of her face. She was young—not more than eighteen—and really the loveliest creature I've ever seen. Rosa Schmitz! Bunk! She was a fairy princess, Aunt Belle. No use in me trying to describe her to you. I couldn't. It's not in my line. I'm trained to describe the things that are real. Well, she just simply wasn't real, that's all.

"I shall only tell you that she was fairly tall—about to my shoulder, and I'm over six feet—slim and graceful, with the carriage of a thoroughbred. Nothing plebeian or

common about Miss Rosa Schmitz, believe me. She was
rather shabbily dressed, to be sure. That's the sort of
clothes all the women wear in Austria and Hungary.
But it was neat and had once been smart. Same with her
out-of-date hat. Afterwards it occurred to me that the
gown hadn't been made for her, but for an older person.
Cast-off or handed down by some friend or relation. All
I can tell you about her features is that she had big dark
blue eyes, and they were full of pain and anxiety. She
wasn't nervous, however. She had all the pluck and
self-possession of a true-blue thoroughbred. Her face was
white and thin, not from illness but from hunger and no
doubt trouble."

"Poor child!" murmured Aunt Belle.

"Aye, poor child," echoed her nephew. "I had the
queerest feeling, Auntie Belle. All of a sudden it came
over me that I ought to pick her up in my arms and start
off afoot for France or England, where she'd be safe."

"Umph!" grunted Uncle George.

"You wouldn't have grunted like that if you'd been
there to see her," retorted his nephew.

"Or if he'd been as young as you were," added Aunt
Belle, putting on the finishing touch.

"The wedding didn't amount to much. We just simply
shook hands and said we were pleased to meet each other
and then Higbee called the advocate in. I've forgotten
to state that she spoke perfect English, with just the
slightest accent. She had a very nice, soft voice, which
trembled a little in spite of her efforts to control it.
Higbee prompted both of us. He had had a lot of experience and he knew the ropes. All I had to say was

'I take you, Rosa, for my wife,' and she said—let me see, just how did she put it?" He frowned thoughtfully.

" 'Same here,' would have been the quickest way," said Uncle George, attempting to be facetious when he really didn't feel that way at all.

"She said, 'I accept you, Pendennis Yorke, as my husband, according to the law.' Didn't overlook the loophole, do you see? I waited for the advocate to pronounce us man and wife, but nothing happened. He simply shook hands with us, gave each of us his business card for future reference, and said good-by very politely. Higbee gave him an American dollar and he almost dropped dead. He was suddenly a rich man. We started off at once to get the passport. It was quite a distance, so I hired a taxi. Horrible extravagance! Cost me a quarter. Higbee went with us—as chaperon, I fancy. I invited my wife and my best man to have luncheon with me. She declined. Said she couldn't think of imposing on my generosity any farther. But Higbee—who loves to eat at some one else's expense—persuaded her to change her mind. Then she had me order the driver of our vehicle—you should have seen that taxi!—she had me order him to turn around and drive back over the route we had come. This was to pick up the old couple who had witnessed the marriage. She frankly informed me that they were far more in need of a good square meal than she was. We found them and, to my amazement, they both were in tears. I don't know what she said to them, but evidently they were pleased. They actually beamed as they bowed to me over and over again, jabbering away in the Magyar tongue. She informed me that she had instructed them to join us at one o'clock at a restaurant across the way from the Opera House. Then she rather timidly, hesitatingly suggested that we make haste, she was most eager to have the passport in her possession. I remember her saying—and I felt very proud of the way she looked up at me with her big blue confiding eyes—'Only an American gentleman could be trusted as I am trusting you, Mr. Yorke. According to the law, I belong to you. I am not so sure that there are many men who would permit me to forget it.'

"Well, we got the passport, permitting Mrs. Pendennis Yorke to leave the country and travel whither she willed. Then the five of us had luncheon. My wife was not talkative. She was silent, anxious, uneasy, I could see. And, hang it all, she seemed to grow lovelier every minute. Even Higbee noticed that. I'll never forget her face— never. Of course, she's five years older now—if she's still alive—and may have lost some of her girlish, tender loveliness—but I doubt it. The chances are that the few years have ripened and glorified her. Rosa Schmitz! Begad, Aunt Belle, she actually had to hide a smile with her hand when she gave that name."

"She may have been a royal princess in disguise," murmured his aunt, in an ecstasy of imagination.

"Incognito, my dear—incognito," corrected her husband, tersely. He had just discovered that his cigar had gone out again.

"Luncheon over, we stood around awkwardly for a little while, not knowing exactly how to begin divorce proceedings. Ridiculous, wasn't it, Auntie? I mean the whole business. Here we were, a couple of civilized, sensible, decent people who believed devoutly in the sacredness of marriage, who—"

"Get on with your story, Penny," interrupted his uncle. "What did you do next?"

"Higbee had an idea. He suggested that it would be quite proper, and at the same time gallant of me, if I were to take Mrs. Yorke to a motion picture show before we got divorced. He could think of no better way for us to spend our honeymoon under the circumstances. Besides it wasn't really necessary for us to be divorced before dinner that evening, unless, of course, one of us happened to have a previous engagement. It was then that I learned she expected to catch a seven o'clock train for Bucharest, over in Rumania. She was a little doubtful at first, but finally said she thought it would be good fun. So—I took my bride to the cinema. She went to sleep in the middle of it. I am obliged to confess that her poor, sleepy little head dropped over against my shoulder."

"Oh, dear!" sighed his aunt.

"You must have been horribly embarrassed," said his uncle, grinning.

"I have never sat through a more thrilling picture," said Denny, quaintly. "But we will skip the minor details. I had to shake her quite violently—it seemed to me cruelly—in order to wake her when the show was over. You see, she hadn't had a wink of sleep in forty-eight hours, Auntie Belle. When we came out of the theater, we found the old couple waiting for us. She didn't seem to be the least bit surprised. Just smiled, thanked me for the treat—ye gods, the only treat she had out of it was an hour's sleep!—and said good-by. I reminded her of dinner. I'll swear I caught a sort of devil-may-care flash in her eyes, as much as to say to the old couple 'Stop me if you can.' They engaged in a brief argument in which it was quite evident that she came out on top. The old people, after first shaking their heads and eyeing me with some disfavor, suddenly ceased their harangue and wilted. I never saw such a change. The old man bent his knee and put his hand to his heart, the old woman following suit. It seemed to me that they looked a trifle scared. As for my wife, she stood very straight and imperious before them for a moment or two, and then calmly turned to me. 'I see no reason why I should not have dinner with my husband,' she said, rather defiantly, it seemed to me. Then, without more ado, she said she would meet me at the same restaurant at six o'clock. If I would excuse her, she would be off now to pack her bags. I offered to take her home in a taxi. She politely but firmly declined. Very sweet and gentle about it, of course, but firm. Then off she went, trailed by the old couple. I had the decency not to follow. I despise a man who spies on his wife, don't you, Auntie Belle?"

Aunt Belle started. "Why, really, Denny, I—I—"

"What I'd like to know," put in Uncle George, hastily, "is whether you held her hand while you were in that dark theater."

"You forget, Uncle George," said Denny, raising his eyebrows, "that about the first thing she did after the ceremony was to boast of the fact that she was married to an American gentleman."

"Ahem! Quite so—eh, quite so," stammered Uncle George. "Can't you take a joke?"

"The old men are the worst," said Aunt Belle, scathingly.

"Oh, now, see here!" began Uncle George, but subsided when both his wife and his nephew began to laugh heartily over his discomfiture.

Pendennis resumed his story. "We had dinner, just the two of us—the best that could be obtained in Hungary at that time, if I do say it as shouldn't. My wife was charming. She cast off much of the reserve that had marked her earlier manner and became quite gay and chatty. There was color in her cheeks, a sparkle in her eyes. She was thrilled and excited and naturally apprehensive over the prospect ahead of her. She wondered whether the passport would really get her safely out of the country—and very much doubted my vainglorious statement that Uncle Sam would blow Mr. Kun off the map if he molested an American subject. I found that she was familiar with Paris and London and all the great European capitals. She had spent a winter in St. Petersburg when she was a little girl, and another on the Riviera. She was frightfully interested in some of my experiences, by the way. Seems that Higbee had told her I was a globe-trotter. I'm sure he told her a good many lies. But she closed up like a clam when I tried to find out something about herself. Just simply implored me to forgive her, but she couldn't talk about herself or her people or her past."

"I just know she was a duchess or something," said

Aunt Belle, positively. "You don't suppose she could have been the Crown Princess of Russia—the Czar's daughter?"

He shook his head.

"Well, just as we were getting on famously with each other—we had got to the demi-tasse stage—she suddenly arose from the table. 'My train leaves at seven, Mr. Yorke,' she said,'blushing like fury, a very pretty picture of confusion. 'I—I think the time has come for us to—to be divorced.' I got up and bowed very gallantly. 'Permit me to suggest, Mrs. Yorke, that the safest time for me to divorce you would be just as you are stepping aboard the train. I could then charge you with desertion. And besides,' I went on, 'if by chance some one undertook to stop you, I would still be your husband and could even ride up the line a short distance with you.' She agreed to put off the divorce till the last minute but she wouldn't listen to me getting on the train with her. So I took her to the East Station in the Kerepeser-Strasse. There we found Higbee and the old couple. The latter were in charge of my wife's luggage—a lot of bags, bundles and boxes, all of them freshly labeled 'Mrs. Pendennis Yorke, U. S. A.'

"The sun was still high at seven o'clock. The same little advocate came up and joined us. Just as she stepped aboard, after bidding the old couple a tearful good-by, she held out her hand to me, shoulder high, mind you, and palm down. I took the hint and did what I was expected to do. I took it in mine and kissed it. On the knuckles, I remember. Then she said, quite distinctly: 'I renounce you as my husband, Pendennis

Yorke. I am no longer your wife.' I stammered something to the same effect. Higbee got his snap-shot from behind a pile of trunks, I believe. The last I saw of her was as the train pulled out. She looked out of the window of her compartment, blew me a kiss, waved her hand and—that's the end of the story, Auntie Belle. I hope, as they used to say in the story-books, that having got married she lived happy ever afterwards."

CHAPTER III

YORKE went down to Southampton the next morning and saw his relatives aboard the steamer, returning at once to London. His outlook upon life had been changed as if by magic. Five thousand guineas made all the difference in the world, so far as a hazy present was concerned, to say nothing of the future. It meant that he could knock off work for awhile, enjoy a real vacation and take things easy. All the way to London he employed his fancy in blissfully conjuring up ways and means to spend the five thousand in absolute idleness. It represented what he called "velvet." His private means and the income from his labors were amply sufficient to keep him in comfort just around the corner from "Easy Street," but not enough to admit of waste or a protracted period of idleness. Now he could gratify a dozen desires and ambitions that heretofore had been denied him; he could sit back for awhile and watch the world go by—something he hadn't been able to do since he left college.

He had always longed for a full, uninterrupted, untrammeled summer of golf—with absolutely nothing on his mind but the game. Then there was that notion of his that he'd like to spend a whole winter in New York with nothing to do but go to bed when he felt like it, get up when he was tired of being in bed, lunch at the Coffee

House Club or The Players, dine out, see a play, go to bed again and in course of time get up again. That was his idea of loafing de luxe. And that other dream of going off into the country and writing a novel!

(He did not think that writing a novel would be work!)

He was within half an hour of London before the thought occurred to him that Aunt Belle perhaps was right. No doubt he ought to get married—or at least be thinking about it. He thereupon began to think about it.

Thirty-two, strong, healthy, active, and sometimes lonely; no one depending on him, out of debt, moderately well off, industrious; of good family, passably decent habits, occasionally lonely, able to earn a living, qualified to support a wife—if he had one who wasn't too extravagant; with a fallow field of oats behind him, frequently lonely—yes, there was something to be said for Aunt Belle's suggestion.

As the train rolled into the station he was thinking of Rosa Schmitz. But, of course, it would be absolutely impossible to find another girl as lovely as she. No use thinking about Rosa.

There was a brief note awaiting him—a brief note from Shelburne, London representative of the New York *Courier-Blade*—urging him to get in touch immediately with the undersigned either in person or by wire. "Very important"—occupied a line all to itself just above Shelburne's signature. Mr. Yorke knew the *Courier-Blade* man and admired him. But with an undeposited check for five thousand guineas in his pocket and a newly formed decision in his mind to be independently rich for at least a year, he sat him down to devise a plausible excuse for rejecting any proposition Shelburne might make in case it represented work. He certainly was not going to work. That was official. Not with five thousand in his pocket, not much. (A momentary suspicion that the check might not be honored, or that the bank might have failed, was readily dissipated.) He would tell Shelburne that his health wasn't what it ought to be— touch of jungle fever. You can fool any one when you spring jungle fever on him. Even the doctors. He would have put off telegraphing until he was sure Shelburne had gone home, had he not remembered in time that there was to be a notable boxing-match that night and that the newspaper man had planned to take him to the first good one that came along. So he called up the *Courier-Blade's* office and asked for the Chief.

"Anything on for to-night?" inquired Shelburne, the instant he was put through.

This sounded auspicious, even promising. It certainly did not sound like the prelude to an invitation to go to work.

"Not a thing, old man," was the prompt reply.' "What's on your mind?"

"Come along and have dinner with me at the Cradle and the Grave. Seven-thirty. Been trying to reach you all afternoon. Got something to talk over with you. Very important. Big idea."

"I was thinking of getting to bed early. Fact is, I'm rather seedy. Not at all up to the mark for the past week or—"

"I shan't keep you from going to bed. Rush cable

from New York this noon. Imperative must see you,"
urged Shelburne, with telegraphic brevity.

"I was thinking of going to the prize fight at—"

"We'll go together. Seven-thirty sharp at the Cradle.
Don't fail. Something big, Yorke. Just in your line.
So long."

Something big, thought Pendennis grumpily, all the
time he was dressing. That meant a job, nothing less.
Well, he'd soon fix that. Simplest thing in the world to
say no, he didn't care to tackle anything at present. No,
nothing could tempt him. Very flattering to be sure, but
he couldn't consider it even if he *were* allowed to name his
own price. Money isn't everything, you know. Thanks
—but count me out on this. Such were his reflections as
he set forth to join Shelburne at the Cradle and the
Grave. Nevertheless, he was curious. What could this
thing be that was "just in his line"? Must be something
big and urgent, to call for a cablegram from New York.
Must be something out of the ordinary. Witness Shelburne's eagerness to get in touch with him. That alone
was enough to excite his curiosity. Never before had he
known an editor to so far forget himself as to seem eager
about anything.

Shelburne was not long in coming to the point. They
had barely seated themselves at a table when he drew a
cablegram from his pocket and passed it over to Yorke.

"Read for yourself, old man," he said. "Nothing up
my sleeve. Cards on the table. You see what the old
man says: 'Let him name his own terms'! He's keen
on this thing or he wouldn't be shooting a cablegram like
that over here. Damn the expense, he must have said,

when he dictated a message as long as that. He makes it very clear, doesn't he, as to what he wants? That's the old man, all over."

Yorke read: "Popular demand for full comprehensive authoritative series of articles on Graustark. Am convinced if properly handled same would be of tremendous interest. Must be exhaustive treatment of conditions before, during and after War with as much personal observation interest as obtainable. Spare no expense in matter and do not delay. Secure Yorke for purpose. Make it worth his while. In order to secure Yorke let him name his own terms if necessary. Put every facility at his command. Impress upon him necessity for quick action. What we want is story of Graustark's activities in War and consequences of same. Full details as to fate of royal family and present condition of same. Prefer accounts of individual members of Court. Economic conditions, political situation and interesting sidelights. Imperative should have some one of Yorke's untheoretical turn of mind on job. Man with vision and imagination and yet to be depended upon for accuracy. Impress importance of keeping project as secret as possible. If Yorke is not in London trace him down and present proposition. Wire result at once."

(What neither of them knew or could have suspected was that this cablegram was written in a New York Club under the able and arbitrary supervision of five or six gentlemen who knew what they wanted.)

Yorke folded the message and handed it back to Shelburne, who restored it to his pocket. Both selected what they desired from the tray of hors d'œuvres presented—and impartially recommended—by the waiter, who saw that they were Americans. As the man wriggled off among the tables, the editor spoke, and there was genuine envy in his voice.

"You lucky dog!"

Pendennis Yorke looked at him in mild astonishment.

"Oh, is that the way I should feel about it?"

"Well, don't you?"

"I'm not so sure that I do," was the other's reply.

"Good Lord! I call it the greatest compliment a fellow could have, coming from the old man himself and—"

"It is a compliment, Shelburne—a great compliment. I certainly appreciate it."

"Can you start at once?"

Yorke leaned back in his chair and laughed.

"By George, you *do* jump to conclusions, don't you? I haven't even said I'd start at all."

Shelburne stared. "You—you don't mean to say you're going to turn it down, Yorke?" he gasped.

"I shall have to think it over."

"Well, I'm damned!"

"Surprised you, eh? Thought I'd jump at it?"

"I sure did. See here, didn't you get that little line— 'name his own terms'? Well, holy smokes! What more do you want?"

"I'll let you know to-morrow afternoon, Shelburne."

"To-morrow aft— Come now, Yorke! A chance like this doesn't come in a—"

"To-morrow afternoon," repeated Yorke, firmly.

"What's the matter with to-morrow morning?" demanded the incredulous Shelburne.

His companion indulged in a slow grin. Then, affecting a bored manner, he announced:

"I'm going to sleep till noon to-morrow, that's what's the matter."

"But, good Lord, to-morrow isn't Sunday."

"You'd sleep for a week, Shelburne, if you were in my boots."

Acting on a sudden impulse, he produced his bill-folder and calmly, deliberately, extracted the check, which he handed to Shelburne.

"I guess you'd sleep well if you had that in your jeans, old top."

Shelburne blinked. "Sleep well? My God, man, I'd never wake up."

"Well, now, you cable your old man that the renowned Mr. Yorke is considering his proposition and promises to set his alarm clock for twelve o'clock sharp, noon, to-morrow, London time. I'll give you a ring at one o'clock. I admit the thing appeals to me. There's a good story in it. And besides, I've always wanted to go to Graustark. Your soup is getting cold, old chap."

The next afternoon at one, Shelburne took down the receiver.

"That you, Mr. Shelburne? Yorke speaking. I have decided to go to Graustark."

"Good," was Shelburne's laconic response. "I thought you would."

"I'll be in to see you as soon as I've been to the bank."

"Righto! By the way, I trust you slept well last night and this morning," sarcastically.

"I didn't sleep a darned wink," cheerfully.

Three days later Pendennis Yorke was on his way to Graustark. Every known convenience had been placed at his command by the powerful newspaper whose influence was not to be denied and whose ramifications reached to the farthermost ends of the earth. As the accredited representative of a great American newspaper he was assured of privileges and courtesies that would have been most grudgingly extended to any European employed in a similar undertaking. Not only was he a citizen of that most envied and at the same time most despised of all countries, but he was plentifully supplied with American gold or its equivalent.

"A dollar bill," Shelburne had said, "is really the only passport you need over in that part of Europe. I've got it figured out, Yorke. If you were to estimate the cost of a trip around the world in marks or kronen or rubles, you could circumnavigate the globe twenty times on a silver dollar and take a side-trip to the moon besides."

Yorke traveled "light." Experience had taught him that one can jump quicker and farther and land nearer the right spot if he keeps his weight down—and by weight he meant luggage. He had once declared that he could go around the world with a kit bag as his sole piece of luggage and be as immaculate at the end of the journey as at the start. For the present journey, however, he was supported by two kit-bags (one brand new), a hat box, a dressing case (very old and disgracefully marred), a "collapsible" typewriter and his dauntless camera. The extra bag and the hat box were concessions to chance; he might be invited to dine at the Royal Palace! Stranger things than that had happened to him. For example, his marriage to Rosa Schmitz. That event most certainly called for a frock coat and a silk hat—and he had had absolutely nothing to wear! Unless you would call a frayed and battered golf suit with army blue stockings something to wear at one's wedding, to say nothing of a cap that had lost some of its youth and all of its pride when he was still in college. On the other hand, it was true that on at least one occasion he had been vulgarly overdressed; an imperial wedding in Central Africa, when the King, his twenty-odd brides and all of his subjects were so simply arrayed that a single cake of soap would have sufficed to disrobe the entire tribe if applied vigorously and individually.

He carried, besides his passports and credentials, a number of letters to prominent personages in Edelweiss, the capital of Graustark. These letters had been procured for him by the energetic and persistent Shelburne, who believed in the principle of asking for what you want and if you can't get it in one way, try another.

It was no easy matter to get into Graustark. The little principality, beset on all sides by rapacious and more or less irresponsible neighbors, had been compelled to adopt strict and, on the whole, drastic regulations governing the admittance of aliens within her borders. Situated as she was in a great bowl surrounded by impassable barrier-mountains, she was in a position to enforce these regulations with the result that only those who came with proper credentials and could offer satisfactory reasons for their presence in the country were permitted to enter. Entrance to the fertile rock-bound valley was to be gained only by means of the jealously guarded mountain passes.

These portals were in charge of the military branch of the government, and while a hostile army could have forced them if attacking in considerable strength, it was next to impossible for any one to pass in time of peace except by permission of the customs officials. Woe betide the adventurer who sought to enter by stealth or the smuggler who dreamed that craft would enable him to cross the border with his contraband wares.

Yorke had soon discovered that but little information was to be gleaned in London official or diplomatic circles concerning Graustark. It was known, of course, that she had cast her lot with Serbia and Russia at the outbreak of the great war, and it was also known that her territory had not been invaded by the enemy. This was due to the fact that she was out of the direct path of Mackensen's armies and to the additional fact that her conquest and occupation would have had no strategic value in the general plan of the Teutonic High Command. Her puny but valiant army was not feared by the Austrian and German hordes that fought back the Muscovites in the early stages of the war, nor was it even considered dangerous by the armies that swept on to Bucharest in the successful campaign against Rumania.

It was of record that Graustarkian troops, together with the friendly armies of Axphain and Dawsbergen, adjoining principalities, had participated in several major engagements as a part of the great Russian Army under the command of Grand Duke Nicholas. Moreover, there was mention in dispatches—brief, it is true—from the Eastern front, of a Graustarkian force holding an important bridgehead until strong Muscovite reënforcements

came up to drive the Hungarians back. Except for such
meager reports as these, Graustark's activities in the war
were unheralded in Great Britain. Close and careful
study of reports from the Russian front revealed the
fact that in every one of the operations mentioned, Graustark troops were commanded by His Serene Highness,
Prince Robin, ruler of the little land on the edge of the
Occident.

The veil of obscurity descended upon Graustark and
its neighbors with the collapse of Russia and the fall of
Rumania. They had been mere specks to begin with;
the world easily lost sight of them in the dust raised by
the crash of Russia. It is even probable that Graustark
and her inconspicuous allies came in for a share of the
scorn and abuse that was heaped upon the faithless Rus-
sians, although no mention of them was to be found in
the press at the time or afterward. They merely dropped
out of notice. The world was not interested in trifles.
If the world gave them a thought at all, it was to hazily
wonder whether they were "red" or "white." Had the
Red Tiger gobbled them up?

The British Foreign Office managed to clear up a little
of the fog just before Yorke left London. They came
forward with the information that the former principality
of Axphain, immediately north of Graustark, had established a Soviet government after overthrowing the thou-
sand-year-old Bolaroz dynasty. There had been at least
two abortive attempts on the part of the Monarchists to
restore the Crown, and there were even now rumors of
an impending movement to overthrow the Communists.

Axphain apparently had succumbed to the influence of

Ukraine, whose able emissaries and propagandists had swooped out of the Northeast to foster discontent and revolution among the people. Graustark and Dawsbergen, so far as known, had maintained their integrity and were now supposed to be independent units in the newly created Confederacy of Czechoslovakia, although Yorke was obliged to accept as a basis for this surmise conditions as they existed at least two years in the past. He had studied maps and Continental time-tables for the better part of a night, devising the most direct and the least arduous route to Edelweiss. The tail end of a severe winter in the upper reaches of the Balkans had greatly impaired the facilities for railway travel. There were but three trains a week from Vienna to Klodso, where passengers changed to a slow, uncertain train that transported them to a division point some sixty miles from the Graustark frontier. Here they took the branch line running direct to the border town of Selnak.

Yorke was considerably dismayed by the prospect ahead. It was certain that there would be many discomforts and even worse, many delays. Nevertheless, he started off from London with a stout heart and a bland faith in the luck that had seldom failed him. He was a light-hearted chap, this Pendennis Yorke; cheerfulness had paid his way on many a weary road.

This was February. He gave himself two months at the outside to complete the task he had set unto himself. The first of May would see him back in London. As he sped down to Dover on this raw, bleak day, it was very pleasant to sink back in his seat and ruminate over future comforts to be derived from the untouched balance of five thousand guineas he had in bank—and more than once he chuckled over the astonishment of the teller who took in his check for deposit. It had been quite a shock to the poor fellow.

But his calculations were wrong. The first of May was not to see him back in London. Indeed, as it turned out, the first of May was to find him in grave doubt as to whether he would ever be in London again.

The cherished though much bethumbed picture of Rosa Schmitz on her wedding day accompanied him on the journey. The custom that tailors have of putting the pocket on the inner right side of a coat instead of the left was all that saved Rosa from reposing snugly against his heart during his waking hours.

The once luxurious Orient Express landed him in Vienna a few nights after his departure from London, and on the following morning he boarded the ramshackle unheated train for Klodso. This stage of the journey, he was informed by a lugubrious, hopeless-eyed railway official, promised to be anything but satisfactory. In the first place it was doubtful if the train would ever get through to the end of the line at all; and, in case it did, it was altogether possible that it might not accomplish the feat in one day. Frequently it took two or three. What with the dilapidated condition of the rolling stock, the wretched state of the roadbed, the shortage of fuel, the shiftlessness of crews, it was more or less certain that something would happen before the day was over, so if the gentleman would be guided by the advice of one who wished him well, although a stranger, he would remain in Vienna and not go to that God-forsaken, accursed town of Klodso. Besides, argued the forlorn official, if the gentleman didn't freeze to death on the trip he would surely starve to death when he got to Klodso. It would be much pleasanter to freeze or starve to death in Vienna, if the gentleman only knew it. A great many people were doing it, so he would not be conspicuous.

Yorke was to discover almost at the outset that the man had not drawn upon his imagination in providing him with these dolorous details. Less than twenty miles out of Vienna, the train stopped on a siding and remained there for three hours, apparently for no reason at all. At the end of that time the engine-driver decided to start up again, a praiseworthy impulse that was, however, almost frustrated by the obstinacy of the locomotive, which had to be coaxed and jerked and belabored for fully half an hour before it could be induced to move. Something, it appears, had frozen up while it loitered. Yorke, the only English-speaking person on the train, said a great many things about the system that pleased his fellow-passengers, notwithstanding the fact that they did not understand a word. It was the way he said them.

At last, after fourteen hours of laborious panting and puffing and creaking, the train finally groveled into the almost lightless depot at Klodso. It was after eleven o'clock. The platform was deserted save for the half-dozen shivering passengers who got off, and a trainman or two. A chill, damp wind smote the tired, unhappy travelers; it came from nowhere out of the black void that seemed actually to be smothering the shadowy station.

The American, with his customary foresight, had forti-

fied himself against emergency by purchasing a well-filled
lunch basket before leaving Vienna. A couple of large
thermos bottles contained hot coffee in quantity. And
yet, despite these precautions, he was almost famished at
the journey's end, for the very good reason that he had,
with true Yankee generosity, shared his provisions with
the other three occupants of the carriage, a man and two
women, all of whom had seen better and no doubt nobler
days.

There is a fine old adage that says "one good turn deserves another." It does not always work out that way,
but in this instance it did. Yorke's guests at the scanty
luncheon and even scantier dinner (the basket had been
stocked for one hearty appetite instead of four) begged
him with unintelligible earnestness to accept a lift in the
dilapidated automobile that had come to the station to
meet them. As there was no other vehicle in sight and
as he had not the remotest idea how to find a hotel, Yorke
piled in with them, bags and all. Off they rattled over
vile pavements, through dark, sinister streets, coming at
last to a dimly lighted plaza, on the far side of which
gleamed windows of what proved to be the principal
hotel in Klodso. He never knew what language it was
that his new acquaintances spoke, but whatever it was
they became suddenly and almost alarmingly prodigal in
the use of it. He gathered that they were saying good-by
to him and perhaps wishing him good luck. They made
a vocal racket of such intensity in front of the hotel that
a startled porter came out to see whether a fresh revolution had started. They had been silent and strangely
aloof up to the moment of parting, and certainly there

had been nothing in their deportment to prepare him for the physical demonstration of gratitude that took place in front of the hotel.

All three of them embraced him. The two women kissed him (he wouldn't have minded that if their lips had been warm) and then the man, apparently overcome by some swift uncontrollable impulse, also kissed him violently on both cheeks. The driver too was talking loudly, earnestly. For a moment Yorke feared that he was about to be favored with a kiss from this bewhiskered menial, but it blew over. He caught one phase that was repeated over and over again, tenderly and solicitously by the women, emphatically by the men. He did not know what it was, but he was pleased to translate it into "God bless you." Later on as he shivered in a hard little bed in an unbelievably vast and icy room, he decided that the second word was "help" instead of "bless."

The next morning he discovered that the head waiter—a one-legged chap—could speak English. He was a Hungarian who had worked for three years at the Waldorf-Astoria in New York, and who wished with great bitterness that he had remained in America instead of hurrying back to the Fatherland only to have his leg shot off at Lemberg. From this repentant individual he ascertained that a train usually left for Selnak at ten o'clock. It would pay the gentleman, however, to inquire at the railway station before making preparations to catch that or any other train leaving Klodso. One never could tell about trains in these days. Sometimes they got stalled up or down the line and were abandoned by the crews.

Any one could see, he went on to explain, that a train could not start out of Klodso unless it first came in from somewhere else. And then there was always the chance that even though the engine was working properly, the crew wouldn't be working at all. Besides, it was said that the tracks were not always to be depended upon because the peasants, being terribly in need of fuel, tore them up, in order to use the ties for home consumption. Also, he had heard from a quite reliable source that the bridges to the North were not safe. Moreover brigands frequently stole entire trains, passengers and all, making off with them into the hills.

"How the deuce could they make off into hills with a railway train?" demanded the skeptical Mr. Yorke.

"It is very simple, gentleman," replied the waiter, shrugging his shoulders. "During the war the government constructed a great many little spurs for the purpose of shifting men and munitions from point to point with the least possible delay. After the war they forgot to remove them. So there you are, gentleman."

"I see," said Mr. Yorke, thoughtfully. "By the way, have you ever been in Edelweiss?"

"Not since the war," replied the waiter, a frown darkening his brow. "I was there when I was a boy living in Buda Pesth, gentleman. In those days all people from my country were welcome in Graustark. Now it is different. They do not receive us with open arms, unless we come with excellent recommendations. They are very strict and very unreasonable, gentleman, at the frontier."

"With reason, perhaps," said Yorke drily, "in view of

what you tell me of the brigands on this side of the border."

The man's eyes narrowed. "The time will surely come, gentleman, when—" He checked the words abruptly and moved off. Yorke observed that his hand was clenched.

CHAPTER IV

A GUARD on the train that afternoon threw considerable light on this cryptic, uncompleted remark. He was a grizzled old fellow, who had been in the service of the Graustark State Railroad for many years. He spoke English fairly well and was not averse to a friendly chat with the young American traveler.

Yorke had been permitted to cross the frontier after a rigid but courteous examination by the customs officials at Selnak, who went to considerable pains to convince him that it was not only a private but a national joy as well to behold an American in the act of setting foot upon the soil of Graustark. The Klodso train, much to its own surprise, had started on schedule and had arrived at the Graustark frontier post almost an hour ahead of time —a feat due solely to bribery on the part of one of its passengers, who, it seems, made judicious use of a handful of silver coins, each of which bore in excellent English the talisman: "In God We Trust."

"You must remember, sir," said the guard, confidentially, "that Graustark is looked upon as the land of plenty. It is not surprising that those worthless pigs down below envy and despise us. They have got their bellies full of Communism and precious little else. It

64

galls them, sir, to know that the people of Graustark subsist upon the grain, while the best they can have is the
husk. I pity them. They are human beings and they
have been betrayed, deceived, defiled. They were promised paradise and what do they get? Purgatory, sir. The
Red Specter stalks among them, keeping them alive with
promises that never can be fulfilled. And when the same
Red Specter comes to our gates it is turned away and has
to fall back among those who created it. So, sir, they
hate us because we have kept our house in order and are
content to toil for our daily bread. If they could they
would break down our walls and scatter desolation
among us. But we have so far succeeded in keeping them
out. They have tried to seduce us, but we still retain our
honor. That irks them, sir. It is the same as if the
wanton and the prostitute scoffed at the virgin. This
fellow who spoke with you in Klodso and had an evil
look in his eye was once a decent, honest man, I have no
doubt. He probably considers himself honest now. But
the Red Specter is behind him and he does not dare look
backward. Beyond these barrier mountains of ours he
knows there is a land of plenty. He is hungry, so he
snarls at us. It is the way with dogs, sir."

"Am I to understand that they have tried to overthrow
your government?"

"Alas, not only have they tried but they are still trying.
You may not know, sir, that north of us lies Axphain,
once a prosperous state, but now a vast pig-sty. The
leading men of that unhappy land are constantly imploring Graustark and Dawsbergen to aid them in the effort
to restore the old government and to crush out Com-

munism. On the other hand, vicious and fanatical agents
of the Communists steal in among our people to spread
the so-called gospel of liberty and equality. They seek
endlessly to corrupt our peasants, to convince them that
they are oppressed by wealth, to show them how to throw
off the yoke and be kings and queens instead of serfs."

"Are they making any headway?"

The guard smiled, a little grimly. "Only last week,
sir, near the town of Ganlook, six Bolshevik agitators
from Axphain were seized by an angry crowd of peasants
and hanged to telegraph poles. In cutting them down
later on, the citizens, realizing that they probably would
have further use for good stout ropes, simply slashed off
the heads and let the bodies drop to the ground. And
the heads, too, for that matter." He hesitated and then
went on drily: "That is the kind of headway they are
making, sir."

Yorke was too wise to question him further about government affairs or to seek information concerning the
royal household. He would have gained nothing by pursuing such a course. On the contrary it is quite probable
that he would have inspired distrust and suspicion in the
mind of the man. Graustark, he reflected, was constantly
on the lookout for spies and mischief-makers, and this
man was a government employee.

The train pounded noisily and laboriously over a ser-
pentine track, along the bank of a turbulent ice-strewn
river, charging down through the gaps in the mountains.
The range over which it was creeping in such a tortuous,
snail-like way was made up of a series of lofty, rugged
peaks whose crests were bare of vegetation and capped

with snow. The railway, following the course of the river, clung precariously to the rocky base of towering eminences, on one side of the sinister defile. Scarce a mile distant on the opposite side of the river, stupendous heights reared themselves with unbelievable abruptness, reflecting in a sense the invisible peaks the train was skirting.

Yorke was impressed by the invulnerable nature of this gigantic barricade protecting the snug little principality of Graustark. What a stronghold it was! What an impregnable barrier God had thrown up about the mysterious, delectable bowl of plenty that lay so safely out of reach of the ravenous world!

The afternoon was well spent before the train began to slip out from among the monster hills, revealing occasional views of the uneven plains and woodlands of Graustark. Presently small farms and fields took their place in the picture; then the spires and towers of hidden villages far off the railway line; then quarries gleaming white in the March sunshine, and the gaunt black chimneys and shafts of mines on the slopes. Wagon roads scarred the open spaces, thin white threads stretching off to the north—always to the north. For in the north, forty miles away, lay Edelweiss, the capital, cradled among the foothills of the encircling range. Herds of cattle, flocks of sheep, ox-drawn carts on the distant knolls and highways; later on human figures in fields and door yards —women in bright colored dresses; men in faded green coats or capes, with dirty white leggings and peaked leathern hats; children in belted smocks of various hues.

The woodlands were of hardy mountain firs and pines, dull green masses under a turquoise sky. There was no snow on the brown, winter-stripped earth, but the ever-narrowing river was filled with swift-moving cakes and floes of ice.

There were but few passengers on the train. Yorke had a compartment all to himself. He was not lonely, however, nor bored. He had his thoughts, his imagination, to keep him company. The latter, at least, was sprightly. It had saved him many a lonely hour in far lonelier places than this. Besides, the friendly guard paid him frequent visits.

They were slowing down for a small mountainside station when the guard came in and closed the corridor door behind him.

"I regret to inform you, sir, that all passengers traveling to the capital must be discharged at Haddok, a station on this side of the river eight kilometers from Edelweiss. The bridge is unsafe. We dare not cross. It has been so for more than a fortnight. The floods and the ice have weakened it dangerously. Up to last week travelers crossed on the ice but now that is impossible. A footpath of timber has been placed across the bridge between the rails. Passengers are expected to cross the bridge afoot. It is quite safe. Diligences meet them at the other end and transfer them to the city. In your case, sir, a motor car will be in waiting."

Yorke's dismay gave way to surprise. "A motor car for me?"

"Yes, Mr. Pendennis Yorke, a motor car."

"You know my name?"

"Most certainly, sir. Is it not revealed on your passport?"

"Of course—to be sure. But why a motor for me? Why this distinction?"

"That question, sir, I cannot answer. I only know that you are to be met at the bridge and driven speedily to the Hotel Regengetz, where suitable accommodations await you."

"But how the devil did any one know I was coming by this train? I did not telegraph ahead."

"I can only say, sir, that we were advised you would arrive in Klodso to-day. Our instructions were to be on the lookout for you and to see that you had every comfort within our means to provide."

"Oho! That accounts for the very excellent luncheon I had after leaving Selnak—for which I was to settle at the end of the journey, I think you said. And also that astonishingly fine bottle of wine that came with it."

The guard smiled. "Yes, sir—and also for this electric heater, without which you would have found the journey most disagreeable."

"Well, I'm blessed! And I daresay we may also include your own polite and friendly company in the list of comforts?"

"If you are pleased to so describe my duties, sir," said the guard modestly. "I may be pardoned for adding, Mr. Yorke, that I happen to be the only guard in the service who speaks English."

"Well, I'll be jiggered!" exclaimed Yorke, surprised into a distinctly American ejaculation. "Gad, you can't beat that for attention, can you?"

"There are two ways of looking at it, sir," said the guard, and Yorke gave him a sharp look.

"I see. They wanted to know what I had to say for myself, eh?"

"Oh, no, sir. You misunderstand me. What I meant was that my efforts to make the journey less lonely may have proved a burden to you. One never can tell, sir. I trust I have not disturbed you with my—"

"Bless you, no! You've been a life-saver."

"I beg your pardon, sir?"

"I mean to say, a great comfort to me. I have enjoyed our little chats. By the way, if you will let me have the bill for my lunch I will settle it now. We must be nearly at the end of the journey."

The guard shook his head. "I am afraid it cannot be done, Mr. Yorke. My orders were plain. At the end of the journey, I was instructed to inform you."

"Well then, would you mind informing me who it is I am to settle with at the end of the journey?"

"My orders are not so elastic as that, sir," replied the guard, something like finality in his tone.

"Far be it for me to complain," exclaimed Yorke. "I partake of a surpassingly fine luncheon—better than anything I've ever seen on a train even in America—and my credit is so good that— By gracious! Now that I think of it, it's a long sight better than it is even in my own country. I'd like to see the dining-car conductor over there who would let me out of his sight till after I'd paid up and tipped the waiter besides."

"You may not have observed, sir, that we carry no restaurant-car on this train," said the man quietly.

Yorke started. "I can't remember rubbing a lamp as Aladdin did, and presto! a magic feast is served. If you haven't a dining-car, where the deuce did my luncheon come from?"

"I am at liberty to state that it came down with us from Edelweiss this morning in charge of a special chef and the waiter who served you. The third compartment back of this was turned into a temporary kitchen for the day, a small campaign stove being installed. I hope you did not notice the smell of cooking, sir."

The American was dumbfounded. "See here," he began seriously. "What does all this mean? Who is back of all this?"

"I am only a servant, Mr. Yorke," replied the guard with dignity.

"I understand," said Yorke, after a moment. "Meaning, I take it, that you are simply obeying orders?"

"Yes, sir. Obeying orders."

"No use asking any more questions, I suppose?"

"May I be pardoned for saying that it would be a waste of breath?"

"You don't look like the Sphinx," said Yorke, whimsically. Suddenly he sat up very straight. "By George, I've got it! It's a case of mistaken identity. They've got me confused with some royal nibs traveling incog. Good Lord! What a situation! Wonderful idea for a farce—if I were only a comedian. See here, my friend, who do they really think I am?"

"There is no mistake," said the guard, quietly. "You are Mr. Pendennis Yorke, plain American citizen. Your name, sir, is very well known in Graustark and has been for quite a long time."

"Great Scott! You don't mean to tell me they read my stuff out here in Graustark!"

"I cannot say as to that. Nevertheless, it is a very well-known name. And now, sir, it is my privilege to instruct you as to how you are to proceed after leaving the train at Haddok. You will confer a favor on the railway officials and accommodate the rest of the passengers if you will be ready to disembark the instant the train stops. There will be persons on hand to take immediate charge of your luggage. You will follow these bearers without delay across the bridge. Not until you are safely over and the motor car is under way will the rest of the passengers be permitted to cross. These are our orders, sir. I trust you will be good enough to assist us in carrying them out."

"Pinch me," was all that Yorke could say.

It was not a dream as he found out the instant the train came to a standstill at Haddok. His bags were snatched up by two uniformed men and whisked forward in the wake of a bobbing lantern.

Night had fallen swiftly, suddenly. Yorke did not hesitate. He promptly fell in behind the two men, keeping close to their heels as they strode off alongside the forward carriages. He was thrilled—he was excited and eager. It was all so very mysterious, so very puzzling, this extraordinary interest that was being taken in his welfare. Who was he that a whole trainload of people should be commanded to sit still while he crossed the trestle without fear of being jostled? Who was he that he should have a special kitchen, a special guard, special porters and a private automobile? Surely he could not be that inconsequential person he had always suspected of being Pendennis Yorke! No, indeed! He must be a person of considerable importance. And such being the case, he couldn't possibly be Pendennis Yorke. That explained everything. He wasn't himself.

They passed the panting locomotive and then took to the center of the track. A short distance ahead of the luggage-carriers walked two men, one of whom carried the lantern. Yorke blinked rapidly. His pace slackened. The headlight of the engine revealed them to be soldiers! A voice behind him called out in English:

"Do not be alarmed. The bridge is quite safe for foot passengers."

He whirled and beheld a tall man in the uniform of an army officer stalking along not ten feet behind him. A swift scrutiny disclosed the somewhat consoling absence of sword or side-arms.

"Hullo!" exclaimed the American, coming to a halt. The officer favored him with a quick, jerky salute, as he drew up beside him.

Yorke took in the uniform at a glance. It recalled the smart, splendid garb of the Austrian officer of the olden days before the war. A red cap trimmed with silver, a short, snug-fitting green overcoat glistening with braid and bedecked with orders; a red belt with a gold scabbard-chain; white trousers and high black cavalry boots. The wearer of this showy raiment was a dark-faced, dashing young man of about his own age. He had a peculiarly engaging smile.

"I am Captain Sambo, Mr. Yorke, of the Graustark Patrol," he announced, extending his hand.

"Sambo?" York repeated, uncertain whether to laugh or not. He grasped the Captain's hand.

"Rodovic Franz Joseph Sambo, at your service. I trust you had a comfortable trip up, sir."

"Very," said Yorke, briefly. "Sambo? The name is very familiar, Captain."

They were walking rapidly toward the bridge now.

"I am of the fourteenth generation," said the other, not without a trace of pride in his voice.

Yorke saw that he was not expected to laugh. He decided that it was better not to remark that there were a great many Sambos in America.

"My word!" he exclaimed. "You certainly do go back a long way over here, Captain. That ought to take the Sambo family back to the flood."

"The first Sambo of record, Mr. Yorke, was a bowman in the service of Black Queen Yanzi, who reigned at the beginning of the fifteenth century. She was called the Black Queen, as you may already know, because the whole world turned black for a short time on her coronation day. A total eclipse of the sun, as we would perfectly well understand in these days. But in those days, a terrifying revelation of God's displeasure. The poor lady was beheaded in the third year of her reign, the people holding her accountable for the pestilence that swept over the country that year. There were Sambos before him no doubt," he went on, smilingly, "but we are afraid to dig them up. He appears to have been an honest fellow. His father—it is only natural that he should have had one—may have been a rascal. Here we are at the bridge. It is quite a long one, just keep to the center of the footway and you will be in no danger. Or if you prefer to take my arm in case the rush of water below should cause you to become nervous or giddy, please do not hesitate to—"

"I will be all right, thanks. Awfully kind of you, Captain, but I'm used to walking the straight and narrow path."

The Captain chuckled softly as he dropped behind.

"Mighty decent, attractive chap," thought Yorke, considerably gratified over that responsive chuckle.

They came in due time to the far end of the long bridge. After proceeding several hundred yards ahead on the permanent way, the soldiers and the carriers turned off the embankment and ran down to the highway below. By the time Yorke and the officer came up with them, the former's bags and belongings had been stowed inside the waiting automobile, the soldiers were standing at attention and a liveried footman was holding open the door of the big limousine. On ahead were a number of smaller cars and several cumbersome-looking horse-drawn diligences, relics of a bygone, turtle-paced era.

"After you, Mr. Yorke," said the Captain, as the American hesitated.

Yorke had noticed a little group of uniformed motorcyclists at the roadside a few rods farther on.

"Is this really intended for me?" he inquired, still incredulous and undecided.

"Most certainly, sir," replied the officer, and Yorke was positive that he caught a note of surprise in the man's voice, as if to say, "For whom else, pray?"

"Well, I'll take your word for it, Captain," said the bewildered American, putting his foot on the running board. "Remember, it's your mistake, not mine, if any-thing comes of this."

"I fear I do not quite grasp you—"

"I mean to say, if we're yanked up and court-mar·· tialed for this."

"Oh?" This was uttered with a coldly rising inflec-tion that left no doubt as to the Captain's disapproval of so flippant a jest.

Yorke entered the car and was followed by Captain Sambo. A moment later the footman sprang up beside the man at the wheel and the car was off. It glided through the lane of cars and diligences and was soon tearing along through the night at a smart clip. Near at hand, but invisible to the occupants of the car, raced the motor-cycle squad, the roar of their machines rising above the muffled thunder of the limousine.

"I don't mind, saying, Captain, that this has got me guessing," ventured Yorke, almost pleadingly, when they had gone a mile or so without speaking.

Captain Sambo relaxed a little. He had stiffened noticeably after Yorke's unintentional reflection upon his official integrity.

"Even so, Mr. Yorke, I cannot see wherein we are lay-ing ourselves open to court-martial or—"

"Oh, my dear fellow," cried his companion, heartily; "you must never take an American seriously on such

short acquaintance. If you should come to know me
better—and I hope you may—you'll learn to pay absolutely no attention to half the things I say."

"I see. Then you were not actually intimating that—"

"Not at all, not at all. I was merely exercising what
is commonly known as our American humor. Sorry it
didn't make a hit with you. You see we Americans are
not supposed to take anything very seriously except our
humor, and when that fails us—well, we're lost, that's
all."

"Ah, now I am beginning to realize how very quaint
your famous American humor can be, Mr. Yorke. We,
of Graustark, should be thoroughly familiar with it by
this time, however. His Serene Highness, Prince Robin,
is half-American by birth. More than half by nature, I
should say. His father, the late Prince Consort, was an
American. The present Princess is half-American. She
is, as you may already know, the daughter of Prince
Dantan of Dawsbergen and his American spouse, the
Princess Beverly. So, you see, we are rather firmly attached to America. Connected, as you might say, by
marriage."

"Would it be *lese Majeste*, Captain, if I were to ask
you a few questions concerning the royal family?"

"That, of course, would depend," replied the Captain,
guardedly.

"I've been reading up on Graustark this past week or
ten days, preparatory to the trip out here. By the way,
I suppose you know why I have come to Graustark?"

"Your credentials explain the nature of your visit to
our country, Mr. Yorke."

"Well, as I was saying, I've read everything I could find concerning your country, and I'm bound to admit I am still considerably in the dark. Hazy, vague, befoggled, as it were. You are pretty much out of things over here in your mountain fastness, Captain Sambo. Prince Robin is still on the throne, I take it?"

Captain Sambo was startled into a quick, searching glance at the indistinct face of his companion.

"Of a certainty, sir," he answered, stiffly. "He is our hereditary ruler. There has been no attempt to overthrow the Crown since he was a very small boy. The Marlanx conspiracy, twenty-five years ago, which you will find upon studying our history, was foiled. I was a lad myself at the time, but I well remember the riots, the pitched battles in the streets and the long siege of the Castle. Yes, Mr. Yorke," he concluded drily, "Prince Robin is still on the throne, as you put it!"

"I put it badly, of course," apologized the American. "I am glad that he still rules, Captain Sambo, and I hope he may continue to reign till he dies of old age."

"Thank you, Mr. Yorke," said the other simply.

"He became ruler when very young, I understand."

"He was a mere babe when his mother, the Princess Yetive, and the Prince Consort were killed in a railway disaster. The affairs of the country were in charge of the Regents until Prince Robin reached the age of fifteen, when he was crowned."

"I trust you will not consider me too inquisitive, but I should like to get this matter of the royal family straightened out in my mind. Prince Robin married the

Crown Princess of Dawsbergen some years ago. Have they any children?"

"The marriage of Prince Robin and Princess Bevra took place on New Year's Day, 1914, at Shenzarm Castle in Serros, the capital of Dawsbergen. They have two children, Prince Dantan and the Princess Yetive, aged eight and three respectively. His Serene Highness was with the army on the Galician front when the heir to the throne was born."

"Are they in Edelweiss at present?"

"Yes. Except for an occasional visit to Dawsbergen, Prince Robin and Princess Bevra have not left Edelweiss since the war. They are now in residence. In these days, Mr. Yorke, no monarch, great or small, can afford to jeopardize his throne by wandering too far away from it. There is grave unrest everywhere. Even in our own land the seeds of revolution are being sown—red seeds that would grow into poisonous weeds in a day if left unwatched."

"The Prince is popular with the people?"

"He is idolized. And yet sometimes we slay the thing we love best," said the soldier bitterly. "It is the way with the world."

"I know the kind of seeds you mean. They are being sown abundantly in my own country, Captain, and I'm afraid that they are left unwatched."

"So we hear, Mr. Yorke," said Captain Sambo, slowly. "You are strengthening the hands that one day will throttle you. Here in Graustark we have a way of stifling these noxious growths. The instant the sprout shows itself it is destroyed—not by the crown as you might suspect, but by the people themselves. It is the wiser way. No longer than a month ago a group of traitors, together with several alien agitators, were hanged by their neighbors. The Crown had no hand in these executions. No malcontent may charge the Crown with oppression or injustice. The government in Graustark very shrewdly contends that our people will protect themselves against ruin; it depends upon them to stamp out the fire ere the wind blows it into a raging conflagration, sweeping everything before it."

"A very sensible idea," said Yorke, thoughtfully. "To kill the snake before it can strike."

"Precisely. It is the only way."

"You have this advantage of us, Captain. You are all Graustarkians. In my country we are not all Americans. They call America the melting pot. But, God help us, we mix a deadly brew. All that goes into the cauldron does not melt. It merely seethes. It is a foul, deadly mess we serve to ourselves. We make a wry face but we still go on adding poison to our gruel."

"We have a saying, sir, that a young cabbage may be transformed into a rosebud by one who is without sight, taste, smell and touch."

"Why not the sense of hearing?"

"Because, even though he be able to hear the opinions of others on the subject, he will not believe."

Yorke was silent for a long time.

"By the way, Captain, is it because I am an American that these most extraordinary courtesies are extended to me?"

The Graustarkian hesitated. "Not exactly, sir," he replied. "By command of His Serene Highness special favors have been accorded you, Mr. Yorke."

"What!" gasped Pendennis Yorke.

"Upon being apprised of the imminence of your arrival, Prince Robin himself issued certain instructions to Baron Gourou."

"The Prince? Why, my dear fellow, Prince Robin has never even heard of me. I'm just—I'm just nobody at all."

"The name of Pendennis Yorke, U.S.A., is very well known in Graustark," declared Captain Sambo. "I may even say, without meaning to give offense, that it is somewhat of a household word at the Castle."

"The—the devil you say!"

The Captain cleared his throat. When he spoke again it was in a more ceremonious manner.

"Upon me, sir, has been conferred the honor of being chosen to act as your personal escort and interpreter during your sojourn in our country. I am, henceforth, at your command, Mr. Yorke."

"Pinch me," commanded Pendennis Yorke for the second time that day.

CHAPTER V

PRESENTLY the car, with its escort, swept out upon the crest of a long, steep hill. Far ahead in the valley below gleamed the city of Edelweiss, a jumbled mass of lights that seemed to mount skyward in the effort to mingle with the stars. The effect was startling.

Captain Sambo, sensing his companion's astonishment, volunteered:

"Edelweiss is the flower of the mountainside, Mr. Yorke. The greater part of the city is built upon the slope of Mount Ganlook. The Castle lies yonder at the extreme left. You can see its lights quite plainly. It stands at the foot of the mountain. Beyond it there are no houses. The whole city lies before the castle. In the foreground, in the lowlands along the river, is the business section of Edelweiss. The residential quarter lies upon the mountainside, extending upward for several thousand feet. Indeed, the topmost houses are fully half a mile above the heart of the city. Those lights you see far above all the others are the windows of the Monastery of St. Valentine at the top of the mountain. Off to the right, in a bend of the river, you see the lights of the fortress. But to-morrow, if you so desire, we will undertake a short tour of the city. I shall be pleased to point out all the places of interest?"

"Thanks so much," was all that Yorke could say. He was beginning to experience the strange, ineffable thrill of romance. His blood was tingling, his imagination was stirred. Mystery had greeted him at the border, mystery had attended him on the road, and mystery still awaited him.

Soon they were jostling over a rough cobblestone street, between quaint little houses from which lights peeped through recessed casement windows under vizor-like thatched roofs. Captain Sambo had lapsed into an alert silence, his gaze fixed steadily on the road ahead. Suddenly the car shot out from the narrow street into a wide, smooth avenue which ended apparently a short distance farther on in an impassable barrier. Not a forbidding obstruction, however, for it was gay with many rows of lighted windows.

"The Hotel Regengetz," said the Captain, briefly.

A few moments later the car swung around the broad circle of the plaza and came to a stop under the porte-cochère of the famous hostelry. Sprightly attendants dashed down the steps, saluting. In a jiffy Yorke's belongings were removed from the car. The Captain stepped out and turned with a ceremonious bow.

"It will not be necessary for you to stop at the office to register, Mr. Yorke. You will be conducted to your suite immediately."

By this time Yorke had joined him on the steps. He experienced a sudden fear that he was about to be deserted.

"I say, Captain," he began hurriedly, "won't you join

me at dinner? It would give me great pleasure—the greatest pleasure."

The Captain bowed again. "It is quite impossible, Mr. Yorke." He coughed discreetly. They were following the attendants up the steps. "Unless I am mistaken, other arrangements have been made."

"Other arrangements?"

"It is now seven o'clock. You are to dine here at eight o'clock, sir, with a lady."

Yorke stopped short. "With a lady! Ye gods, man, is there no limit to Graustark's hospitality?"

"The situation may prove embarrassing, Mr. Yorke," said the officer, with a smile; "but I daresay you will survive it."

"Just a moment, please," insisted Yorke, laying a hand on the other's arm. "I don't want to appear ungracious or finicky or anything of the sort, but I came to Graustark on business—strictly business. I—"

"In that case, Mr. Yorke, I should advise you not to offend the Crown by declining to dine with a lady of the Royal Household."

"Holy—" began Pendennis Yorke, and gulped down the "mackerel" that ordinarily completed the ejaculation.

"Come, sir; you have but an hour to spare. It is not wise to keep a princess waiting."

He was chuckling softly.

They passed through the lobby and mounted a broad staircase, pursued by a number of interested eyes. At the top of the steps they were met by the manager, who with many bows and polite exclamations conducted them down the corridor and ushered them into a commodious,

luxuriantly appointed "sitting room." Mr. Yorke's bags
were already there, waiting to be disposed of as he saw
fit by the valet who stood guard over them. The "bell-
hops" had vanished. Afterwards, Yorke remembered
that they had gone away without their tips. Proof positive that it was all a dream.

"The royal suite," announced Captain Sambo, with a
wave of his hand as the manager bowed himself out.

"Say, does this chap understand English?" demanded
the American abruptly, indicating the valet.

"He does," replied the Captain.

"Then go into the bedroom with these things and—
and close the door," ordered Yorke, tossing his keys to
the man.

When they were alone, he turned upon Captain Sambo.

"Did you say a princess?"

"I did, Mr. Yorke."

"Do—do you mean to say I'm to dine with a—with a
royal princess? Here in this hotel? All alone?"

"Not quite alone," said the Captain, with a slight lifting of the eyebrows albeit he smiled good-naturedly.
"You are to have dinner in the *salle à manger*. At a
near-by table you will, if you deign to look in that direction, behold your humble servant seated with several other
officers. At another table close by will be several ladies
and gentlemen of the Court. Should your curiosity
prompt you to peer out of the windows overlooking the
Platz you will discover an escort of six Castle Guardsmen. But I must detain you no longer. At five minutes
before eight I shall be here to conduct you downstairs.
Now—how is it you say in America? Get busy?"

With that the elegant Captain Sambo departed, leaving his charge in a deeper state of perplexity than ever before in all his eventful life.

Vastly excited and not a little perturbed, he dashed into the bedchamber. There he found the nimble valet already in the act of pressing his full dress trousers. He stopped in amazement. Never had he known such celerity as this.

"Your bath is drawn, sir," announced the man, barely looking up from the ironing board that reposed upon the arms of two regal looking chairs. "We anticipated your arrival, sir. If the temperature is not just to your liking—"

"It will be all right," interrupted Yorke, gazing about him with interest. "I shan't notice whether it is hot or cold."

"I beg pardon, sir?"

"I mean to say, I don't mind which it is. I take 'em both ways."

"When you are ready, sir, I shall fetch your shaving things. Beg pardon, sir; shall I find your studs in this little black case?"

Yorke nodded as he sat down on the edge of the great canopied bed.

"I don't see how I'm ever going to live up to this," he murmured, weakly.

"I think, sir, I have found everything else. Will you wear the black studs, sir, or the white?"

"I—I leave it entirely to you—er—ah—"

"My name is Sharpe, sir."

"English?"

"Yes, sir; thank you, sir."

"I suppose I ought to be manicured," ventured Yorke, dubiously regarding his nails. "And a hair-cut wouldn't— "

"There will hardly be time, sir," suggested the valet, scrutinizing him with a critical, appraising eye. "I daresay both your nails and your hair will do quite well as they are, if I may be permitted to so decide, sir. The black studs, then. Thank you, sir."

Sharpe resumed the interrupted process of pressing. After a moment of indecision, Yorke nervously began to divest himself of his travel-creased garments.

"Is she young or old?" he inquired, his voice muffled by the undervest he was at the moment pulling over his head.

"If you refer to the hotel, sir," said the valet, very distinctly, "she is. Very old, sir."

At a quarter before eight, Yorke surveyed himself in the tall, gold-framed cheval glass over in a corner of the bed-chamber. He could not recall that he had ever before taken such a keen, critical interest in his personal appearance. He was surprised and gratified by the inspection. In that short period of contemplation he came to a decision: henceforth he would see to it that his dress suit was properly pressed before he put it on. He rubbed his clean-shaven cheek and chin, readjusted his white tie, gave his waistcoat a needless hitch or two.

"Well, Sharpe, do you think I'll—er—do?" he inquired.

"Quite, sir," coming forward to flick a particle of dust from the shoulder of his creation. "And now the boutonnière, sir."

He forthwith produced a fragrant gardenia, astoundingly after the manner of the prestidigitator who garners posies and bunnies and silver coins at will out of the supposedly empty air. This he proceeded deftly to insert in Yorke's buttonhole.

"You are a bright chap, Sharpe. I'll give you one chance to guess who I remind myself of at this moment."

"I couldn't possibly guess, sir."

"Cinderella," said the stalwart Mr. Yorke.

"I shouldn't have guessed it, sir, if you'd given me a thousand chances," said Sharpe, with a twitch—a very slight twitch—of the lips. He strode over and opened the door for Yorke to pass into the sitting-room. As the American sauntered through, the valet's practiced eye traversed his long, well set-up figure. "Very good, sir," he said, but whether in the nature of comment or merely because it was his way of temporarily dismissing himself it would be useless to discuss.

On the wall opposite the door hung a half-length portrait of a very good-looking young man in the vivid full-dress uniform of a high army official. Yorke paused to study the patrician features of this handsome young man, whose painted eyes seemed singularly to regard him with an interest as keen as his own.

"The Prince," he decided, and forthwith straightened himself to his full height. On second thought, he crossed over to peer closely at the date in the lower corner of the canvas, and was relieved to find that it was 1920. "He looks noble enough to be an ancestor," was his silent, admiring comment, as he turned away for a hasty inspection of the regally furnished room.

Almost the first object his gaze fell upon brought forth a sharp exclamation of dismay, and caused him to glance hurriedly and somewhat agitatedly about the room. This object was a large black portmanteau—a disreputable-looking bag it was, scuffed and scarred by many a vicious buffeting and seamed with the cracks of decrepitude. It lay upon the floor just inside the corridor door.

His searching glance revealed no other occupant of the room—but whose bag was it? An uneasy thought shot through his brain. Were they planning to have some one else share the suite with him? Some one to spy upon his every— The flash of annoyance that leaped into his eyes gave way to one of sheer astonishment as he made out the name crudely painted in white letters on the end of the bag. His own name! "Pendennis Yorke!" No! He clapped his hand to his forehead and stared incredulously.

"MRS. PENDENNIS YORKE, U.S.A."

He gaped for a moment or two as if stupefied, doubting his senses. Good Lord! Were these cordial Graustarkians actually providing him with a wife! That would be the quintessence of— And then, with the force of a sharp blow, came the staggering solution.

He recognized that clumsy, middle-class "valise." He remembered the lettering; he recalled his own emotions when for the first—and only—time he beheld the name of "Mrs. Pendennis Yorke" in print; his memory sped back to an unforgettable scene in the railway station at

Buda Pesth. Rosa Schmitz's bag! But what was the meaning—

"By gosh!" he gasped, dropping limply into a chair, comprehension smiting him with such force that his brain reeled. With all the startling swiftness of a lightning flash the truth was revealed to him. Rosa Schmitz and the Princess! One and the same!

Now he knew why his name was so familiar to the Court of Graustark. Now he knew why it was a household word! A Princess of the Realm had taken it as her own— Good Heavens, was Rosa Schmitz going to turn out to be no other than the Royal Princess herself, the wife of Graustark's ruler? Or was she— Thunder! Why hadn't he asked if the Prince had a sister? Or a cousin?

There was not the slightest doubt in his mind that the Princess with whom he was to have dinner would prove to be Rosa Schmitz. It was she who had planned everything—even to the shock he was bound to experience on finding the historic bag in his apartment.

A royal jest! A royal bit of comedy! A royal prank over which they both would be laughing in—he glanced at his watch—in less than seven minutes. But, he wondered uneasily, would this royal princess and simple Rosa Schmitz be the same after all? This was not Buda Pesth in the grim days of Bela Kun; no more was this princess the timorous, harassed young girl of that bygone day when he was the prince and she the grateful mendicant. Would she laugh and make merry? Wouldn't she, on the contrary, be stiff and imperious and composedly superior, as befitted her station— No! He banged his fist on the arm of his chair. No, she wouldn't! She could not have sent that bag up to the apartment except in a spirit of mischief; and that being the case, she most certainly was not looking forward to a dull and formal evening.

His speculations were running riot when Captain Sambo entered the room.

"Whose bag is that?" he demanded, springing to his feet, determined to straighten out at least one thread of the tangle.

The Captain inserted a monocle in his right eye and calmly inspected the object on the floor.

"That, I should say, Mr. Yorke, is the property of your wife."

"Come, now, Captain, the truth, if you please."

"Perhaps I should have said your divorced wife," said Sambo drily. "You may recall my saying that the situation might prove embarrassing to you. It is possible that you do not care to meet your former wife."

"The Mrs. Pendennis Yorke whose name you see on that bag was a Miss Rosa Schmitz before I married her. I'll be obliged to you if you will tell me what it is now."

The Captain drew himself up. "It is my privilege, sir, to acquaint you with the fact that you are dining tonight with Princess Virginia Louise, second daughter of His Highness, Prince Dantan, of Dawsbergen, and Princess Beverly. She is the sister of our own most gracious sovereign, the Princess Bevra, with whom she has been spending the winter at the Castle. It is my further privilege to inform you that for a period of some six or seven hours, the Princess Virginia was the wife of one Pendennis Yorke, an American gentleman, from whom by mutual consent she was divorced on a Buda Pesth railway platform in the year of our Lord, nineteen hundred and nineteen, but toward whom she harbors no ill-will notwithstanding the fact that he cruelly, brutally and maliciously attempted to kill her on at least two occasions —once at luncheon and once at dinner, when he cunningly induced her to eat more than was good for her. But come, Mr. Yorke, we must not tarry. I trust that my carefully rehearsed speech has prepared you for what is about to follow. I do not mind confessing," he went on guiltily, as they stepped out into the corridor, "that I had some difficulty in memorizing it. I was compelled to repeat it several times before the Princess was satisfied with my manner of delivery. She wrote it out for me herself on the typewriter."

They had reached the top of the great staircase before Yorke felt confident of controlling his voice. His heart was pounding so furiously and he was so light-headed from the shock of these revelations that his voice seemed muffled and far away when he finally succeeded in saying to his companion:

"You might at least tell me whether—whether my wife ever married again."

"The Princess Virginia is a spinster, Mr. Yorke," said the Captain. Then hastily he added: "At least, she is a divorced spinster, if you see what I mean."

Yorke pulled himself together as he caught sight of a small group of army officers in the lobby. An invisible orchestra was playing "The Star Spangled Banner" in some remote musicians' gallery. His heart swelled. . . .

The officers saluted. . . . He had himself in hand now. He did not return the salute. That would have been the most grotesque exhibition of conceit on his part. He merely threw back his shoulders and inserted his thumb into the right hand pocket of his waist-coat, thereby indicating to all beholders that he was perfectly at ease and quite accustomed to this sort of thing!

His guide conducted him through the practically empty lounge, past the open doors of the main dining hall, and into a narrow passage beyond. Here, in front of a door opening off to the left, stood a liveried flunkey, who, as they approached, bowed stiffly and stepped to one side.

"I leave you here," said Captain Sambo, in a low tone, signifying by a gesture that Yorke was to pass within.

Yorke clutched his arm, detaining him in order to whisper in some agitation:

"Good Heaven! I almost forgot. How am I to address my ex-wife? Has she resumed her maiden name?"

"I have had no instructions, Mr. Yorke, but I fancy you will be on the safe side if you address her as Princess."

With that, he turned on his heel and walked rapidly away. Yorke took a full breath, as one about to dive off into deep water, and passed through the door. He found himself in a small, daintily furnished ante-chamber. On the opposite side of this room was an open door through which the crowded dining-room was partly visible. He took in his surroundings at a glance and found that he was quite alone. Just as he was beginning to wonder what he was to do next, a mirrored panel in the wall to his right swung slowly outward and—into the room stepped a slender young woman, whose graceful figure was enveloped in a long, closely held chinchilla wrap. She paused just inside the door to regard the tall young man with frank, undisguised eagerness. Then her lips parted in a faint smile, a warm glow crept into her cheeks, her dark, inquiring eyes softened. She held out a slim gloved hand as she advanced.

"It is really you, Mr. Yorke," she said, a little tremor of excitement in her voice.

He lifted her hand to his lips.

"I cannot be sure, Princess," he said, shaking his head doubtfully. "I have a strange feeling that I am not Pendennis Yorke."

"Ah, but you are," she cried. "I should have known you anywhere."

"I, myself, have a staunch, abiding memory for faces," said he, risking a smile. "I have never for one instant forgotten the face of Rosa Schmitz."

"You don't expect me to believe that, Mr. Yorke."

She was looking up into his eyes, a challenging light in her own.

"You haven't the slightest idea, Princess, how unforgettably lovely Rosa was on the day she married me," he went on, growing bolder under the challenge. "You will forgive me for saying that I shall always be haunted by the fear in her dark eyes, by the wanness of her cheek, the courage of her smile. Yet, after all, why should I expect the Princess Virginia to believe me?"

She laid her hand on his arm.

"We speak lightly to-night of a day that poor Rosa Schmitz will not permit the Princess to forget. Your memory harbors a frightened, half-starved, helpless girl,

Mr. Yorke. I remember a strong, generous, gallant gentleman to whom Rosa Schmitz owes a debt that the Princess never can repay."

"Rosa Schmitz owes me nothing that the Princess has not already paid by graciously remembering me."

Her eyes suddenly sparkled with mirth. (Never, never had he dreamed—and he had dreamed many a time of Rosa Schmitz—never had he dreamed of anything so lovely as this radiant upturned face, nestling like a flower in a soft gray bed of fur.)

"And you *will* forgive me for the trick I played tonight?" she cried. "It was most unseemly, most unmaidenly, most undignified, but I simply couldn't help it."

"Bless my soul, I can't see anything unseemly about it, or unmaidenly, for that matter. I should say it was perfect," he exclaimed, with enthusiasm.

"Oh, I am not referring to all this," she said, with a toss of her head. "Nor to the things Prince Robin so gladly did for me when I took him into my little conspiracy. I mean the—that dreadful old bag with my name printed on it." She flushed. "I mean with *your* name on it."

(He liked the curve of her smooth round chin as it was fashioned against the warm chinchilla, and the red of her smiling lips.)

"It came very near to being the death of me," he confessed. "How I managed to keep from dropping dead I'll never understand. And, now that I think of it, it *was* your name at one time, wasn't it?"

"Indeed it was," she said promptly. "Even to this day

my sister and my mother—they are frightful teases—
sometimes call me Mrs. Yorke."

(And the way her wavy brown hair grew about her
temples, and the carefree lock that seemed on the point
of stealing down on to her forehead.)

"For five long years I've called you Rosa Schmitz,"
said he. "And for that many years I've wondered
whether you were alive or dead, happy or miserable,
married or single. I am not surprised to find that you
are a princess. Somehow I sensed it five years ago. I
never expected to see you again, however. I can't believe it, even now."

"I could hardly believe my ears when they told me you
were coming to Edelweiss. It seemed incredible. And I
wondered—yes, I wondered a great deal."

"You wondered?"

"Yes. Whether you had found out who Rosa Schmitz
really was and were coming here to—" She checked the
words, noting the expression in his eyes.

"I should not have dared to presume upon so slight an
acquaintance," said he, stiffly, after a moment.

"Forgive me," she said, flushing again. "But," she
went on defensively, "it wouldn't have been surprising if
you had found out, would it?"

"I suppose not," he admitted, smiling. "I have a
peculiar gift for unearthing things."

"If I were Pharaoh's daughter, dead and buried for
thousands of years, I am sure you would have gone to no
end of trouble to unearth me."

He was surprised. "You don't mean to say you have

read what I wrote about the bottomless pit of old King Tut?"

"Why not? Wasn't it intended for general circulation?" she countered, lightly.

"Permit me," he said, as she partially turned her back to him in order that he might relieve her of the wrap.

It slipped from her shoulders, revealing a slender, erect figure, smartly arrayed in what he would have been pardoned for describing as a gown direct from the most fashionable modiste's in all Paris, but which she afterwards took pains to inform him was two seasons old, ready to fall to pieces, horribly out of date, and conceived by a little seamstress in Serros instead of by the mighty Poiret in Paris. He marveled at the smooth, white shoulders, the proud, graceful neck—aye, marveled despite the fact that he had seen hundreds no less beautiful. He marveled because of the pinched, drooping shoulders and the flat, sunken chest of the half-starved girl who was Rosa Schmitz. Here was the perfection of full-blown, glorious womanhood; there, far back in his memory, the vision of a slim, haggard young girl whose eyes were as blue as these and far more wistful, whose cheeks were wan but as smooth as these, whose chin quivered yet was held as high as this one. The Princess was lovely but his heart was true to Rosa Schmitz. The Princess could never drive the appealing vision of Rosa out of his mind's eye. It was there to stay forever.

"Thank you," said the Princess. "Shall we go in now? Throw it on a chair, anywhere, Mr. Yorke. It will be safe here. No one is permitted to enter this room, you see. I hope you are hungry. You ought to be. I suppose I should have consulted you before ordering dinner, but turn about is fair play. You did not consult me that day in Buda Pesth. You just ordered everything on the menu. And, I am not ashamed to say, I ate it. I was nearly starved, Mr. Yorke."

The presence of a bowing, obsequious maître d'hôtel who confronted them just inside the private entrance to the dining-room alone saved Yorke from uttering the fatuous though obvious rejoinder that she certainly had looked it.

His gaze swept the room as he followed her toward a plant-guarded recess a short distance to the left of the door. If he expected all of the diners to arise with the entrance of royalty he was disappointed—or rather, he was relieved. There was a discreet craning of necks, testimony of polite whisperings; other than that, the appearance in the crowded restaurant of so noble a lady as the sister-in-law of the Prince of Graustark created no appreciable flutter.

She nodded to acquaintances at near-by tables; the men got to their feet and made profound obeisance. Yorke's attention was held for a fleeting moment by a party of six seated almost directly in front of the green bower to which he was being conducted. There was no mistaking the character of this little group. The Princess turned to wave a jaunty hand to them as she passed through the screen of potted plants.

"My chaperones," she remarked to Yorke, with a faint grimace. "It is dreadfully shocking of me to be dining in a public restaurant with a young man," she went on gayly. "Do you know what my venerable cousin, the Dowager Duchess of Halfont, said to me when I reminded her that I had dined quite alone with you before I was eighteen? The dear old thing declared that it was entirely proper at the time, because you were my husband. She is the one who shook her fan at me, Mr. Yorke. She's loads of fun. I am sure she is more thrilled and excited over all this than I am myself."

As she sat down at the daintily arranged table in this bower of enchantment, she smiled up at him, shyly, diffidently—and suddenly he realized that after all it was Rosa Schmitz into whose eyes he was looking. Time, environment and the plumage of a Princess had wrought many changes in her but her eyes were those of Rosa Schmitz and always would be.

"The worst of this wonderful dream, Princess, is that I've still got to wake up in that awful bed at Klodso," said he, shaking his head mournfully as he sat down opposite her.

"Have you tried pinching yourself?" she asked, her smile deepening.

"Have I?" he exclaimed. "I've done nothing else for hours."

"I've never seen any one who appeared to be more wide awake than you are at this moment," she declared, breaking into a laugh of sheer enjoyment. Then her eyes sobered and the smile gave way to a rueful expression. "Oh, dear! How difficult it is to be a princess sometimes, Mr. Yorke," she complained. "I am not behaving at all like a princess, am I?"

"You are!" he explained and with conviction. "You

are behaving just as I've always imagined a fairy princess ought to behave."

"You see," she went on to explain in self-defense, "I am half American. That should cover a multitude of my sins, shouldn't it?"

"Far be it from me to find fault with the half of you that is not American," said he, with his most engaging smile. "It would seem too much like boasting."

"I suppose you are wondering why I planned all this, Mr. Yorke," she began seriously. "First, because you were my friend in a time of great trouble. Second, because I owe you more than you would ever suspect. Third, I wanted to be the one to welcome you here. Graustark is not my own country. I too am what you might call an alien. If we were in Dawsbergen instead of here in Graustark, you would have been received and entertained at the Castle by my father, Prince Dantan. But we are not in Dawsbergen, so I have insisted that I, of all people, should be the one to greet you. No doubt I have taken a theatric way to do it, Mr. Yorke—but, alas for convention, it is my way. I shall never forget the dinner we had together in Buda Pesth. We were alone. You were what you now are and I was no less a Princess, even then." Abruptly her manner changed. The seriousness dropped from her as a discarded mantle falls from the shoulders. "So here is poor Rosa Schmitz," she cried, her eyes dancing, "playing hob with the serenity of ages, upsetting tradition and getting the Princess Virginia into hot water, all for the sake of a madcap whim!"

"Hot water?" he ejaculated. "Do you mean to say you—er—you will be criticized for this?"

She leaned forward to direct his attention to the party of six just outside the sylvan retreat.

"Can you see the man sitting at the right of the Duchess of Halfont?" she inquired, lowering her voice.

"The dark, rather—" He was about to say "sullen-looking chap," but fortunately stopped in time.

"Yes," she said, as he hesitated. "The dark, rather unpleasant-looking man. Well, he is the heir-apparent to the throne of Axphain—if Axphain ever has a throne again—Prince Hubert. He is a refugee here in Edelweiss. The Bolsheviki have driven the royal family out of Axphain. Prince Hubert, you will be interested to learn, Mr. Yorke, is a suitor for the hand of your divorced wife."

CHAPTER VI

PRINCESS VIRGINIA

FROM time to time Yorke found his gaze wandering from the lovely high-bred face of the Princess to that of the royal exile. Hubert was swarthy. His raven black hair grew low upon his forehead, separated from the heavy, undivided eyebrows by a pallid streak scarce half an inch in width. A tiny mustache nestled in the shelter of a broad, flat nose, leaving most of the thick upper lip bare. His mouth was wide, the lips full, the blue-black chin square and domineering. His eyes curiously were light gray, or pale blue in color, noticeably out of key with his swarthy complexion; they were icy, unblinking, and rather prominent even though they were set deep in the sockets.

He was a big man. His clothes did not fit him. The coat hung loosely upon his huge, sloping shoulders; his pleated silk shirt bulged far out from the confines of his waistcoat, creased and wrinkled, and there were ruby or garnet studs down the front of it which sparkled when the light played upon them. An eight-pointed decoration of rubies and diamonds, incongruously small and chaste against so gross a background, adorned the lapel of his coat. He took but little part in the conversation that went on at the table. If he at any time smiled, it must have been when Yorke was not observing him. The latter experienced an ever-increasing growth of revulsion as he pictured this man as the lord and master of the exquisite girl who sat opposite him, she whose eyes were like the violet and whose smiling lips were as tender as the petals of a rose.

Having made the calm announcement, Princess Virginia dismissed Prince Hubert without further comment, and proceeded forthwith to devote herself to a subject in which she obviously was more interested. The color in her cheek, the glow in her eyes betrayed an inward excitement that did not escape the notice of the alert diagnostician of the human emotions who watched her with fascinated interest. After a very few minutes he decided that she was making a determined effort to conceal the fact that she was ill at ease and self-conscious. Perhaps she was even repenting the reckless impulse that had led her into this pleasant though flagrant violation of royal decorum. There was something in her manner that suggested the naughty child who seeks to avoid the consequences of mischief by resorting to the time-honored expedient best described as "talking against time." She had started the fire and now was forced to play with it, regardless, perhaps, of warnings and despite her own secret misgivings.

As for Yorke, the whole delectable adventure was still in a process of transformation from the unreal to the real. He was still figuratively pinching himself.

The champagne, she confessed, was from the Castle. "With Prince Robin's compliments," she explained, as it was being served by a quaint, leather-aproned cellarman from whose belt dangled a huge iron key. Yorke arose and held his glass aloft.

"To His Serene Highness, the Prince of Graustark," he said, looking down into her eyes; "and to Rosa Schmitz," he added, as he drained the glass.

"When you dine at the Castle, Mr. Yorke, you will drink with your eyes until they are completely intoxicated," she said. "My sister will dazzle you. She is the loveliest thing in all the world."

"I prefer, if it's all the same to you, to accept your sister's opinion as to that, rather than yours, Princess."

"Pooh!"

"I hope I have not offended you," he cried, with mock concern.

"Not at all," she assured him, airily. "My sister considers her baby daughter the loveliest thing that God ever created."

"In that case, I fear I am doomed to stand alone and unsupported."

At this she laughed gayly. From that moment on the tension lessened perceptibly. Whatever doubts or misgivings she may have had at the outset were being rapidly dispelled. So, when he complained that he, being a poor man, could not afford the splendor of the royal suite in the Regengetz, she glibly informed him that it was the cheapest apartment in the house—because, she went on naïvely, hotel managers invariably make a special rate for kings and consider themselves extremely fortunate if their majesties do not walk off without paying anything at all. Besides, she argued, queens and kings and all such things are very much out of fashion in these days and hotel managers are only too happy to let their empty and profitless suites at tremendously reduced rates. His face brightened.

"I've often wondered how it would feel to live like a king," he said. "Now that I have the chance to find out at bargain prices, I suppose I'd be foolish to move into an expensive hall bedroom without bath, don't you?"

"It would be a vulgar display of wealth, Mr. Yorke," said she.

They were half way through dinner before he undertook to lead the sprightly conversation into more serious channels. He was curious about her presence in Buda Pesth during the days of the Commune. Why was she, a Princess of Dawsbergen, in that turbulent city at such a time and what were the conditions under which she was living when he first encountered her?

Higbee had refused point-blank to enlighten him at the time. He had known who she was, of course, and he must also have been pretty well acquainted with her previous circumstances.

"It didn't require much in the way of intelligence to see that you were not a native Hungarian," he was saying. "Nor, despite your name, a German. But now that I know who Rosa Schmitz really is—or was, I should say— I am more puzzled than ever. What were you, a foreign princess, doing in Buda Pesth at such a time?"

Her eyes clouded. "Will you consider me rude, Mr. Yorke, and ungracious, if I remind you of my reluctance to answer any questions at that time?"

"Certainly not, Princess," he said instantly. "I beg your pardon."

She was silent for a moment. "You need not apologize, my friend. It is only natural that you should ask that and many more questions. I am sorry that I am no more at liberty to answer them now than I was five years ago. You will understand, I am sure, and forgive me."

"There is nothing to forgive, Princess, except my own unpardonable impudence," said he, quite gravely.

She rewarded him with a dazzling smile. "Then, since we have nothing to forgive each other for, let's talk about something else. You, for example."

"If you don't mind, I'd rather talk about you," he said, daringly.

"Oh, but we've talked altogether too much about me," she protested. "Besides, I'm not at all interested in me. I haven't gone down into anybody's tomb, I haven't explored anything except some frightfully dull castles, and the only wild quadrupeds I've encountered are mice, which scare me almost to death. To be sure, I have seen a number of two-legged beasts, but I don't like to talk about them."

"I can understand that, Princess. The two-legged beast is the most savage of all God's creatures."

"And nothing could be truer than the saying that the female of the species is the worst," she declared, and while she spoke lightly there was a world of significance in the momentary hardening of her eyes.

He observed this passing shadow and instantly associated it with the forbidden topic: her experiences in Buda Pesth. It was jumping at a conclusion, of course, but somehow he felt sure that her story of those troublous days would reveal ill-treatment and perhaps treachery at the hands of her own sex. He resolved, then and there, that one day he would have the story from her own lips.

"I'll tell you what," said he, as if inspired, "let's compromise. Suppose we talk about Prince Hubert."

"In confidential undertones," she agreed without hesitation, casting an amused glance over her shoulder in the direction of the proposed subject. "He has very sharp ears," she went on whimsically, "and very large ones, as you may have observed. Well?"

"You say he has been banished from his own country?"

"Kicked out, as Prince Robin puts it when the American half of him gets the upper hand of the Graustark half. Poor Hubert! If it wasn't for the half million gavvos he managed to smuggle out of Axphain before the revolution he would be horribly annoyed by the present state of affairs over there. Especially so when you stop to consider that the Communists might have shot him as they did his father and his elder brother, both of whom made the grievous mistake of electing to defend the crown instead of running away. You see, he probably is very much annoyed by the thought that if he'd stayed at home and, like Jack the giant-killer, sallied forth single-handed to slay all the Bolsheviks, he might now be on the throne instead of trying to subsist on a beggarly half million."

The contempt in her voice surprised and pleased him. He discreetly decided not to refer to it, however.

"Half a million gavvos?" he queried. "What does that come to in real money?"

"Real money?" she cried, indignantly. "My dear Mr. Yorke, our money is worth as much to-day as it was

before the war. The gavvo of Graustark and Dawsbergen in pre-war days was the equivalent of one dollar
and a half in your money. To-day it is practically the
same. There is no longer any such coin as the one gavvo
piece, however. It was abolished almost a hundred years
ago. A gavvo to-day, strictly speaking, is really five
gavvos, if you see what I mean. So when I say Prince
Hubert has half a million gavvos stored away or safely
invested, I mean over three million and a half in your
money. Please do not misunderstand me. Prince Hubert
is the rightful owner of this money. You may have
thought he robbed the treasury or something of the sort.
He simply converted his share of the crown holdings into
cash when he saw the storm approaching and got it out
of Axphain. I daresay it was a clever thing to do. Certainly, it was a wise thing to do in the light of subsequent
events. The crown estates are wiped out. The people
have inherited them, so to speak. They didn't even wait
until Hubert's father and the Crown Prince died to claim
the legacy. They were, as you may know, brutally assassinated."

She spoke with real feeling now. He caught a fleeting
shadow of dread in her eyes. He glanced out of the
corner of his eye at the son and brother of those mur-
dered princes and somehow their tragic end was brought
very close to him. This man, for all he knew, was all
that was left of a once powerful family. And this fair,
gentle, young girl—was she even now standing on the edge
of the grave, afraid of death?

"Were they all killed—the women and children of the
House of Axphain?" he asked, leaning toward her. There

was a strange hush in his voice as he added: "Like the
Czar of Russia and his—"

She broke in stonily: "Hubert is the only one of the
Royal family alive to-day. His mother, his sisters and
the wife of the Crown Prince were—were executed, Mr.
Yorke. Some members of the Court escaped. Others
are still in the prisons of Axphain. Some are beggars in
the streets and some are working as servants in the houses
and on the farms of people who once were their servants.
Twice Prince Hubert has sought to bring about a counter
revolution. In both instances his plans were thwarted.
And why? Because he chose to be a follower rather than
a leader in the cause. His place was at the head of his
forces. Instead he trusted other men with the leadership
—and they failed him."

Yorke made no effort to conceal the sneer that twisted
his lips.

"And he is a suitor for your hand in marriage,
Princess?"

She laughed lightly. "Why not?"

Yorke flushed. "And—and do you intend to marry
him?"

"Oh, heavens, no! May not a girl have suitors without
accepting them? What a dreadful predicament she would
be in if she accepted every suitor who came along! Law-
zee!" she cried, resorting to a Southern expression picked
up from her mother, the former Beverly Calhoun of Virginia. "Didn't I marry you? And you weren't even pre-
tending to be a suitor."

"That was a marriage of convenience if there ever was
one," said he. "You must not forget that I didn't have a

chance to become a suitor. I married in haste and alas, I've never had the slightest indication of repenting at leisure."

Her eyes were sparkling with fun. "But you never would have become a suitor for the hand of poor Rosa Schmitz, even though you'd had the chance."

"I'm not so sure about that," was his cool retort.

A faint color stole into her cheeks. "You can well afford to be polite now, Mr. Yorke."

He hesitated a moment before taking the risk and then said: "No longer than a week ago I told my aunt that I could hardly resist the temptation to pick Rosa Schmitz up in my arms and carry her all the way to Paris, on foot if necessary."

She started. "You—you told your aunt about me?" she cried.

"I told her about poor little Rosa Schmitz," he corrected hastily. "Surely there was no harm in that. She was tremendously interested. And she agreed with me that Rosa Schmitz was an amazingly pretty girl. So did my Uncle George."

A puzzled expression came into her eyes. "But how on earth were they to know what I looked like?"

For answer he drew a small leather case from his pocket, extracted an oblong bit of paper and passed it over to her.

"Higbee took it," he said briefly.

She held it up to one of the candles, squinting her eyes as she studied the picture closely. The color deepened in her cheeks. She was silent for so long a time that he began to regret his temerity.

"I did not know about this," she said at last, without lifting her eyes from the print.

"Nor did I for many days," said he. "Higbee gave it to me a week after it was taken."

Now she looked up at him, meeting his gaze fairly.

"And you have kept it all these years?"

"Yes."

He expected her to tear it to pieces. Serve him right, he thought.

"Thank you," she said, and calmly handed it back to him. "I see you did, after all, carry Rosa Schmitz all the way to Paris. In your pocket, to be sure, where she wasn't as much of a burden as you might have found her if you had followed your first inclination."

"I carried her into the jungles of Africa. I carried her to far-off Patagonia. I took her down into King Tut's tomb and across the blazing Sahara. I carried her completely around the globe. I hope the Princess Virginia is not annoyed because I have done all these things for Rosa Schmitz?"

"On the contrary, the Princess Virginia is exceedingly envious," she declared, all traces of confusion gone from her manner. She watched him restore the picture to his pocket. Then she abruptly turned the conversation back into its old channel.

"A royal courtship, Mr. Yorke, is invariably conducted by proxy," she announced. "The parents of the parties to said courtship put their heads together and say, 'Well, if your son will marry my daughter, my daughter will marry your son,' and that's all there is to it. It's very simple. No trouble at all to either of the aforesaid parties, meaning, of course, said son and daughter."

"It *is* simple," said he, a trifle ironically. "I suppose your father and Prince Hubert's father put their heads together and—"

"Not at all. Prince Hubert's father, poor man, hasn't got any head, and my father isn't that sort of a prince anyhow. No; Hubert is merely a suitor on his own account. I daresay he thinks the safest and easiest way to get onto a throne is to marry me."

"From all I hear, the royal families of Graustark and Dawsbergen haven't paid much attention to tradition of late years. Prince Robin's mother married an American, and Prince Danton, your father, also married one."

"Yes," she said, with a whimsical smile; "they took it upon themselves to put the necessary heads together."

"That's ripping!" he cried, admiringly. "Awfully jolly."

"You have been picking up things from the English, haven't you?" she chided.

He beamed. "I had no idea we should get on so famously. I confess I was horribly afraid of you at first."

She shrugged her shoulders. "Hubert is still horribly afraid of me, and he has known me for years. So don't consider yourself out of danger yet, my friend."

"I say, I'm glad you're not going to marry Prince Hubert. I don't like his looks. I'm sure you wouldn't be happy with him. I admire the Princess Yetive enormously for having had the courage and the backbone to marry the man she loved, even though he was a—er—Commoner."

"Well, for that matter, I once had the temerity to marry a man of humble origin," she countered lightly. "To be sure, I got rid of him before you could say Jack Robinson, but, even so, he was an uncommonly nice husband while he lasted."

He lowered his voice. "Does—Prince Hubert know about me?" he asked.

"Oh, yes. Everybody knows about you, Mr. Yorke."

"I mean, does he know about you and me?" he persisted.

"That's the funny part of it," she said, affecting a confidential air. "He's such a queer person. He believes our marriage was legal. But he doesn't believe the divorce was legal."

Yorke so far forgot himself as to exclaim: "The deuce you say!"

"Well, it seems he has heard or read of a sect in Europe and America whose members get married in pretty much the same way, and it's frightfully legal. But it's just as difficult for them to obtain divorces as it is for anybody else."

"I know of that religious sect. It's one of their doctrines. Nobody ever questions the validity of such marriages."

"That's just what Hubert says. He maintains that you and I were legally married in the sight of God. He insists that God leaves the matter of divorce entirely in the hands of man. And so he says I ought to go into a court and have the marriage dissolved or annulled or whatever they do in such cases. Then it would be legal in the sight of man. Isn't it ridiculous?"

He frowned. "There is something to be said for his contention. And you've never done this? I mean, you haven't taken steps to obtain a legal—"

"Certainly not. Good heavens!" she exclaimed, her eyes widening. "You can't possibly think there is anything in it, Mr. Yorke! You don't believe we are still married to each other, do you?"

"Of course not," he assured her. "That's preposterous. On the other hand, Princess," he went on seriously, "the laws of Hungary in the days of Bela Kun were not recognized by other nations, you must remember. It is true that in some countries the mere declaration of two persons that they are man and wife has been held to constitute a lawful marriage. I don't believe, however, that divorce by declaration is valid in a single country in the world to-day."

"My goodness!" gasped the Princess Virginia, the picture of dismay.

"What does your father say about it?"

"Father? Oh, he regards the whole thing as a joke."

He pondered. "If you don't mind my making a suggestion, I think I should consult some high legal authority on the question, Princess."

"Dear me," she cried, impatiently; "why do you put all the responsibility on me? Aren't you in just as bad a fix as I am? That is, assuming that we are not legally divorced."

"I hadn't thought of it in that light," said he.

Suddenly her face brightened. She drew a deep breath of relief.

"But you didn't marry me at all," she cried. "You married Rosa Schmitz. And there wasn't any such person as Rosa Schmitz. So, don't you see, the marriage itself couldn't possibly be legal. Therefore, a divorce isn't necessary."

"The trouble with that argument, Princess, is that marriage is not a union of names. It is the union of two human beings."

She dismissed the subject with a flaunt of her hand. "Pooh! Let's not worry about it, Mr. Yorke. I'll ask father to get you out of the scrape. It will be quite simple."

"My innate gallantry revolts against the word scrape," said he, assuming an air of injured dignity. "Besides, I haven't said I wanted to be got out of it, have I?"

"I have no fault to find with your gallantry, Mr. Yorke," she said, so gently that he reddened with mortification. Noting his change of expression, she instantly sought to put him at his ease once more. "We must not make mountains out of mole hills," she said, smiling. "In any case, I do not intend to go through the divorce mill just to please old Hubert. I'd much sooner remain an old maid all my life."

"If you stick to that decision, Princess," said he gallantly, "I shall consider it a great privilege to remain a bachelor to the end of my days."

"Splendid," she cried, enthusiastically. "Married though single! Wasn't there a book of that name?"

"A far greater book was called 'Paradise Lost,'" said he, in the same spirit.

Presently, as the delectable feast (for he had feasted in more ways than one) drew near the end, she said to him:

"My little escapade is about over, Mr. Yorke. I see the Duchess fidgeting—she's putting on her gloves for the second time, I'm sure. It has been delightful, seeing you again. I've been shockingly unconventional, frightfully self-willed, and—and all that—but I am sure you will think none the less of me for being just myself for a little while to-night. You are to remain in Graustark for some weeks, I understand. Prince Robin has asked me to present his compliments and to assure you that he will do everything in his power to make your stay here an agreeable as well as a profitable one." Her manner had become distinctly formal. "Captain Sambo has been directed to assist you in every way possible. Every courtesy that Graustark can think of will be cheerfully and gladly extended to the representative of the great newspaper in whose interests you come."

He was not guilty of committing the obvious and fatuous error that might have been expected under the circumstances. He forbore asking whether he was to see her again and if so, when.

"Please thank His Highness for me, Princess, and say to him that I greatly appreciate his kindness to me."

She signaled to the waiter who hovered outside the recess. To him she spoke briefly in the language of the country. The man glided away and a moment later Yorke saw him bowing obsequiously as he addressed himself to the Duchess of Halfont. Signs of departure followed almost instantly. Waiters dashed up to withdraw chairs; the maître d'hôtel appeared from nowhere, like Jack-in-the-box; the orchestra broke off in the middle of a lively tune and after the briefest of intervals struck up a weird, ringing air that thrilled Yorke to the bone.

"The Graustark Anthem," said the Princess, as she arose from her chair. He sprang to his feet, with shoulders thrown back, chin lifted, and turned to face the music. The few diners who were left in the restaurant at the time were on their feet.

The Duchess's party were leaving their table. The Princess, however, did not move. She remained standing, her gaze fixed on the musicians in their gallery at the far end of the long dining-room. Yorke found himself wondering at the moment whether she intended to present him to the Duchess and her companions. Or—and he felt the blood mounting to his face—were they there merely as spectators to watch a pretty little scene from a much talked-of comedy? The good American blood in his veins was prepared to boil. Who were these noble puppets that they should disdain to meet the free-born descendant of a Sixteenth Century English Earl? Even as his choler rose the Princess smiled up into his eyes and said:

"I am sure the Duchess approves of you. She is a very keen old lady. She nodded her head to me a little while ago as much as to say, 'Your American is all right, Virgie Lou!' So you must reconcile yourself to the inevitable, Mr. Yorke. She will ask you to dinner at Halfont Palace before long—and you will be bored stiff.

She's a perfect dear—but heavens, those dinners of hers!
If Methuselah and Noah and old King Solomon were alive
to-day she'd have them to dinner as representatives of
the younger set. I am a beast to be saying such things,
Mr. Yorke, because I am devoted to her and I know she
loves me—and, what is more to the point, she approves
of what I've done to-night."

"Then I am for her, first, last and all the time," said he,
as they made their way past empty tables to the ante-
chamber.

Her friends had already disappeared. He looked about
the room in search of Captain Sambo and his fellow
officers. They too had gone.

He placed the luxurious chinchilla wrap about her
shoulders, and was surprised when she thanked him. The
thought flashed through his brain: "She's had a darned
good bringing up for a princess, I'll say that for Virgie
Lou's mother."

"Good night," she said, holding out her hand, not high
as Rosa Schmitz had done years before but on a level to
meet his own. Her handclasp was warm, firm, friendly.

"Good night, Princess—and thank you," said he.

The mirrored frame swung open noiselessly, as if by
magic, and a tall guardsman entered the room. He took
two steps to the right, wheeled, stood at attention as she
passed through the door, and then followed close behind
her. The mirror swung noiselessly back into place—and
it was all over! Like the fairy princess, she had vanished
before his eyes.

There were perhaps half a dozen people in the lobby as
he walked briskly through on his way to his room, and

they appeared to be attachés of the hotel. Nothing there—absolutely nothing—to prove that it wasn't all a dream. But as he entered his sitting-room he heard the clatter of horses' hoofs on the pavement outside. He rushed to the window and witnessed the departure of a big automobile from what he decided was the entrance reserved for royalty, almost directly beneath his rooms. A small detachment of mounted guardsmen rode off in its wake.

"Rosa Schmitz!" he sighed, a smile on his lips.

He suddenly thought of the portmanteau. It was nowhere in sight, whisked away during his absence—but Sharpe was standing in the bedroom door. He stared at the valet rather blankly for a few moments before realizing why the fellow was there.

"Never mind, Sharpe. I am in the habit of undressing myself," he said, his lips tightening. Now was the time to nip this sort of thing in the bud. Sharpe must not be permitted to get the upper hand of him. That would be fatal.

"Very good, sir," said Sharpe, calmly. "What suit shall I have ready for you in—"

Yorke broke in hastily: "And I am also capable of dressing myself in the morning, Sharpe."

"Quite so, sir. I understand, sir. But is it to be the gray tweed or the—ah—suit you were wearing when you arrived, sir?"

"The gray tweed, Sharpe."

"Very good, sir. Pardon me for having already thought so, sir. It has been laid out for you. Good night, sir."

"Good night, Sharpe."

CHAPTER VII

RODKIN THE RED

YORKE was sleeping soundly the next morning when Sharpe, after rapping lightly, unlocked the door and entered the apartment. Peeping into the inner chamber the valet discovered that the occupant of the great bed was still asleep. He frowned, perhaps a little impatiently, certainly in open perplexity. Even a well-trained valet may frown when he is perplexed, particularly when he is sure that his lapse from serenity is not likely to be detected. There was righteous cause for Sharpe's concern—or, for that matter, his vexation. In the first place it was after ten o'clock, and in the second place he was the bearer of a verbal message from Captain Sambo, who had been cooling his heels downstairs for the better part of an hour.

At the same time there was excellent cause for Mr. Yorke's tardy awakening. He had not gone to sleep until nearly five o'clock and he was therefore entitled to the belated slumber he was now enjoying, notwithstanding the fact that all unbeknownst to him at least two cabinet ministers of Graustark were expecting a call from him during the forenoon.

That an American could sleep till ten o'clock was something no Graustarkian—least of all, Captain Sambo—was willing or prepared to believe. It was generally accepted

as a fact in Graustark that all Americans were up and
doing at sunrise or a little thereafter, and that they were
in the habit of successfully accomplishing more by ten
o'clock in the morning than any half dozen Europeans put
together could have managed in a whole day. America
was supposed to be wide awake while all the rest of the
world was snoozing.

But here was an American who, far from being wide
awake, was magnificently sound asleep fully two hours
after the whole kingdom of Graustark was on the move.
This was Sharpe's third visit to the apartment. Twice
he had reported to Captain Sambo. On each of these
previous occasions he had taken it for granted that Mr.
Yorke was merely asleep. Now he listened intently, his
hand to his ear. He was apprehensive. This singular
inactivity on the part of an American suggested something sinister to the mind of the excellent Sharpe; the poor
man must be dead! Auricular testimony convinced him,
however, that this passing suspicion was groundless. And
this, of course, increased his dilemma. Should he arouse
Mr. Yorke or should he let him sleep? He was confronted by a most unexpected conflict in the matter of
instructions. On the one hand there was Captain Sambo's
command to notify Mr. Yorke that Captain Sambo was
waiting below to escort him to the office of the Minister of
War, while on the other hand were the positive, definite
and imperative orders that Mr. Yorke's comfort was to
be considered above everything else—and if sleeping till
ten o'clock wasn't a comfort, he'd like to know what
you'd call it.

Sharpe first tried dropping a military hairbrush on the

floor. No good. Then he permitted a window-shade to fly to the top with a great clatter. No good. Slamming the bedroom door had the same effect. Slamming it twice in rapid succession was no better. He thought of the bathtub, and proceeded to turn both faucets on full force. Sticking his nose around the corner of the door-jamb he looked to see what effect the roar of rushing water was having upon the sleeper. None whatever. Then his eyes brightened. He went out into the corridor and inaugurated a prolonged and violent assault upon the big brass door-knocker. That, he was confident, would disturb anything short of death itself.

And it did, as a matter of fact, disturb Yorke. When Sharpe looked in to observe the result of his experiment, he found that Mr. Yorke had turned over in bed, but, alas, probably in his sleep. The situation called for something drastic. Never in all his career as a valet had Sharpe been forced to lay hands upon a sleeping master, but now it had come to that pass. So he walked over and shook Mr. Yorke gently by the shoulder. He shook him again, this time a little more vigorously. Mr. Yorke's shoulder was large and hard but unresisting. It would stand a great deal of shaking. So Sharpe laid both hands upon the sleeper and shook with all his might. That did it. Mr. Yorke opened his eyes and blinked at Sharpe.

"Beg pardon, sir, but it's time to get up, sir," said Sharpe, a strong note of exasperation in his voice.

"All right, all right," said Yorke, cheerfully. " But say!" he exclaimed, sitting up suddenly. "I'm going to dress myself, understand that, Sharpe."

"Your bath is drawn, sir," said the imperturbable

Sharpe, and bolted into the bathroom to prevent its being disastrously overdrawn.

Fifteen minutes later Yorke was on his way downstairs. He had vindicated all American manhood in the judgment of the temporarily doubting Sharpe. He had given an example of speed, proficiency and adroitness in dressing himself that fairly staggered the valet, who couldn't believe his eyes when the tall young man strode briskly into the sitting-room, fully clad, when by all rights he should have been no farther along than the fourteenth or fifteenth yawn and the merest contemplation of a suit of still undisturbed underwear.

"My word, sir!" gasped Sharpe, involuntarily.

"You say Captain Sambo is waiting for me?"

"He is, sir."

At the door Yorke turned, surprising the valet in a stare of astonishment. "I can undress and get into bed in just half the time," he announced, meaningly.

Now Yorke had spent the greater part of the sleepless night in pleasant cogitation. Chief among his thoughts was the highly satisfactory reflection that Princess Virginia of Dawsbergen, for all her royal antecedents, was just like any other girl: bright and merry, fun-loving and gay, not a bit uppish or formal, just a regular girl. Like any other girl save in one particular, he qualified. She was prettier than any of the rest of them. He had rather hoped he might go on dreaming about her after he fell asleep, but no such luck. It rather disgusted him to think that he didn't dream about anything at all. Still he had some wonderful dreams about her while he lay awake. He wondered if it were possible for them ever to come true.

Hardly. He had been in love with Rosa Schmitz for five years—and that's a long time to be in love with a girl you've seen only once—but it was a far cry from simple Rosa to imperial Virginia.

Captain Sambo was nervously pacing the lobby.

"Have you breakfasted?" he inquired as he greeted the delinquent Yorke. Yorke's reply caused him to throw up his hands in a gesture of despair. "Good heavens! We are due at Count Quinnox's in precisely thirty minutes."

"That doesn't stump me," said Yorke, cheerfully. "Come and sit with me while I bolt a cup of coffee. That's all I need. How far is it to the Count's?"

They were out of the hotel and entering the Captain's automobile in less than fifteen minutes.

"You see what can be done when you put your mind to it," the American was saying. "I not only had toast and coffee, but fried eggs as well. And we have eight minutes to spare."

"I wonder if there is anything that can stump you Americans," said the Captain, shaking his head hopelessly.

The short drive to the War Office gave Yorke his first impression of the quaint old city. On every hand were signs of extreme antiquity: staunch old houses unlike anything he had ever seen before, rugged, age-polished and gray from the scourings of countless tempests and the bleachings of incalculable suns; queer, lop-sided doors and windows and rusty multangular roofs with shaggy stone chimneys; tiny balconies clinging like lichens to grim and battered façades; on the more pretentious buildings, turrets, with sinister-looking slits up and down their

several sides. Here and there Mosque-like domes lifted
their oval splendor above the humble surroundings, revealing the presence of temples that had been built in an
era when the city was dominated by Tartar, Semitic or
even Mohammedan influence.

The stone-paved streets were narrow, barely wide
enough for two vehicles to pass, and were bewilderingly
erratic in their wanderings. They roved in angles, bends,
twists and curlycues over an area that seemed as great
as all New York but which probably could have been set
down in Central Park with room to spare—a tangle of
walled-in lanes as baffling and as confusing as the paths
of a goldfish in an aquarium.

The sidewalks in that part of Edelweiss through which
Captain Sambo's car was weaving its way were a scant
four feet in width, but they were absolutely clear of fixed
obstacles. The windows in the shops could never have
been called "show windows" in the accepted meaning of
the term. They were intended for ventilation rather than
for display. A few of the shops exhibited articles characteristic of the commerce carried on inside, but as a
general thing signboards above or alongside the doors
served as guides to the public. Push-carts, mule-carts
and an occasional reminder of new-world audacity in
the shape of a Ford delivery wagon constituted what may
be described as the transport system of the City of Edelweiss. Police regulations and a no doubt inherent regard
for orderliness on the part of the people confined pedes-
trianism to the narrow sidewalks.

Never in all his travels had Yorke found himself in a
place so medieval as this, or so superior to the ravages

of decay. Egypt the mysterious, the magic, with all its vanquished glories, its shattered antiquity, its crumbling testimonials to the magnificence of long dead Pharaohs, could not—to quote the vastly interested American— hold a candle to Edelweiss when it came to visible, substantial evidence to support the fancy that he had been transported bodily back to the Middle Ages.

The people in the streets were not medieval in their physical aspect however. Most of them were dressed after the fashion of continental Europeans, both the men and the women. Occasionally one saw men, evidently peasants from the outlying districts, who still clung to the native costume as worn by their fathers and forefathers, but they were few and far between. There was indeed something surprisingly cosmopolitan about the throngs. Even in this busy, crowded district known as the "Lower City," one might easily have been persuaded to believe that he was in Vienna or Paris or even New York, that great Metropolis where foreign visages predominate. The true New Yorker, however, would have remarked this distinction: the faces of these people were clean whereas cleanliness of person in the foreign districts of his home city is an almost totally unrecognizable virtue.

Captain Sambo explained that this part of Edelweiss was at least seven hundred years old. The "Upper City," or the region bounded on the west by Castle Avenue, was quite modern; very few of the houses there were more than two hundred years old, some of them, indeed, having been built as recently as the early part of the nineteenth century. Of course, he went on to say rather apologetically, there were a number of so-called palaces in Edelweiss, put up by the *nouveau riche* since the beginning of the present century, parvenus being something that even the oldest of civilizations was powerless to suppress. And over beyond the Regengetz Circus, on which the hotel was situated, Mr. Yorke presently would see a few American-designed office buildings, to say nothing of the handsome structure formerly occupied by the American Club but now used as an Art Museum.

What he drily described as the "American invasion" had followed close upon the elevation of Mr. Grenfell Lorry to the exalted position of Prince Consort, some thirty-four or -five years ago. With the outbreak of the Great War many of the Americans—the engineers, architects, builders and railway men who came over at the beginning of the century—left Edelweiss to return to their own country or to join the Foreign Legion in France. The "invasion," he explained, was almost exclusively a young man's affair. These men never returned to Graustark. And so the Club became a thing of the joyous past.

"There are very few Jews in Edelweiss," he said. "We have here a number of citizens who call themselves Jews but we know their origin. In religion only are they Jews, Mr. Yorke. Centuries ago their forebears were Tartars —flat-nosed Tartars—who, being hunted and driven from one land to another by relentless foes, sought refuge with the true Hebrews, fastened themselves upon that devout and resourceful race and in course of time came to be known as Jews. Russia swarms with Jews of that type. They are not descended from the ancient Hebrews. They were outcasts, remnants of shattered tribes, barterers, traders, wandering merchants, poachers. And to-day they are called Hebrews the world over, God save the name! They multiply as no other branch of the human race multiplies and they have followed civilization only when the path leads to security. It is this element that we fear in Graustark. They preach communism and talk of the Brotherhood of man with but one object in view: the overthrow of established order and the creation of a new chaos from which they, being shrewd traders in human emotions and human frailty, may arise with their hands clutching not the empty air but all the physical wealth of the world. Ah! Here we are, Mr. Yorke. The citadel confronts you."

The car, turning sharply out of what appeared to be a *cul de sac*, entered a wide, grass-covered square or plaza on the far side of which loomed the walls and towers of the ancient fortress of Edelweiss. The flag of Graustark floated from the central tower. Sentries paced to and fro before the huge, iron-studded gates; obsolete cannon, posted along the base of the wall, pointed their ugly noses toward the peaceful city; a squad of mounted patrol guards, awaiting orders, formed a gaudy, picturesque group over against the farthermost corner of the gray mass of stone.

"Relics of the twelve-year war with Axphain back in the seventeenth century," said Captain Sambo, indicating the ridiculous old siege guns.

Being admitted without delay to the fortress, they were in a very few minutes ushered into the office of the Commander-in-chief of the Graustark Army, the tall, white-haired Count Quinnox. Never had Yorke looked upon a finer specimen of soldier than the man who rose to greet them as they entered the room. He was seventy or more, yet as erect as a pine; his figure was young and vigorous and full of a supple grace; his scarred face was lean and bronzed and singularly handsome despite its disfigurements.

Count Quinnox shook hands warmly with the young American. His smile was friendly, his eyes searching in their scrutiny of his visitor's face.

"And if there is anything that I can do, Mr. Yorke," he was saying after the first few minutes of polite conversation, "anything at all that will be of help to you in your mission here you may be assured of my readiness and willingness up to that point where military obstinacy intervenes on the side of discretion. Your father, I understand, was an officer in the United States Army a number of years ago."

"Yes. He was a Colonel."

"Colonel Randolph Yorke, if my memory serves me faithfully. He died, I believe, when you were but a few weeks old."

Yorke was startled. "You appear to have investigated me pretty thoroughly in a very short space of time," said he, smiling. "Ten days at the outside."

The Count raised his hand in protest. "You do our secret service more honor than it deserves, Mr. Yorke. In the first place, our knowledge of you is derived almost entirely from facts gleaned by our neighbor, Dawsbergen, and I may add for your edification that Prince Dantan began his inquiries at least five years ago."

"The deuce you say," murmured Yorke, rather blankly.

"It is to Dawsbergen that we are indebted for a fairly complete history of you and your forefathers," said the Count, enjoying the young man's astonishment. "We know that your mother was Miss Emily Margaret Fortune, of Washington, second daughter of Mr. John K. Fortune, and a granddaughter of Judge Robert Fortune. Her brother is Mr. George Fortune, of Montana. We know your college, the year you were graduated, your athletic as well as your scholastic record. We know something of your habits, your work, your adventures and your record in the Navy. In short, Mr. Yorke, we know a great deal more about you than you know about us, although I trust you may become better acquainted with us before long. You see, my dear sir, Prince Dantan had an excellent reason for inquiring into the personal and private life of Mr. Pendennis Yorke."

Whereupon the speaker and Captain Sambo joined in a hearty laugh. Mr. Yorke perforce laughed also, but somewhat lamely.

"I hope with all my soul that Prince Dantan found out nothing that would prejudice him against me, because, you see, I expect to go from here to Dawsbergen in the same capacity that brings me to Graustark. It would be extremely awkward if I got there only to have the door slammed in my face by an irate ruler who had found out a good many things about me that had somehow managed to escape the notice of a watchful college faculty."

"It may comfort you, my young friend, to know that Prince Dantan was once a college student," said the Count, most affably. "In fact, he was thrice a college student. The records will show that he was sent down from Oxford in his second year and that he subsequently experienced grave difficulty in staying at both Heidelberg and the University of Vienna for any considerable length of time."

"Well, I'm glad to hear that," said Yorke, relieved. "He seems to be human, at any rate."

The Count himself conducted his visitor over the fortress. The view from the battlements was magnificent. Situated on the brow of a rather pronounced eminence, the fortress looked down upon a wide bend of the river and far out across the lowlands to the snow-capped mountains that ringed the massive bowl. As far as the eye could reach were lofty mountains, peak above peak, until the farthermost crests were like sunlit, cone-shaped clouds resting immovable upon the deceptive mist created by vast distances.

"Wonderful!" exclaimed Yorke.

"It would not last an hour against the fire of modern guns," said Count Quinnox, who was not thinking of the view.

Before taking his departure, Yorke made an early appointment with the Commander-in-chief of the army for an interview concerning the military affairs of the country.

"You do not let the grass grow under your feet, I perceive," said the Count, drily.

"It's my early training, sir," explained Yorke, with his most engaging smile. "I was what is known as a sprinter in college."

From the fortress Captain Sambo conducted his charge

to the Tower, where he was introduced to Baron Gourou, Chief of Police and Commander of the Tower, a thin-faced, keen-eyed man who, while courteous, was nevertheless wary. He was the successor to the famous Baron Jasto Dangloss, who for nearly half a century had held this position of trust and who was known far and wide as head of one of the most efficient secret service organizations in all Europe.

It was said of Gourou that he had eyes in the back of his head, ears that could hear through walls ten feet thick, a nose like a bloodhound's, and, greater than all these, the power to render himself invisible! To this astute gentleman Yorke frankly bared his intentions. He announced that it was not his plan to confine his study of conditions in Graustark to the upper classes alone.

"It is much simpler, Baron, for the well-to-do, the powerful and the satisfied upper classes to put their best foot forward than it is for the lower and supposedly down-trodden classes. I have learned that there are usually two truths to every question, assuming that the truth is something that one tells when he is absolutely honest in his convictions. Well, if the rich believe one thing to be true and the poor believe another thing to be true, it stands to reason that there are two truths to be considered instead of one. I have been sent here to get the real story of Graustark for my paper. By putting together the truth as told by the bourgeoisie and that told by the so-named proletariat I have an idea I can weave them into the whole truth and nothing but the truth, and that's what we are after, isn't it?"

"I daresay," replied Baron Gourou briefly.

Captain Sambo seemed a trifle uneasy. He was asking himself the question: Is this fellow Yorke, after all, one of those meddlesome literary fanatics who are turning the world upside down with their silly views? Yorke's next remark cleared the atmosphere considerably.

"I shall pay no more heed to your unbalanced radicals than I would to their soap-box counterparts in New York or London, Baron. I come from a free country where alas, we have entirely too much freedom. I have heard men spouting on street corners who ought to have been shot dead where they stood. All I ask, Baron Gourou, is the privilege of studying conditions here from all angles, and I would appreciate your coöperation. If at any time I should ignorantly overstep the bounds of discretion, in your opinion, I shall expect you to fetch me up with a jerk, and I promise you not to resent it."

Baron Gourou had not taken his eyes from the young man's face. Yorke had the feeling that his innermost thoughts were being read. Perhaps they were, for suddenly the Commander of the Tower smiled and held out his hand.

"It will give me great pleasure, Mr. Yorke, to assist you in every way. When in doubt, come to me. I understand you contemplate a month's stay in Graustark. I trust you will not take it amiss if I assure you that in two days' time, if you so desire, you could be in possession of all the data you need concerning our little country. You will find the task a simple one. Our problems are easy ones, our solutions prompt. The Minister of the Treasury will show you that our national debt is insignificant, that our people are prosperous and not overburdened by taxes, and that our credit, paradoxically, is much too good. That is an economical misfortune, strange as it may appear, Mr. Yorke. Our war records are available. We did our bit, as the English say, and we came out of the maelstrom right side up. We have our radical element, to be sure. I maintain that it is a necessary evil. It would be a very tiresome world if there were no screws loose in it. No country can survive universal contentment. Remember there were angels cast out of heaven. To-day the world is more restless than ever before. Restlessness is in the air. We in Graustark breathe the same air that keeps the rest of the world alive. And so we have traces here of the greatest of all plagues—unrest. Writers of sea tales speak of the cloud no larger than a man's hand appearing on the face of the calm blue sky, and they tell you that in an hour's time that same little cloud produces a tempest violent enough to convulse an entire ocean. The wise mariner does not despise the little cloud. He battens down his hatches, reefs his sails, and waits. There is nothing else for him to do. He cannot turn the tempest aside with a wave of his feeble hand, nor can he evade it, so he makes ready to meet it when the time comes. So it is with us in Graustark, Mr. Yorke. We keep an eye on the little white cloud and wait. Come in and see me often. I may be able to add a little spice to your articles. Captain Sambo will tell you that I am a great chatterbox, an inveterate scandalmonger."

As they left the Tower, Captain Sambo shrugged his shapely shoulders and said: "Mount Ganlook up there is a magpie compared to Baron Gourou. If you can get anything out of him, Yorke, you are truly a wizard. But, I must say this. He has taken a fancy to you. And I suppose, after all, he is only a shade less human than the rest of us. He will not be in the least displeased at having his name and his exploits published in a great American newspaper."

They spent the remainder of the morning sight-seeing. Yorke was vastly impressed by the handsome houses and private parks of the nobility which lined the eastern side of Castle Avenue, a magnificent two mile boulevard that had its beginning in Regengetz Circus and ended in a wide plaza before the enormous gates leading to the castle grounds. Above the treetops in the foreground rose the weather-beaten, time-worn stone towers of the ancient castle, standing far back in the royal park, screened from intimate view by the high, sinister walls that had guarded the home of all the Princes and Princesses of Graustark for centuries.

"Grim," was the single word uttered by Yorke as he gazed upon the forbidding walls, the massive gates and the distant gray towers.

"Grim without but glorious within," said Captain Sambo, rather curtly. "These walls, my friend, have withstood many an ancient siege, have turned back many a gallant foe. Those towers have felt the touch of cannon balls but never the scratch of spears. Valiant men have scaled these walls, sir, but not one has ever fought his way to the base of those historic towers. One day I will show you the moat guarding the northern side of the castle. You will then understand why innumerable attempts to force the castle from that direction ended in disaster for the enemy." He shrugged his shoulders again. "What was impossible in the olden days would, of course, be ridiculously easy to-day. Long range guns in the hills across the valley could blow the castle to pieces in half an hour. But in those good old days, sir, when men fought hand-to-hand with battle-ax and spear and sent their own bodies against impregnable walls instead of hurling substitutes in the shape of shells from a distance of five leagues or more—ah, then the Castle of Graustark was as strong as Gibraltar."

"Those good old days," mused Yorke. "You speak feelingly, Captain. As if you regret that we do not fight our battles now as they did in the good old days."

The Captain stared at him in astonishment. "Good God, sir, what soldier doesn't regret it?" he exclaimed, bitterly.

Later on, as the two men were having luncheon at Pingari's, a fashionable restaurant far up the steep slope of Mount Ganlook, Yorke brought up the subject of Prince Hubert.

"Is there any likelihood that he may some day succeed in regaining the throne of his ancestors? The Princess informs me that he has made several attempts to bring about a counter-revolution but always without getting anywhere."

Captain Sambo glanced over his shoulder before answering. When he spoke it was in a low, guarded tone.

"I beg of you to be careful, Mr. Yorke. The Soviets in Axphain have spies scattered throughout Edelweiss, watching every move of Prince Hubert, catching every

word they possibly can that might indicate activity on
the part of the monarchists. Baron Gourou has reason
to believe that several of the waiters in this café are
Axphainian agents." Apparently satisfied that no one
was listening, he went on: "Prince Hubert is not popular
with his own party. The monarchists do not like him.
Conditions are so bad in Axphain that I am convinced
the people themselves would welcome the reëstablish-
ment of the monarchy. If a leader were to spring up in
whom all parties had confidence, the coup would be
simple."

"Is there no one?"

Sambo's eyes narrowed. "Are you interviewing me,
Mr. Yorke, for newspaper publication?"

"You have only to say that it is confidential, Captain
Sambo, and it will go no farther," replied Yorke, stiffly.
"If there can be honor among thieves, there certainly can
be honor among newspaper men."

"I beg your pardon, sir," said the officer promptly.
"Since it is not for publication, I may tell you that there
is but one man who can lead Axphain out of the morass.
Hubert's half-brother, the illegitimate offspring of the late
Prince and a certain noble lady of Axphain. There is no
secret about it. Prince Hedrik long ago proclaimed this
boy to be his son. Whereupon the people at once gave
their hearts to the young man. He enjoyed a popularity
that was never accorded the legal heirs to the throne.
The people sympathized with him, they loved him and
they would have rejoiced to see him, bastard though he
is, succeed to the throne rather than the Crown Prince or

his brother Hubert. He was what you might well call
an idol—a besmirched idol, you will say—but still an
idol."

"Where is he now?"

"He is with his mother in Italy. When the revolution
came, they were permitted to leave Axphain without interference. Indeed, they were given a special escort and
many favors. The lady of whom I speak is the Countess
Valerie Yanzi, sister of a mighty and a well-beloved nobleman, the Duke of Mizrox, who died some years ago." He
hesitated a moment before continuing. "She never married, Mr. Yorke. It has been said that one of her own
servants, a faithful fellow indeed, was the man who
wielded the ax when Prince Hedrik was beheaded."

"Why don't the monarchists get hold of this young
fellow and bring him back to lead the—"

"I thought you would ask that question," interrupted
the other. "The young fellow, as you call him, refuses
to come back. He will not listen to their pleas, their
blandishments, their promises. In short, he prefers to
remain what he now is, a beloved outcast rather than
become the questionable ruler of Axphain. I rather admire his stand. He says it is Hubert's job, not his."

"I don't know but that he's right," said Yorke, after a
moment's thought. "I shouldn't care to sit on a throne
my father had debased."

"Those are rather strong words."

"He has probably used stronger," said Yorke, succinctly.

They were sitting at a table on the glass-enclosed terrace which looked down upon the city two thousand feet

below. Over a winding, zigzag course they had ascended the mountainside, passing scores of houses perched on the slope in such seemingly precarious fashion that Yorke wondered why they did not topple over and go rattling down like avalanches into the serenely indifferent heart of Edelweiss. There were times, too, where he shrank back from the window of the car, confident that the next turn of the wheels would plunge them over the low protecting wall that guarded the hair-raising curves. He was devoutly thankful when the car swung out upon the little plateau on which Pingari's was situated, and was soon lost in admiration of the wonderful picture to be seen from the café terrace. Now, after an excellent luncheon, he was wondering how they could possibly get down the steep mountain without disaster. However, he did not mention his fears to the complacent officer who looked dreamily out over the rockbound valley. He remembered Captain Sambo saying as the car started to climb the slanting, serpentinous road that very few people had ever motored up. Only a high-powered car could make the grade. Fashionable Edelweiss preferred the slower, more leisurely means of travel: they made the ascent in vehicles drawn by horse or donkey.

"But we will come down much faster than we go up," he had promised, and Yorke was now wondering if it would not turn out to be a prophecy rather than a promise. At three o'clock he was to appear with his credentials at the office of the Prime Minister, where certain formalities were necessary before permission could be granted him, as an alien, to remain in Graustark for a period longer than six days. "Don't be uneasy about the time," Sambo had said reassuringly. "I will have you at the Prime Minister's on the minute if I have to break my neck doing it."

Yorke sighed deeply as he recalled these words—in fact, he had sighed repeatedly.

Now there had been a definite purpose in his mind when he broached the subject of Hubert. So, as he re-lighted his cigar, he inquired with commendable unconcern:

"Wouldn't Prince Hubert solve a great many of his difficulties if he were to marry—er—some one like the Princess of Dawsbergen, for instance?"

The Captain's smile was ironical. "He would, indeed. He would much prefer doing that than to go out and fight for a throne."

Yorke hesitated a few seconds. "Do you think he has a chance?"

"Who knows? Is there a man in all this world so wise that he can guess what is in a woman's mind?"

"Does that mean, Captain, that you wouldn't be surprised if—so to speak—if she accepted him?"

"She might," answered the officer, with irritating calmness. "God knows that stranger things have happened."

"It would be terrible," announced Pendennis Yorke, with sudden vehemence.

The Captain leaned forward. "Grewsome is the better word, Yorke," he said, a hard note in his voice. "Thirty odd years ago in the Hotel Regengetz, Prince Hubert's uncle was assassinated in cold blood by Prince Gabriel, brother of Princess Virginia's father, the present ruler of Dawsbergen. Since that day Axphainian princes have thirsted for the royal blood of Dawsbergen. I shudder, sir, when I think of Princess Virginia married to a blood hungry Prince of Axphain."

"There was a blood feud between the Montagues and the Capulets," Yorke reminded him, "and it was in a fair way to being wiped out by the loves of Romeo and Juliet."

"Ah, but theirs was the most beautiful love story ever conceived. Prince Hubert is not a Romeo, Mr. Yorke, nor is the daughter of Dantan a Juliet. Bless my soul, it is ten minutes of three!" he exclaimed, looking at his watch. "We must be off at once."

As Yorke entered the Regengetz shortly before six o'clock he was accosted by a man whose face was strangely familiar and who held out his hand in greeting. He was short, thin and bespectacled. His features were sharp, his complexion pallid, his eyes behind the horn-rimmed glasses singularly large and alert.

He was holding his hat in his hand, uncovering a thick, bushy mass of oily black hair. The lips, spread in a smile, were thin and red, the teeth white and even. He had a broad, low brow, from which the rest of his face tapered to a sharp chin.

"You don't remember me, Yorke," he said, and his smile was wistful.

"Good Lord!" exclaimed Yorke, grasping the other's hand. "Rodkin! What the devil are you doing here?"

He had recognized the man as a classmate, one of the brightest men in college. Michael Rodkin!

"Forgive me for tackling you in this manner, Yorke," apologized the other. "But I couldn't resist coming to see you. It has been a long time since I've run across any one from college—and I don't mind confessing I was hungry for the sight of you. What am I doing here? Ask that chap standing over there by the window. He isn't looking at us, but I fancy he sees us just the same. He is one of Gourou's smartest agents."

"By thunder, Michael! I remember now. You were the red-hottest little socialist going when you were in college. Don't tell me you're over here cooking up revolutions and all that sort of thing."

Rodkin laughed. "You don't imagine I came around to ask you to be one of my pall-bearers, do you? To be sure I am a Communist, I belong to the Internationale, and I am what is generally known as an agitator. A Red, if you like, Denny. And I make speeches on street corners occasionally, ripping the rich up the back. Right under the old Baron's nose, too. But I am hardly what you'd call a revolutionary leader. I am simply an educator. I've never thrown a bomb in my life, but I've hurled bales of communistic literature in my time. Everybody knows me here. They all know I am a jolly little Red. I suppose I've got you in Dutch with the police by coming to see you as a friend. I heard you were here to write up Graustark for a New York paper; so I hurried around to shake hands with you before you found out too much about me. Don't you worry, old chap. I'll give you a clean bill if they come to me. They will believe me. I've never lied to them."

"Do you mean to tell me you are preaching Bolshevism openly here in Edelweiss, Rodkin?"

"Certainly. If I preached it secretly they'd hang me."

"But why the deuce do they allow it? Why don't they chase you out of the country?"

"My dear fellow, you must not forget that I am an American citizen," said Rodkin, a mocking light in his big, black eyes. "I also am an American correspondent, the same as you, if you please."

"The dickens you are!"

"I am the Edelweiss representative of the largest American news service bureau in Moscow. We send reams of stuff to the U. S. A. every month. There must be a couple of hundred honest American citizens employed by our bureau up there in Moscow."

"What kind of Americans?" demanded Yorke, his lip curling.

Rodkin did not take offense. He was used to being badgered. "Intelligent Americans, old man—if you see what I mean."

"I'm damned if I do, Michael. And why is it that I've never seen anything about Graustark in the stuff you are circulating over there in America?"

"I daresay it is because you don't read the language in which it is printed," replied Rodkin coolly. "I've shot hundreds of columns about Graustark to the United States in the last year or two, and here you are telling me you've never read a line of it. Come, old man, is that fair? I've read every line you've written since you took up the game."

"Yes, but, thank God, I write only in English."

"Let's not quarrel, Denny. You think one way, I think another. We're both honest. We both manage to get our stuff printed—and that's all there is to it. If I

am willing to shake hands with an enemy I don't see
why you should object to shaking hands with a friend."

"By gad, Rodkin, you always did have a smart way of
pullings things," said Yorke, not without a trace of admiration in his voice. "You haven't lost any of your infernal cleverness, have you?"

"Am I to consider that a compliment? Don't answer.
I'll take it as such, Denny, for the sake of old times. But
no more politics, if you please. You don't seem a day
older than when I saw you last in New York. That was
seven years ago, wasn't it?"

"I think so. You have aged, Michael. Gad, it's no
wonder I didn't recognize you at first. We're about the
same age, aren't we?"

"My dear fellow, I am at least a hundred years older
than you are. As a matter of fact, you aren't even born
yet. Well, it's good to see you, Denny. I'd ask you to
drop in and see me if I thought you'd care to take the
risk. I am in lodgings down near the railway station.
Any policeman can point out the place. If there is anything I can do to be of assistance to you, don't hesitate
to call on me. You might even want to get an angle on
our side of the great problem, you know."

He held out his hand again, and, to save his life, Yorke
could not resist taking it. He had always liked the mild-
mannered, brilliant Rodkin.

"I'll look in on you one day, Michael," he said. "They
can't hang me for that, can they?"

"They would have to hang me first," said Rodkin, a
glitter in his eyes.

The man at the window had left his place and was passing by them on his way to the door. Rodkin spoke to him.

"I say, Landos, I'll stroll along with you, if you don't mind. I want to tell you something about my good friend Yorke."

CHAPTER VIII

YORKE had a busy week. He met and interviewed a number of the leading men of Graustark, visited various institutions, obtained valuable and interesting statistics from government sources, filling half a dozen notebooks with data of an exceedingly tiresome nature. Figures, facts and nothing else—certainly nothing from which he could hope to construct the thrilling story he was expected and virtually commanded to write.

His orders had been explicit. "Give us something snappy, something that will make 'em sit up and take notice. Inside stuff, with a lot of zip to it."

He had to laugh every time he thought of his notes. How was he to make a snappy, zippy story out of the material he had collected? Tax figures, crop statistics, rates of exchange, visible resources and practically invisible liabilities, contentment, the cost of living, winter sports (which he had missed), war stories that nobody would read, police exploits that New York would laugh at, the death rate and the birth rate, health conditions (which were so good that people wouldn't be interested in them at all), the quality of light wines and beer, customs and costumes of the people, the size of the standing army— Good heavens! Nobody would read such drivel! The only thing about Graustark that distinguished it from

146

the rest of eastern Europe, was its disgusting serenity. Nobody in America—absolutely nobody—wanted to read about serenity! And if he were to report that Graustark did not owe a penny to the United States—which was quite true—there wouldn't be the slightest reason in the world for mentioning the fact that she was prosperous. Nevertheless, despite the sparse gleanings, his typewriter rattled on with deceptive energy, sometimes late into the night. He rejoiced that the faithful machine was blissfully ignorant of what he was writing. Also that it did not possess a sense of the ridiculous.

He lunched almost daily with smart young officers, dined at Pingari's with some lively married friends of Sambo's and spent a full day in the mining town of Ganlook. But not once during the week did he have so much as a glimpse of the Princess Virginia or any member of the royal family. Nor word of any kind from the erstwhile Rosa Schmitz. He saw a great deal of Sharpe, however. Every evening, without fail, the valet stuck a fresh gardenia in his buttonhole.

"See here, Sharpe," said Yorke on the eighth evening, "where do you get these gardenias?"

"Sir?"

"I say, where do you get them?"

"The gardenias, sir?"

"Yes, the gardenias. Don't you know they are out of season and as rare as hen's teeth?"

Sharpe cleared his throat. "I am aware of that, sir." He seemed a trifle confused, a most uncommon thing for Sharpe. "As a matter of fact, I really can't say that I get them anywhere, if you see what I mean, sir."

"No, I don't see what you mean."

"Well, sir, the fact is, if I may speak of it in confidence, a gardener's boy from the Castle fetches them every day, just as he would fetch the milk, sir, if that was his job."

Mr. Yorke's face brightened instantly. His spirits shot upward with a velocity that left him dizzy for a moment or two.

"Is—is there anything else you would care to tell me in confidence, Sharpe?"

"Of course, sir, it is only hearsay and perhaps not to be relied upon, but I understand Her Highness, Princess Virginia, has given special orders to the Chief Gardener to send a gardenia to you every day, Mr. Yorke, as long as they last."

"Hearsay? May I inquire from whom you heard all this?"

"From the gardener's boy, sir."

"Is he in the habit of lying?"

"If I ever caught him at it, I'd give him a good strapping," said Sharpe, sternly. "You see, sir, he is my son. I have decided to bring him up in a manner of speaking to be a gardener. It's not quite so confining an occupation as valeting, you understand, and besides my wife happens to be the Chief Gardener's only daughter. I might mention, sir, that only this morning Her Highness asked me if the gardenias the gardener's boy was delivering were perfectly fresh."

"You saw the Princess Virginia this morning, Sharpe?"

"Quite by accident, sir. Her car bumped into me as I was crossing Castle Avenue. She was driving her father, sir, to the railway station."

"Her father? The Prince of Dawsbergen?" exclaimed Yorke.

"Yes, sir. He has been a guest at the Castle for two or three days." A thoroughly human smile illuminated Sharpe's usually sober face. "You may recall him, sir, as the gentleman who lunched at the Tower with you and Baron Gourou quite informally yesterday."

"What!"

"In a manner of speaking, sir, very much after the fashion of the celebrated Caliph of Baghdad," volunteered Sharpe. "In cog, as it were."

Yorke stared. "You must be crazy, Sharpe. The man you refer to was the Chief Forester of Graustark, Colonel Baldos. I've never seen the Prince of—"

"Pardon the interruption, sir, but you have," said Sharpe firmly. "When you come to know royalty as I know it, sir—by means of a more or less personal contact, you will not be surprised by anything they may take it into their heads to do. It pleased His Highness to pose as a Forester, leggings, shooting-jacket, pipe and all—and there you are, sir. If I may be permitted to offer a suggestion I should say that it was uncommonly decent of him. It is a rather jolly way that royalty some time has of putting the—ah—the common people, so to speak, at their ease, sir. Makes them act natural and all that sort of thing, if you see what I mean. I daresay you talked to him as free and easy as you would to me, sir."

Yorke sat down limply on the edge of the bed. "A damned sight more so," he exclaimed, adding: "If you see what I mean."

It was true that Prince Dantan had assumed the rather humble rôle of Chief Forester of Graustark. He had journeyed from Serros in haste upon receipt of a letter from his youngest daughter. A single sentence toward the end was responsible for his sudden unannounced visit. "I know I shall fall heels over head in love with him all over again if I see very much of him and that would be simply shocking, wouldn't it?" The next sentence, while not quite so flattering to Mr. Yorke, in that it ignored him altogether, was not without its significance. "By the way, before I forget it, I had to borrow two hundred gavvos from Bevra, who is awfully hard-up just now, so please advance me a thousand if convenient, because if you don't I shall have to come home much sooner than I expected. Your loving and devoted daughter, Virginia."

Now Dantan was a man of action. More than that, he was a man of vision. So, foreseeing complications, he hurried off to Graustark. There was great commotion at the Castle when he turned up one morning in time for breakfast and announced that he was hungry for the sight of his grandchildren. His son-in-law, Prince Robin, was properly deceived and delighted, but his two daughters, possessing that strange gift peculiar to their sex, instantly divined the true purpose behind his visit.

Pursuing a wily course in strategy, he spent the better part of the forenoon romping in a most unmajestic fashion with the small heir to the throne of Graustark and his even smaller sister.

"And now, my dear," he said to Virginia, as the royal

family sat down to luncheon, "where am I to find this agreeable ex-husband of yours?"

"So *that's* why you've come," cried Virginia, who had known all the time.

"By Jove!" exclaimed Prince Robin, his jaw falling.

"I was sure you were up to something, daddy," said Princess Bevra, severely.

"So was I," cried Virginia. "But I thought it was only because you didn't think it would be safe to let anybody else bring me the godsend. I mean the thousand."

"And it wasn't the children at all," pouted Bevra. "You are a dreadfully unreliable grandparent."

"He is at the Regengetz," said Virginia, answering her father's question. "But," she went on, frowning dubiously, "if you want to see him, Your Majesty, it will be necessary to make an appointment. He is a very busy man and can't afford to waste much time on incidentals."

"Incidentals! I like that!"

"Nothing could be more incidental than you as a parent-in-law, daddy. You are a wonderful grandparent, but as a father-in-law you don't amount to a row of pins."

"Nevertheless," began Prince Dantan, firmly, "I mean to have a look at the young man and a chat with him as well."

"If you fancy you can frighten him or bluff him by looking at him regally, daddy, you will have the surprise of your life," announced Virginia.

"What do you think of him, Robin?"

"From all accounts, Sir, he is a most attractive chap. I haven't seen him myself, but he has made a very favorable impression on several members of the Cabinet. And Sharpe, the shrewdest of Baron Gourou's agents, reports that he is all he claims to be and a gentleman in every sense of the word. And Sharpe has seen a great deal of him. We intend asking him to dinner one night next week, Sir."

"Just a little family dinner," added Bevra, maliciously.

"Don't be silly, Bevra," commanded her father. "It isn't the subject for jest, you know." He leaned forward, a dark frown on his brow. "I fear we have all been treating the matter too lightly."

"What do you mean, Sir?" asked Robin, struck by his father-in-law's seriousness.

"I have had Mavorak, of the Department of Justice, go into the question thoroughly. Yesterday he advised me that if this young American should decide to stand upon his rights he can make trouble for Virginia. Mavorak says that they declared themselves to be husband and wife before witnesses in the presence of a notary who held his seal of office under the old régime in Hungary and who still holds it to-day. It was not absolutely necessary for the notary to pronounce them man and wife it appears. Their own declarations constitute a marriage, the pronouncement of justice or priest being no more than a form by which the state and church puts its sanction and approval upon the union. As for the divorce, the facts are these: if proof of marriage be established a decree of court is necessary to dissolve it. In short, Robin, a man and a woman may be united by God but they must be divorced by man. A rare anomaly, isn't it? Every country has its own marriage laws, and they are bound to be recognized by all other countries. It seems, however, that the laws regarding divorce are comparatively uniform. There must be an official decree, granted by a person authorized by the state—not by the church, mind you, nor by the individual—to grant such decree. Mavorak has ascertained that at no time was it legal for persons to be divorced in Hungary by merely signifying the intention, not even in Bela Kun's day. He says there is no doubt about that. The people, it seems, assumed that because they could be legally married by declaration they could also be divorced in the same manner. So we are confronted by a very definite situation. Virginia and Yorke were legally married and they are not legally divorced."

The statement was not the bombshell that he may have expected it to be. He had made it to three young people in whose veins coursed a fair share of American blood unhampered by that sluggish factor known as the imperial strain. His daughters and his son-in-law laughed delightedly!

"What the devil is there to laugh at?" he demanded, more exasperated than astonished. He had long since gotten over being astonished by anything these whilom young people did or said. His own wife, the mother of the two girls, had given him many a lesson in deportment. Sometimes, when sorely tried, he threw up his hands and hopelessly but lovingly declared all three of them to be "half-breeds."

"I was only wondering, daddy, what Mr. Yorke will say when we break the awful news to him," said his daughter Virginia, her eyes sparkling.

"Gosh!" exclaimed the American side of Prince Robin. "I can't help laughing, Sir, when I think of Yorke having to support Virginia for the rest of his natural life. Still, on second thought, he's had a pretty easy time of it for the first five years. One luncheon, one dinner, one cinema and a couple of taxi rides in all that time—"

"It is a very serious matter, Bobbie," broke in Prince Dantan, sternly. "Suppose he concludes to be—well, a blackguard?"

Here Virginia's eyes flashed. "Father! That is a most disgusting word."

"I am perfectly aware of that, my dear. But, after all, there *is* such a word, you know, and there *are* blackguards in the world, millions of them."

"Mr. Yorke isn't one," said she, hotly.

"I think," said Bevra, soberly, "that if we agree to let Mr. Yorke off scot-free, he would condescend to be equally charitable to us."

"Confound you, Bevra," began her father, explosively; "do you mean to suggest that I—"

"I'm not going to have you bullying Mr. Yorke, daddy," said Virginia, darkly.

"It is not my intention to bully him, Virginia. Will you be good enough to tell me what objection you have to my seeing him?"

"Oh, goodness, I don't object to that," she cried quickly. "You can't help liking him. He has the truest, finest eyes and the most—"

"Spare me!" interrupted her parent. "I've been hearing all that for the past five years. Now see here, Bobbie, I have a plan. I should like to meet this engaging Mr.

Yorke, but I don't want him to know who I am. Can we arrange it?"

"Easily, Sir. Leave it to me."

"The sooner the better."

"To-morrow."

"Do you really believe, daddy, that they are still married?" asked Bevra, her brow puckered.

"We must be on the safe side, my dear. Mavorak advises me to institute proceedings in Serros for a divorce."

"I don't think it is quite fair to drag Mr. Yorke into a divorce court when he only meant to be kind to me," protested Virginia.

"Good heavens, child, what would you have me do? Drop the matter? Let it stand as it is? Why, if it is as Mavorak says, you are married to this man. Don't you realize what that means? Don't you— And besides," he interrupted himself to growl, "when you have the confounded impudence to say to me in a letter that you are likely to fall heels over head in love with him, I submit it is time for me to take steps of some sort."

"Pray tell me, daddy," said she, sweetly, "what would be wrong with my falling heels over head in love with him? Doesn't that sometimes happen even in the best regulated of families?"

"Don't be vulgar!"

"See here, Virgie," put in Robin, seriously; "you're not falling in love with this chap, are you?"

"Certainly not!" she exclaimed, indignantly.

"Then what do you mean by writing such silly nonsense to me—"

"Father dear, the most important thing in the letter,

the only important thing in it, in fact, you choose to completely ignore," said Virginia, eyeing him with cold disfavor. "It seems to me you are doing it intentionally, deliberately."

"Good God! What could be more important than your—"

"You have been here since eight o'clock this morning and you haven't once peeped about the two thousand I implored you to advance against my next year's allowance."   .

"You distinctly mentioned one thousand."

"Ah, now we're getting somewhere at last. How about it?"

"No wonder the Bolsheviks cry out against the grasping, mercenary upper classes," groaned her father.

Two days later she accompanied him to the railway station. It was early in the morning. She drove the car, the chauffeur sitting behind on the rumble. From time to time Prince Dantan glanced at her tenderly, almost wonderingly out of the corner of his eye. She was so fresh and exquisite, so joyous, so adorably and so tantalizingly feminine, that he wondered how she could be all these and still be the daughter of a mere mortal like himself. And to make the mystery all the deeper, she was said to bear a pronounced though glorified resemblance to her father. Her sister Bevra was like her mother; it was easy for him to understand why she was lovely. But that this one, who "took after" her father, should be so superlatively beautiful—well, somehow it did not seem quite right or just that she should look like him instead of like her mother. It wasn't fair.

What was in store for her? What would the future bring to his Virginia? She would marry—but where in all this world was there another Robin of Graustark to whom Fate in its rarest mood had given his daughter Bevra? He knew them all, these princes. He knew many of them personally, all of them by reputation. They were either stupid or vile. Not one was fit to touch the hem of her garment, much less to lay hands upon her body, nor even to breathe words of love into her ear. Once upon a time there were noble young princes in the land, strong and good and valiant, but alas, they were of a passing generation. A sorry brood had come along to take their places—insignificant, headstrong, gloating young rakes whose souls were small and whose bodies were gross from reckless indulgences. There were few young men of royal blood who rose above the blighting estimate Prince Dantan put upon their class.

His soul rebelled against the mere thought of giving his beloved Virginia in marriage to one of these pusillanimous (the word was a favorite of his) young bounders whom destiny had set aside long before they were born to compose the list of men eligible for the hand of a Princess of Dawsbergen. Triflers, ignoramuses, pinheads! (He had picked up "pinhead" from Prince Robin.)

And, as he stole these sly, puzzled glances at her, he realized for the thousandth time that he would never be able to give away the American part of her in any case! She would have something to say about that! He could, no doubt, direct the fate of the Dawsbergen part, but what would be the use? She was unquestionably more than half Dawsbergen—that could be seen at a glance or divined in a second—aye, the blood of her father was dominant—but what chance would Dawsbergen have if it came to a tussle with America? None whatever!

Time and again he had seen American independence triumph over Dawsbergen arrogance in both of his daughters. For that matter, he himself had long ago surrendered to a delicate, far from formidable American, and he had been her slave ever since. Then there was the Princess Yetive of Graustark, hadn't she and all her proud little kingdom fallen before the assault of a single American? What was it in his daughters and in Robin, the son of Yetive and her conquering American, what was it in them that made them so different, so amazingly superior in every way? He knew. The strain of clean, fresh, virile blood that came out of the veins of strong people from across the sea, the beat of a free heart, the glow of renewed vitality.

Prince Dantan, as was often the case with him, sighed deeply—and, strangely enough, contentedly.

This American, Yorke. He had seen him, had spoken with him, and secretly confessed to a liking for him. The young man was as clean as a whistle, mentally and physically and beyond a doubt morally. It was impossible to think of him as otherwise. He looked straight into your eye with an eye that was clear and alert and straightforward. He was a thoroughbred. He was keen, eager, sensitive. There was strength in his lean, handsome face; strength in his fine body.

Heigh-ho, sighed poor Prince Dantan. Far worse things could happen to his beloved Virginia than going to America to live!

As for Virginia, she was blithe and gay on this bright, crisp morning. The luster of the turquoise was in her eyes, the bloom of the rose on her cheeks; and somehow the air seemed to be filled with the perfume of her. She had her father's promise to take no action in the matter of the silly old divorce until she had consulted with Pendennis Yorke. Moreover, she did not owe Bevra a penny; she had told Prince Hubert for the tenth and last time that she couldn't and wouldn't marry him if he were the only man on earth; she had forced her father to grudgingly admit that Yorke was an uncommonly attractive chap; and, best of all, the Graustark Minister of Justice had unhesitatingly concurred in the opinion of the Dawsbergen Minister of Justice! It was indeed a blithe and cheerful morning for her.

"Why are you so solemn, daddy?" she inquired, as they neared the railway station. "You haven't spoken a word in the last ten minutes."

"Neither have you, for that matter," said he. "And God knows it never would have occurred to me to charge you with being solemn."

"Oh, I never talk when I am driving the car, especially if I have a nice, adorable, paternal old Prince for a passenger."

"And I make a point of never talking to the driver, especially if she happens to be a reckless, devil-may-care young Princess who has a reputation for not keeping to the middle of the road at any time."

"Sometimes it is much safer to skim along the edge, daddy, and certainly there are times where one is better off if he scoots clear down into the ditch," said she, smiling, but still with a serious note in her voice. "There are more accidents happening in the middle of the road than anywhere else."

"A fine philosophy!"

"And besides, one is really much more careful when running along the edge or in the ditch."

"You are speaking in parables, I presume?"

"Robin says that prize-fighters manage to escape defeat by side-stepping or something like that," she went on.

"Just what are you trying to get at, Virginia?"

"I am simply endeavoring to get it through your dear, thick old head that I never skip out of the middle of the road unless I see danger ahead."

"You are seeking, I presume, to convince me that you are a very wise and prudent young woman."

"Oh, dear me, no. Only the most foolish of young women are wise and prudent, daddy."

"Bless my soul!"

She slowed the car down to a snail's pace. A small detachment of the Royal Mounted Patrol was lined up alongside the station platform.

"Because," she explained brightly, "they are so frightfully lonely, only they haven't sense enough to know it." She leaned closer to him and, remembering the chauffeur, lowered her voice almost to a whisper. "I am so glad you like him, daddy."

He regarded her sternly. "Watch where you're going, Virgie. You almost ran over that man. He is the second one this morning."

"I didn't come within a mile of him," she cried, loftily. "Besides," she continued, as she turned to look after the pedestrian who had stepped leisurely aside to let them pass and was now regarding her with undisguised interest, "he is one of my most eloquent admirers, although he has never spoken a word to me in his life. His eyes speak for him. That is Michael Rodkin, the anarchist, and we should have been blown to smithereens if I had hit him. His pockets are probably full of bombs.

"Rodkin? I have heard Gourou speak of him. A clever and a very dangerous man. What do you mean when you say that he is one of your admirers?"

"Have you never held a piece of meat beyond the reach of a hungry dog?" she contended.

"I would not describe the look in a hungry dog's eyes as one of affection," said her father, frowning.

"Well, that's the way Rodkin always looks at me, daddy. I call it admiration."

"The insolent scoundrel!" grated Prince Dantan, clenching his hand.

"I daresay he has already picked me as his own special share of the loot if the Reds ever come into power," she said calmly, even airily.

"And the damned rascal calls himself an American!"

"Well," she argued, demurely, "Hubert calls himself a gentleman, daddy."

A strange haggardness suddenly crept into the rugged face of Virginia's father. His jaw was set, his brow was dark with trouble.

"I am afraid, sorely afraid," he muttered.

The car had come to a stop. She was warming her gloved hands by clapping them together.

"Of the Reds? Pooh! They say there are not more
than a handful of them in Edelweiss."

"A pinch of salt will season a whole roast, my child,"
was his cryptic rejoinder. "A single match is sufficient
to fire a forest. A lone wolf may stampede a vast herd
of cattle. So it is with your handful of Reds. Those
few can transform quiet into riot, they can sway the
masses, they can turn sheep into wolves. We do not
know—"

"Are you really worried, father?" she broke in, laying
her hand on his rigid arm. Her thoughts went flying
back to those black days in Hungary. She shuddered.

He hesitated a moment before replying. "I wish you
and Bevra and your mother were in—in England," he
said.

"Or America," said she, softly.

CHAPTER IX

CONCERNING A DIVORCE

THE same day that Yorke's invitation to dine at the Castle was delivered to him by a Court Messenger he also received a brief note from Princess Virginia. The first was presented to him by a liveried functionary and was not in the ordinary sense of the word an invitation: it was virtually a command. Mr. Pendennis Yorke's "presence" at dinner was not requested, nor was the "pleasure of his company desired" by their Serene Highnesses; he was formally notified by the Lord Chamberlain that on a certain date and at a certain hour he was "expected" to dine at the Castle, the "enclosed ticket to be presented in person at the postern gate." The second was delivered by the postman and there was nothing formal about it.

"Dear Mr. Yorke," wrote Virginia in a dashingly upright hand, with steeples and elbows and angles racing in legible confusion across two sheets of note paper bearing the crest of Dawsbergen; "I want very much to see you about a matter which concerns us both. If you can find it convenient to come to the Castle to-morrow afternoon at four, you will hear something to your advantage, as they say when they are advertising for lost persons. I will be at the gatehouse, so you will not require a pass to get by the guard. In case you cannot spare the time from your arduous labors, won't you be good enough to

163

drop me a line to say when you can come? It really is
not imperative that I see you to-morrow, however. Any
other day will do. I know you are frightfully busy. Sincerely yours, Virginia."

"P.S.—The dear old Duchess has been laid up with
tonsilitis. I went to see her yesterday. She was quite
feverish and out of her head. She asked me if you were
related to the Duke of York. Not wishing her to suspect
that I noticed how her mind was wandering, I said yes,
you DO like fresh strawberries very much, and that pleased
her immensely. She is frightfully proud of the strawberries that come out of her hothouses. So I made a
little memorandum on a pad she keeps on her night-table,
just to remind her that she promised to send you a basket
of them in a day or two. They are huge and perfectly
delicious. Five or six good-sized bites to each one of
them!!! I also jotted down a line to remind her that
she asked me to bring you up one day to go through her
picture gallery. That will please her too when she is able
to be up and around, because she is very proud of the
Halfont collection and wouldn't in the least object if you
were to write something about it for your newspaper! Of
course, the poor dear will cudgel her brain trying to recall
when she made these promises, but there they are in black
and white and she can't go back on them!"

Yorke was in a fine humor when he set forth the next
afternoon. Acting on Sharpe's advice, he wore his gray
tweed suit, his tan shoes and his brown fedora. He also
purchased a smart walking-stick for the occasion. His
brown suit, Sharpe explained, seemed a trifle small for
him, due, no doubt to the fact that he must have grown

considerably since it was made for him back in 1914. The obliging valet also gave him a number of "pointers" on how to behave in an inhabited castle. Mr. Yorke, who had explored numerous uninhabited castles, confessed to a woeful though wholesome lack of confidence when it came to tackling one peopled by ladies-in-waiting, gentlemen-of-the-bedchamber, major-domos, footmen, lackeys, pages, nursemaids, warders, dragoons, princes, princesses and suits of armor that might resent being inquisitively tapped in the midriff with a cane.

"Is it your purpose, sir, to walk to the Castle?" inquired Sharpe, as he helped Mr. Yorke on with his overcoat. It was then precisely five minutes past three.

"I shall take a taxi," replied his master, eyeing him with considerable severity.

Sharpe merely glanced at his wrist-watch and said nothing.

"I'm glad you spoke of it, Sharpe," said Yorke, turning a bit red in the face. "As a matter of fact, I had planned to walk to the Castle. But my mind is so full of other things that I completely forgot it."

"Quite so, sir."

"A good, brisk walk will clear the cobwebs out of my brain, you see. That was what I really figured on. Lucky you reminded me in time." He laughed rather boisterously. "I need a guardian, don't I, Sharpe?"

Sharpe had the grace to smile, perhaps a trifle too broadly. "Oh, I shouldn't say you were as bad as all that, sir. Still a brisk walk will do you good. I shouldn't make it too brisk, however. Might easily arrive half an hour too soon. Have you your gloves, sir?"

Yorke was as excited as any schoolboy as he strode up Castle Avenue. His heart was thumping buoyantly, his blood was singing. He was to see her again—he glanced at his watch—in three-quarters of an hour. "You will hear something to your advantage." "A matter that concerns us both." And she would be at the gates to meet him! He wondered why the birds were not singing in the trees.

He met Michael Rodkin in the Avenue. He had not seen him since that day at the Regengetz. Rodkin's face lighted with pleasure, albeit his smile was satirical.

"Behold me, Denny, a varlet poaching on the preserves of the good-godly," he said, as they stopped and shook hands. "I walk here nearly every day and yet no earthquake follows. My tread is heavy with evil portent, my lungs breathe fire and brimstone, but no one shakes in his boots, so far as I can see. If I were to stamp my feet in mighty anger the complacent earth would not even tremble. All I should get for my pains would be a pitying glance from the passers-by and the mortifying verdict that my shoes were too tight or my toes were cold. Well, old chap, how are you?"

"Never better. I see they haven't shot you at sunrise yet, Michael."

"The weather is too fine. They wouldn't risk spoiling a pleasant day by shooting me at sunrise. Whither are you bound, my gay, gray cavalier?"

"I'm on my way to hob-nob with your hated nabobs. I'm going to the Castle."

Rodkin grinned good-humoredly. "If you stick around

Edelweiss long enough, old top, I'll be pleased to rent you a front room in the Castle, overlooking the parade ground."

"See here, Michael, that's rather a stupid thing to say, even in jest. These stone walls may have ears."

"Serve them jolly well right," jeered Rodkin. "They're likely to hear something to their advantage if they listen sharply. Do you mind if I turn back and stroll along with you? I like to be seen in good company once in a while. Besides, I will have to admit that the air is better along Castle Avenue than it is down in my neighborhood. Seems that the nabobs have a monopoly on all the fresh air going."

"Come along. I am perfectly willing to share the air with you, Michael."

"You've got damn long legs, remember," protested the other, as he fell in beside his tall companion. "I suggested a stroll, old chap, not a race. Slack up a bit, can't you? Or are you late for your date with His Highness?"

"Bless you, no! I am interminably early. Not due there till four o'clock. Seriously, Michael, do you really believe this country will ever go Bolshevik?"

"In time," declared the other, conviction in his tone. "Graustark will have to keep step with the rest of the world. As certain as we are walking here together, Denny, the whole world will some day go Bolshevik, as you call it. It is inevitable. The people are bound to squirm out from under the iron heel."

"But, hang it all, why should you and your kind set

about deliberately to breed dissatisfaction among a happy, contented people, such as these Graustarkians are?   What do you offer them in exchange?"

"It would be useless for me to harangue you as I would a street corner crowd, Denny.   You are too thick-headed. You simply wouldn't understand."

"I can understand this much of your beautiful dream. You first completely wreck a country, prostitute its people, destroy its integrity, and then call upon the rest of the world to applaud what you are pleased to describe as progress."

Rodkin frowned.   "I suppose you would say I was lying or talking through my hat if I were to tell you that the only way to convert the base metal into shining gold is by putting it through a rather drastic process of refinement," he said ironically.

"On the contrary, I should say you were talking sense, Michael.   You forget, however, that shining gold is a thing that endures forever.   You don't destroy it in the process, you know.   But how about these poor, unfortunate, ignorant human beings that you destroy in your efforts to justify the similitude?   You don't make them over into new and perfect and glittering men and women, do you?   I should say not!   You first make fools of them, then fiends, and in the end, skeletons.   There is a wide difference between refining gold and starving to death, Michael."

"The end justifies the means," said Rodkin quietly.   "A hundred years from now the world will be a paradise."

"At considerable cost to those who at present are finding it a hell of a world to live in."

"It has always been a hell of a world to live in. That's the very thing we're trying to prove."

"Well, you are proving it all right, all right," said Yorke, with a bitter laugh. "Does it never occur to your otherwise normal and at times exalted intelligence, Michael, that these poor devils won't be in a position one hundred years hence to enjoy the paradise they now contemplate through a glass darkly obscured by murder, rapine, hate, revenge, greed and all that sort of thing?"

"Their spirits will survive the test," retorted Rodkin patiently. "You give us a lovely vista to look back upon, Denny."

"I am less of a visionary than you, my dear Michael. You are seeing things one hundred years ahead, I am seeing only the things that are about us now. To-day, for example, I see a happy, prosperous, contented people here in Graustark. It is rather a paradise as things go. You would destroy paradise, such as it is—to what end? Merely to create another paradise in its place. Where is the gain? You know as well as I do, my friend, that the strong will always rule. One hundred years from now there will still be despotism. You merely take the power from one hand and put it into the other. You say the people will rule, but don't forget that some of the people are strong and some are weak. Your wonderful paradise will still be for the mighty."

"Have it your way, Denny," said Rodkin, shrugging his thin shoulders. "Nevertheless, I prophesy that there will be a soviet government of the whole world in less than a quarter of a century."

"The United States included, I suppose," said Yorke, scoffingly.

"Beyond the slightest doubt," declared Michael Rodkin, slowly and deliberately.

"Bunk!"

"A short, inelegant word supposed to express contempt, I believe. It is used almost exclusively by persons desiring to terminate a discussion in which they are getting the worst of it. By the way, has your good friend Gourou said anything to you about me? Has he warned you to beware the dog?"

"He pays you the highest of compliments by subsiding into an inscrutable silence when your name is mentioned."

"Ha! That *is* a compliment. It's plain to be seen that he fears even though he pretends not to notice me. Most people have eyes only for the mighty oak and none at all for the tiny acorn. Not so Gourou. He keeps his nose to the ground, like a pig, nibbling the acorns. The easiest and simplest way to cut down a mighty oak, according to the astute Baron, is to devour it while it is still an acorn. But possess your soul in peace, Denny. The Commune is a long way off in Graustark. The people love their Prince too well. This is unfavorable soil for the seeds of Communism. But the seeds are being sown, just the same. Harvest is bound to come. Graustark has survived centuries of blind idolatry. She has had smart, cunning rulers. They have pulled the wool over the eyes of all the people. But just remember what Lincoln said about fooling all of the people all of the time, my boy. It can't be done."

"Were you in Axphain, Michael, when the revolution came?"

"I was."

"Do you know the conditions there now?"

"I do."

"And yet you have the face to tell me you believe the world would be better off for Communism?"

"Hang it all, Denny," said Rodkin, with real feeling; "the people of Axphain have laid down on the job. They refuse to work. They feel that Communism is something one can eat instead of something that has to be fed. I have no sympathy for the whining fools. Oh, yes, while I think of it, Denny," he broke off suddenly, his expression undergoing a lightning change, from anger to anxiety, "keep your eye cocked for this fellow Hubert. He's got it in for you."

"What do you mean? He doesn't even know me."

"He was pretty well jingled the other night up at Pingari's. Somebody I know overheard him say that you were a cheap adventurer and that he was going to make it his business to show you up in your true colors."

Yorke laughed, "Gad, Michael, if you tell me such things as that I'll soon begin to believe I am as important a person as you are."

"It's no joke, Denny. This Hubert fellow is a born conspirator, and he's a dirty coward. He will frame you if it's a possible thing to do. I guess you know why he's got it in for you."

"You mean—ahem!—the Princess Virginia?"

"Yes. Hubert has always been pretty keen on widows, you know."

"Widows? What's the matter with you, Michael? She isn't a widow."

"I know she isn't—*yet.*"

"You mean he wouldn't be above making a widow of her?" said Yorke, slowly comprehending.

"Gad, man, if it were possible he'd also make an orphan of her. That's the sort of gentleman. he is."

"But, hang it, Michael, she isn't really married to me."

"I'm not so sure about that, Denny," said Rodkin, a trifle sententiously. "Anyhow, keep your eye peeled. Well, so long. I'll leave you here. This is as close to the gates as I ever venture—halfway. Glad to have seen you again. Come and see me. Old Gourou won't mind, and I'll promise not to leave any bombs lying around for you to stub your toe against."

"I'd hate to make a widow of the Princess by stubbing my toe," said Yorke, holding out his hand with a smile.

They parted, Rodkin sauntering off in the direction from which they came. Yorke's face was a study as he strode up the Avenue. He was not thinking of Rodkin's warning. He was wondering just what he meant when he said: "I'm not so sure about that, Denny."

He was within a few hundred yards of the Gates Plaza, walking slowly along the edge of the grass plot in the center of the street, when he was sharply aroused from his smiling fit of abstraction by the loud snort of an automobile horn, alarmingly close at hand. There was peril in that sharp, sudden blast. He sprang frantically toward the middle of the parkway, conscious even as he did so of the spectacle he made of himself and anticipating the shrieks of mirth that would go up from the occupants of the car as they whizzed by.

Notwithstanding the swiftness of his leap, the fenders of a big car grazed him as it shot over the sloping cement curb onto the grass. His heart stood still! God! Half a foot, the hundredth part of a second, and he would have been directly in the path of that charging monster. And he would now be lying, smashed and lifeless many feet from the spot where he stood as if petrified.

The car, after tearing along the grass plot for fifty yards or more, responded to the wheel and bounded back into the roadway again. A man in the seat beside the driver half arose and looked back. Yorke had seen his face only once before, but it was unforgettable. The man who looked back was Prince Hubert.

He leaned weakly against a small tree, his hand to his heart, his knees trembling. Despite the fact that he was shaken by the narrow squeak he had had, his brain entertained but one thought as he stood there looking after the motorists; was the swerving of the car unavoidable or was it deliberate? He had not heard it as it came up the Avenue behind him, but that was not surprising. Strange that the steering gear should have gone wrong just as— Then suddenly Rodkin's warning flashed into his mind. Good God! A gust of fury swept over him, almost blinding him. His fists were clenched, his face disfigured by a savage scowl. In that instant he grasped the truth. Hubert had tried to kill him! Providence alone had saved him.

"You filthy coward!" he shouted impotently after the car, which had not even slowed down. It was already crossing the Gates Plaza, and uniformed warders had sprung forward to throw open the huge portals.

Half a dozen pedestrians came running up to Yorke, witnesses to the incident. Two automobiles on the opposite side of the Avenue halted and several men jumped out and rushed over to where he was standing. They were all talking excitedly, but he could not understand what they were saying.

As suddenly as his anger rose, just as abruptly did it subside. He realized his helplessness. He could not prove that Hubert had tried to run him down, he could not even accuse him of the intent. He could only complain of the driver's carelessness! So he began to grin sheepishly, as one does who finds himself an object of curiosity or concern. But his face was white and his hands were still clenched. Some one picked up his cane and solicitously examined it before handing it back to him. Then, apparently satisfied that the gentleman was neither killed nor injured, the rapidly increasing crowd began to inspect the tire-scraped curb and the slithered course of the wheels over the moist soil. Yorke heard the name of Prince Hubert repeated many times and gratefully took note of dour frowns and portentous head-shakings. Presently he resumed his jaunty stroll! The spectators favored him with individual smiles of felicitation and followed him with a collective stare of admiration as he strode off.

Meanwhile, Prince Hubert's car had passed through the Gates; they were ponderously closing behind him. The Axphainian, apart from that hurried glance over his shoulder, had paid no more attention to Yorke than he would have granted a scurrying dog or a fluttering hen. The American, reflecting somewhat blasphemously upon Hubert's shortcomings, wondered whether he would have paused long enough to do his victim the honor of inquiring what he would like to have done with his remains now that he was as dead as a mackerel.

It was a significant and a sinister fact that Hubert was not driving the car himself. The man at the wheel, whoever he may have been, was the one to be blamed for the accident, and he, supported by the Prince, would have had no difficulty in proving that the car had suddenly become unmanageable—the old story of the faulty steering gear or the skidding forewheel. In any event, the driver was undoubtedly in the employ of Prince Hubert, and therein lay the sinister aspect of the case. A cohort, a paid assassin! Rodkin was right.

Coming to the gates, Yorke accosted one of the four warders who stood guard. The Princess was nowhere in sight. He had looked at his watch; he was precisely on time.

"I am Mr. Yorke," he said, and at once decided from the expression on the warder's face that he was politely interested but nothing more. Slightly embarrassed, he bethought himself to inquire: "Do you speak English?"

"I do, sir. French and German and Russian as well," replied the man.

"I was informed that—er—some one from the Castle would meet me here and that I would not require a pass to enter the grounds."

The man shook his head, "I regret, sir, that we have

had no instructions to admit Mr. Pendennis Yorke.
We—"

He was interrupted by a small page who dashed breathlessly out of the gatehouse hard-by. He halted abruptly
on catching sight of Yorke, clicked his heels together,
saluted and burst into a shrill, agitated torrent of words,
the outcome of which was an astonishing display of activity on the part of the four warders. Two of them
sprang to the gates and stood at attention, a third leaped
forward and turned the huge key in the lock, while the
man who could speak in five languages bowed very low
to Mr. Yorke and, straightening up, shouted something
very sharply in one of them. Whereupon the first two
seized the gate handles and yanked, the third jumped
nimbly to one side, and with a rush, the great portals
swung wide on their creaking hinges, presenting an orifice
through which a troop of cavalry could have ridden eight
abreast.

And straight through the middle of this commodious
opening marched Pendennis Yorke into the garden of
dreams. He did not glance backward, nor to right or
left, but he was aware of the squealing of hinges, the
thud of heavy iron-studded timber and the grinding of
a key. He was locked inside the Castle grounds; his own
world was locked outside. His gaze, set ahead of him,
searched eagerly, perhaps a trifle anxiously for a figure
that was certain to be unfamiliar to him notwithstanding
its permanence in his thoughts. She would not appear
before him to-day in the form of Rosa Schmitz, nor as the
Princess Virginia of that memorable night at the Regengetz. Instead he must expect a trig young person in furs

and boots and one of those snug-fitting little hats of the
period—a figure familiar enough on any crisp afternoon
in Hyde Park or the Bois du Boulogne where she was so
multitudinous that one met her at every turn. Virginia
would be like one of those to-day. He was rather pleased
by the thought. He liked girls in smart, out-of-door
get-ups.

Far ahead, above the green tops of the firs and spruces
and through the stripped branches of less hardy trees
could be seen the towers of the castle. He trod a winding road, bordered by shrubbery; at his side marched
the page, whose short legs twinkled in the shadow cast
by his own long-striding body. A sharp wind blew out
of a distant gap in the mountains and smote his tingling
face as it swept by on its way down the valley.

They came to a fork in the driveway. Here the page
bounced out in front of him and pointed to the left, uttering at the same time an absolutely unintelligible bit of
information—which Mr. Yorke promptly accepted as official. Then, with a fresh salute, a clicking of heels, the
youngster proceeded at a swift run down the right fork,
leaving his charge alone in a world which became drearily
unpopulated the instant that flying figure disappeared
around a bend. Following the road to the left, Yorke soon
swung around a bend and there ahead of him, some distance away, stood a man and a woman. Beyond them,
motionless at the roadside, was a large green automobile.
He recognized the car and the man at a glance, and then
he recognized Virginia. She *was* a trig figure in furs and
boots and a snug little hat. He would have known her
anywhere! She was precisely what he expected her to be.

His pace slackened. He had not included Hubert in the mental picture he had been drawing since noon the day before. He had counted on something far more enchanting.

The Princess, evidently on the lookout for him, greeted him with a long-range smile, but did not advance to meet him. Hubert, huge and overpowering in his sable coat, had his back to Yorke and was talking earnestly to her. Her smile caused him to turn his head. His queer lightish eyes flew open in a stare of amazement as he beheld the slowly approaching American. Breaking off in the middle of a sentence, he left Virginia and strode toward Yorke.

"I say!" he exclaimed loudly. "What the devil do you mean by coming in here? Don't you know that you are not allowed to enter the Castle grounds? Get out! Confound your impudence! Get out, I say, or I will call the guard and have you kicked out!"

Yorke did not hesitate. He strode coolly, deliberately forward, his hat in his hand, a smile for Virginia on his lips.

"I say!" roared Hubert, this time in some surprise. "Did you hear me? It's time you damned Americans were taught that you cannot— Stop where you are, sir! Get out of here!"

"I am glad you understand English," said Yorke, coolly, levelly. "You will know what I mean when I tell you to go to hell."

Hubert's face turned purple. "You—you insolent dog! Herman!" he shouted to the chauffeur. "Summon the guard at once!"

"Be careful, Herman," called out the American.

"Don't run anybody down in your haste to obey orders!"

Virginia held out her hand to him. She was very pale and there was angry humiliation in her big blue eyes.

"Welcome, Mr. Yorke," she cried, clearly, distinctly. "I am sorry not to have met you at the gates as I promised. I was unavoidably detained." Turning to the astonished Hubert, she said: "Mr. Yorke is here, Prince Hubert, at my request. He is going on to the Castle with me—at Prince Robin's request. And I am also sorry, Mr. Yorke, that you should have been subjected to such cavalier treatment on your first visit to us. I hope you will be generous enough to overlook it."

She had turned her back on Hubert, who was speechless with rage. Yorke, looking straight into his pale blue eyes, experienced a queer, unaccountable shock. He had seen the glittering, unwavering eyes of trapped reptiles in the jungle, but never had he beheld anything so venomous as the steady glare in Hubert's. They were curiously like those of a rattlesnake.

"Cheerfully and gladly, Princess," said Yorke. "Pray do not give it another thought. I am lucky to be here at all. God has been good to me to-day."

Struck by the significant note in his voice, she exclaimed:

"Why do you say that, Mr. Yorke?"

By this time, Hubert had recovered his speech. He answered for Yorke.

"So you are the man who nearly caused us to turn over in Castle Avenue," he exclaimed, affecting surprise. "Confound you! Don't you know enough to stay on the sidewalk?"

There was not a flicker in Yorke's eyes. "I repeat, God has been good to me to-day."

"My man lost control of the car. He—"

"Permit me to say that I never saw a man handle a car with greater skill," interrupted Yorke, meaningly. "He missed me only by inches."

"Do you mean to insinuate, sir, that—"

"What is all this about?" demanded Virginia, turning to Hubert, her eyes narrowing.

"This blundering fool seems to think that I—" began the Prince, haughtily.

"Stop!" she cried. Her eyes were blazing. "That will do, Prince Hubert! Be good enough to leave us."

He started as if struck in the face. His heavy jaw dropped, his lips fell apart, and again the dark, purplish hue spread over his face.

"My dear Virginia—I—do you know what you are saying?" he fairly gulped in his astonishment.

"I do—perfectly," was her cold, emphatic reply.

His mouth worked fantastically, hideously for a moment. Then, without another word, he swung on his heel and strode off toward the waiting motor, his great shoulders hunched forward, his head lowered like that of a tormented bull. They watched him in silence as he climbed heavily, clumsily, as if blind, into the seat beside the driver. He uttered a short, guttural command and the car was off, roaring around a bend in the road.

"I am so sorry," murmured Virginia, as the sound of grinding gears died away, "I am so terribly sorry that this should have happened to you. It was all my fault."

He looked down into the distressed, rueful eyes and forced a smile. His face was still pale.

"My only concern is for you, Princess. I fear you have lost a noble suitor."

"Please don't be sarcastic, Mr. Yorke!"

"I ought to be kicked for having said that," he exclaimed remorsefully.

She smiled, a little tremulously, he thought. "But there isn't any one near enough to kick you, Mr. Yorke, except me, and I am desperately afraid of you. Goodness, the way you looked at Hubert!"

"Did you notice the way he looked at me?" he asked, wryly.

A slight shudder passed over her face. "He is a beast. Tell me, did he attempt to run you down with his car?"

"I prefer not to make a charge that I cannot prove," he replied, after a moment's hesitation. "However, I don't mind saying that I should have liked nothing better than to take a punch at his nose a moment ago. In fact, I had great difficulty in keeping from doing it."

An expression of dread flashed into her eyes. "Oh!" she exclaimed. "He is as strong as Samson. They say he has killed an ox with a blow of his fist."

"Oxen are notoriously poor dodgers," he informed her, laughingly. "And besides, you will be interested to know, I am an exceptionally artful dodger and a very fast runner," he went on, now quite gayly. "But let us forget Prince Hubert. You sent for me, Princess. On a matter concerning both of us, you said. I am at your service. Command me."

"Very well," she said, her face clearing. The color was fast returning to her cheeks. "I planned to meet you at the gates so that we could have time for a little talk before going to the Castle. We can talk as we stroll, Mr. Yorke—and get it over with," she concluded, in a hurried, embarrassed manner. To cover her momentary confusion she drew his attention to the surroundings. "The park is wonderful in the spring, but isn't it dreary and—and naked now?"

"I hadn't noticed it," said he, gazing into her eyes.

"We will walk round by the grotto first," she said, looking away; "and down past the barracks and stables. My sister would like us to be in for tea by five o'clock."

"My cup is already full," said he, gallantly. "I fear it will overflow before the day is over, Princess."

"You do know how to make nice speeches!"

"You said in your note I should hear something to my advantage," he reminded her, as they sauntered side by side through a narrow, hedge-lined path. "I have already heard it."

She sighed. "I suppose we'd better talk things over, Mr. Yorke. Don't you think so?"

"It sounds ominous."

"Well, it's about—our—about you and me," she hurried on, realizing that this wasn't at all the way she had intended to introduce the subject. She had meant to go about it lightly, gayly, even jestingly.

"I think I understand, Princess," said he gently. "Pray do not be distressed or uneasy. There is nothing for you to be afraid of."

"It seems, Mr. Yorke, that we are not entirely out of our difficulties. My father has been here. He says that the highest legal authority in Serros is of the opinion that we—that you and I are still married to each other. It is only fair that I should take the first opportunity to break the news to you. That is why I sent for you. It wasn't the joke we thought it was, that strange marriage of ours. It was real, it was binding. And we are not divorced. That is the dreadful part of it. Justice Mavorak says that people cannot be divorced in that way. Now you know the worst. I promised my father that I would explain the situation to you. We must decide on some plan of action, Mr. Yorke, to—to get out of the pickle we are in."

She knew she was doing it very badly. She felt that her face was crimson.

He did not speak at once. His heart was thumping violently—he would have said it was thumping noisily.

"It should be very simple, Princess," he said at last. "If what they say is true—it seems incredible to me— but if what they say is true, there is a very simple remedy. We went about it innocently, unwittingly, with no thought in our minds of making a sacred bargain. We were misled. Others are undoubtedly in the same boat, if what Higbee said was true. Under the circumstances, there will not be the slightest difficulty in having the preposterous marriage annulled. I don't know what your laws are over here, but I am sure you would only have to ask a court or a tribunal to set the marriage aside and it would all be over in a jiffy. It would only be necessary for you to state the case exactly as it is and that would be the end of it." He paused and then went on drily, humorously: "I daresay your father has sufficient influence in his own country to see to it that the affair is settled behind closed doors and without the slightest publicity."

"It all seems so foolish, so childish," she lamented.

"Even so, Princess, we seem to be in the clutches of the law," he reminded her, whimsically. "I was of some small help to you in Buda Pesth that day. Inadvertently I—"

"You were of great help to me. I shall never forget it, Mr. Yorke. I shall never be able to thank you enough."

"You may still count on my help," he said, but his heart had suddenly turned to lead. The dream was over. "If you should need me in the new emergency, pray do not hesitate to command me. My testimony, or my statement rather, may be necessary."

"You are—very good," she said, without enthusiasm. "I—I assured my father that you would be—that you would be reasonable."

"If your father thought for an instant that I would cause you any trouble or annoyance in your predicament, he did me a wrong," said he stiffly. "Please convey my respects to him and inform him that my support is pledged to any action you may decide to take. Nothing could be farther from my thoughts than the desire to make capital of—"

"Oh, please don't think for a moment that he—"

"Nevertheless, I should like you to make my position clear to him. For all I know—or for all you know—he may harbor in the back of his mind the suspicion that I am something of a blackguard. I wish to disabuse him of that—"

"A blackguard?" she cried, and again her face reddened.

"A bounder, if you prefer the word."

"Oh!"

"And now, may I ask when and where the next step is to be taken? You may be assured of my coöperation, but I should like to know just what is to be expected of me."

She was silent for a long time. She was, truth to tell, piqued. He was taking it much too unconcernedly to please her. When she spoke again there was a perceptible chill in her voice.

"Nothing is expected of you, Mr. Yorke. The matter can be arranged without dragging you into it at all. As you were saying a moment ago, my father has sufficient influence to—"

"Then, may I be permitted to inquire," he broke in, "why you deemed it necessary to consult me about it, Princess?"

She looked straight into his eyes. "You must not overlook the fact, Mr. Yorke, that I have accepted you as my friend as well as my—my husband."

"A well-deserved rebuke. I beg your pardon. I shall go on being your friend forever."

Her laugh was scornful. "A far pleasanter responsibility than the other," she scoffed.

"In any case, it is a privilege that the law cannot take away from me."

"Am I to have no thanks for setting you free?" she cried, with some heat.

"None whatever," he replied promptly.

She gasped. "But—but you seem to be blaming me for having the—the decency to consult your feelings in the matter," she stammered, struggling to regain her lost composure.

"By no means! I am just a little bit puzzled, that's all."

"Puzzled?"

"Yes, you said I was to hear something to my advantage. That's what puzzles me."

"Well, for goodness' sake," she cried, perversely; "what more could you ask than to be set free, Mr. Yorke?"

"Your forgiveness, Princess, for my churlishness," he replied, suddenly contrite and humbled. "I fear we are both making too much of a trifling yet extraordinary situation. So far as I am concerned, we were divorced the same day that we were married. I have never been in any doubt as to that. On the other hand, I appreciate your position. My saying and believing that we were divorced that day isn't sufficient. Nor does it help matters any, it would seem, that both of us looked upon the comedy as ended when we said good-by at the station. It's rather a shock, Princess, for a chap to wake up after five years and find he's been married all that time without knowing it. Good heavens!" he cried in mock consternation. "I might even have committed bigamy without knowing it."

She glanced at him quickly, and as quickly looked away.

"If that is the way you feel about it—" she began, coldly.

"I assure you I've never for an instant felt like committing bigamy, Princess."

"But you just now said you might have done it!" she argued. "I don't see how you have resisted temptation all these years." There was a trace of mockery in her voice.

"It is impossible to commit bigamy without the aid of a confederate, you see."

"It shouldn't have been difficult for you to find an accomplice. The world is full of them." She thought that sounded a little spiteful, so she added: "I shudder when I think of all the trouble I might have got you into."

"Well, the peril will soon be behind me—and you too, for that matter—so let's not worry over the past and what's left of the present. The future is the thing that counts. Let's wish each other good luck, Princess. I can't tell you how many times in the past five years I have wished Rosa Schmitz the very best of luck—and, thank God, she's had it."

She lowered her eyes. "You were very good to Rosa Schmitz."

He shrugged his shoulders. "No better than Higbee was to a lot of others. I daresay if it hadn't been Rosa Schmitz it would have been some one else. More than that, I probably would have married a dozen or more harassed young ladies in similar straits if I'd stayed long enough in Buda Pesth."

Then and there, Princess Virginia of Dawsbergen, one of the most assiduously courted young women in the near

East, arrived at the astounding conclusion that Pendennis Yorke did not care a tuppence about her! Not a tuppence! And she had been fondly coddling the belief that he cared a great deal. It was really a rather staggering discovery. She was suddenly conscious of a queer little feeling of desolation—and a desire to be alone in her room.

For, down in her heart, she had begun to love this tall American on the day that she married him!

CHAPTER X

TEA at the Castle was a delightful, informal little function, shorn completely of the ceremony and severity that one would naturally expect in a royal household. The only shadow of constraint was that cast by the pair who had just come in from a stroll through the grounds—and even that was rendered unnoticeable by the extremely clever acting of the pair themselves.

Virginia was especially gay—a circumstance which added considerably to the depression that had settled down upon her fellow-performer. However, his own well-simulated air of indifference had an equally distressing effect on her. Each therefore was wholly successful in deceiving the other, and each was inwardly miserable. Outwardly both of them were without a care in the world. Standing in their own shadows, each gazed disconsolately into the sunshine that surrounded the other.

She was sorely afflicted with self-pity growing out of the consciousness that she had made a fool of herself in his eyes. She had behaved in a most undignified manner. She had been very silly and school-girlish in prompting the now detestable scheme that had succeeded so happily on the day of his arrival in Graustark. What a fool she had been to even imagine that he was heart-whole and fancy free! Of course he was in love with some one else. There must surely be a girl at home—an American girl. It was all poppycock his saying—or if not actually saying at any rate implying—that he had been true to Rosa Schmitz all these years. Persiflage! Idle flattery! Testing her vanity as if she were a hare-brained, unsophisticated ninny! Somehow chagrin was uppermost over regret in her meditations.

Yorke, on the other hand, by a singular coincidence in speculation, attributed her eagerness to have the ridiculous marriage legally dissolved as quickly as possible to a decision on her part to marry some one else. No doubt the husband already had been selected; plans probably were fairly under way for the royal nuptials; all that remained to be done was to get rid of a pernicious obstacle bearing the name of Yorke. There was something significant, and decidedly nauseating as well, in her request that he refrain from mentioning the scene with Prince Hubert in the park. Now that he had had time to think it over, the reason she had given was an exceedingly flimsy one. She had said:

"I think it would be a mistake for you to complain, Mr. Yorke. Let me be the tale-bearer. Prince Hubert, after all, is the guest of Graustark. If any one is to report him, I think it would be much better if I did it, rather than you."

Was Hubert the husband they had chosen for her? Was that the reason why she seemed so nervous and self-conscious when she asked him to say nothing about the brute's conduct? Hubert! That gorilla? Good Lord, what was the matter with Virginia's mother that she could countenance such a hideous sacrifice?

Under other conditions, Yorke would have enjoyed the cozy, informal little tea for four, served in Princess Bevra's boudoir. He would have been able to more fully appreciate the delicate attention his charming hostess had paid him when she admitted him, a wayfaring stranger, to the privacy of an apartment in which none save the most intimate of her friends were received or entertained.

He was not, of course, unmindful of the distinction accorded him, nor was he without a very deep and glowing sense of satisfaction. He was conscious of a feeling of exaltation such as he had never known before. He had been secretly apprehensive. He had anticipated something stiff and formal and, in a manner of speaking, starchy. He found exactly the reverse. After what he had seen of the great castle, in all its lofty, somewhat somber stateliness, this warm, friendly little room was a surprise and a delight. Virginia had hurried him through spacious halls and galleries, peopled by glittering attendants, rigid guardsmen and forbidding vacuums accoutered in suits of mail; up the long, gorgeous stairway that ascended from these overpowering regions of pomp to vast carpeted corridors whose turns and angles seemed endless and confusing; and in time to what she described as the left wing, where generations of Graustark's princes and princesses had lived and died "just like other people."

Here, at the end of the impressive journey, they came to the real domicile of the princess, a home within a home. Here was Graustark's hearthstone, her nursery, her sanctuary. And here he found a cheerful, unregal welcome that banished all his misgivings; here was an amazing contrast to the frigorific austerity that had daunted him below, that had made him feel small and insignificant.

A wood fire blazed merrily in a shallow brick fireplace, incongruously reminiscent of flat life in New York. Nothing medieval about that saucy little fireplace, nor about the things that stood on the white mantelpiece above it. Dainty, up-to-the-minute little things that bore testimony to the extreme modernity of the fastidious young woman who reigned over this bright corner of the grim old pile. A rich Chinese rug of a delicate rose hue covered the floor; the hangings were exquisite, the few pictures on the walls were gay in color and subject, the furbishings were bright and jaunty; the chairs comfortable, the chaise-longue seductive, the divan luxurious.

An escritoire over near the window revealed a condition of disorderliness that existed nowhere else in the room; it was littered with letters, note paper, envelopes, blotters, pens and pencils, to say nothing of a partially obscured engagement book, a calendar and a small but well-worn dictionary—that most indispensable friend of all females in distress. Altogether an ineffably feminine room and therefore appealing to men.

A fender-bench guarded the fireplace. On this Virginia sat down, her back to the fire, her legs outstretched, propping herself with her hands. From time to time she altered her position to crack her heels against the frame of the fender as if beating time to some mute melody that was running through her head. She had not removed her smart little hat. Her coat and gloves had been carelessly cast on a chair just inside the door. Her

cheeks were still tinged with the rosy flush that the kiss
of the wind had kindled.

"Would you prefer something else?" Prince Robin had
thoughtfully inquired of Yorke, as tea was being brought
in by a flunkey.

"Tea, thank you, Your Highness."

"All you have to do is to say the word," continued the
Prince, lifting his eyebrows encouragingly—and hos-
pitably.

"Mr. Yorke prefers tea, Bobby," announced Princess
Bevra. "Didn't you hear him say so?"

"I heard him say he'd take tea, but I didn't hear him
say he preferred it, my dear."

"But I do prefer it," Yorke made haste to assert. "I
am already intoxicated with joy, of course."

It was at this precise juncture that Princess Virginia
first began to beat time with her heels against the fender.

"We thought you would like it much better if just we
four made a little family party of it, Mr. Yorke," Bevra
had explained, as he was presented by her sister. "Much
nicer than a regular tea battle, especially when two-thirds
of the enemy forces can tear you to shreds without your
understanding a word they're saying. Besides," she had
gone on, with the most disarming smile he had ever seen,
"you are a sort of brother-in-law, don't you know."

"What one might call a sort of foster-husband," added
Prince Robin, laughing.

"Don't be idiotic," said Virginia.

Yorke could not help comparing the two sisters.
Bevra was beautiful, fascinating. She was several years
older than Virginia, slender and graceful, merry-eyed, soft

voiced and with the most infectious of gurgles when she laughed. She lacked the vivid, radiant coloring of her sister—but there he stopped, realizing that he was prejudiced. She was exquisite in a filmy tea gown of azure blue. Her arms and neck were perfect.

Prince Robin was a strikingly handsome fellow with dark, smiling eyes and a joyous laugh. He was not more than thirty-two or -three, tall, smooth-shaven, clear-skinned and—at the moment—as rumpled-haired as a boy. His greenish, sun-stained Norfolk jacket was sadly in need of cleansing and repair; a jagged rent just above the right knee of his knickerbockers bore evidence of having been hurriedly mended by an unskilled tailor—(who, in this case, happened to be his wife), and one of the side patch-pockets of his jacket bulged with a pair of heavy, fleece-lined gloves. There were mud streaks and splotches on his golf stockings, and the pumps in which his feet were incased had seen better days but not recently. He wore a soft collar and a rather gay striped necktie. Certainly in a sartorial sense he fell far short of typifying royalty as we commoners are prone to look upon it from an ancient conception of purple and fine raiment. He slumped indolently down into his chair, one knee crossed over the other, his long body relaxed in most unkingly comfort.

Yorke took a tremendous liking to him from the start. He was a "regular fellow," to quote from the American's stock of unvoiced impressions. He possessed a rare charm and the even rarer faculty for making it felt without the faintest trace of condescension. He treated Yorke as if he were an equal in all respects. Something passed between these two young men as they shook hands and looked into each other's eyes that made them bond-fellows in spirit.

Yorke was not long in discovering that the homelife of royal families differs very little from that of ordinary beings. He was permitted to witness a rather unconventional little scene between the rulers of Graustark. Bevra had taken Robin to task for appearing in such an outlandish costume—especially "those disreputable pumps."

"Really, Bobby, you ought to be ashamed of yourself. You are perfectly disgraceful."

"But, hang it all, Bevvy, I was late. I didn't have time to change anything except my shoes. You ought to thank your lucky stars I didn't blunder in here tracking mud all over the place."

"But you've got a dozen pairs of decent looking shoes, old dear."

"Takes time to lace 'em. I'm sure Mr. Yorke doesn't think the less of me for putting on a comfortable pair of pumps. He's a man. He knows."

"Even muddy boots would have been better than those awful things."

"Lord, I've seen you take Danny over your knee many a time for coming in here with muddy shoes."

"Virgie, don't forget to remind me to have them thrown into the fire to-night."

"He's got a worse pair than those, Bev. The ones you gave him for Christmas the first year you were married."

"Nobody shall destroy *that* pair," declared Robin. "They are going to become the most cherished of our family heirlooms. My great grandchildren— Oh, I'm sorry, Mr. Yorke, I forgot to offer you a cigarette. We all smoke in here. It's good for the ceiling."

Whereupon Bevra pinched his ear and announced that if it took her last penny he should have a new pair of carpet slippers for his next birthday.

It developed later on that the Prince was not only a great admirer of Colonel Roosevelt but an emulator as well. He had been off in the hills with some woodsmen that afternoon chopping down trees!

When, after a most charming and delightful hour, Yorke rose to take his departure, Prince Robin volunteered to conduct him on a sight-seeing tour of the castle, after which a car would be in readiness to take him to the Regengetz.

Left alone with her sister, Virginia's demeanor underwent a swift and startling change. Her gayety forsook her almost as soon as the two men disappeared down the corridor.

"Bevvy dear," she said, solemn-eyed and serious; "you remember what I told you a long time ago? Well, it's true."

"I don't know what you are talking about. You've told me a lot of things, you know."

"I mean about him."

"Oh? Well, he is all you said he was, dear—perfectly delightful, and—"

"For heaven's sake, don't you remember me telling you that I was in love with him?" cried Virginia, impatiently.

"Oh, *that!* Certainly I remember it." She looked deeply into her sister's eyes, and then said slowly: "And you are still in love with him? Is that what you mean?"

"Yes—that's just it, Bev. I am in love with him—only more so than ever. For a long, long time he was a —well, a phantom, a sort of dream man. I never expected to see him again. And now he isn't a phantom nor is he a dream any longer. He is real, and he is here where I can touch him with my hands, and speak to him, and hear his voice, and—"

"Go on, dear. Why do you pause?"

"I was just about to say precious little good it does me," sighed Virginia. "I think—in fact, I am sure—he loves some one else. Oh, don't laugh, Bevvy! I'm frightfully unhappy."

"But, Virginia dear," cried the Princess, instantly sober; "what difference could it possibly make to you if he were in love with you and not with some one else? You couldn't—you couldn't marry him, you know."

"Oh, I couldn't, couldn't I?" cried Virginia, a combined note of triumph and defiance in her voice. "Why, bless your stupid old heart, I don't have to marry him. I am already married to him. That's what all the hullabaloo is about, isn't it? Don't say I *couldn't* marry him. It has been proved that I can."

"Please don't jump down my throat, Virgie! In any event, if he is in love with some one else—why, that settles it, doesn't it?"

"I suppose it does," admitted Virginia. "But now that he knows he is married to me, he hasn't any right to be in love with another girl," she argued stubbornly.

"It seems to me," said Bevra, with a faint yawn, "that it's the other woman's place to worry."

"That's all very well, but why should she worry when she doesn't know anything about it?"

"Did you talk it over with him, as you promised father you would?"

"Certainly."

"Doesn't he agree that the only thing to do is to go through with the form of a divorce?"

"I never knew anybody to agree to anything so quickly as he did. You would have thought he'd say his heart was broken or something like that, wouldn't you? I gave him the chance and all he said was that he'd be delighted to help me out of the scrape. He even said the sooner the better. He doesn't care the snap of his finger for me, Bevvy. There is some one else. He pretended to be flippant about it, but—"

"Did he say there was another woman?"

"Heavens, no! Even though he'd only known for five minutes that he was a married man he ran true to form, as Bobby would say. He never so much as peeped about the other woman. He's just like all husbands. It's second nature with them. They never admit there is another woman."

Bevra laughed. "You are perfectly delicious, Virg. He falls in with the plan you suggest to him, agrees to everything as a gentleman should, and now you treat him as if he were a real husband. You suspect him. You—"

Virginia sprang to her feet, the light of a new and inspired determination in her eyes.

"Listen, Bev. I've made up my mind. I shan't go on with this stupid divorce business!"

"What!" cried her sister, her eyes flying wide open.

"I've been thinking it over, and now I've decided—positively. If he wants a divorce, he'll have to apply for it himself. He can't marry any one else till he's been divorced from me. So that's that!"

Her sister was aghast. "You must be crazy, Virginia. Of course you are going to have the marriage annulled. It wasn't a marriage in the first place. It was a—a what-do-you-call-it? A subterfuge. You surely can't—"

"I don't care what it was in the first place," retorted Virginia. "It's what it is now that matters to me. I love him and I always have loved him. You can tell father and mother whatever you please, Bevra, but I'm not going through the divorce courts just to please Mr. Pendennis Yorke or anybody else!"

With that she flounced out of the room, leaving her sister to recover from the shock as best she could. That she recovered quickly was manifest. A soft, wondering light filled her eyes and a little smile played about her tender lips as she gazed dreamily into the fire. She too was young and she knew what it was to love a man. Slowly her ruminations took definite form. She was arguing with herself as follows:

"I don't believe father would really mind. I'm sure mother wouldn't. Under the skin he is as good as any of us. The prince business is in an awful slump. The bottom has dropped out of it. Busted flat, is what I'd call it. What it needs is less preferred stock and a lot more common stock. Father realizes it more than anybody. Something that will pay dividends in fresh, clean, sterling blood. See what good, rich American blood has done for Robin—and see what it has done for Virginia and me   Nothing worn-out or impoverished or bankrupt about us. And look at my babies. Good gracious, the more I think of it, the more I hope he isn't in love with some one else."

And while all this was going on in the privacy of the Princess's boudoir and at the same time in the brains of two more or less revolutionary young women of royal blood, the young man of common stock was traversing the halls of kings in the company of the most promising issue of preferred stock the European market had known in many years.

"You know," Prince Robin was saying, rather eagerly, as they stood inside the doors of the great, gloomy throne room—his hands were jammed deep into his trousers pockets—"my name is Lorry. They called me Bob Lorry at Eton. I suppose you know my father's name was Lorry. He was an American—born and bred."

"I know, Your Highness."

"I never knew him. He was killed in a railway accident when I was a tiny kid. I wish I had known him. They say he was fine."

"My father died when I was only a few weeks old," said Yorke, and then, with a humorous twist of the lips: "They say he was fine."

"I'll bet he was," said the Prince of Graustark, warmly. "Come along; I want you to see the gun room before it gets too dark. This isn't very interesting."

In the gun room, Yorke naturally found an opening for an allusion to Graustark's part in the Great War.

"We couldn't do much," said the Prince modestly. "We weren't big enough. Small guns, that's what we were. But we lost a lot of men just the same. Our share, I mean. The full strength of our Army was considerably under fifty thousand. Our job was to hold the passes in this part of the Carpathians, and we somehow managed to do it. Of course, we couldn't have lasted a week if they'd sent a big force against us. In any case, they didn't go through us to get to Rumania. I guess they figured we'd delay 'em a little longer than they liked. So they went around us to the South."

"You were in personal command, I understand, Your Highness," said the American, encouraging the unexpected.

"Only figuratively," replied the Prince, with becoming candor. "Count Quinnox was, of course, Chief of Staff and the actual Commander of our army. I am not a real soldier, you see. But I saw considerable action, if that's what you mean. Several chunks of shrapnel in one of my legs and a bullet through my shoulder while I was being carried back. Hospital for a couple of months. It was all over before I came out. I mean to say, Russia had quit and was making a separate peace. We three little countries up here were helpless after that, so we signed a treaty of peace ourselves. Making peace was all the rage just then, so far as this neck of the woods was concerned," he concluded, with a wry grimace.

"Well, Graustark seems to have come out of it in much better shape than the rest of the belligerents," remarked the American.

The Prince hesitated for a moment, his brow darkening.

"I will have to confess that we made a bargain with

Russia before abandoning our original stand of armed neutrality. My ministers were canny, they were wise, and as it turns out, they were far-sighted. Please do not gather that we intended to remain neutral for any length of time. The Prime Minister saw a way to wipe out our debt to Russia. Graustark owed the Russian government several million dollars. Strangely enough the debt had been guaranteed by Germany, who had pulled the wool over the eyes of a former Cabinet. We saw through her scheme too late. She hoped in course of time to force us to grant her the right to extend her railway system through our valley in a grand project to gain control of the Persian and the India seaboards. You know what I mean. My cabinet seized the opportunity to do what nearly every other nation did in the great crisis. They bargained. Frankly, Mr. Yorke, they demanded that Russia cancel our debt in return for our aid in the war. Russia jumped at the chance. She saw the opportunity to get something for nothing—because, if Germany were to win the war the guarantee of our debt wouldn't amount to a pinch of snuff and she would grab Graustark into the bargain. Well, the debt was cancelled. It was a robber's claim to begin with, I may say in defense of Graustark's apparent act of cupidity. We promptly went into the war on the side of Serbia, as we had intended doing all along. We did our best. It wasn't much, but it helped. Germany forgot all about us in the haste to make advantageous peace terms with Russia. She ignored us, thank God for the slight. If she had won the war, however, she would have remembered us, you may be sure. She would have taken her pound of flesh.

So, you will perceive, in a way the war was actually a benefit to us. We made peace about the same time that Russia did—and we've had it ever since, which is more than can be said for the great and powerful nation that had crumbled from within and came near to burying all of her allies under the ruins. By the way, are you obtaining all the information you desire for your articles on Graustark?"

"I am getting much more than I expected, Your Highness."

"This is what we call the Room of Wrangles," announced the Prince, pausing before a door. "It is here that the cabinet meets twice a month." An attendant threw open the door and they stepped inside the lofty, vaulted chamber. "Over there at the end of the table I signed the declaration of war. My hand shook a little. It shook worse when I signed the treaty of peace, however. It was a confession of defeat when as a matter of fact we were not conquered. One doesn't mind admitting he's been licked when he's down on his back after a good thumping, but it's pretty hard to acknowledge defeat when you're still on your feet and fighting for all you're worth. That little chamber over there is my private office. May I offer you a highball? No trouble at all and it's not bootleg stuff. Come along, let's have one. I drink very little myself but I find a nip now and then doesn't hurt my conscience."

A few minutes later they raised tall glasses to each other and murmured the customary "Here's how."

Robin cleared his throat. "Ahem! I trust you will pardon my curiosity, but I'd rather like to know the result of the confab you had with Virginia this afternoon I assume you came to some decision."

"We did. Naturally, there is only one thing to be done. I hadn't the remotest idea that our marriage was legal, Your Highness. But it seems that it was. It's preposterous, of course—the whole affair. We hadn't the slightest suspicion of what we were getting into. I advised Princess Virginia to proceed without delay in the matter of having the marriage annulled."

"It's a shame to cause you all this trouble, Mr. Yorke, after what you did for Virginia out of the kindness of your heart."

"It hasn't caused me the least bit of trouble, Your Highness."

Silence fell between them. They emptied their glasses with what appeared to be a calculated slowness. Yorke sighed deeply as he set his glass down on the table.

"Why the sigh?" inquired the Prince, eyeing him narrowly, speculatively.

"Did I sigh?"

"Profoundly."

"I'm sorry. It was unconscious."

"Isn't the liquor all right?"

"It's wonderful."

"Are you in—er—in trouble of any kind, Mr. Yorke?"

"Good God, do I give you the impression of being in—"

"It struck me a moment ago that you looked quite troubled and unhappy."

Yorke was startled into a quick, uneasy glance at his royal host. "I never was so happy in my life," he said, affecting surprise.

Prince Robin shook his head, smiling faintly. "I don't believe a damned word of it," said he.

"I—I beg your pardon, Your—"

"I don't believe you are happy, Yorke. Just now I caught a look in your eyes that—and, what's more, I was observing you pretty closely upstairs a while ago. When Virginia was with us, I mean. I saw the expression in your eyes when you looked at her. You can't fool me. You're hard hit, Yorke. It's as plain as the nose on your face. I don't blame you. Now, let's have the truth."

"Sometimes the truth were better left untold," said Yorke, rather gruffly.

"I'm sorry if I have offended you, Yorke."

Yorke's jaw was set. "What would be the use of my telling you that I love her?" he blurted out, suddenly. "Fat lot of good it would do me!"

"Then I was right. You are in love with her."

"Of course I am—damn the luck! I never realized it until a week or so ago, but I've been in love with her for five years. Can you beat it? Can you think of a rottener piece of luck than to accidentally fall in love with a princess?"

Prince Robin threw back his head and laughed. "Well, I like that!" he exclaimed. "Yes," he went on, soberly, "I can think of a worse bit of luck. It would be for a princess to deliberately fall in love with a commoner."

"They don't often do anything as foolish as that."

"They don't, eh?" scoffed Robin. "My dear fellow, that's just what every single one of 'em does. They rarely if ever fall in love with men of their own station. That's the pity of it. They love the commoner and they marry the prince. You don't suppose Princess Bevra fell in love with me because I am a prince, do you? Well, she didn't. She fell in love with me because I happen to be blessed with what is described in monarchist circles as a common streak. Now, what I should like to know, Yorke, is this: Do you willingly consent to this divorce?"

"I would be lying like the devil, Your Highness, if I were to answer yes to that question. I agree to the divorce because she wishes it, and furthermore because there is nothing else for us to do in the circumstances. I'd be a dog to stand in her way in case she wants to marry some one else, or even in case her father has arranged one of your happy alliances.. But, just the same, I'd give my very soul to be in a position to say, 'No; you're mine. You belong to me. I'm hanged if I'll give you up!' "

"Have you, by any chance, told her that you love her?"

"Certainly not, Your Highness!"

"I am sure she would take it as a great compliment. All women are alike. Princesses are no different in that respect from their more fortunate sisters. They like to be told. It pleases their vanity, even though nothing can come of it."

"I couldn't even think of it," said Yorke firmly. "She'd only laugh at me."

"Well, you wouldn't begrudge the poor girl a good laugh, would you, Yorke?" demanded the Prince, in high good humor. He took his arm as they strolled forth into the great, vaulted audience room where for centuries men had bent the knee before the Princes of Graustark.

CHAPTER XI

THE fifth day after his visit to Edelweiss Castle, Yorke received a short, formal letter from Virginia. It came by post and was a polite though rather imperious request for him to send to her immediately a certain snapshot which had been taken by Mr. Higbee in Buda Pesth some five years ago. She curtly informed him that she wished to destroy the silly thing! He promptly sent it to her by special messenger.

Now this demand of hers was not the result of prolonged deliberation. It came as a sort of inspiration on the morning of that self-same day. For four days and nights she had been in a turmoil of uncertainty, decision succeeding indecision over and over again with exasperating constancy. In the first place, she had gone to bed the night after his visit firmly and unalterably resolved not to be the one to appeal for a legal dissolution of the tie that bound them. She awoke the next morning in a completely altered frame of mind. She *would* set him free. It was only fair and just and—she employed the word herself—decent. Especially so, she reasoned, when it was plain to be seen that he wanted to be free and besides—this was the deciding point—she wasn't sure that she loved him anyhow. That point, however, she soon discovered, was debatable. In any case, she would be only making herself ridiculous in his eyes if she allowed him to even suspect that she wasn't willing and eager to release him.

So she sat down that very morning and wrote a long letter to her father, advising him to start proceedings at once. Then, before noon, she decided there was no occasion for haste; she destroyed the letter. She knew she was being very silly and unwomanly about it and perhaps a little shameless, but somehow the hope persisted that she might, after all, be wrong in assuming that Yorke was in love with some one else and that he was indifferent to her. Not that anything could come of it—of course not—but still— Here her reflections became lost in a maze from which there was no pleasant or direct outlet.

The second day she was discussing with herself the advisability of returning immediately to her home in Serros; and practically all of the third day was spent in wondering why she had been such a goose as to tell Bevra all that rubbish about being in love with him. She had by now gained the impression that her sister and Robin were secretly laughing at her; quite naturally the former would have confided the sickening details to her husband and no doubt they had nothing better to do than to discuss her affairs behind her back. The thought of this irritated her beyond words. There were times when she considered them with unmistakably black looks—or at least looks as black as one with such tender blue eyes was capable of producing.

On the fourth day she screwed up the courage to ask Robin whether he and Mr. Yorke had settled upon the day when the latter was to come to the Castle for breakfast preliminary to a day's shooting in the hills. Upon receiving the answer she at once expressed an opinion of Mr. Yorke's manners, turning a deaf ear to her brother-in-law's highly edifying announcement that Mr. Yorke's manners were of a quality that forbade his coming to the Castle for breakfast in the random sort of way she seemed to advocate. That same afternoon she wrote another letter to her father—and destroyed it—and was rather sharp and captious at dinner; a most unusual and therefore noticeable mood for her to be in. She had, it seems, waylaid the gardener's boy, from whom she had gleaned the somewhat disturbing information that Mr. Yorke was in the best of health and exceedingly cheerful. A similar report from Captain Sambo was direfully augmented by the statement that his American friend was in better spirits than at any time since his arrival in Edelweiss. This disgusting news was further embellished by an account of a jolly little dinner at Pingari's the night before, when "Denny" Yorke was the life of the party. Moreover, quoth the Captain, practically all of the women had lost their hearts to him—and some of them were in danger of losing their heads.

Bright and early on the fifth morning she thought of the snapshot picture. What right had he to be carrying around in his pocket a cheap little kodak picture of her? A disgusting thing depicting him in the act of kissing her hand—bucolic, common, coarse, plebeian! What had possessed her that she did not tear it to bits and throw it in his face that night at the Regengetz? (But always when she thought of that night at the Regengetz, a pensive, wistful light stole into her eyes and she was distressingly aware of an unaccountable difficulty in steeling her heart against him.) The vacillation that had attended her efforts to despatch a message to her father was significantly absent when it came to writing to Yorke. She dashed off her letter hurriedly, stamped it, and, as if fearing she might waver in her resolution, motored in to the city and posted it herself at the Tower Station.

As she emerged from the post-office she saw Michael Rodkin. He was standing on the curb not far from her car. His dark eyes were fixed on her from the instant she came out of the door until the car turned the corner, a block away. She was alone. She was aware of the unswerving gaze with which he devoured her. It was not the first time she had experienced a queer, creepy little sensation; of late it had constantly assailed her when she felt herself subjected to his rapt, avid stare. Time and again she had encountered the man in the street and always he had looked at her with those hungry, covetous eyes—eyes that seemed strangely to be stripping her of every vestige of raiment. He frightened her. She had seen that look in men's eyes before. In Buda Pesth, when she was eighteen. . . .

She soon forgot Rodkin. Governed by a sudden impulse she drove to Regengetz Circus. Something told her that her face was scarlet as she circled the Plaza; at any rate, it was burning. Passing the Hotel she kept her gaze fixed rigidly ahead. Only at the very instant of turning off into Castle Avenue did she allow it to relax. Then she sent a swift, searching glance over her right shoulder. Her heart gave a mighty thump—and kept on thumping as she shot up Castle Avenue as if pursued by demons. That fleeting glance had taken in a tall, motionless figure on the steps, a white face turned in her direction. She could not be sure, but—well, whoever he was, he was wearing a gray suit of clothes and a brown fedora hat.

She suffered a disappointment later on. Down in her heart she had hoped that Pendennis (what was it that Captain Sambo had called him? "Denny?" She rather liked it) Yorke would refuse to surrender the picture. She secretly longed for a letter from him setting forth his reluctance to part with the souvenir—a letter in which he would plead earnestly and perhaps a trifle tenderly for permission to retain the picture. She hoped for a letter from which she could derive a little comfort by reading between the lines.

Instead of that kind of a letter, however, she received a polite note, enclosed with the photograph, delivered by a paid messenger from the Regengetz, with absolutely nothing between the lines. It was as follows:

"Dear Princess: I fully appreciate your desire to have the picture destroyed—and by your own trustworthy hands, as you so ingenuously state in your note. I have no right to it, of course, and had I been less contemptible than I must seem to you, I would have insisted on your keeping it that night at the Regengetz, thereby sparing you the embarrassment of having to ask me for it. It would be idle for me to say that I relinquish it without regret. I shall miss it after all these years. But you have asked for it, and here it is with my compliments and apologies. Hold it over your lighted candle. It will soon be ashes. Permit me, Princess, to subscribe myself, Your devoted servant, Pendennis Yorke.

"P.S.—I am wondering whether, after having deprived me of a cherished memento, you will continue to preserve the only thing you possess that may serve to remind you of the day on which this picture was taken. I refer to a certain time-honored traveling bag on which my humble name is painted in rather imposing characters. P.Y."

She was furious. The insolence of him! She shed a few tears over that postscript. For, when all is said and done, a princess may be quite as sensitive as even the lowliest of her sex and as prone to heartaches and—tempers.

Shortly after this she began to show a most extraordinary interest in Bevra's children. She had always adored them but now her devotion seemed to be turning into a tender, jolly sort of slavery. She spent much of her spare time playing with them. She walked in the Park with them, told them fairy stories, came in with their mother to hear their prayers and to kiss them good night as their eyes were closing in sleep, got up much earlier than usual in the morning to romp with them, and twice saved young Prince Dantan from a paddling at the hands of his strict though loving mother.

It was and always had been the custom in Edelweiss Castle to paddle naughty little princes and princesses, just as other little boys and girls are paddled or ought to be paddled when they misbehave. And the naughty little princes and princesses howled just as lustily under the slipper as the humblest wrongdoer in the land, proving that all mortals are made in the same mold and that purple and fine raiment are no protection against the law. Parents in Graustark were humane. They believed in swift punishment, getting it over with as quickly as possible; they did not believe in such prolonged cruelties as sending children to bed supperless, locking them up for determinate periods in dark closets, depriving them of cherished playthings, sentencing them to heart-breaking hours in which they were made to feel that mother no longer loved them. Prince Robin had been paddled by an adoring great-aunt, the Duchess of Halfont; Princess Bevra had been soundly paddled by her mother, and so had Princess Virginia. It is worthy of note that these punitive measures invariably were attended to by the mothers; they know how to administer a paddling without giving offense!

There were times, however, when Virginia's restlessness got the better of her. At such times she took the car out for a spin, disregarding imperial precedent by driving in solitary defiance of custom up and down Castle Avenue and through the upper streets of the city. Citizens accustomed to seeing royalty only when it was attended by flunkeys, bodyguards and the strictest decorum were at first amazed by the extraordinary digressions of Dawsbergen's daughter, but soon began to nudge each other and smile as they followed her with admiring eyes.

"It is the American blood that's in her," was the sage verdict of the people of Edelweiss.

She confined her little excursions to precincts adjacent to the Castle, thereby conscientiously observing the law as laid down by the wise and cautious Baron Gourou, head of the Police Department of Graustark, who pointedly declared that he would not be responsible for her safety if she roamed too far afield.

On several of these "spins" she was accompanied by the bulky Prince Hubert. She did not like him but he served a purpose. It had something to do with Pendennis Yorke's peace of mind. She frequently passed Michael Rodkin in the street and was always conscious of his pursuing gaze. This in itself was not sufficient cause for complaint on her part. He had as much right to gaze at her as any other man or woman in the street—and they all gazed at her, you may be sure. Only once did she catch him in the act of smiling at her, and that was when she stopped the car one day in Regengetz Circus to pick up Prince Hubert! She was not offended by his smile however, for there was an open sneer in it, there was mockery in it; she was honest enough with herself to admit that there was some excuse for his sneer. It was his way of proclaiming what she knew to be the truth. Hubert, for all that he wore the insignia of a Prince, was less worthy to sit beside her than the commonest man in Edelweiss.

Hubert, who was living at the Hotel Regengetz, did not rise any higher in her estimation when, on this particular occasion, he remarked as they drove off:

"I passed that bounder Yorke in the lobby just now, Virginia."

"*Did* you?" she said, coldly.

"I complained to the manager the other day about that infernal typewriter of his. He keeps banging away on it till long past midnight."

"How interesting! And what did the manager say?"

Hubert scowled. "He said he'd speak to him about it."

"I suppose Mr. Yorke stopped his racket at once?"

"He did not. The damned bounder paid no attention to the manager's request. He ought to be thrown out of the hotel."

"Are you sure the manager spoke to him about it?"

"Absolutely. In writing. He showed me the note the fellow wrote in reply—on his beastly typewriter, too. He said that any one of his own sex who reported that he used the machine after six o'clock in the evening was a liar."

"Goodness! That *was* being definite, wasn't it? I should say, Hubert, that it is up to you to get some one of the opposite sex to report him. That would simplify matters tremendously. He wouldn't dare call a woman a liar, you know."

The irony escaped him. "He's got all the fool women about the place eating out of his hand," he growled. Then scornfully: "Lord, how they do fall for him! Somebody's husband will blow his brains out if he hangs around Edelweiss— Hey! Easy! This isn't a country road, Virginia! Good Lord, you're up to fifty-five—"

"If you don't like the way I am driving this car, Hubert," she flung over her shoulder into the rush of the wind, "you can just hop out!"

That same evening Captain Sambo dropped in for dinner with Yorke. He found that gentleman pacing the room, his brows knit in thought.

"Hello! What's up?" demanded the Captain. Sharpe had taken his coat and cap into the bedroom.

"One of my fellow-lodgers has been trying to have me

kicked out of the hotel," replied Yorke, who rarely
wasted words. "Prince Hubert. He complained about
the typewriter the other day. This evening he informed
the management that I have been hobnobbing with
Michael Rodkin, the Red, and that I am not what I claim
to be. The manager came to me a while ago in great
agitation. He doesn't believe a word of what the prince
says, but it seems the fellow has been telling a lot to other
patrons of the place."

"Don't let it worry you, Denny. You have excellent
sponsors. Prince Robin, Gourou, Quinnox and— See
here, old man, you don't mean to say the management
is hinting that you ought to get out?"

"All I can say is that Grossman appears to be nervous
and embarrassed. He may have something of the sort in
mind."

"We'll soon get it out of his mind," declared Sambo,
warmly. "Don't think anything more about it."

"There's another thing," resumed Yorke. "I went
down to call on Rodkin at his diggings this afternoon.
I'd been promising to go. I think I've told you we were
in college together. He's a radical all right enough and
I've no doubt would like to see the government over-
thrown. There on the table is a lot of literature he's been
getting out for the enlightenment of the masses. Baron
Gourou knows all about it. In fact, Rodkin sends most
of the stuff to him as soon as it's off the press. No secret
about it. Well, Rodkin told me to-day that one of his
acquaintances, a Red of the deepest dye, came to him
last night with a rather ugly story. It seems that a day
or two ago a stranger—an Axphainian, I gather—ap-

proached this fellow and coolly offered him a thousand gavvos if he would do a little private job of assassinating. The man refused to consider the proposition. The stranger mentioned no names but he did say that the intended victim was not a member of the royal family, nor was he a citizen of Graustark. Rodkin is firm in his belief that I am the mán whose death is desired. He also suspects that a certain visiting prince is the man higher up. Rodkin knows no more than I have told you. His friend is positive that the man who made the proposal to him is a stranger in Edelweiss. He never saw him before and, so far as he is able to report, he has disappeared as if swallowed by the earth. He describes him as a frail, sickly looking young fellow, extremely nervous and—"

"It's as plain as the nose on my face," broke in the Captain. "This fellow, whoever he is, has been hired to do the job himself. He's in a funk. Can't go through with it. Lost his nerve. So he's trying to hire some one to take the dirty job off his hands. Gourou must be told at once. He—"

"That has already been attended to," interrupted the other.

"Have you see Gourou?"

"No, Michael Rodkin went straight to him with the story. I'm bound to tell you, old man, just what Rodkin said to me. He said that he wouldn't have breathed a word of this to Gourou if he hadn't believed it was me they are after and not Prince Robin or some one else among the All-Highest."

"Gad, he's a frank devil, isn't he? He gave you to

understand, did he, that he wouldn't have put a thing in their way if their plot called for the assassination of His Highness?"

"One of Gourou's men was discussing the matter with me just before you came in," said Yorke, slowly. "He says that Rodkin made practically the same statement to the Baron."

"Which one of Gourou's men was here to see you?"

"He's in the next room now," replied Yorke, with a queer smile. "My valet, Sharpe."

Captain Sambo started. He allowed a guilty look to flash across his face and then heaved a sigh of relief.

"So you have tumbled to Sharpe's real job, have you?" Captain Sambo was picking up some excellent English through his association with Pendennis Yorke.

"I must confess that I was beginning to suspect him. He is much too good a valet to be the real article. What do you make of Rodkin's story?"

"It is not for me to say, Yorke. My position denies me the privilege of making a definite accusation. Just the same, I am glad that Rodkin warned you. Be on your guard, Denny. You need not be afraid of Prince Hubert attacking you himself. He isn't built that way. But the world is full of men who can be hired to commit murder. I am saying more than I should, I suppose, but I happen to know that Prince Hubert looks upon you as the only obstacle between him and—er—victory."

"I understand. He goes on the principle that death is surer than divorce. Isn't that it?"

"At any rate, it is swifter," said Captain Sambo, significantly. "He is a coward, despite his size and pro-

digious strength. He will not fight. There is a story that
a Russian nobleman once slapped his face in a restaurant.
He was half Hubert's size. According to witnesses, the
Prince, instead of retaliating with his fist, leaped behind
a table, white with fear, and shot the man dead. So now
you know what kind of a fighter he is."

"Where I came from we don't slap men in the face,"
said Yorke, rather grimly. "We swing for the jaw with
all we've got."

"That's what I've heard," said Sambo, his eyes resting
for a moment on Yorke's broad shoulders as he followed
him through the door.

The following day Prince Robin and the American
started out bright and early on a shooting expedition into
the hills near Ganlook, accompanied by huntsmen and
beaters. Pendennis breakfasted at the Castle and they
were off shortly after sunrise, long before the household
was astir. The Prince supplied the guns. They were
after pheasants.

Virginia ambled leisurely into Bevra's breakfast room
as usual, soon after eight o'clock to have coffee and toast
with her sister. It was not until then that she learned
of the shooting trip, which obviously had been planned
beforehand and without her knowledge.

"Don't blame me, Virgie," protested Bevra, when taken
to task by her sister. "I knew nothing about it till late
last night when Robin told me he was getting up at four
this morning to go off shooting with Mr. Yorke. I don't
know when they arranged it. Besides, dear, what possible difference could it have made to you? Surely you
wouldn't have been such a goose as to get up at four

o'clock to have breakfast with a couple of grouchy men."

"I call it sneaking, that's what I call it," flamed Virginia, stormily. Then suddenly her anger gave way to smiles. "You old dear, I don't blame you. You are only a poor little wifey. You're not supposed to be consulted about anything your high and mighty lord and master chooses to do. And if Robin didn't consider it worth while to mention it to you, I daresay he thought it was even less important to mention it to me. Goodness, this coffee is hot!"

And when the hunters returned at six o'clock that evening, leg-sore but triumphant, she was not present to congratulate them on their luck. She was up at the Halfont mansion, whither she had hastened at mid-afternoon, impelled by the praiseworthy object of delighting the venerable lady with a proposal to make her dinner more cheerful by sharing it with her in the privacy of the ducal bedchamber, to which the duchess was still confined by her diminishing attack of tonsilitis. The duchess had never known her to be so tenderly thoughtful nor her conversation to be so sprightly.

"You are a sweetheart, Virginia," cried the pleased old woman as her self-invited guest was taking her departure. "I feel twenty years younger and I shan't have my tonsils out—not by any means. I am looking forward to another attack, my dear—and you shall be my physician. By the way, how is your friend Mr. Yorke?"

"Who?" inquired Virginia, puckering her brow.

"Isn't his name Yorke? The man you are married to, I mean."

"Oh, Mr. *Yorke*. I wasn't listening, I fear, Duchess.

He is very well, I hear. I haven't seen anything of him for ages."

"Dear me! What kind of a simpleton is he, may I ask? If I were a man and married to you, my dear, you'd never see anything else but me."

"That's awfully sweet of you, Duchess, but I am afraid your fever is coming up again."

"It isn't a circumstance to the fever I'd be having if I were—"

"Good night, you old darling! I really must be running along now. They'll lock the gates on me."

The next afternoon she came face to face with Pendennis in Castle Avenue. Dusk fell early upon Edelweiss, screened as it was on all sides by towering mountains; and night came swiftly even while the sun shone brightly, on lands not many leagues away. She was hurrying homeward in the little car, when she beheld him walking from the direction of the Castle. Her first thought was to speed by as if she had not observed him, but it was instantly dismissed. She hated herself for the thought. She was ashamed of the childish motive.

So she swung in toward the curb, bringing the car to a stop with more haste than was good for it. Her smile was warm and friendly as she leaned over and held out her hand to him.

"How do you do, stranger," was her gay greeting. Her heart was beating rapidly, although to all outward appearances she was as calm and serene as the proverbial May morning. If she noticed the eager, searching look in his eyes as his big hand engulfed hers in a grip that should have caused pain, but did not, she gave no sign.

"This is a most unexpected pleasure, Princess," he said, still holding her hand.

He appeared to have forgotten to release it. She was conscious of a strange, warm current coursing through her veins; she felt her whole body sag a little as if by some mysterious, though pleasant process, it was being denuded of all its strength, all its resistance. She felt this warm current clear to the tips of her toes. Suddenly he remembered, and released her little gloved hand. But he could not withdraw the legacy left by that brief, highly sensitized moment of contact. She still tingled—deliciously.

"I haven't seen you in ages," she said, and was afraid that he would detect the queer breathlessness that attended the effort. She was beginning to regret that she had not hurried on without stopping to speak to him.

"I have been terribly busy," he explained, almost inarticulate except for his eyes, which were still eloquent.

"So I hear," said she, equally at a loss for words.

He waited for a moment, collecting himself. "I walk out this way every afternoon. Clearing the cobwebs out of my brain. The Avenue is wonderful. I've never seen a more splendid—er—magnificent Avenue."

"It is magnificent, isn't it? I love it. I am not supposed to be out driving alone at this time of day, with night coming on. But, you see, I too need something to clear the cobwebs away, so I violate all rules, all precedent, all of the conventions, and—and— Oh, what did I tell you?" she broke off to exclaim, pointing up the Avenue.

She hadn't told him anything, to be sure; still he graciously overlooked the omission and turned his head to look in the direction indicated.

Half a dozen mounted guardsmen were cantering toward them on the opposite side of the dividing parkway.

"Ostensibly exercising their horses," she commented with a shrug of her shoulders; "but in reality looking for me. They will pass by without the slightest sign of having perceived me. Nevertheless, in a very few minutes they will come riding up behind us. They will salute and a few rods farther on they will come to rest. And there they will wait until I am ready to precede them through the Castle gates. You see, I know their habits. They are very faithful watchdogs and this isn't the first time they've ridden out on the trail of bothersome me."

"It will soon be dark, Princess. Isn't it a little unsafe, I mean to say unwise, for you to be out alone—"

"I am not afraid," she broke in.

"These are evil days."

"All the more reason why I should not be a coward, Mr. Yorke. Go on—don't be afraid to say it."

"Say what?"

"What was on the tip of your tongue. 'All the more reason why you should not be a fool!' Wasn't that on the top of your tongue?"

"It was," he replied succinctly.

"I thought it was. How is the work getting on?"

"Splendidly. I shall be through much sooner than I anticipated."

"Really?"

"A couple of weeks more will finish the job."

She took that moment to lean forward and fumble with the switch regulating the headlights.

"And then I suppose you will return at once to London," she said, still bending forward—a circumstance which may have accounted for the muffled tone in which she spoke.

"Oh, no, I am going on to Dawsbergen for a couple of weeks. After that I shall go to Axphain to study conditions there."

"How—very interesting."

A brief silence ensued. She found herself looking, not into his eyes, but at the red carnation on his coat lapel. She was not thinking of the flower, however. In fact, it is doubtful if she saw it at all, the intentness of her gaze notwithstanding.

He misinterpreted her interest. "Gardenias are my favorites," he said, with a whimsical smile. "But the boy who has been supplying me with them notified my valet the other day that he couldn't bring any more of them to me."

"Indeed?" she said, a trifle coldly.

"I miss them terribly. Still, I like carnations for a change."

She felt the flush mounting to her face. The words came out before she could check them. "There are no more gardenias. Didn't the gardener's boy tell you?"

"I have never seen the gardener's boy, Princess."

"Do you—do you doubt that there *is* a gardener's boy?" she demanded, indignantly.

"No, indeed. I know you sent them to me by Sharpe's

son. I would thank you if I believed that you wished to be thanked."

"Oh!"

He leaned closer and said, a thrill in his voice: "Is that the only reason why the gardener's boy ceased bringing them to me?"

"I—I don't understand." (But she did.)

"Because there were no more to be had?"

"What other reason could there be, Mr. Yorke?" she asked, raising her eyebrows slightly.

"The extinction of a whim," he replied, looking straight into her eyes.

She flared. "How dare you speak of it as a whim! That is a nice way to thank me! I did it because I knew you liked them. Now you make me sorry that I even tried to be kind and—"

"Please don't be angry!"

"I am very angry, Mr. Yorke."

"Forgive me—Rosa!"

It was daring, but he said it so gently, so softly that it was little more than a whisper. She started, her lips fell slightly apart, and again her body experienced that quick sagging sensation as of complete surrender to a bewildering, unexplicable languor. Then she laughed uncertainly, confusedly.

"How—how funny that sounded," she cried, struggling bravely to recover her composure. Then, in sheer desperation: "I must not keep those men waiting. My sister will be wondering what has become of me. Good-by, Mr. Yorke."

"You are no longer angry with me?" He did not remove his foot from the running-board.

"Of course I am, frightfully," she said, making no further move to start the car.

"You will be amused to know that I have pressed a number of those gardenias between the leaves of a book." He laughed awkwardly. "Silly, isn't it?"

"Very," she answered, now quite cool and collected. "I thought only disappointed old maids pressed flowers in books. It does seem silly for a man to do it."

"Well, anyhow, I did it."

"I suppose you will be taking them down into somebody's tomb with you one of these days," she said, mockingly.

"Certainly. Down into my own, Princess."

Her hand was on the clutch. She grasped it nervously, rather convulsively.

"Good-by! I really must be going. It is nice to have seen you again. So sorry to have missed you after the hunt yesterday."

He stood back, lifting his hat. She hesitated a moment and then impulsively cried:

"I was mean and cattish about that picture, Mr. Yorke, and I've been awfully ashamed. Would you like to have it back?"

In the gathering gloom she saw his white teeth as his lips broke into a broad, pleased smile.

"Then you haven't destroyed it?"

She ignored the question. "Would you like to have it?" she demanded, a querulous note in her voice.

"I should say I would!" he cried.

"You shall have it to-morrow morning," she called over her shoulder, as the car got under way.

Not a word from either about the subject that was uppermost in their thoughts: the divorce.

CHAPTER XII

THE crash came on the twenty-third of March. Axphainian hordes invaded northern Graustark, sweeping down through the supposedly well-guarded mountain passes with the resistless force of a tidal wave. By nightfall of that memorable day many farms and villages were in the hands of the invaders; the fortress and city of Ganlook were besieged. The attack had come with the swiftness, the unexpectedness of a lightning bolt—a bolt out of a clear sky, at that.

Wires were down; means of communication with Edelweiss had been destroyed by scouting parties that had stolen down from the mountains some time in advance of the carefully calculated assault. Subsequent developments revealed the fact that these stealthy agents had secreted themselves in the dense forests several days before the sudden coup was to be undertaken. Their plans were so skillfully and so effectively consummated that hours passed before news of the invasion reached the capital, scarce forty miles away. Small but adequately armed bands of Red soldiers appeared from nowhere, springing up out of the earth like overnight fungi, to bar the highways and to tear up the railway tracks of the single line that ran through Ganlook to the heart of Graustark.

It was on the night of the twenty-third that Pendennis Yorke, at a certain hour, presented his pass to the guardian of the postern gate of Edelweiss Castle and was admitted to the private gardens immediately adjacent to the huge, brilliantly lighted structure. He came alone in a hired car and he was wearing the despised silk hat and his carefully doctored "spike-tail" coat. For this was the night of the long-anticipated and secretly dreaded dinner. He felt like a boy going to his first real party in his first tuxedo as the car passed the portcullis and swung around the circular driveway up to the great carriage porch, where a pair of resplendent footmen were stationed.

As he stepped down from the car he was startled almost out of his pumps. Standing in the shadow of one of the columns was Sharpe, his valet. Now he had left Sharpe in his rooms at the Regengetz not ten minutes before— yet here was Sharpe nonchalantly loitering under the very doors of the Castle Royal. How the deuce had he managed to get there ahead of him and what was he doing there, anyhow? Then suddenly the solution came—or at least the mystery was partly solved. He remembered that Sharpe was a secret service man, which, in a sense, accounted for the fact that he betrayed not the slightest sign of having recognized his master—his pseudo-master, as Yorke was pleased to describe himself in the amusing circumstances.

Yorke was too full of his own affairs, however, to devote further speculation to the shadowy, ubiquitous Sharpe; he was not to know for full many a day that the fellow had merely obeyed orders from Baron Gourou when he joined several other men who had been detailed

to act as a special guard for the American on this particular occasion. And most certainly Yorke had had no
suspicion at the time that the touring car which followed
him so closely almost to the castle gates and then.shot
through ahead of him contained men whose eyes searched
the pavements for a lurking, sickly looking stranger who
might be keeping his right hand well concealed inside the
breast of his overcoat. These men knew the postures of
street assassins.

Pendennis shortly found himself mingling with a brilliant throng in the Hall of Nobles, time-honored wait-
ing-room where generations of Graustarkian rulers had
received their banquet guests. He saw but few familiar
faces—four or five beautifully dressed young matrons and
as many men in whose company he had at one time or
another dined at Pingari's. The gay set, he classed them,
and with but one or two exceptions not of the nobility.
These erstwhile merry acquaintances greeted him in a dis-
hearteningly ceremonious manner. They were at ease,
however, and perfectly at home in surroundings where he
was lost.

A somewhat charitably inclined young widow whose
husband, Count Boske Danke, had lost his life in the war,
attached herself to him. He had met her twice at Pingari's, and had found her gay and amusing, and pretty as
well. She undertook to point out the "notables" to him;
she was guarded however in her manner and in her com-
ments. There were perhaps fifty people already in the
room and more were entering all the time. No one was
seated.

It was a striking assemblage and a stately one. There

were startlingly beautiful women and smart looking men, many of the latter in the full uniform of the Army. There were red-ribboned shirt fronts, there were shimmering decorations and diadems; there were old men and old women who looked more like monarchs than Robin or Bevra; there were radiant young women—but not one of them could hold a candle to the sisters who came out of Dawsbergen. A band was playing somewhere off in the vasty recesses of the castle—a Czech band playing the jaunty, fantastic gypsy airs that stir the senses and put life into the most sedate of feet.

"Good Lord!" reflected Yorke. "Call this a dinner party?"

A banquet, that's what it was going to be—and he loathed banquets. This wasn't at all what he had hoped for, nor, as a matter of fact was it what he had rather conceitedly expected. Catching a glimpse of himself in one of the long mirrors set in the walls, he felt more out of place than ever. His gaze rested upon a white, hang-dog, rather stupid-looking face, in which anxiety was so markedly revealed that all observers must have pitied him. Or, at least he would have felt sorry for any one who looked as he did to that truthful mirror.

He regretted his hitherto consoling stature. His six-feet-two rendered him disgustingly visible to all beholders. That silly-looking cranium of his stood up like an excrescence, a parapatetic knob, above the heads of four-score noble ladies and gentlemen. He had the uncanny notion that he must have grown many inches since entering the room—and most assuredly he had become uglier. He hadn't by any means been as homely as all this when he surveyed himself in the glass just before leaving the Regengetz. Indeed, he had rather prided himself on his physical appearance; and besides, that lying Sharpe had gone out of his way to encourage the delusion.

All around him were dark, vivid, clear-cut faces; vivacious, semi-oriental women in vivid gowns, with gleaming shoulders, red lips, and soft, alluring eyes; lithe, medium-sized men who carried themselves like soldiers all. Above them all protruded his pallid, bald, characterless visage —an alien weed in a bed of flowers. He searched the assemblage for the familiar face and figure of Captain Sambo, whose good six feet would have been a welcome relief to him in his peculiar isolation. He caught a glimpse of a very tall, white haired man on the opposite side of the room—Count Quinnox, Commander-in-Chief of the Army—but he was too far away to be of much use and besides he possessed a face that would have caused his own to pale into even more ignominious mediocrity.

"These affairs bore me almost to death," the Countess was saying, even as he regarded himself ruefully over the top of her sleek black head. "Once a month in the season they pull off something like this at the Castle."

"Pull off?" murmured Yorke, who thought he had not heard aright. He was conscious of a strange, grateful warmth stealing through his gelid diaphragm. For the first time since he entered the room he felt that he was not hopelessly alone. It was good to hear his own language spoken—the language of uncouth America!

"It has been the custom for hundreds of years," she went on, imperviously. "The Prince and Princess hate it, but what can the poor things do? Tradition has them in its grip. They— Are you looking for some one, Mr. Yorke?" she broke off to inquire rather coldly.

He hastily interrupted the forlorn contemplation of himself in the glass and, in some confusion, devoted his attention to his fair companion. The coldness faded from her dark eyes as she looked into his, and she smiled.

"If you were a little taller, Countess, you could see the person at whom I have been staring," he said, with a grimace. "He's over there in that mirror. A great big gawk of a fellow with awful ears and a putty-colored face. The sort of a face you'd say looked perfectly natural if he were dead and you wanted to say something pleasant for the family to hear."

"You do not look like a dead one to me," said this amazing Countess, and he forthwith found a cozy place for her in his reviving heart.

At this juncture, the boom of a deep, melodious gong was heard. Once, twice, thrice it sounded, and an instantaneous hush fell upon the company. Every voice was stilled and every eye was turned toward the upper end of the room where two lofty doors were slowly swinging open.

"Sh!" warned the Countess under her breath. Then in an almost inaudible whisper: "Face the door, Mr. Yorke."

The backs of two score men suddenly were bent and two score women sank into a deep, graceful curtsey as if controlled by a single mechanical device, manipulated by some unseen operators. Yorke, being a trifle slower than the rest—and considerably higher—allowed his gaze to rest for an appreciable length of time upon their Serene

Highnesses as they appeared in the massive gold frame of the doorway. Then he also lowered his eyes, painfully conscious of his transgression.

As suddenly the masculine backs straightened to military erectness; the curtseying figures, to the accompaniment of the swish and rustle of silk, rose like a many-colored wave. Then from every throat issued a subdued, almost toneless salutation, reminding Pendennis of nothing so much as the passive, indivisible responses of the Episcopal Church. Translated, the salutation was: "God be with your Highness!"

Prince Robin and Princess Bevra, moving with stately tread, crossed over and took their stand under a golden canopy. Close behind them followed Princess Virginia and Prince Hubert of Axphain. They remained slightly apart from their Serene Highnesses and in the background.

Yorke started. The thought flashed through his brain that here at last was confirmation of his fears. Was this to be the occasion of a public acknowledgment of Virginia's betrothal to— No, that was most unlikely. His mind worked rapidly. The announcement would come from the Castle in Serros. Still there was something vitally significant to be derived from the inclusion of Hubert in the royal party.

"The Princess looks tired, doesn't she?" the Countess was saying, in lowered tones.

He swallowed hard before replying, somewhat hazily:
"I think she looks—radiant." He was referring to Virginia.

"She is worn out with all her charity work, her interest

in the soldiers' hospitals, these tiresome audiences and state dinners. But isn't she beautiful?"

"Su-superlatively," muttered Yorke, his eyes on Virginia.

"I am speaking of Princess Bevra," said the Countess, a trifle severely.

"To be sure—to be sure," said he, hastily. "Superlatively beautiful."

He fell to contrasting the royal couple with the delightfully unassuming pair he had known under far pleasanter conditions. An incredible metamorphosis had taken place. Could it be possible that this imperious, dignified young man in the brilliant court apparel was the same unconventional chap with whom he had hunted, the same fellow who had appeared in the Princess's boudoir in a slouchy golf suit and pumps, and who had stood with his hands in his pockets and a pipe in his mouth on the threshold of the sacred throne-room? And was this regal creature with the jeweled coronet on her head, the ropes of pearls about her neck, the same as the charming, vivacious young person who, in a filmy blue gown, had given him tea and cigarettes, and sat with her legs crossed in a low rocking chair, revealing more than a shapely azure ankle?

He realized the truth. Now he was beholding these young people as circumstance had shaped them and not as God had made them—happy, light-hearted, insouciant mortals who loved life and love.

The company, strictly observing the rules of precedence, began to file past the royal couple. The Countess gave whispered instructions to Yorke.

"Watch what the others do—and do thou likewise. Remember, one does not shake hands with royalty. You are not in America, Mr. Yorke, where, I understand, everybody shakes hands with your president. Do not say 'Good evening, I hope you are well, Prince.' Do not say to the Princess: 'How charming you are looking this evening,' or 'And how are the kiddies, my dear?' No, Mr. Yorke—nothing like that. Being a stranger at court, it would be proper for you to bow and say 'I am conscious of the great honor your highness has conferred on me by—' You will get no farther than that, so don't feel it is necessary to commit the speech to memory. The next person in line will bump you along in the middle of the sentence. It's all very much cut-and-dried, you see. Prince Robin will not be paying attention to what any one says. He will probably be thinking of the blisters he has on his hands from chopping down trees, and all that sort of thing. And the Princess will be wondering if the children are asleep and haven't kicked the coverings off."

"Thanks! You are an awfully jolly guide, Countess. I couldn't possible have gone through it without you."

She crinkled up her pretty nose. "How I loathe the sight of that man Hubert!" Then, with a mischievous smile up into his eyes: "If she were *my* wife, even on probation, I should— Oh, dear me, Mr. Yorke! Don't scowl like that! People will think you are angry with *me!*"

"Was I scowling, Countess?"

"Diabolically," she assured him.

They moved along a few paces before he felt able to inquire in a manner sufficiently casual to deceive her:

"Do you suppose there is any truth in the report that she is going to marry him?"

Her face clouded. "I wonder. This is the first time he has been included in the royal party on an occasion as formal as this. Heavens! I would jump into the river if I were she. I'd sooner be married to a Congo ape than to that awful beast. Don't be uneasy. No one near us understands a word of English, Mr. Yorke."

"Thank God, handshaking is not required," was his fervent comment.

"You do not fancy the heir-presumptive to your throne?" she ventured.

He glanced down at her humorously. "You have a wonderful imagination, Countess," he drawled.

Presently they were face to face with Prince Robin and the Princess. Yorke looked for the light of friendly interest in the former's eyes as he mumbled the words the Countess had put into his head. The smile with which the Prince received the unheard little speech was utterly without warmth. It was the same perfunctory smile that one sees on the lips of the stage dancer as she turns her face toward the audience. A sort of stamped, rigid smile that had been put on like a mask for the occasion. It did not vary. It was the same smile that had greeted the Countess and all those who preceded her. The smile of a Monarch on display. A Jarley Waxworks smile.

Yorke hoped for something different in Bevra's smile, something intimate, something real. He was disappointed. She held her head high and—could it be true?—looked at him as if she had never seen him before in her life. He passed on, bewildered, and came to Princess Virginia. Here, at least, would be recognition, a friendly little smile, a word or two of— But there was not even the flicker of an eyelid! The same set smile, the same immobility of feature; the same flawless, unwavering graciousness that caused his soul to smart with scorn and the blood to mount to his face. Insufferable! From exalted heights they were looking down with tolerant eyes upon the salt of the earth, and not upon the worms thereof; they were looking down upon men and women whose loyal hearts and hands kept their little kingdom safe for them. And the devil of it, mused the indignant Yorke—whose quick American pride was hurt —the devil of it was that these subjects of theirs loved it all! Groveling sycophants!

And when the monstrous Hubert leered unctuously in his direction as if he were looking into space, he could have smashed his face with joy.

Out of the red haze of anger he groped. The Countess was speaking.

"We must find our places. Over here, Mr. Yorke."

She laid her fingers on his arm and guided him toward a long table about which the guests were clustered.

"Wouldn't it be great luck," she cried; "if you were to take me in?"

"The best luck I've ever had," he said, spurring up his gallantry. "What am I to do next?"

"I daresay all this is strange to you. Our customs are queer and primitive. You ask the man in charge for your ticket. On it you will find a number and the name of the woman you are to take in. The numbering begins at the top of the table, where their highnesses sit. If your num-

ber is 25 R, you will sit in place 25 on the right side of
the table, and the person you take in will occupy the next
seat beyond, which is unnumbered. Run along now and
get your ticket. I will wait here for you."

. He edged up to the lacquered table behind which sat
two ancient, bespectacled men upon whose russet tunics
was embroidered in blue the crest of the House of Ganlook. The Countess explained to him later on that they
were pensioners who had served for fifty years or more
in the office of the Castle steward.

When Yorke gave his name, both of the old men looked
up at him quickly, squinting their eyes in a near-sighted
effort to satisfy their curiosity. Then one of them extracted a card from the bunch he was holding in his hand,
turning to it with unerring dexterity. In a low voice he
called off the name of Pendennis Yorke and his companion put a check mark against it on the table chart
spread out before him.

Yorke glanced at the name and number on his card.
His place at table was No. 5 R, and he was to take in the
friendly Countess Danke. When he showed her the card
she uttered a little squeal of surprise and delight.

"Five? Who are you, Mr. Yorke? A great potentate
in disguise? No one outside of the royal line *ever* gets
nearer than ten or twelve. Oh, I forgot! You are a sort
of unrecognized member of the family, aren't you? Will
you believe me when I tell you that I have never been
nearer than No. 11 before? Heavens, I am thrilled. 1
feel like Cinderella. Have you the glass slipper in your
pocket?"

He was calculating rapidly. Virginia would most certainly be several seats removed from Prince Robin. He remembered the Countess Danke mentioning and pointing out at least three doughty-looking old duchesses and expressing sympathy for His Highness. These grande dames naturally would be placed at the top of the table. Virginia would be sent down the line a few seats. It was not unprobable that he would find her next to him— but he dared not hope.

He felt the Countess's fingers suddenly, convulsively tighten on his arm.

"What can have happened?" she cried out anxiously. "See! Count Quinnox is hurrying out of the room. Look at his face, Mr. Yorke! Something terrible has happened. And Colonel Minchin and— There! Do you see the Captain of the Castle Guard speaking to Prince Robin? He would not dare approach his highness at such a time unless— Yes! It is bad news! The Prince's face is as white as chalk!"

And so it was that the news from the North reached the Castle in time to spoil the feast.

There was but little confusion. The whispered word went round; faces blanched and then became grim and set; vacancies occurred in the resplendent throng; certain brilliantly clad men vanished; Prince Robin held up his hand at last and there was silence in the room. He spoke.

"There is bad news from Ganlook. Messengers have this instant arrived. They have been hours making their way to the city. Count Quinnox has gone to receive their report. I can only say that the news is disturbing. It is serious. We have been invaded. Thousands of armed men have crossed the border from Axphain. They have seized farms and villages and, if report be true, have invested Ganlook. So far, I am informed, there has been but little bloodshed. The attack was swift and found the people unprepared. Fighting has begun around Ganlook, however. Peasants who were able to make their way into Ganlook report pillage and destruction all along the border." He hesitated a moment, and then resumed, a deep, solemn note in his voice: "My friends, the starving people of Axphain have come to us for food, but they come with the sword and gun in hand. We shall drive them off and they will be but a little less hungry 'than when they came. Hunger and disillusionment have turned our neighbors into savage beasts. We shall kill many of them and they will kill many of us, I fear, before they can be driven from Graustark's sacred soil. We would not war upon those unhappy people, but our homes, our women, our honor, must be safeguarded. In the circumstances I feel that none of us is in the mood to feast and make merry to-night. We would not eat when starving men are killing our people for the bread that Graustark has in abundance. It would be mockery. Most of us are needed elsewhere. I hereby release you, one and all, from any obligation to remain here, in the Castle. The dinner—ah—naturally is—is"—he seemed at a loss for a proper and dignified conclusion, so he wound up with a rush—"called off!"

Then the Prince, after a brief, low-toned conference with the Prime Minister and Princess Bevra, strode swiftly from the room with the former. Pendennis Yorke felt his heart swell with a mighty fullness.

Not until then did the Countess Danke relax her grasp on his arm. He looked down at her. A deathly pallor had spread over her face. In a dull, monotonous tone she repeated the news from the North.

Yorke had watched Robin as if fascinated throughout the little speech; he had not understood a word of it and yet in those few tense moments all of his false impressions were swept away. He dismissed the scornful judgment he had rendered against these royal snobs. He saw in a flash the vast gulf that lay between the well-named commoner and the god to whom that commoner bent the knee. He knew now that he was looking upon the real prince of the blood, the descendant of a hundred rulers of men.

Now he understood why all these people humbled themselves before him—and why he, a lordly American, was suddenly shorn of his belief that all men are born equal! He, with the rest of them, stood in the presence of a Monarch. And the same astounding discovery embraced the two lovely young women whose heads were high and in whose serene eyes there was no alarm. They, too, had suddenly stepped outside the common fold into the isolation of Queens. No doubt their hearts were beating as tumultuously, no doubt their consternation was as great as that of any woman in the room; if so, they had command of themselves. Fear, anxiety, alarm, filled the eyes of the other women; the eyes of Bevra and Virginia, daughters of Dawsbergen, revealed only supreme trust in the everlasting strength of their forefathers.

"Would you like me to take you somewhere away from the crowd, Countess?" he asked, quickly, anxiously.

"No," she replied, with a calmness that belied her appearance. "I prefer to stay here as long as possible. I want to be with people." Her voice took on a strange hoarseness and she continued with difficulty. "My little boy is up there—with his grandparents—near the border above Ganlook. My father is Baron Brodrik. He is the burgrave of the province. The Castle is directly in the path of the—"

Princess Virginia stood before her, holding out her hands.

"Come with me, Karina," she said, an ineffable tenderness in her voice. "Be not afraid, dear. God will not let anything happen to your little boy. Come! We will go up to my room for a while. It is terrible, I know, but I am sure it isn't as black as it looks, Karina. Good night, Mr. Yorke."

There was a strangely wistful light in her now troubled eyes as she held out her hand to him. He would never forget the gentleness with which she spoke to the Countess.

"Good night, Princess. I hope to-morrow will prove that the reports are exaggerated and that the trouble will soon be over. If there is anything I can do, Countess, pray command me. When you are ready to go home—"

"I intend to keep her with me to-night," interrupted Virginia. "There will be further news during the night. Let us pray that it will be encouraging."

"I know the Axphainians," said the Countess, in a hard, choked voice. "They are cruel. They are beasts."

"Not all of them, dear," said Virginia, gently.

Yorke followed them with his eyes as they threaded

their way among the seemingly petrified guests and vanished through a door at the upper end of the room. Hubert had already disappeared. Princess Bevra alone of the royal party remained. She was now speaking rapidly, earnestly, in a voice that carried throughout the room. The company listened in stolid silence until she concluded what she had set out to say and then they broke into excited cries and cheers. As the Princess retired by the upper door, a woman whom he knew spoke to Yorke.

"Do not go away, Mr. Yorke," she said in her poor English. "Her Highness requests us all to remain as long as we please. There will be news from the north. It will be received here as it comes in and will be repeated to us. There will be bulletins in front of the Tower down in the City. Those who wish to do so, may partake of the food that has been prepared. But I fear no one will have the stomach for food to-night. Still, you are an American; you may feel that you have been cheated out of a good dinner. So, in case you feel hungry, you have only to—"

"Thank you," interrupted Yorke, courteously, but drily; "but like all the rest of you, madam, I am hungry only for news. You do my sensitive American stomach a grave injustice."

By this time the Hall of Nobles was in an uproar. Every one was talking; shrill, high-voiced women and loud, excited men; a clatter and babble of absolutely unintelligible words. Pendennis found himself suddenly alone and at sea in this agitated throng. He was making his way somewhat aimlessly toward the door by which he had entered when he was confronted by an impassive footman.

"Your pardon, sir," said this well-trained individual. "I am directed to conduct you to His Highness. If you will be so good as to follow me, sir."

A few minutes later he was admitted to the antechamber off the Hall of Nobles, where a small group of tense-faced men were gathered about the Prince. Among them was Prince Hubert, whose cheeks were livid. Prince Robin greeted Yorke with a faint smile and a sober shake of the head.

"Well, Yorke, you are in luck after all," he said, rather grimly. "Now you will have something really worth while to write about. You must have been born under a lucky star. Instead of a lot of dull, dry statistics to give your readers, you happen upon the most thrilling, the most important event that has befallen Graustark in a great many years. We are invaded. We shall have to fight hard to drive the invaders out. It is hardly necessary for me to tell you that the situation is serious. There are at least fifteen thousand Axphainians already on Graustark territory. Most of them saw service in the Great War. They are experienced soldiers. They have joined the Red army of Axphain and are commanded by capable and ruthless officers. Reports are far more complete than I have given out. Ganlook is cut off, the mines have been seized, peasants have been butchered, houses burned, farms sacked. I saw you were with the Countess Danke. Her father's castle has been taken and"—here his voice broke—"the inmates have either been killed or carried off as hostages. This is the outcome of failure,

Mr. Yorke. The Commune has failed. The Red Terror is out of hand, unleashed, desperate." Then abruptly: "How long have you known Michael Rodkin and what do you know of his record in the United States?"

Yorke started. "Rodkin? We were in college together, Your Highness. He was always a radical, I may even say a potential anarchist. I have not seen or heard of him in seven or eight years until I ran across him here in Edelweiss. I don't believe he has had a hand in this move of Axphain's, if you would care for my honest opinion."

Prince Robin was not the kind to beat about the bush.

"I shall be perfectly frank with you," he said. "Prince Hubert has to-night accused you of being in league with this man Rodkin. He charges you with being in the conspiracy to overthrow this government. What have you to say to these charges, Mr. Yorke?"

Yorke was cool despite the sudden fury that filled his soul.

"Does Prince Hubert expect me to oblige him by admitting that what he says is true?" he demanded, turning to Hubert with a withering smile on his lips. "And do you, Your Highness, expect me to humiliate myself by denying these charges?" he went on, as he drew himself erect, his chin held high. "What would be the result if I were to say to Prince Hubert's face, here before you all, that he is a liar?"

"I can answer that question," boomed Prince Hubert, lowering his head and sticking out his jaw. "You would have to pay for it with your life's blood."

"Very well," said Yorke, coolly. "With your permission, Prince Robin, I take great pleasure in calling this man a damned, white-livered liar. The cheapest way for him to get my life's blood is to hire some one to shoot me in the back, and the safest, I may add."

Hubert's lips worked convulsively. His great shoulders hunched forward. He had convinced himself in one swift, wary look that Yorke was unarmed. He could crush this contemptible American in his mighty arms—he could squeeze the life out of him as a bear puts an end to his adversary. But even as the will to do this flashed into momentary existence it was quelled by a restraining doubt. There was something in those cool gray eyes of Pendennis Yorke that caused him to hesitate, and besides, Yorke's shoulders were broad. He had not noticed before how broad they were. He took refuge behind a convenient deference to his host, the Prince of Graustark. Drawing himself up, he said, as if his self-restraint were costing him a mighty effort:

"This is neither the time nor the place for me to thrash you, Mr. Yorke. But you may rest assured that at the first opportunity I shall break every bone in your sneaking, treacherous body."

Yorke contemptuously turned his back on him.

"Your Highness, may I be permitted to ask if you take this man's charges seriously?" he inquired, his face set.

"I do not," replied Robin promptly. "I have said as much to Prince Hubert. He is in no doubt as to how I feel about the matter."

"I have it from the most trustworthy source that this

man Yorke is constantly in the company of Rodkin, sometimes openly but as a rule under cover of secrecy," began Hubert.

He was curtly interrupted by the Prince. "I think we understand each other, Prince Hubert. If I have not made myself clear to you, I am sorry. I have the utmost faith and confidence in Pendennis Yorke. There is nothing more to be said on the subject. I had two objects in asking you to come to this room, Mr. Yorke. The first has been disposed of so far as I am concerned. The second is to grant you the privilege of accompanying our troops to the front. You will this night be presented with special credentials entitling you to every consideration at general headquarters. I am assuming, of course, that you desire this privilege."

"I do, indeed," cried Yorke, eagerly.

Hubert stared at the prince.

"Do—do you mean this, Robin?" he gasped.

"Certainly," replied Robin, rather sharply.

"I consider your action an unpardonable affront," exploded the other thickly. "You take the word of this adventurer in preference to mine. You discredit me, you hold me up to scorn and ridicule. You—"

"One moment, Hubert! You have made your home in Edelweiss for many months, you have accepted Graustark's protection and her hospitality, you have found refuge here. It ill becomes you to question my judgment in this or any other matter. We are hereditary foes—you and I. Your misguided countrymen are to-day ravaging my lands and killing my people. And yet I would not ask you to seek refuge elsewhere. You are at liberty to remain in Graustark as long as you choose."

Hubert actually snorted. "Remain here? After this? What do you think I am? I shall leave Graustark tomorrow. A haven is open to me in Dawsbergen. Before another night has fallen I shall be in Serros. Prince Dantan—"

"As you please, Hubert," broke in Robin, his lip curling. "You will be safer in Serros than here, I apprehend. There is less danger of meeting your own countrymen in Dawsbergen."

"What do you mean by that, sir?"

"I leave it to your imagination," replied Robin, levelly.

The big Axphainian shot a look of hatred at the speaker.

"I hope to God my countrymen—" he began, but caught himself up in time. The sentence died away in an inarticulate rumble.

"Your countrymen would like nothing better than to overtake you before you reach Serros," said Robin, after a pause. He gave vent to a short, hard laugh. "I should advise you not to let the grass grow under your feet, Hubert, once you find yourself outside the city walls."

The dark red in Hubert's cheeks began to ebb. A hunted look came into his eyes despite the angry snarl that issued from his twisted lips.

"It is your pleasure to goad me, Robin. If I remain longer I shall lose my temper. Permit me to retire. We will meet another day under different conditions, I promise you. In the meantime, I shall make it my duty to escort Princess Virginia to her home in Dawsbergen. Prince Dantan would be justified in turning me away from his door if I came away without her. I demand the right to see her to-night and—"

"You have my permission to retire, Prince Hubert," interrupted Robin. "Princess Virginia must decide for herself just which is the safer thing for her to do—remain here in Edelweiss or undertake the journey to Serros alone with you."

Hubert swung on his heel and strode to the door, where he turned to fling a challenge to Pendennis Yorke.

"As for you, I shall not forget my promise. Every bone in your body. Remember that, my fine bird."

He yanked open the heavy door and slammed it violently behind him.

The Prime Minister, an old man, winced.

"What damned bad manners he has," was all he said, however—and that rather peevishly.

CHAPTER XIII

A COLD spring rain was falling. Pendennis Yorke, astride a jaded horse, rode alone through one of the somber mountain defiles many miles to the east of Ganlook. He was making his way toward the village of Arlak, where there had been hard fighting the day before. A strong Graustark force under Colonel Radd had driven the Axphainians out of the town with severe losses to the disheartened enemy.

The section through which he now rode had been cleared of the Red rabble earlier in the week. A fortnight had passed since the beginning of hostilities. The Axphainians, beaten on all sides by the hardy defenders, were retreating in disorder. A few of the mountainside farms and villages near the border still remained in their stubborn hands, however. Count Quinnox, after three days of sanguinary fighting, had relieved the beleaguered fortress of Ganlook and had driven the enemy pell-mell from the environs of the town, following them doggedly through the passes to within sight of the open country beyond, where lay the barren, wind-swept plains of Axphain. Before and during the retreat, hundreds of groveling, half-starved men had crawled to the Graustark lines, surrendering in the hope that they would be cast into prison camps where food and shelter would be provided.

Few of these unhappy creatures were in the regulation uniform of the Axphain army. They represented that misguided element lusciously designated by the Bolshevik leaders as the "proletariat." They were the plundered, deceived peasants and laborers who had been promised the Elysium of peace and contentment and who had found instead havoc and despair as the reward for their fatuity. Tattered remnants of once stout and durable uniforms hung upon their emaciated bodies—it were almost safe to speak of them as carcasses; the feet of many were bare or clumsily wrapped in ragged, trailing strips of cloth that had not been removed or changed in months; now and then battered trench helmets or service caps were to be seen perched upon shaggy, unkempt heads. Always there were haggard, bleak-eyed faces; sunken chests, concave abdomens, bony arms; sepulchral, racking coughs that ripped and tore their way to freedom through stretched lips and hairy, cramped throats.

A sorry lot of warriors! The Reds in all their glory!

The advancing Graustark troops, sweeping on through the passes in swift pursuit, hourly came upon grewsome signs of revolt among the rank and file of the baffled, embittered army of Axphain—if indeed it could be called an army. Fat, well-nourished officers in warm garments lay sprawling in heaps beside the roadway, shot down or bayoneted by their own men. The wiping out of the Red Terror! A general here, colonels and captains there, piles of brutish-looking sergeants who had been ripped wide open by the steel of vengeance. The latter were Muscovite soldiers from the pampered armies of Russia, sent down to bolster up the morale of their less-favored

acolytes, and they had been butchered like hogs in return
for their tyranny. And the red flag of the Commune
trampled in the mud!   Ghastly signs of a second uprising
of the peasants, ghastly proof of the strength of the weak!

Yorke had seen these things. He had paused beside
grim-visaged Graustark officers to gaze in horror upon
these prophetic spectacles. He had watched the soldiers
bury those massacred officers in trenches that had been
dug by the men who slew them. He was sensible of the
new chapter of history that was being written in his presence, pages of far greater moment to the world than
the insignificant little conflict of a fortnight's duration
between Graustark and Axphain. These wretched peasants were throwing off the Red yoke. He was witnessing
the death struggle of Communism in the principality of
Axphain.

But he had seen worse things than these, he had heard
stories infinitely more harrowing than the ones that were
written in blood. He had seen and heard the women of
Axphain!

Gaunt, wild-eyed women who had followed the soldiers
into the land of promise, which was Graustark, and who,
fierce and more ravenous than the men, were the last to
retreat. They were trampled under foot by the retreating hordes, kicked aside, but they rose again to face the
oncoming troops of Graustark. Hundreds of them!
Starving women who prayed and cursed and wept and
wailed, and who had the look of cannibals in their faces
as they dragged their dead men back into the forests.
He would never forget those scuttling, flapping scare-
crows of women; half-naked creatures whose voices when

they cried out their woe were singularly like that of the crow—hoarse and raucous. The wives and sisters and mothers of the men who had come down into Graustark to wrest food and fuel and treasure by force from the land of plenty. Gibbering furies who had laughed at the slaughter of women and children on the farms above Ganlook, who had shrieked with glee at the sight of burning houses in which the trapped inmates were roasted alive! The horrible, pitiable women from the fields and towns of Axphain—he would dream of them to his dying day.

With the relief of Ganlook, the invasion showed immediate signs of collapse. There had been bitter fighting and many casualties on both sides. The better-armed, better-trained troops of Graustark had suffered less than the surprisingly undisciplined though remarkably courageous enemy. Yorke had spent several days with Prince Robin at headquarters. Once the acute peril was past, the Prince issued an order directing his officers to instruct their men not to kill unless absolutely necessary to gain an objective, and then only when the disorganized Axphainians made a desperate stand in the effort to hold or recover lost ground.

"Drive them out of Graustark!" he had commanded. "But do not shoot the miserable creatures in the back. Axphain will have need for backbone before many days —unless I am badly mistaken. You have heard what many of the prisoners are saying, gentlemen. They speak of the rumor that a young man is on his way up from the South to save Axphain. We all know what that means. They do not speak his name but we know who this young man is. He is the son of Valerie Yanzi. His sire was Prince Hedrik. He was born out of wedlock—a bastard, if you will—but he was born to rule these people. We know him. He can save Axphain. And these men we are pursuing to-day are all that is left from which to make a backbone strong enough to support young Gregory's cause. As for the women—feed them!"

There was wisdom as well as compassion in the edict of the Prince of Graustark.

The pass through which Pendennis Yorke was riding on this rainy April day ran well eastward through the barrier range. The pillaged town of Arlak stood on the farther slope of the mountain, overlooking the land of Axphain. He had traveled by this long, circuitous route in order to avoid the still occupied territory between Ganlook and the scene of the recent and what was conceivably the most significant engagement of the brief war, for it was at Arlak that the discouraged invaders had made their most desperate stand. It was here, according to report, that the flower of the Red army had concentrated under able and desperate leaders. Prisoners taken at Ganlook described them with great bitterness as the fattest and cleanest officers in the army!—the commander-in-chief and his staff.

The road which he followed through this gloomy gap in the mountains—known even in ancient times as "The Pass of the Two Kings"—ran to the Black Sea and to the Russian City of Odessa. According to the map he carried he would branch off to the left at the northern mouth of the pass and travel four or five miles westward to Arlak. The right fork of the road led to Russia, many leagues away. It was a wild region; a mighty and lofty jungle that ran skyward to the crest of stupendous peaks.

The journey by horse from a point near Ganlook required a good twelve hours of steady riding, although the distance as the eagle flies was a scant fifteen miles. After dropping down into the defile some distance from its most southerly extremity, Yorke had seen but few human beings; only an occasional hunter or woodsman, since leaving the last of the patrol posts behind.

He was not very cheerful. There still remained two hours between him and the camp of the Graustark troops and he was wet and tired and hungry. Unless delayed he would reach the camp shortly after dark. There was small danger of losing his way as long as he kept to the indicated highway and avoided the confusing little by-roads that shot off into the lateral gulches and ravines.

Strange to say, his mind was particularly at rest so far as the thought of ambush was concerned.

He was not afraid of being shot at by some hidden marksman. It would not be a new experience. He had been shot at on the night of the cancelled dinner; the luck that attended him on that occasion was not likely to desert him now—an optimist's view, to be sure, but one calculated to sustain a lone traveler venturing into unfamiliar fastnesses. His cherished silk hat had been shot from his head on that memorable night.

It had happened long after midnight as he was hurrying up the steps of the Regengetz, under the glare of the porch lights. Simultaneously with the crack of a rifle his hat flew off and went bounding down the steps. Realizing that the shot from the dark was intended for him, he instantly sank to his knees and then sprawled out in grotesque simulation of death. Sharpe and others, piling out of an automobile, rushed up to him and he was carried into the hotel—convulsed with laughter! The next morning the police, ransacking the buildings bordering on Regengetz Circus, found in a high garret the dead body of a frail, emaciated stranger. He had been strangled. There were marks of huge fingers on his throat. A ghastly illustration of the infallibility of the old saw that dead men tell no tales.

He was studying his map as he rode slowly up a long incline skirting the shoulder of one of the lesser peaks. Suddenly, above the gentle swish of the rain on tree and road, there came to his ears the sound of a stalled automobile engine striving frantically to negotiate a grade or to extricate its heavy burden from the mire in which it had become embedded. He drew rein and listened. The road, as far as he could see, revealed no sign of a car in distress. Yet there was no mistaking the close proximity of that laboring engine. He rode on, his senses alert, and came abruptly upon a narrow, almost hidden road branching off to the left. It ran down the side of the natural embankment to the bed of the valley below, a gradual, winding descent among the trees of several hundred feet and evidently an outlet by which carters brought their loads of stone for the quarry on the opposite side of the pass. He had been told of this abandoned quarry; a circle had been drawn about it on his map with a marginal note advising him that the fork to Arlak was the first road to the left, five kilometers further on.

Drawing his army revolver, he halted just beyond the

mouth of the road, ready at an instant's warning to gallop off and yet intensely curious to know more about the car and the reason for its being on this practically unused and seemingly impassable by-road. Presently he was aware that the machine was slowly making progress up the steep, and with a vast amount of noisy energy. It came into sight at last, reeling and jerking in the deep, mud-filled ruts. A man was plodding wearily up the road some rods ahead of the car, which proved to be a big, gray limousine with one man at the wheel and another walking alongside.

The foremost figure wore a heavy ulster, buttoned close about the throat, the collar turned up to meet the slouch hat that was pulled well down over his eyes. A glance was sufficient to disclose the fact that these men were not soldiers. They were in civilian clothes and there was nothing to indicate that they were armed. On catching sight of the horseman at the top of the road, the man in the long ulster came to an abrupt halt. After a moment's hesitation, due to surprise and perhaps dismay, he turned and shouted a command to the driver, who, with an execration, stopped the car.

Yorke gave a violent start and then stared intently at the leader, who was now facing him. There was no mistaking the pallid face and the black, horn-rimmed eyes.

"Michael!" he shouted. "What the devil are you doing up here in—" He broke off suddenly, silenced by a staggering suspicion. An instant later he put this suspicion into words. "Damn you, Rodkin, are you mixed up in this Axphain outrage? Just stop where you are! I'll be obliged to you if you'll give an account of yourself. I've got a gun, Michael, and I'll shoot as sure as—"

"Put up your gun, Denny," called out Rodkin, huskily.
"I'm not concerned in this Axphain business. I am trying
to get out of Graustark, that's all. Take my word for it,
or not, just as you please. I am on my way to Russia.
As for what the devil I am doing here, that's easy. You
don't imagine I am such a fool as to take the highroad,
do you? With patrols all along the gap? Give me credit
for having the sense to worm my way out rather than at
tempt to fly high, as you are flying, old chap. 'You take
the high road, I'll take the low.' And a gosh-awful road
it is, let me tell you—that antediluvian cow-trail back
there."

He advanced slowly, his hands in his coat pockets.
There was a furtive, uneasy expression in his black eyes.

"I gave you credit for more sense than to try to get
anywhere in that tank," said Yorke, with a jerk of his
head in the direction of the car. "Lord, man, what have
you got in it? All the gold in Edelweiss?"

Rodkin regarded him soberly for a moment before
replying.

"I don't believe I have told you that I am a married
man," he said. "My wife is in the car. All the gold in
Edelweiss couldn't have tempted me to leave her behind."

"I never dreamed that you were married, Rodkin."

"Well, I am—this long time. Three years ago, Denny.
In Moscow," explained Rodkin, jerkily. "I don't know
how I happened not to mention it to you. Still, I suppose
when a man's been married for three years he doesn't go
around talking about it. I daresay I took it for granted
you knew. But, I say, old man, I can't stop here talking

with you. We've simply got to be moving. I must be across the frontier before dark. If we delay here too long—I stand a chance of being nabbed from behind. So, if you'll forgive me, Denny, I'll—"

"I've bad news for you, Michael," broke in Yorke, slowly, all the while eyeing Rodkin narrowly. He was not satisfied. "You'll never get into Axphain by this road. When did you leave Edelweiss?"

"Last night. What do you mean I can't get into Axphain by this road?"

"Because the other end of the pass is stuffed with Graustark troops. Haven't you heard of the scrap at Arlak? Colonel Radd took the town yesterday. That's why you can't get into Axphain by this road."

Rodkin uttered a muffled ejaculation. His face gleamed livid in the shadows.

"Good God! Are you telling me the truth, Yorke?" he cried out.

"I'm playing fair with you, Michael, for the sake of old times. I suppose it's all wrong for me to assist you in getting out of the country, but my best excuse is that you are three to one and I can't stop you. Aha! I see your two friends have guns, after all. Rifles. I'd stand a poor chance against—"

"See here, Denny, I'm desperate," broke in Rodkin, rapidly. "For God's sake, don't try to stop me. If you do—well, something will happen that I'll regret all the rest of my life. These men will shoot, Denny. Much as I love you, old man, I—I'd have to order them to shoot you if you attempt to stop me—or even delay me much longer. My own life is at stake, Denny. There's

an order from Gourou to round up all the radicals in
Edelweiss and—and—five of my friends were executed
early last night. They want me. They're after me,
Denny. So, you see, I have no time to waste. God knows
I don't want to kill you, old friend—but—but those men
will shoot!"

Yorke stood his ground. "What has happened in Edelweiss that would cause Gourou to round up all the radicals
—and execute some of them? Have you and your gang
been throwing bombs? Good God, Michael! Have they
got Prince Robin? Has he been assassinated?"

"No, no, no!" cried Rodkin, shrilly. "Nothing like
that. I give you my word. A couple of fools set off a
bomb last night at the railroad station. I knew nothing
about it, I swear to heaven, Denny. Several people were
killed. I am looked upon as the leader of the radicals.
They want me. I got wind of the man-hunt in time to
escape with my wife. This car belongs to the man who
is driving. We managed to reach his home outside the
city walls before our flight could be intercepted. His
wife is in the car with mine. They're both ill—ill with
terror and—and his wife's going to have a baby soon.
Now you know all I have to tell you, Denny. You can
see how desperate the situation is. Turn back a little
way and wait till we're out of sight around the bend.
If you don't, I—I cannot answer for your safety."

Pendennis was in a quandary. Something told him
that Rodkin was lying, that he was fleeing from justice,
that he had committed some heinous crime—mayhap the
murder of the Prince of Graustark. This talk about a
wife! He didn't believe a word of it. Rodkin and his

sinister looking companions were making off with something more valuable than wives! Loot! Suddenly his heart seemed to have stopped beating. A sickening, horrible thought flashed through his brain. Prince Robin's children! In that car! Kidnaped!

"Good God!" burst from his lips. His eyes, glaring with horror, were fixed on the curtained windows of the car.

Rodkin, struck by the American's expression, shot a startled, apprehensive look over his shoulder. The next instant he barked a command to the two men. Then as both men leveled their rifles at Yorke, he jerked a revolver from his coat pocket and faced the man on horseback. His eyes were glittering behind his glasses, his teeth were showing between his stretched lips.

"Get out of the way, Yorke," he almost screamed. "I don't want to kill you but—"

"Who have you got in that car?" shouted the other peremptorily. "Come now! The truth, damn you, Rodkin! If you've got those two helpless little kids there you'll have to kill me before you can get away with them. You—"

"Kids?" gasped Rodkin, blankly.

"You know who I mean. Prince Robin's babies. My God, man, have you stolen those—"

Rodkin's laugh was shrill, almost maniacal.

"Oh, Lord!" he cried out, lowering his pistol, as he doubled up in a fit of laughter. "What—what do you think I am, Denny? A child-stealer? Well, that's the limit! Ha! Ha! Bless your heart, old man, I shouldn't mind blowing up the castle with everybody in it, but I'm damned if I'm rotten enough to steal children. If that's in your mind—"

"Who is in that car?" repeated Yorke, white-faced and resolute.

Rodkin did not answer at once. He studied Yorke's face long and seriously. Then abruptly his whole manner changed. He returned the weapon to his pocket and, holding out his empty hands, advanced to the roadside.

"You want the truth, Denny, so I'll give it to you," he said slowly. "No use stalling any longer. I've got a woman in that car. I'm taking her to Russia. If you make a move to raise that revolver, those men down there will drill a couple of holes through your head." He showed his teeth again in a ghastly smile. "I don't suppose you will care to congratulate me, old man, but you ought to, all the same. I'm doing you a good turn. I'm making things easy for you." He hesitated a moment before venturing the next remark. "Your wife is eloping with me."

"What!" gasped Yorke, and suddenly jumped to the conclusion that the man was stark, staring mad.

"Not willingly, I must confess, but still unresistingly. She's trussed and gagged, and for a while she was drugged. In view of the fact that you don't want her, and what is more to the point, couldn't have her if you did happen to want her, you might at least felicitate me on having taken a long step toward obtaining the desire of my life. I've got her and that's more than all the king's horses and all the king's men have been able to accomplish."

"Michael!" cried Yorke, unwilling to believe his ears. "What stupid jest is this? Do you think you are being funny—"

"It is no jest," interrupted Rodkin, exultingly. "I don't know why I am telling you this, Denny, unless it's because I am beside myself with joy. I daresay I am a fool. Perhaps it's a form of bravado on my part. Perhaps I have become a braggart. Maybe I am crazy. Anyhow, I've got her safe and sound and if fortune continues to favor me she will be mine in body if not in soul before many hours have—"

"You dirty dog!" shouted Yorke, convinced at last that the man was speaking the truth.

"Look out!" warned Rodkin. "Put up that revolver! I've warned you, Denny. They will shoot at a word from me."

Pendennis sagged limply in the saddle. A cold perspiration broke out all over his body. He realized his helplessness. He was powerless. For an instant everything went black before his staring eyes. She was down there in that car, bound and gagged and terrified—the woman he loved better than life. Life! What would his life be worth if he risked it in an attempt to rescue her? They would shoot if he made a single threatening move. Of what avail, his dead body lying in the road? Not a formidable obstacle in their path: a mere log to be rolled aside, a pool of blood to drive through, and Virginia's fate still in doubt—no, not at all in doubt!

Rodkin was speaking, hurriedly, nervously, but Yorke's brain was not taking in his words. It was working feverishly on its own problem. How to circumvent, how to frustrate the diabolical design of the love-crazed Michael; how to save her from unspeakable horrors.

Occasionally his whirling brain grasped a sentence or a few words of the jumbled harangue:

"I would sell my soul for her. . . . I will make her happy . . . die for her . . . devotion such as mine . . . I was to have been the Lenine of Graustark . . . lead the people . . . all over now . . . Axphain imbeciles! . . . Graustark is lost to us. . . . But I have her at last for my own . . . my heart's desire . . . wasting precious time . . . kill you, Denny, God forgive me . . . old friend . . . your dear mother was kind to me . . ."

Yorke's only chance rested upon his powers of persuasion. He could accomplish nothing by force. If he could bring Rodkin to his senses, if he could reason with him, if he could only make him realize the fiendishness of his undertaking, if he could reach him through an appeal to his honor—there was no other way.

"Michael!" he cried out, pleadingly. "Listen to me—please!"

Something in Yorke's voice—a note of compassion, a touch of the old-time kindness—must have found its way to Rodkin's craven soul, for he checked the torrent that was pouring from his lips.

"Be—be quick," he mumbled, as he shot a look over his shoulder. "We are wasting time. And it has stopped raining. We ought to be—"

"Have you—have you harmed her, Michael?"

"You mean . . . no! What do you think I am? She is going to become my wife. Would—"

"Consider, Michael, consider what you are doing. You

are destroying her. You are dragging her down into the very pits of hell. You—"

"Don't talk to me! I love her. I worship her. What do you mean by the pits of hell?" An exalted light glowed in his eyes, he straightened his figure, an amazing dignity seemed suddenly to lay its calming influence upon him. "I shall be her slave, Denny. I shall devote my life, my love to her. She will love me in time. It is inevitable. Such love as mine cannot be—"

"Love! Give it the true name, Michael. Call it lust. That's what it is. Be honest."

"I—I ought to shoot you for that!"

"For the love of God, Michael, set her free. Spare her! Don't torture her proud, innocent young soul by making her body an unfit place for it to live in. Give her back to me, Michael. She is my wife. She—"

"Your wife! Bosh! To use your own word—bunk!" exclaimed Rodkin, with a raucous laugh.

"Tell your friends to put down their guns. I am not going to put up a fight, Michael. We can talk better if we—"

"I don't want to talk to you. I've got to be moving. I'll take a chance on getting past Radd's men. I know of another road."

"You've got to talk. You've got to listen to me, Michael."

For five minutes or longer he used every argument, every plea, he could bring to bear upon the little anarchist. Finally he was rewarded by signs of weakening. Rodkin hung his head and stared at the ground. He was trembling. His voice was no longer hard and defiant.

Instead there was a petulant, querulous note in it that augured well for the success of Yorke's patience and discretion. Suddenly he began to cry. He could hardly speak for the sobs that shook his frame. He took to beating his hands together, distractedly.

"My God! My God! Denny, I—I can't—give her up. I have wanted her so long. I cannot live without her. I'd sooner die—a thousand deaths. There is nothing for me to live for if—if she is taken away from me —if I give her up to you—after all I have risked to get her."

"You are not a bad man, Michael. You are a decent man. You have decent instincts. You were my friend —and I was proud to call you friend. My mother liked you. She used to defend you when I held forth against your radical views. She believed that you were honest, that you were sincere. And, Michael, she always said you were a boy with the highest ideals, the loftiest motives. She did not agree with you but she did respect you. And so did I, Michael Rodkin. If all the people in the world had come to me and said that you could even think of doing such a dastardly thing as this I would have stood up for you, I would have fought for you, Michael, no matter—"

"Well, I have done this dastardly thing," cried Rodkin, straightening up. "Now you know what I really am. But there is one thing I want you to know. I am not a coward. I am not afraid to die. I hope your dear mother is where she can see and hear me now. A moment ago you said you would die for the woman we both love. I did not know, I did not dream that you love her, Denny.

You would die for her—and I cannot live without her. I have the cards in my hand. It is not necessary for me to compromise with you. Time is short. We must settle this business at once, Denny. I will take the sporting chance if you will, my old friend, and my chance will be a slim one. Luck may be with me, however. We will fight for her. It is the only way. If I fall, well and good. I am out of it. I shall not have given her up. It won't be so hard to lose her, Denny—if I am dead."

Yorke, who had been staring at him, first in bewilderment, then in a sort of horror, marveled at the whimsical smile that played about Rodkin's lips as he uttered the last four words.

"Good Lord, Michael! Do you mean a duel? Do you mean that we are to stand up and shoot at each other until—"

"It's the only alternative," said Rodkin, so calmly, so levelly that there was nothing ludicrous in the noisy way he sniffed back the tears that coursed down through his nostrils. "Get down from your horse. I mean it. If you don't, I will order those men to shoot. Better take the same chance that I am fool enough to take. It's a hundred to one shot you'll get me, Denny, but never mind. If you want her as much as you say you do, you'll accept the challenge. There is only one other way out of it for you, Denny, and that is to turn your horse's head and ride as hard as you can back over the road you've traveled. You don't *have* to fight me, you know. You can be out of danger in two minutes if you'll ride away—"

"I'm damned if I'll do that!" shouted Yorke. "So call off your men! Give me a fair chance. This is mad-

ness, Michael—sheer madness—but if you will have it
so, all right. Your blood will be on your own head. I'll
shoot to kill and—"

"Shut up!" commanded Rodkin. "You shall have a
fair chance."

Deliberately turning away, he strode back to where his
puzzled companions were waiting. A brief confab ensued—the two men expostulating violently. In the end,
however, they shrugged their shoulders and appeared to
wash their hands of the whole affair. Rodkin was removing his heavy, clumsy overcoat as he approached
Yorke.

The latter, pale but determined, had started to dismount. As he hurriedly swung his leg over the saddle
he glanced from Michael to the two men. For an instant
his body remained rigid as if arrested by paralysis. He
sensed the thing seconds before it happened. The men
were whispering fiercely to each other in one second, in
the next the man nearest the car had his rifle pointed at
Rodkin's back.

"Look out, Michael!" Yorke fairly screamed.

Before the words were out of his mouth the fellow
fired. Pendennis did not wait to see the result of the
shot. Self-preservation was his first and only thought.
The other man was raising his gun to his shoulder as the
American threw himself clear of the saddle and dropped
to the ground. The horse, frightened by the discharge
of the weapon, jerked up its head and leaped frantically
forward. Yorke, clinging to the bridle rein, was dragged
a few yards, screened by the body of the plunging animal.
But even before his feet touched the ground, he heard

the second report. Another followed instantly. The horse gave an almost human scream. A moment later the animal's head fell forward and his legs began to crumple up. As the stricken beast crashed to earth, Yorke sprawled frantically into a shallow crevice at the roadside: countless floods pouring down the steep side of the mountain had burrowed a path along the obstructing highway.

His brain was working like lightning. Crouching down in this imperfect trench, he covered the mouth of the narrow road with his revolver, prepared to fire as the first of the treacherous rascals bounded into view. He had but a few seconds to wait. One of them came leaping up the slope, his rifle held in readiness for instant action. He caught sight of Yorke's head and stopped short, throwing his gun to his shoulder.

Yorke fired. He was less than twenty feet away. He had practiced shooting with a revolver for many years. Hundreds of times he had fired at a piece of paper pinned to a board or a tree, and scores of times he had seen a small black spot appear as if by magic on the white surface of the mark. That had been sport, fun—but now in the blink of an eyelid a black spot appeared in the white space between the man's beard and his eye. As if by magic! The rifle was discharged as its owner plunged forward upon his face. No need to be wary of him any longer! Something had gone out of him—as if by magic.

His companion, close behind, fired wildly at the man in the trench. The trench! The fellow knew about trenches. A bullet from Yorke's revolver sang past his

ear. Yes, he knew about trenches. Like a scared rabbit
he turned and darted down the quarry road. Apprehen-
sion of an entirely different nature caused Yorke to forget
his own peril. Throwing discretion to the winds, he
leaped out of the ditch and dashed after the man, bent
on frustrating any attempt at reprisal on the ruffian's
part. The smashing of a car window, a shot into the
interior at the huddled form of the captive princess . . .

Yorke did not even see the crumbled figure of Michael
Rodkin as he raced wildly past it in the fear that he
might be too late. He fired again at the fleeing figure and
missed. The fugitive was nearing the car when he slackened his speed and turned to send two shots at his pursuer. He was backing away rapidly as he fired and both
bullets went wild. Then, in a panic of terror as he realized that bullets could not check the oncoming giant, he
abandoned the open road and went crashing off through
the thick underbrush, yelling like a whipped dog.

His pursuer did not stop. Yorke dashed into the wood,
determined to bring his man down if possible, thereby
removing any immediate danger of interference with the
rescue. He was in time to see the fellow stumble over a
rock and go sprawling to the ground. In an instant he
scrambled to his feet and was off again, using hands and
arms to beat his way through the tanglewood. He had
dropped his gun. Yorke fired again. A squeal of pain
was the reward of that chance shot, and one of the man's
arms fell limp and useless as he leaped down a sharp
declivity into a small ravine. He was nowhere in sight
when Yorke came to the spot, but he could be heard

running down the rock-strewn bed of the gully. Pendennis snatched up the discarded rifle as he dashed back
to the car, his heart in his mouth. All else was forgotten
in his anxiety. Dropping the rifle and his own revolver,
he jerked open the door, calling out as he did so:

"Virginia!"

CHAPTER XIV

SHE was sitting bolt upright in the far corner of the seat. In the dim light of the curtained interior her face was indistinct save for the wide, terrified eyes.

"It is I, Pendennis Yorke," he cried, suddenly realizing that she could not know whether he was friend or foe. "You are safe! Don't be afraid, Virginia. Everything is all right now."

He did not clamber into the tonneau at once, holding back a moment to allow her to at least partially overcome any doubt as to his identity. She moaned—a strangled, sobbing moan that brought a shout of joy from him, for it was a muffled cry of recognition.

Instantly he was in beside her, tearing the curtains away to let in the waning light of day. All the while he was crying out reassuring words to her. If one or two of those words constituted a bitter imprecation, he was never called upon to account for his fervent profanity.

The lower portion of her face was covered with a tightly drawn towel or napkin which was knotted at the back of her head. Her wide-open blue eyes were streaming with tears while she looked mutely into his face as he sat down beside her and began clumsily to untie the coarse bandage. Strands of her dark disordered hair brushed softly against his face as he leaned close in his

efforts to undo the stubborn knot. Her arms were bound
to her sides at the elbows in a not uncomfortable position. The wrists, however, were strapped tightly together, one on top of the other. A rope, wound loosely
about her ankles, was fastened securely to the footrail,
allowing a few inches of play to her legs. A skillful and
even considerate job, thought Yorke, perceiving the hand
and mind of Rodkin, the lover, in the fettering of the
captive.

Presently the bandage came away. As he flung it from
him, he heard her murmuring thickly through dry, para-
lyzed lips:

"Oh, God be praised! Thank God! Thank God!"

She was moistening her lips with her tongue, working
them grotesquely as she tried to smile.

"Don't try to speak—yet. Take it easy, Princess. Be
patient just a few minutes longer. I'll soon have these
beastly things undone."

"Water!" she half sobbed. "Please—first of all—give
me some water."

Dropping everything else, he unslung his small army
canteen and a moment later was holding the dripping
nozzle to her lips. She gulped thirstily, eagerly, unmindful of the stream that trickled down her chin and coursed
on unchecked to her bosom.

"Thank you," she gasped, as he withdrew the container.

In silence—a bewildered silence—she watched him
untie the bonds.

"There!" he cried, straightening up. "You—you are
free!"

"Where are we?"

"Never mind now. I'll tell you everything by and by."

"There was shooting. Are you—hurt?"

"Not a scratch. That's the ticket. Move 'em a little. The blood will soon be going through them again. Try your legs. Good! Now, you stay right here while I have a look outside. That fellow may take it into his head to come back and—"

"Are you alone?"

"Yes. I just happened to be riding past when they came up this road. They—"

She began to tremble as if in the throes of a mighty chill.

"Where—where is he? Michael Rodkin? Don't leave me! I am afraid of him. He—"

"He will not trouble you again, Princess. Rest assured of that. He's gone. You are absolutely safe so far as Rodkin is concerned. Here! Take a nip of this. It will buck you up a lot. Brandy. Can't hurt you. Come on, now—there's a good girl." He was speaking to her as if she were a child.

She drank a little from his flask, coughed and made a wry face.

"Let me get out of this car," she cried, chokingly. "I cannot bear it any longer. Help me out. My legs feel as if they were dead. I—"

"No! You stay right here," he ordered, more sternly than he thought. "I must have a look around first. Don't be afraid. I'll not be gone more than a minute or two. Then I'll get this car started and we'll be off for Edelweiss in no time."

He thrilled under the touch of her hand on his arm. If

she swayed a little toward him—and he was sure she did—he attributed the action to weakness. (There was a faint odor of chloroform in the car.) He was always to wonder at the tremendous self-restraint that had kept him from clasping her in his arms and from pouring out words of love to her when he first flung himself in beside her. The impulse, the desire, to strain her to his heart was so well-nigh irresistible that he marveled at his strength— or was it his weakness? Was it not that down in his soul he was still afraid of her?

If he had but known that she was prevented from throwing her arms about his neck only because of her inability to use them, or that had she been able to utter an articulate sound when she realized who he was, he would not have been forced to exert his self-control at all. After the first few moments of complete surrender to her emotions—many emotions among which ecstasy was uppermost—she succeeded in mastering her unruly impulse and was able to think and act sensibly.

As for the man, he appreciated the delicacy of this extraordinary situation. She had suffered the terror and anguish wrought by the passion of one man; it would be worse than cowardly to subject her to a similar ordeal at the hands of another, even though his motives be of the best. She was alone and helpless and at his mercy. Only a dastard would take advantage of her plight. To her dying day she would loathe him if he so much as touched her, if he so much as breathed a word of love into her defenseless ear.

He found Michael Rodkin's lifeless body at the edge of the road. He had been shot through the head. For a

few seconds he stood looking down at the sprawling figure
of his one-time friend; it was rendered weirdly grotesque
by the empty sleeve of the partially removed overcoat
and the spraddled legs, evidence of an attempt to struggle
to his feet after pitching forward on his face.

Unconsciously Yorke spoke aloud as he gazed upon the
dead man.

"Thank God, I didn't have to kill you, Michael. So
you have met the fate that befalls all those who lead in
this mad scheme to make the world better. You, the man
of brains, the man of vision, the man with an ideal, are
struck down from behind by the very creatures you would
lead out of the wilderness into the light. 'Gad, Michael,
of what use is a brain like yours to a people who have
no more sense than to blow it out when it happens to
please them to do so?"

He carried the body off into the underbrush, arranged
the garments and covered the face with the empty sleeve.
Then he hurried up to the highway. With scant ceremony
he dragged the victim of his own bullet out of sight among
the bushes lining the road, but not before he had con-
fiscated the well-stocked cartridge belt.

His horse was dead. Hastily removing his pack from
the saddle, he grabbed up the assassin's rifle and rushed
back to the car. There was nothing now for Virginia to
see except the carcass of a horse—and he could make
light of that!

She was rubbing her wrists vigorously when he appeared at the open door. Her hair had been hastily put
in some sort of order during his brief absence; a tight-
fitting little brown hat was pulled well down upon her

head, and a feminine observer would have remarked other signs of a reviving interest in her personal appearance. She leaned forward eagerly.

"Are we quite safe? Have they really fled?" she asked in a tremulous half-whisper.

"We are safe from Rodkin and his friends," he replied. "But it will soon be dark, Princess. We must be on our way. It's forty miles or more to Edelweiss—"

"How did you happen to be here, Mr. Yorke?" she broke in. "When did you hear that I had been carried away? Have you been trailing us since last night? Please tell me—everything."

In as few words as possible he related his story, reserving certain grewsome details for another day's recital.

"Just the sheerest luck, Princess. Five minutes later and I should have missed you—you would be far away and I would still be jogging along toward Arlak on my trusty steed. It seems like a miracle. To think that I should be the one who . . . But we haven't time to talk about it now. Time enough to talk later on. And at the same time you can tell me how all this came about. You poor girl! 'Gad, I—I could . . ."

He swallowed hard and abruptly withdrew from the door. As he stooped over to pick up the weapons and other objects lying on the ground, he heard her getting out of the car.

"I heard them talking only a few minutes before the shooting began," she was saying. "The man who was driving shouted back to Rodkin that the gasoline tank was almost empty. He was urging Rodkin to let him fill it up from one of the reserve cans they've got strapped on the roof of the car. But Rodkin wouldn't consent to the delay. So you'd better see how much there is, Mr. Yorke. Oh, it feels good to stretch my poor aching legs and back! I wonder if I'll ever be able to walk again."

Yorke found the gasoline very low and was preparing to climb up onto the roof of the car for one of the cans she had spoken about when it occurred to him that he would have observed them before if they were up there. Stepping back for a view of the roof, he was dismayed to find that it was absolutely bare, except for a luggage protection rail and net. He sprang upon the front seat ·for a hasty examination. Mute testimony of disaster was revealed in a glance. The rail at the back had been torn away, evidently by the heavy oil cans as they were swept off the roof by the limb of a tree. Loose strands of twine lay upon the roof; they were attached at one end to the guard-rail and had given way under the strain of impact.

He was lowering the hood after an inspection of the engine, when Virginia came hobbling down from the high road.

"Bad news," he called out grimly, as he pointed to the top of the car.

She stopped, aghast.

"Gone? Isn't there any— Oh, I remember! Sometime this afternoon I heard an awful ripping and scratching on the top of the car. Rodkin and one of the men had run on ahead to see if the road was passable. I heard them talking about the damage the mountain torrents had done. Well? What are we to do about it?" She seemed to be quite unconcerned—singularly unruffled by calamity, he could not help thinking.

"It's the deuce of a fix we're in," he said, frowning darkly. "There isn't enough gas to take us a mile—if that. And no way to get any, or to find help, so far as I can see."

"Heaven knows we can't walk back to Edelweiss," she mused aloud. "Goodness, Mr. Yorke; I am always getting you into a mess, am I not?"

It struck him that she was in surprisingly buoyant spirits for one who so recently had experienced all that she had been through, and who was still in a far from comfortable situation.

"Never mind about me," he said, rather gruffly. "Really, you know, Princess, it isn't a laughing matter."

"I know it isn't, Mr. Yorke," she admitted, contritely—and rather plaintively.

"We're likely to be here all night."

"And it has started to drizzle again! Oh, dear me, I thought it had stopped raining for good."

"You'd better hop into the car. I'll see if I can start her up. Maybe I can get her up to the main road where—"

"Where some motor lorry would smash us all to splinters if it happened to come along," she interrupted. "No, Mr. Yorke; I think it would be safer to stay right where we are—unless, of course, you want to go back over the road to see if you can find a gasoline can."

"I don't dare leave you alone."

"I was only joking. I wouldn't be left alone for worlds "

"I can't for the life of me see what there is to joke about, Princess. You seem to find the situation amusing."

She was by now inside the car, arranging herself snugly in the far corner of the seat.

"It is a great deal more amusing than it was," she retorted, and then sighed comfortably. "Do come in out of the rain, Mr. Yorke."

He was perplexed. He was willing to admit that he was puzzled but it never would have occurred to him that he was dense.

"This Burberry is water-proof," he muttered, and proceeded to climb into the driver's seat. For five minutes he tried in vain to start the engine. Finally he looked over his shoulder and shouted through the glass window: "No use! Dead as Rameses the First. We are—" He stopped in amazement, blinking.

By the rapidly failing light he made out a large, unwieldy box or basket on her knees. She was studying the contents, occasionally inserting her hand for the obvious purpose of exploration. Suddenly she looked up smiling and, catching his eye, beckoned to him with her forefinger.

"What have you got there?" he called out.

"Come in and see," she replied, raising her voice.

In an instant he was at the door.

"Food!" she cried. "Thank heaven, they didn't put this basket on top of the car. Take off that wet coat before you come in here with me! Yes," she went on, as he slid in beside her after tossing the Burberry into the front seat; "Michael Rodkin had no intention of starving me into submission. He had two baskets of sandwiches and cold chicken and ham and—see! Two bottles of red wine. They emptied one of the baskets this morning—he and his companions. They tried to force me to eat but I—I couldn't. I haven't been hungry till this minute—and now I am as hungry as a bear."

"Did Michael do this? Did he think of this?" cried Yorke, his thoughts going to that soaked, distorted object lying out there in the bushes.

"Yes," she answered in an almost inaudible tone. He could see that she was shivering.

"You are all right now, Princess," he said, soothingly, reassuringly. "All that is behind you."

"I shall never forget it," she moaned, covering her eyes with her hands.

He would have given his soul at that moment to take her in his arms and— But he remembered that he was her protector, not her profaner. She must not for an instant feel that she was unsafe with him.

"You said something about being as hungry as a bear," he reminded her, briskly. "So am I. I hope you are going to invite me to have dinner with you, Princess. Or is there enough for two bears?"

He waited many seconds for her to answer. Then he gently grasped her hands and drew them away from her eyes.

"I know it was dreadful, Princess—but it's all over. You are safe. Try not to think about it." He floundered his words. "Brace up! I mean to say—er—try one of these sandwiches. Oh, Lord! It isn't a sandwich. It's a pickle."

His confusion acted as a tonic to her. She laughed when he held up a huge pickle for her to see.

"Come to think of it," he explained, eagerly, "there

must still be some hot coffee left in my thermos bottle, and I know I have a corkscrew in my pack. My word!" he went on, rather fatuously, "we're as snug as a bug in a rug, aren't we? Listen to that rain trying to get at us! Cats and dogs! Pitchforks! All that sort of thing."

(Michael Rodkin lying out there in the deluge!)

"Of course there is plenty for both of us," she cried, a new thrill in her voice. "We may eat and drink, but how can we be merry?"

"Well, to be sure, it isn't the Regengetz, or even that queer little café in Buda Pesth," he acknowledged, "but it's rather jolly just the same. We seem fated to dine with each other in awfully unexpected places, don't we?"

"This *is* a sandwich, Mr. Yorke," she said, quite gayly, as she fished the article out of the basket and thrust it into his hand. "You wouldn't mind eating a few mouthfuls just to see if it's poisoned? You are always going about saving me from some dreadful fate, you know—and what could be more chivalrous than to save me from an ignominious death by poison? Take a big bite out of this end—please." He did so and she instantly snatched the sandwich from his fingers and sank her teeth into the side of the commodious crescent he had created. She smiled up into his eyes and her mouth was full as she purled: "We can be silly, even if we can't be merry."

"Hand that sandwich back to me," he commanded, thickly. "You've no right to be swallowing my poison." He was desperately afraid that he wasn't going to be able to withstand the shock to his noble intentions. Tantalus was never so tormented as he.

She obediently gave it back to him and experienced a

distinct sensation of giddiness when after inspecting the sandwich he deliberately included in his next prodigious mouthful the dainty little gap her teeth had left.

"This will never do," he muttered, despairingly.

"What did you say?"

"I—why, I—oh, yes; the coffee," he fenced, and, springing up, began to yank at the forward window strap. His belongings were piled on the front seat.

"And the corkscrew," she sang out.

"Heaven help me!" he groaned to himself.

He took what seemed to be a preposterously long time in locating and producing the things he was searching for. When he sat down beside her again he had considerably more confidence in his ability to resist temptation. Still, he meditated, there was a long night ahead of them.

"It's almost dark," she said, munching a sandwich in her corner of the seat. "I can barely see your face."

"See here, Princess," he burst out, desperately, "I've just got to do something about this car. We can't stay here all night. It's out of the—"

"Can't you wait till after we've finished our dinner?" she inquired, with provoking calmness. "You haven't eaten a thing, you haven't opened the thermos bottle and you haven't— Will you please tell me what we gain by worrying? It seems to me we will just simply have to trust to luck. It's dry and warm in here and if Michael Rodkin and his men don't return to—"

"I may as well tell you, Princess, that Michael Rodkin is dead and so is one of his men. The other has fled. I didn't mean to tell you now, but—"

She grasped his arm. "Did you kill Michael Rodkin?" she whispered shrilly.

"No. He was shot from behind by one of his own men. Thank God, I did not have to kill him—and I should if it hadn't been for that treacherous shot. They killed my horse. I got one of the scoundrels. He's dead. The other escaped—wounded, I am sure. Now you know the situation. You have nothing to fear from Michael Rodkin."

She was silent for a long time—and motionless. Finally she said:

"I don't believe I can eat any more. Those—those dead men lying out there—so near."

He busied himself pouring the hot coffee into the cup of the thermos bottle.

"You must drink this, Princess. I was a fool to tell you before you had finished your supper. I might have known. My own appetite is— Well, I haven't much to speak of."

She drank the coffee without protest. "I am glad you did not kill him," she murmured faintly. "He was your friend. He really loved you—Denny."

"He was out of his mind. He wouldn't have done this if he had been sane. It wasn't like—"

"I must differ with you there, Mr. Yorke," she said quietly. "He had this thing in mind for months."

"Even so, he did not—abuse you?"

"No. He was as gentle, as considerate as he could be under the circumstances."

"I shudder when I think of what would have happened

to you if those two men had succeeded in killing both Rodkin and me," he said, more to himself than to her.

Silence fell between them. She was so still that he began to fear that she had dropped off into a swoon, and was vastly relieved when at last she spoke in a calm, natural voice. Then it was that he came to a full understanding of the quality of courage that elevates these women of the royal breed to a plane far above their lowlier sisters.

"He is dead. I have no hatred for him now. It would please his mother, if she is still living, to learn that he was not allowed to lie out there in the rain and the mud. I will help you, Mr. Yorke, to carry his body to some sheltered place where you can cover it with these laprobes and blankets."

He was staring at her in the semi-darkness.

"And they say there are wolves and wild hogs in the mountains," she continued. "I should not like to think of animals fighting over—"

"You are wonderful!" he exclaimed. "But it's out of the question. Michael Rodkin is no better than thousands of men who fell on the field of battle and lay for days in the mud and rain. He deserves less consideration than the worst of them. Let him lie where he is, Princess. He came to an ignoble end. Perhaps I am a little calloused. Most men are in these days. Try to put him out of your thoughts. You must eat, you must drink some of this wine. You—you are all shot to pieces, Princess. And you must try to sleep. I will—"

"Sleep! Good gracious! I never was so wide-awake in all my born days," she cried, in the vernacular that always pleased and surprised him. "You are right. We must forget. We must eat. But I shan't sleep a wink to-night. Open the wine, please."

Presently they fell to discussing the prospect ahead of them. There was not a doubt in the mind of either as to the immediate future; they were beyond question doomed to spend the night in this wild, unfrequented part of the pass. There was the possibility, but a remote one, of their being discovered by a patrol party or by a detachment of troops moving down from Arlak. There was comfort in their conviction that Graustark forces lay between them and the Axphainians; the likelihood of raiders venturing this far into the pass was dismissed by Yorke.

Virginia was completely in the dark as to the activities of the authorities in Edelweiss. She had not the faintest knowledge of what was happening there, nor could she give an intelligent account of the movements of her abductors for a long time after she was seized. The means and the route they took in leaving the city were unknown to her. They must have passed through one of the four gates in the city wall—and that was no simple matter in these days of caution.

Food and wine were reviving her spirits. She insisted on relating the story of her capture, contrary to his earnest plea that she wait till another time. It appears that she and Princess Bevra, with many other noble ladies, devoted a great deal of time to the care of wounded soldiers brought down from the front to the military hospital. Her custom was to go to the hospital at four every afternoon and remain until eight o'clock, when a squad

of guardsmen came to escort her back to the castle. Yesterday she started out alone in her car shortly after three,
meaning to visit the home of a young woman whose husband ‑had been killed a few days before at Ganlook.
This young woman was a volunteer nurse at the hospital
and Virginia happened to be with her when the news came
of her husband's death. She had taken the distracted
young wife home in her car and had remained with her
all that night, sending word to Bevra by the corporal of
the guard.

Since that first day she had made daily visits to the
home of this young woman, who lived in what was known
as the "Twin Gates Quarter," a district of somewhat
humble character in the vicinity of the most westerly gate
in the city wall. She remembered seeing a big gray car
standing in the quiet street almost directly in front of
the house when she drove up yesterday—or was it yesterday? A man and a boy were loitering on the curb
near by. As she got down from her roadster, the former
approached and informed her that a young woman was
very ill in the house and advised her not to enter. There
was some talk, he said, of the plague. His car had been
engaged to convey the patient out of the city, so from
that he judged that she must be afflicted with the black
disease. The boy strode up and said Mrs. Ober had been
having fits and spasms and the doctors had been in there
for a long time and that everybody had been warned to
keep away from the house.

Undaunted, Virginia hurried into the house. She recalled young Mrs. Ober's repeated threat to take her own
life, now that it could no longer be shared with the man

she loved. In a flash she realized what had happened. The half-crazed girl had taken poison and was in convulsions. A strange man, evidently a doctor or an assistant, opened the door for her. She turned to question him as he closed the door quickly behind her. At that very instant she was seized and a thick cloth thrown over her head; as she struggled to cry out, a hand was pressed against her mouth and the stifling fumes of chloroform assailed her.

She knew nothing of what transpired after that until she came out of the stupor and slowly realized that she was in what appeared to be a dark, swaying, jostling little room. After a time she became aware of the presence of the man who was seated beside her, and presently discovered him to be Michael Rodkin the Red.

From that time on she existed as if in a nightmare. She remembered traveling at high speed for what seemed to be ages; stopping at a peasant's hut far along in the night, where Rodkin pleaded with her to partake of food; the resumption of the journey, the coming of daybreak, the progress over deep-rutted wagon-roads, the delay of several hours due to a fallen tree which blocked their path and had to be chopped away by the swearing henchmen; Rodkin's dread of being overtaken, his solicitude for her, his arguments with the men; the never-ceasing patter of rain on the roof of the car; the wild hope that sprang up within her when the car stopped and she heard loud voices on ahead; then the shooting.

"And you looking in at the door and calling out my name," she concluded. "I thought I was dreaming. It couldn't be real—but it was!"

(What she did not know and therefore was unable to incorporate in her account may be told in very few words. Michael Rodkin was aware of her daily visits to the house of Mrs. Ober. He planned cunningly and daringly. The young widow and her mother were surprised to receive a call from three agents of the war insurance department—a clerk and two doctors. They came at half-past two o'clock in the afternoon, announcing that they had been commanded to take depositions. By this ruse they gained admittance to the house. They overpowered the women, bound and gagged them and locked them in an upstairs room. A few inquisitive neighbors were informed that Mrs. Ober was ill of the plague and was to be removed to the pesthouse outside the city walls. It was, of course, Princess Virginia who was bundled up and carried out to the big gray car. Her own little runabout was found the next day in an alley not far from the scene of the abduction. A forged order from the health department enabled the conspirators to pass through the city gates.)

"I've been dreaming ever since I crossed the Graustark frontier weeks ago," said he.

"Then, my dear man, it's time you woke up," she cried, breathlessly. There was a queer, agitated flutter in her voice, as of one about to dive into cold water.

He utterly misconstrued the sense of that capitulating admonition. He took it as a rebuff. She must have guessed his secret and—well, it *was* time he woke up!

"You're right," he agreed, somewhat harshly, and was thankful that she could not see his face. "It's time I stopped dreaming. I—"

"Shall I pinch you?" she half-whispered out of her corner.

He said something under his breath and then incontinently bolted out of the car, mumbling gruffly that he would have a look around to see whether that fellow had taken it into his head to come back with reënforcements! A moment later he stuck his head in through the door to say:

"Here is my electric torch, Princess. Take it. Now, curl up on the seat and go to sleep. Don't be afraid. I'll keep watch—eh? Yes, I know it's raining—but it's letting up. I will sit out here in the front seat and—I beg pardon? No, I'm not foolish!"

And while he was splashing around in the wind and rain she was saying to herself in an ecstasy that seemed to be suffocating her:

"He *does* love me! I know he does! I know it—I know it at last! But why can't he see? How can he be so blind?" A strange exasperation possessed her. "Oh, what a stupid thing he is! The most hopeless idiot in all the world would have seen through me long ago. Good heavens! I wonder what he expects? Does he expect me to throw my arms around his neck and— Oh, dear! If he only *would* wake up!"

So, from these reflections, it may be seen that the patrician Princess Virginia was quite as elemental in her thoughts and desires as any other maiden in all the land— and no doubt as illogical.

She furtively studied her wrist-watch by the aid of the little pocket torch. Eight o'clock. The long night had just begun. Heigh-ho!

Ten minutes later he slid into the front seat and resumed his futile efforts to start the car. She settled back
in the corner and smiled faintly as she watched him.
After a while he gave up in despair and prepared to make
himself snug in the partially exposed front seat. Her
eyes, accustomed to the darkness, took in these preparations. First, he fastened a rain curtain in place on the
right-hand side; then he unrolled his pack and produced
a pair of army blankets, one of which he proceeded to
wrap around his legs; the two rifles he placed beside the
wheel within easy and instant reach. After wasting half
a dozen matches in his cupped hands, he succeeded in
lighting his pipe. This accomplished, he turned his head
to peer intently into the interior of the car. It was too
dark for him to see her face; his contemplation of the
motionless, indistinct figure, however, was needlessly prolonged. Satisfied that she was asleep, he continued to
gaze pensively at a vague, shadowy patch somewhat
lighter than its surroundings and which he was content
to believe was her dear, troubled face. He pictured the
lowered lids and the long dark lashes, the gentle rise and
fall of her breast, the relaxed droop of her head—and his
sense of desolation grew and grew and grew.

But she was not asleep. She was gazing straight into
his eyes out of the favoring darkness and there was a
soft, dreamy appeal in her own.

Presently the wild denizens of the mountains began to
make themselves heard. The sharp, staccato bark of
the fox, the sinister howl of the great black wolf, the
hideous screams of foraging birds of prey, the weird
scramble of unseen things through the branches of trees

close by, the cries and calls of night-birds—a terrifying chorus of musicians whose song was always of death. And there were dead men close at hand, listening out there in the dark to sounds no mortal ear could catch.

Down through the gap from the north came a freshening wind, bringing with it a new downpour. The wind, increasing in violence, sent swirling sprays of rain into Yorke's shelter; it began to tear savagely at the protecting rain-curtain. In an incredibly short time—seconds it seemed—it had grown to the fury of a gale, shrieking and roaring through the trees, battering all creation with a remorseless, unending volley of liquid canister.

He was struggling with the curtain when he heard a sharp rat-a-tat on the glass behind him. At the same moment a wavering circle of light played about him. Looking over his shoulder, he beheld her face close to the window—a thrilled, eager, excited face it was in the glow of the torch-light which she held above her head. She was smiling—it seemed delightedly—as she beckoned to him with her forefinger.

He was still clutching the curtain when she began lowering the window.

"Come in here, Denny!" she cried the instant she could make herself heard. "Crawl in through the window. Do as I command you! This instant! *Please,* Denny!"

Flop went the curtain. He cast off his raincoat and started to wriggle awkwardly through the window. When he was halfway through the light went out.

"Where are you?" he cried a moment later, as he stooped, blinking and irresolute in the darkness.

"Here!" came the answer in a faint, almost inaudible voice.

He was vaguely aware of stumbling over the forgotten basket as he dropped down beside her on the seat. Their knees touched. The contact broke down every barrier. She was in his arms, panting, almost whimpering.

"Virginia! Virginia!" he whispered, giddily. "Forgive me! I—I can't help it. I—"

"Oh, Denny—Denny, my dear, my dear," she cried, trembling with the rapture of complete surrender. Her free arm stole up about his neck—and their lips met in the kiss that every drop of blood in their bodies had craved so long and so fiercely.

A long time afterward she gently, even reluctantly, withdrew from his embrace and sank back into the corner of the seat, a sigh as of exhaustion issuing from her lips. They had murmured countless words during that incalculable period of oblivion, but her beatific remark from the corner was the first to indicate the return of what may well be described as lucidity or that either of them was likely to remember in future efforts to chronicle the primitive sayings of two very modern young people in the first transports of love. What she now said was astonishingly material and beyond a doubt rational. It betrayed her innermost thoughts.

"Thank goodness, dearest, now we sha'n't have to go on with that wretched divorce. We can just stay married."

Pendennis was startled. He seemed suddenly to come to his senses.

"Oh, Lord! But that's just what your father will in-sist on our doing, Virginia," he groaned. "He will never let me have you. You will have to—"

"I daresay we shall have to be married all over again," she went on dreamily, paying no heed to his lamentation; "just for the sake of appearances and all that. But, Denny, dearest, we *are* married—now. I am—your wife."

"You darling!" he cried, lifting her hand to his lips. "So we are, if we are to believe the learned justices. But I've still got to ask the Prince of Dawsbergen for the hand of his daughter Virginia in marriage. And he is set on our being divorced. It looks hopeless to me."

She was silent for a long time. Then she said:

"When he comes to know what a true gentleman you are, Pendennis Yorke, my father will not ask me to give you up."

CHAPTER XV

THE STORY OF VIRGINIA LOUISE

THE city of Edelweiss was in the throes of an excitement almost as great as when the news of the invasion spread like wildfire from the riverside hovels to the monastery of St. Valentine on the top of Mount Ganlook. In less than twelve hours after it became known that Princess Virginia was missing, every man, woman and child in the city not only was aware of the fact but was interested in the search being made for her.

When the Castle guardsmen appeared at the hospital at eight o'clock to escort her home, they were told by the surprised officials that she had telephoned sometime during the afternoon to say that she would be unable to report that day because of a hastily arranged trip that she and the Princess of Graustark were to make to one of the field stations not far from the front. The officer in command of the squad, knowing that Princess Bevra had not left the city, promptly telephoned to the Castle. He was put through to the Princess herself, who immediately became panic-stricken. Within the hour Baron Gourou's men were scouring the city, messages had gone through the war office to Prince Robin at Ganlook headquarters, the city gates were closed and guarded by troops, every house in town where Virginia might possibly have de-

cided to spend the evening had been reached by telephone. Bevra herself spoke with Robin, who late in the
night reported to her that his sister-in-law had not appeared at either of the temporary field hospitals. A large
force of men had been sent out from army headquarters
to search the highways between Ganlook and Edelweiss.

Long before this, however, Gourou himself had traced
Virginia to the home of Mrs. Ober. He discovered the
two women bound and imprisoned in an upstairs room.
Their story was illuminating, although they knew nothing of what had transpired below-stairs. The men who
overpowered them were strangers; they had never seen
them before. Gourou jumped at once to the conclusion
that they were in the employ of Prince Hubert, who
was known to be in Vienna. The crafty Baron never for
an instant considered Michael Rodkin in his swift deduc-
tions. He was convinced that Hubert had planned the
abduction and that he was waiting at some point along
the southern frontier for his hirelings and their captive.
People living in Mrs. Ober's neighborhood were uncere-
moniously routed out of bed and questioned by the police.
The story of the bogus doctors, the black plague warning
and the removal of the sick woman came out. A small
boy told of seeing the fine young lady enter Mrs. Ober's
house just before Mrs. Ober was taken away to the pesthouse, and a number of people observed a short, black-
whiskered man driving off in a little runabout directly
behind the big gray car. The keepers of the Twin Gates
reported the passage of the gray machine and produced
the forged order from the health authorities directing
them to permit the car to go through without delay and

to keep as far away from it as possible in view of the nature of the malady with which its occupant was afflicted: the bubonic plague! After passing the gates the car sped northward in the direction of the bridge which spanned the river half a mile above.

Inside of an hour after these facts became known to Gourou, every town and post along the southern and western frontiers had been warned to be on the lookout for the abductors; a number of high-powered automobiles, filled with armed men, were off on a wild goose chase in exactly the opposite direction to that taken by Michael Rodkin. So it was that the great Baron Gourou lost many precious hours because of his very astuteness! It was not until late the following day that woodsmen in the foothills reported having seen a strange gray car creeping up one of the rarely traversed wagon-roads far to the north of Edelweiss, headed toward Axphain.

The waning struggle along the Axphain frontier was overshadowed in importance by the new sensation—indeed, the latter took on the momentousness of a real calamity. A royal princess had been seized and spirited away; a royal visitor from the friendly house of Dawsbergen had been carried off under the very noses of the vaunted police force of Edelweiss! A ghastly blemish on the proud name of Graustark! But as the day wore on there was much head-shaking among the people, and many were the wiseacres who professed to have said over and over again that something was sure to happen to the beautiful, head-strong Princess if she kept on gallivanting about all alone in that little car of hers.

Prince Dantan and Princess Beverly were on their way

to Edelweiss by special train, summoned by the distracted Bevra, and Prince Robin had hurried down from Ganlook in response to her appeal. It was he who headed the company of soldiers that set forth late in the afternoon to follow the now accepted trail of the abductors. Troops engaged in the Arlak sector were ordered by wire from the Castle to block all of the roads leading to Axphain, and to invade that principality in force if the fugitives had succeeded in crossing the border before the instructions could be put into effect.

It is easy to account for Pendennis Yorke's ignorance of all that had happened during the twenty-four hours immediately prior to his encounter with Rodkin at the top of the quarry road. He had left army headquarters early in the evening of the preceding day, going by motor to the Castle of Baron Brodrik, northeast of Ganlook. Captain Sambo and a detachment of soldiers were occupying the castle, which had been retaken from the enemy a few days before. It was Yorke's intention to start early the next morning from this point on his solitary ride to Arlak. He had a double objective in visiting the burgrave's castle. He wanted first-hand information as to the condition of the castle and the fate of its occupants to carry down to the Countess Danke when he made his next trip from the front to Edelweiss.

By starting from the burgrave's castle he could travel by motor to one of the posts in the mountains, where he was to begin his horseback journey over narrow, winding roads to the main highway through the Pass of the Two Kings. The hue and cry occasioned by the disappearance of Princess Virginia did not reach Captain Sambo's quarters until some time after the American's departure at daybreak. The latter had seen and talked with the wounded burgrave and had held the Countess Danke's little boy on his knee, so his heart was lighter than it had been for days as he started for the Arlak front.

The first glimmer of dawn was filtering down into the Pass of the Two Kings when Prince Robin's outriders came to the rim of the forsaken quarry and dismounted. There was unmistakable evidence here that the car they were following had taken the wrong fork and had been backed with considerable difficulty down to the junction where it was turned into the road that wound up the steep trail to the main highway over the mountains. All night long the pursuers had blundered through the darkness and the rain over the treacherous lower road, urged and encouraged by signs that proved they were on the right track.

By the light of lanterns they had found the battered can of gasoline and portions of guard net; they had come upon the fallen tree through whose trunk a gate had been hewn; a discarded tire, a basket containing broken dishes and the soggy remnants of sandwiches; great gashes in the earth where the car had slid off the edge of the road; and at one place, a few miles back, indications that the fugitives had attempted to turn the car around in the narrow road with the obvious intention of seeking a less hazardous way out of the valley.

The tired outriders waited at the quarry until Prince Robin joined them with the rest of his party. It was the general opinion that the kidnapers had been forced to delay their flight here until daylight came to their relief. If such were the case, they must now be close at hand. Indeed, it was more than likely that they had taken alarm but a few minutes before the first of the dragoons rode up to the dilapidated sheds and shanties constituting the stone-cutters' camp, and were even now making their way up the quarry road to the main highway.

Just as the jaded but now hopeful pursuers were on the point of starting up the wretched wagon trail, shouts from one of the shanties detained them. Men assigned to the task of searching these ramshackle buildings had come upon a wounded man hiding in one of them. He had been shot through the right arm, and was too faint from loss of blood to either resist or make any effort to evade the searchers.

He was at once recognized as a "Red" of the most virulent type, one Nicholas Spantz, whose uncle many years before had been one of the leaders in what was known historically as the Marlanx conspiracy. He refused to talk.

"Put him up on a horse," commanded Prince Robin, "and bring him along. Waste no time with him. Forward! We are hot on their heels."

Half an hour later the leaders of the toiling cavalcade drew rein and excitedly signaled to those behind. Rounding a bend, they had sighted the big gray car in the road not a hundred yards ahead, stationary and apparently deserted.

"Dismount!" was Robin's command. "Spread out! Close in on them from all sides. They will put up a fight. There will be shooting, men. But, on your lives, do not fire in return. The Princess is in the car with them. We must rush them. If—"

He was interrupted by a loud, sardonic laugh from the wounded "Red."

The advance was slow and wary. At any moment a fusillade might be expected from the interior of the seemingly empty car. Not a sign of human life was visible, not a thing to indicate that the car was occupied or that the fugitives were aware of the proximity of their pursuers. Creeping cautiously up to within a few yards of the car, a dozen men at a sharp command from Robin hurled themselves forward. Springing upon the running boards from both sides of the road, the leaders, with revolvers ready for instant use, peered inside the car.

All the time these valiant though apprehensive troopers were creeping up so stealthily to take the occupants of the car by surprise, those self-same occupants were sound asleep!

The first men to gaze in upon them were arrested in the very act of jerking open the doors. They stared hard and long and in utter bewilderment; then with one accord, they lowered their pistols and stepped down into the road, crowding their companions back. Half a dozen hands flew up in salute to Prince Robin as he came hurrying up, puzzled and alarmed by the extraordinary conduct of his men.

A stern-visaged sergeant stepped forward.

"Your Highness," he began, in hushed tones; "I beg leave to report that Her Serene Highness has been found. I fear, sire, that we are too late."

"Good God!" gasped Robin, in horror. "Do you mean
—that—she is—"

"Yes, sire—the worst has happened. She is dead. One
of the scoundrels has met the same . . ."

Robin rushed past the speaker and threw open the door.
Instantly the supposed corpses opened their eyes and
started up in alarm.

Now this is what the doughty sergeant and his fellows
beheld: the Princess Virginia and a strange man huddled
down in the corner of the seat, the former's head pillowed
in the hollow of the latter's shoulder, the latter's head
drooping limply over till it rested against the crown of
rumpled brown. The bodies mercifully had been covered
with a blanket by the slayers! The same vandals, no
doubt possessed of a fantastic sort of humor, had taken
the trouble to drape one of the man's arms over the shoulder of the Princess.

Suffice it to say, the occupants of the car came to life
with startling alacrity. Before Robin had even partially
recovered from his stupefaction, Virginia was sitting bolt
upright and gazing at him with blinking eyes.

"Robin!" she cried out, wonderingly.

But Robin's face was stern and forbidding. Like the
great Baron Gourou he too had jumped to a conclusion.

"So-ho!" he ejaculated, fixing the dazed Yorke with
angry, accusing eyes. "It's you, is it? You are back of
all this damnable—"

"Oh, Robin, is it really you?" broke in Virginia, joy-
ously.

"Don't move, Yorke!" commanded His Highness.
"Stay where you are, sir. Come out, Virginia! Of all

the scurvy, contemptible—good God, Virginia, how could you have done this thing? Bevra is almost crazy, your father and mother are—"

"What the devil are you talking about?" demanded Yorke, with scant courtesy.

"I was damned badly mistaken in you," grated the Prince. "I thought you were a gentleman. And now I catch you running away with this foolish girl who hasn't—"

"Robin!" cried Virginia, her eyes blazing. "How dare you say such a thing?"

She pushed her way past him and sprang to the ground. Facing him with a hauteur that would have shriveled an ordinary mortal, she exclaimed:

"Apologize at once, sir! Running away with me! Foolish girl, am I? Haven't you a grain of intelligence in that head of yours, Robin Lorry?" She waved her hand spaciously, taking in all visible creation. "Search! Look about you! You will find the man who was back of all this, my dear Robin. And when you have found him you will go down on your knees to Pendennis Yorke. Go now and—ah!" Her eyes had fallen upon the pallid face of Nicholas Spantz. "Look, Denny!" she cried, pointing. "The man who ran away!"

Even as the words left her lips, men came running out of the underbrush, saluting awkwardly in their haste.

"A dead man, Your Highness," shouted one.

Yorke was standing beside Virginia now, a hard smile on his lips.

"One Michael Rodkin, Your Highness," he said, stiffly. "A classmate of mine in college—you may remember. He did not fall by my hand—but his assassin did. You will find him up yonder by the road."

"And you dare, Robin Lorry, to accuse Pendennis Yorke of planning this—" began Virginia, furiously. "Why, if it had not been for him I should now be . . . God knows where and God only knows what my fate would have been. And listen to me, all of you. I love Pendennis Yorke. I am going to be his wife . . . his real wife. Hand me my hat, Robin," she went on, loftily, quite as if he were the humblest of menials. "It's pinned to the back of the front seat."

In due course, the Prince of Graustark apologized to Pendennis Yorke, fairly hugging him in his fervor.

"I am terribly sorry to have made that crack," he said, so feelingly that he allowed the American half of him to speak for the Graustark half. "I'd let you kick me if I weren't afraid these fellows would stop cheering you and fill you full of bullets."

"They certainly wouldn't shoot me if I were to kick you, Bobby," said Virginia, and immediately favored her brother-in-law with a kiss. "There! Let them shoot me!"

"Do you call that a kick, Virg?"

"Good gracious! I'm so happy I don't know whether I am standing on my feet or my head," she cried, rapturously.

Messengers mounted on the strongest and swiftest horses in the command were soon galloping off down the pass to the nearest patrol post, to flash the news of the rescue to Edelweiss Castle. Shortly afterward Prince Robin set off in more leisurely fashion with a dozen men.

Perched behind him on the charger rode Virginia, clinging to his waist with one arm while with the other hand she threw kisses to Pendennis Yorke, who stubbornly had refused to abandon his trip to Arlak!

"I can't allow a little mishap like this to divert me from the path of duty," he declared, whimsically. "My natural chivalry interfered with my progress yesterday and last night, but now that it isn't necessary for me to be gallant any longer I must perforce resume the humdrum life of a war correspondent. My motto is and always shall be: 'Never lie down on a job.' I witnessed the beginning of the war and I want to be in at the finish. I rather suspect that the next day or two in the Arlak sector will see the end of hostilities. You wouldn't have me miss the last and best act of the show, would you, Princess?"

For ten minutes she had pleaded and importuned and cajoled, all to no avail. Most of this time had been spent in walking back and forth—and arm-in-arm—in the highway a short distance beyond the spot where the Prince and his men impatiently awaited her pleasure. She had made the mistake of picturing to him the ovation he would receive when they entered the city together; how the people would hail him as a mighty hero and perhaps carry him through the streets on their shoulders; how her father and mother would embrace him in public, and Bevra would kiss him, and Robin would issue an edict proclaiming a holiday. The rejoicing, she prophesied, would be even greater than that accorded the news of victories at Ganlook and Arlak!

Alas! It was her undoing. The picture she painted

in her enthusiasm terrified him. Not even the loving
pressure on his tingling arm, nor the pleading look in her
adoring eyes, nor the kiss that lay so promising on her
eager lips—not all of them could give him the courage
needed to face the ordeal. For, as has been said before
in the course of this narrative, Pendennis Yorke was
rather a shy young man and a modest one. He did not
in the least mind being a conspicuous unit in a maniacal
throng of hero-worshipers—he could, indeed, make himself the most conspicuous imbecile of them all—but when
it came to being the principal attraction in the show—
well, he shivered in his boots at the mere thought of it.
His notion—as a matter of fact, it was an intention—of
entering Edelweiss was to slip in when nobody was looking—when there were no brass bands or rejoicing potentates obstructing the way.

He made the foregoing speech to Prince Robin and the
still imploring Virginia as they were on the point of starting off down the pass—and this was the answer she resignedly gave to his question:

"I suppose I must let you have your own way, Denny.
My sister says it's the only way to keep a husband in
good humor. Heigh-ho! Poor dear, she's had a lot of
experience." She leaned over and reached her hand down
to him. As he pressed his lips to it, she sighed again,
rather breathlessly, and then with a mischievous little
smile: "Don't get your feet wet, dear, and be sure to
come home early."

"Regular wife stuff," remarked the Prince, soulfully if
inelegantly. "However, I believe she'll make you a good
wife, Yorke."

"At any rate," said she, "I've been a good one for the first five years. And they say they're the most difficult."

Yorke watched them until they rounded a bend in the road far below. Then he spoke to the trooper who was holding the horse he was to mount.

"My God, I'm happy!" was his rapt though perfectly incomprehensible exclamation. The unenlightened trooper had the grace, however, to beam as he exclaimed in return:

"Allode da sarra da moddif volenz fella da yank."

Which Yorke, on his part, had the grace to accept as a rather jolly sort of compliment, not being by way of knowing that "yank" in the Graustark language means horse and "fella," translated, was an insult to the steed itself. It was a term of opprobrium bearing a close relationship to the American word "punk."

Three of the soldiers remained to guard the big gray machine until gasoline was sent down from the camp at Arlak. A cold chill ran down Yorke's spine when he peered in through the window of the car just before leaving the scene. With no thought of achieving a grewsome effect, the soldiers had placed the bodies of Michael Rodkin and his accomplice in opposite corners of the back seat, stiffly upright and facing each other!

Accompanied by the two remaining troopers, Yorke rode off toward Arlak within ten minutes after the departure of Prince Robin's party. The sun had broken through the morning mists; the air was laden with the mild, dank breath of the steaming earth and the pungent odor of sweating pines. And song birds were caroling gayly and sweetly in the leafy treetops, where the night

before there had been naught but hideous screams and
yaups and the shrieks of things being cruelly done to
death.

It was close upon noon when Princess Virginia and her
escort rode wearily up to the military station near the
mouth of the Pass of the Two Kings, where they were
received with much excitement and the word that Prince
Dantan was hastening from Edelweiss by motor to meet
his daughter.

Prince Robin and his troopers fairly dropped out of
their saddles. They were too tired to partake of the
feast that had been prepared for them; within five minutes they were all fast asleep in the patrol barracks. Not
so the Princess Virginia. She was very wide-awake and
ravenously hungry. Robin fell asleep on a couch in the
Commandant's office while that worthy was earnestly advising him that a breakfast fit for a king was ready and
awaiting his pleasure.

"Do go to sleep, Robin dear," said Virginia, passing
her fingers through his disheveled hair with loving gentleness. "Poor boy, you've had a horrid time of it—bless
his heart, Colonel, he's sound asleep already. Sh! Please
don't rattle your spurs and scabbard like that. And *do*
tip-toe, Colonel—like this," she whispered, suiting the
action to the word by tip-toeing daintily out of the room,
an example that the stalwart soldier tried his best to
follow but with such ill success that a fierce, sibilant hiss
was his reward.

A couple of hours later Virginia, physically refreshed
and mentally rehabilitated, sat in the watch-tower regarding with some trepidation the approach of three

motor cars which could be seen far below in the distance winding their way up the mountain road.

Nevertheless, there was resolution in her soul and defiance in her eyes. She was prepared for battle. She had made up her mind to throw down the gauntlet at once. No use skirmishing for position, no use waiting for a more auspicious occasion to cast her bombshell. Right at the outset—when she was being fondled and embraced by her father—she would come straight out with it; she would go farther and say that there wasn't the slightest use of his kicking up a row about it, or being nasty or obstreperous or even pathetic. No matter what he said or did, she was going to marry Pendennis Yorke and "live happily ever afterward"! Indeed, if he became too troublesome about it, it was her intention to remind her father that no less a person than the great Chief Justice Mavorak was of the opinion that she could "live happily ever afterward" with Pendennis Yorke without bothering about getting married to him—*again*. But, to please the family (and incidentally to please the righteous Mr. Yorke), she would consent to a state marriage and all that sort of thing. Under no circumstances, however, would she consent to a divorce!

Nevertheless, when the time came, she failed in every one of these highfalutin resolves. She wept unrestrainedly in his embrace, and was so meek and docile in the presence of his great joy that she forgot everything else. She hugged him and kissed him and petted him—as if he were the hurt child, not she.

And all because he too was crying and blubbering and calling her "my poor little lamb" and "my precious" and "my own little baby," and sniffling in a most un-majestic way.

Certainly this was no way for a stern, overbearing, obstinate parent to be acting! How could she defy a father who was so glad to see her that the tears streamed down his cheeks; and how could she possibly be defiant if she were laughing and crying at the same time, and couldn't find her pocket handkerchief—nor her voice, for that matter! So it was necessary to indefinitely postpone Prince Dantan's evil hour; for the time being she was too well satisfied with being his "poor little lamb."

And she was strangely humble and subdued most the way down to Edelweiss. She had heard from her father's lips a great deal about the agony her mother had suffered; how she had stayed up all night praying, how she swooned with joy when the news came that her darling had been found and was safe, and how she had charged him to restore the lost one to her arms with all possible speed lest she die of suspense and anxiety. No, thought Virginia, now was no time to be selfish or high-and-mighty or even argumentative. So she was very quiet and very thoughtful as she sat between the two princes all the way to Edelweiss and listened dreamily to the conversation that went on between them and the redoubtable Baron Gourou, who sat facing them on one of the little front seats, and who for once in his life was acutely garrulous. He dwelt at great length upon the situation at the front and the latest inside news from Axphain; not once, be it said to his credit, did he allow the conversation to revert to Michael Rodkin or to the experience through which Virginia had just passed.

His spies in Axphain were authority for the news that young Gregory, heir presumptive to the throne, was already in the capital, where he was awaiting the psychological moment to wrest the reins of government from the tottering Commune and restore the monarchy. The people were ready and eager for the return to old conditions and they were clamoring for Gregory, the bastard prince, to lead them out of the morass into which their own greed and stupidity had led them.

He watched Virginia furtively out of the corner of his eye—or perhaps it was through the fabled eye he was credited with having in the back of his head; he watched for any sign of interest or agitation on her part at the mention of Gregory's name. He was rewarded by the most pronounced indifference. She was staring moodily out of the car window. Finally Prince Dantan cleared his throat and said:

"That is all over, Baron—years ago. My daughter is no longer interested in Gregory."

"I am glad to hear it, sire."

"A passing fancy, inspired by a young girl's sympathy, Baron."

"I understand—quite."

"It has long been regarded as a closed incident."

Here Virginia squeezed her father's arm and murmured:

"Wasn't I a dreadful little idiot, daddy?"

"You were," said he, very succinctly.

"But you must admit that Gregory was a nice boy and —and frightfully good-looking."

"I grant you all that, my dear."

"And everybody was fond of him—including you, daddy—and everybody was sorry for him, isn't that true?"

All three of the men nodded their heads and smiled.

"Fate had played him an abominable trick, hadn't it?"

"Well, I am not so sure that fate had anything to do with it," began her father, drily.

"Anyhow, it wasn't Gregory's fault, was it?" she persisted.

"Certainly not. I, for one, will be glad to see him where he illegitimately belongs—on the throne of Axphain. Still, my dear, I am even more glad that you are not to share it with him."

"And so am I," said Baron Gourou, feelingly.

"Oh, dear!" she sighed. "When I think of what might have happened, I—wake up, Bobby!" She nudged her brother-in-law violently. "I want you to promise me one thing. You're a member of the family, you know. Promise me you'll not tell Pendennis Yorke about Gregory and me. He—he might put it in his old newspaper."

"Nonsense!" exclaimed her father.

"Bosh!" grunted Robin, and subsided into silence upon catching a look of warning in her eyes.

"The Americans have very queer ideas about things," said she, sagely. "They're awfully old-fashioned in spite of their newness. I am afraid Mr. Yorke wouldn't understand. In any case, I don't see any reason why he should be let into the family secret."

"I don't think that's fair, Virginia," said Robin, grinning. "He's supposed to be a sort of a member of the family, you know."

"Vicariously," said Baron Gourou.

"I see no reason why he should be told," said Prince Dantan seriously. "We have kept it to ourselves all these years and—"

"I never could look him in the face again, Robin," declared Virginia.

"Don't look at me like that, please," said Robin. "I've not said I was going to tell him, have I?"

"No—but you might. You've taken quite a fancy to him."

"Oh, I have, have I?" cried he, ironically.

"I mean, just at this time when Gregory is bound to be in the limelight, with everybody talking about him and hailing him as the man of the hour, you might let something slip about Gregory and me, Robin, without thinking, you see. And Mr. Yorke would probably jump at the chance to get what he calls heart interest into the story he will have to write about the new Prince of Axphain. He says no story is complete without heart interest and—"

Her father interrupted her. "I think, Virginia, Mr. Yorke has proved himself to be a very gallant gentleman. It ill becomes you to—"

"Don't you worry, Virgie," broke in Prince Robin, a twinkle in his eyes. "If Mr. Pendennis Yorke prints anything scandalous about you in his newspaper, I'll call him out and run him through. I'll challenge him to mortal combat, and before I've finished with him he'll wish he'd never seen or heard of my little sister-in-law."

"Idiot!"

"My dear Robin," said Prince Dantan, rather severely;

"there was nothing scandalous in what Virginia did. She was headstrong and all that, to be sure, but as for—"

"And she was very young and impressionable and—" began Baron Gourou.

"Good Lord!" cried Robin, throwing up his hands in despair. "Is it possible that neither of you understands that I'm trying to be funny?"

"Ahem!" coughed Baron Gourou.

Virginia now squeezed Robin's arm. "They're both frightfully old and dense, Bobby," she cried. Then she suddenly became serious. "It wasn't fair of me to say that Mr. Yorke would print anything about that silly affair, even if he were to find out about it. I'm not afraid of that. But I am afraid that he might not understand the—the circumstances. He asked me once—and only once—how I came to be in Buda Pesth. When he realized that I did not want to explain, he never referred to it again."

No one spoke for a long time. Each was occupied with thoughts of a remote day when the royal houses of Dawsbergen and Graustark were racked by anxiety and despair over the whereabouts and the fate of the self-same girl who for the second time had just been delivered out of peril by Pendennis Yorke. The unwritten history of Dawsbergen contains the following chapter:

In the winter of 1919, Gregory, the son of the Countess Valerie Yanzi, came with his mother to Shenzarm Castle, the ancient home of the rulers of Dawsbergen. It was no secret that the beautiful Countess, a sister of the Duke of Mizrox, one of Axphain's most beloved noblemen, had once been the mistress of Prince Hedrik of that principality. In justice to the lady it may be said that she was in love with and secretly betrothed to the Prince long before his ambitious and avaricious father succeeded in bringing about a loveless marriage between the young man and a Montenegrin princess, an alliance which was expected to be of vast consequence in course of time. Hedrik was the second son of old Prince Bolaroz. At this time, the Crown Prince was living and still unmarried. Shortly after the marriage of his younger brother, Hedrik, to the Montenegrin, the Crown Prince was assassinated while on a visit to the capital of Graustark. Whereupon Hedrik automatically became the heir to the throne and soon afterward succeeded his father. But the love story of Hedrik and Valerie did not end with the former's marriage and subsequent elevation. She lived abroad for several years. When she thought she had conquered her love for him, she returned to Axphain. She had reckoned without his fiery, undiminished passion, and without her own, for that matter.

But this is not supposed to be the chronicle of Court life in Axphain, nor is it the story of the loves of Hedrik and Valerie Yanzi. Suffice it to say that Gregory was born on a December day at Castle Mizrox and that all Axphain knew who was his father. The Crown Prince was four years old and his brother Hubert was two when their illegitimate half-brother came into the world. Shortly after Gregory's birth, Prince Hedrik became infatuated with a Viennese dancer. This liaison continued for several years. Valerie was forgotten, ignored. The people of Axphain never forgave Hedrik for being unfaithful to the sister of the Duke of Mizrox! They were

content to overlook and even condone his disloyalty to
the Montenegrin princess, his wife, who had always been
looked upon as an interloper and was despised! But
when he proved himself false to his noble mistress, he
was secretly excoriated on all sides, high and low. For
the people loved the Mizrox family and they were bitter
over the conscienceless marriage that had placed a for-
eigner on the throne instead of the beloved, popular sister
of the Duke.

Young Gregory grew up at Castle Mizrox. He was
recognized and acknowledged throughout the land as the
son of the Prince of Axphain, although his name was
Gregory Yanzi, Yanzi being the Mizrox family name.
He was popular, he was received everywhere; the bar
sinister was ignored. His mother, though not a wife,
was adored and respected by the people. When he was
eighteen she established a residence in Italy and they
spent most of their time in that country. It was from
Rome that he and his mother came to visit at friendly
Shenzarm Castle in the winter of 1919, at a time when
there were vague rumors that Hedrik and his sons were
about to be forced to abdicate in favor of the bastard
prince.

Now at that time Virginia was eighteen. Gregory
was twenty-three. They fell in love with each other—
or at least they imagined they were in love. When the
time came for the Countess and Gregory to return to
Rome, the former prevailed upon Virginia's parents to
allow her to accompany them for a month's visit.
Neither Prince Dantan nor Princess Beverly suspected
the existence of a love affair between the two young

people. They still looked upon Virginia as a child; and while they admired Gregory, nothing could have been farther from their minds than the thought of permitting their daughter to become his wife. If the Countess Yanzi had any such thought in mind, she was careful not to reveal it by word or action.

Virginia was tender-hearted. She easily persuaded herself that Gregory was the victim of a most unkind fate; pity and resentment served jointly to aggravate what she was pleased in her romantic soul to define as love. True, there were times when she was sure that she did not love him; times when she realized that a jolly, affectionate friendship was all that she felt for him. If she had been certain that it was love, she would have gone to her parents with the confession. Nevertheless, she had half promised Gregory that she would be his wife— and he, being wiser than she, was importuning her to marry him secretly in Rome. He at least knew that her parents would object to him as a son-in-law.

Now Gregory was not unlike other young men of his age and propensities. He had not led the immaculate life that Virginia, in her innocence, attributed to him. The awakening was very much of a shock to her.

He had induced his mother to stop off for a few days in Belgrave on the way down to Rome, explaining that he had business matters of importance to transact in the Serbian capital. It transpired, however, that a certain young and very attractive Italian singer was playing an engagement in Belgrade at that time. Virginia was not long in discovering the true nature of his business matters of importance. She was stunned, disillusioned, revolted.

And when she learned from Gregory's own mother that the singer had been his mistress for many months, her disgust and mortification were complete. She hated Gregory and she despised all princes! For, she argued to herself, they were *all* cut to the same pattern—at least, all that she had ever heard discussed by tactless ladies of the Court.

Without saying a word to the Countess about her intentions, she boarded a train for Vienna, accompanied by her maid, who had surreptitiously packed a few bags for the hurried flight. She left a letter for the Countess, explaining her action and requesting her to forward her trunks to Serros.

Traveling northward from Belgrade, she reached Buda Pesth on the day of the revolution. She could go no farther. Train service was disrupted and travel by any form of conveyance was practically impossible. Virginia bethought herself of a Hungarian Countess who had visited at the Court of Dawsbergen on several occasions prior to the war, and announced to her maid that they would both set forth in quest of this lady, who was known to reside in a fashionable part of the city.

The maid was a native of Buda Pesth. Her parents, she said, lived in one of the river streets. She suggested that they first seek their house for refuge, the city being then in a state of riotous turmoil. She conducted the frightened princess to a rather pretentious looking house down by the river, and there Virginia remained for nearly a month, virtually a prisoner. The treacherous maid had delivered her into the hands of a couple with whom she had lived in service before going to Serros, a broken-down sportsman and his wife, whose reputations had never been any too good and were fast becoming worse. Like others who fall from comparatively high places, they had not attempted to regain the lost position. On the contrary, they were content to sink below the surface into what may be described as an upper-class underworld. For years they had lived by blackmail.

But it was not they who conceived the idea of profiting by the temporary misfortune of the young Princess Virginia. To their former maid-servant belonged most of the credit. She showed them the light and they were soon basking in it. Ransom, heavy ransom from the golden coffers of Dawsbergen—that was her original idea. Failing in this, the sale of the lovely young Princess to the highest bidder!

Virginia was in ignorance of the plot for many days. She believed the stories they told her of vain efforts to communicate with her father by telegraph or post. The letters she wrote were never posted, nor were her telegrams sent. She believed them when they said that if she ventured from the house she would be seized by the "communist devils" and—well, they did not leave anything to her imagination. Particularly did they impress upon her the fate that would befall her if it ever became known to the rabble that she was of royal birth. And terrible would be the price that her protectors would have to pay if it were discovered that they sheltered a princess! That was the excuse they gave for taking away all of her own garments and supplying her with dresses which they declared to be from the wardrobe of a niece.

Meanwhile, the whole of Europe was being combed by

the cleverest men in the Secret Service of Dawsbergen
and Graustark, aided by the police departments of every
city in that section of the continent. In Buda Pesth and
other Hungarian cities controlled by the Bela Kun government search was practically impossible, owing to the
prevailing conditions. If the authorities in those cities
were aware of the efforts being made to find the missing
girl, they paid no heed to them nor did they allow the
news to be published in the press. The royal houses
of Dawsbergen and Graustark—and even of Axphain in
those days—were not only in disfavor with the Red government but the people of those principalities were still
looked upon as enemies. The conspirators bided their
time. They could afford to wait until the searchers were
ready to give up the task as hopeless. When all hope was
lost, then would be their time to move. One hundred
thousand gavvos was to be their price.

Virginia seldom left her room, except at mealtime. She
preferred solitude to the companionship of such visitors
as occasionally appeared at the home of the Braggas.
One man in particular she disliked; a bold-eyed, insolent
fellow whose name was Spreck. Sometimes frightened,
nervous young girls came there with men old enough to
be their fathers, but who, it appeared, were their husbands.

Then came a night when she happened to overhear
a conversation between the man Spreck and the two
Braggas. They addressed him as "Count." What she
heard of that conversation from the top of the dark stairway filled her with terror. They were talking about her.
She stole up to her room and bolted the door. Now she

knew the meaning of the screams she had heard more than once in that house. The next morning, long before the household was astir, she crept downstairs and escaped into the street by means of a window.

Somehow she succeeded, hours afterwards, in finding the home of the Countess to whom she originally had decided to appeal for help. The palace itself was closed but the lodgekeeper and his wife took her into their cottage and made her comfortable. The Countess and her family had fled at the beginning of the revolution and were now in Bucharest. Virginia remained hidden in the lodge for several days, and it was only when the aged servitor brought the news that the Braggas had been thrown into prison that she plucked up the courage to venture into the streets. At the old man's suggestion she posed as their niece, Rosa Schmitz, and it was he who earnestly advised her not to reveal her identity nor to attempt to communicate with the Castle at Serros. Through a friend he learned of the kindly offices of certain Americans and after long deliberation went timorously to Ethelbert Higbee to solicit his aid in getting Virginia out of Hungary. In course of time—a fortnight, more or less—the strange marriage of Pendennis Yorke and Rosa Schmitz took place, and thereby hangs the tale that is now approaching its end.

CHAPTER XVI

THE third night after her safe return to Edelweiss Castle, Virginia sat in the presence of a very distinguished company and calmly announced her intention to become the wife of Pendennis Yorke.

In that company were her father and mother, her sister and Prince Robin, the venerable Duchess of Halfont, the Prime Minister of Graustark and his wife, Baron Gourou and the Minister of War, the latter having arrived that day from Ganlook to report that an armistice had been signed and that the Monarchists, with the new Prince Gregory at their head, were in power again in the unhappy principality of Axphain.

It was while they were at dinner that Count Quinnox casually remarked that he had ordered Pendennis Yorke into hospital at Ganlook. He was threatened with pneumonia. It appears that he had turned up with a heavy cold at Arlak; he was in rather a serious condition when he returned to Ganlook in order to be present at the armistice meeting.

At least two pairs of eyes were focussed upon Virginia as the Count made the announcement. She caught her breath, paled, and instantly leaned forward to fix the War Minister with wide, anxious eyes.

"Oh, Count Quinnox," she cried, "do you really think it is serious?"

"The doctors were not sure when I left, Princess. They could only say that there was danger of pneumonia. I did not see him myself."

"I hope they are mistaken," said Virginia's mother, gravely. "It would be terrible if he were to—"

Prince Dantan interrupted her. He had been watching Virginia's face.

"We must send doctors and nurses up to Ganlook at once, Quinnox," he said. "The best in Edelweiss, Robin. We owe him more than we can ever repay. If it is possible to prevent pneumonia, we—"

Virginia straightened up in her chair, the light of unalterable decision in her eyes.

"I shall go to Ganlook to-morrow," she announced. "To-night if it is possible, Count Quinnox."

"Virginia!" exclaimed her mother.

"He caught this cold looking after me, mother. He was out in the rain, he was shivering, he gave me the blanket and sat up in . . . Anyhow, I shall go to him. That's settled. I shall nurse him—oh, you needn't smile, Bev. I did my share of nursing during the war and I've been fairly useful around the hospital these past two weeks. Is there a train going up to-night, Count Quinnox?"

"But, my darling, we—we've just got you back . . ." began Princess Beverly, agitatedly.

"If you think I am going to let him die up there in Ganlook for want of proper nursing, you don't know me, mother."

"But, my dear," protested her father, "there will be competent nurses there to look after him, and all the doctors in town if they are needed. He will have the best of care. You would only be in the way . . ."

"My place is with my husband," said Virginia, calmly and distinctly.

There was an amazed silence. Even the servants stood as if petrified.

"Your husband?" finally fell from the lips of her mother.

"Oh, I say, Virgie!" exclaimed Prince Robin. "That's all tommy-rot, you know."

She flashed a scornful look at him. "I thought you were my friend, Robin."

"Good heavens, of course I am. But I'm hanged if I'll allow you to make any such statement as that—especially when I happen to know that Pendennis Yorke doesn't consider himself your husband. He's no fool, you know."

"Well, then," began Virginia, taking the plunge, "you force me to announce that he is going to be my husband. And so far as the law is concerned—if Justice Mavorak knows his A B C's *about* the law—he is already my husband. I think we're all agreed on that. Even you, father. I am sorry, mother, if—if you are shocked. I wouldn't hurt you for anything in all this world. But the truth is, I love him. We need not go into that now, however. I will tell you all about it, mother darling, when we are alone. Oh, goodness! you're not going to cry, are you, dearest?"

"Cry?" exclaimed her mother. "Of course I am not going to cry. I cried for two whole days and nights over you and it's time I had a good laugh."

"You may laugh at me as much as you please—all of you—but you'll see! I am perfectly calm and I wish all the rest of you were. I did not mean to speak about this to-night. I—I simply couldn't help it, that's all. It came out before I knew what I was saying." She stiffened perceptibly. "I think we would better drop the subject until we are in a position to talk it over in—in private."

"I see no reason why we should not discuss the situation now," said the old Duchess of Halfont, speaking for the first time. Her eyes were twinkling. "We are all interested, we are all more or less in the family, and I submit that now is as good a time to thresh the matter out as any other. Permit me to remind you, Virginia dear, that you will need support in your conflict with authority. So you would better be nice to me if you want me to stand behind you. I do not know this young man of yours, but I must say that I like the looks of him. Naturally I should prefer to see you married to some one of your own station in life, but so far as I am able to ascertain there isn't a prince or a duke or even a count of the proper generation who amounts to a pinch of salt. If I had a daughter I'd sooner see her married to an American any day than to one of these lollipop libertines we have—"

"My dear Duchess," broke in Prince Dantan, hastily; "don't you think we ought to wait until the servants have left the room?"

"My dear Dantan, experience has taught me that the less servants hear the more they talk, and the more they hear the less they talk. I daresay it's human nature. These servants were in the castle doing precisely what they are doing now—waiting on table—before Prince

Robin was born, and that's thirty odd years ago. They've been in the family longer than he has. I think we can trust them to be quite as discreet as the rest of us. Now, Virginia, my dear, speak up plainly and a little louder, please. I can't hear you unless you do. You say you are going to marry this young man, whether or no?"

"I am," replied Virginia, bright spots in her cheeks. "And thank you, Duchess, for—for sticking up for me."

"Umph!" grunted Prince Dantan, frowning. "She's been sticking up for the servants too."

"What I should like to ask before we go any farther," said Virginia, sweeping the group with a calm and superior gaze, "is this: Is there any one here who has ever been in love?"

Eight backs stiffened a little as eight persons sat up very abruptly and gasped. Baron Gourou, alone, slumped a little deeper into his chair. He was a bachelor.

"Great Scott!" ejaculated Prince Robin.

"That's a polite little question to ask, Virginia," cried her sister Bevra, staring.

"Well—*has* any one here ever been in love?" repeated Virginia.

"Don't be silly, Virginia Louise," said her mother sharply. "Of course, everybody here has been in love —and you know it. Aren't we all married—all except you, I mean?"

"And I suppose every single one of you—male and female—married for love? Don't answer! We'll take it for granted. Well, now, will somebody tell me why I shouldn't marry the person I love—just the same as all the rest of you have done?"

"My dear Princess," said the Prime Minister, on whose forehead a little moisture had suddenly appeared; "don't look at me as if I were the only one guilty of marrying for love. I fancy the same thing happened to your parents and to your sister and Prince Robin, and—er—in the same way that it happened to me. Ahem!"

He laughed but did not look at his wife. If he had done so he would have noticed the faint, sardonic smile on her lips. A little later on he found the opportunity to use his handkerchief on his forehead when no one was looking in his direction—that is, no one save his wife, who knew of at least two persons in the room who had not married for love.

"See here, Virginia," said Prince Dantan, bluntly; "do you mean to tell me that you will marry this man Yorke against my wishes—and your mother's?"

"I wish you wouldn't speak of him as 'this man Yorke,' " she complained. "What has he done to deserve being spoken of as 'this man Yorke'?"

"Your rebuke is just," said her father, promptly. "I am sorry, Virginia. It shan't happen again. Now, will you answer my question?"

"I do not intend to marry him without your approval," said she, composedly. "I expect to marry him *with* your approval."

"Bless my soul!"

"This is what you get, Dantan, for marrying an American yourself," observed the Duchess of Halfont, drily. "You can't blame Virginia for having a little spunk and independence."

"And as for mother," pursued Virginia, with a loving

glance at Princess Beverly, who was biting her lip;
"I am absolutely sure that she wants me to be happy—
to be as happy as Bevra is, and that's saying a great
deal."

"Stick to the point! Bevra did not marry against our
wishes. She—"

"No, but she married the man she was in love with
and wanted to marry, didn't she?"

"Oh, I say, Virgie, this is getting a bit—er—embarrassing," put in Prince Robin. "Leave Bevra and me
out of it."

"There's no sense blushing, Robin, as if you'd done
something you were ashamed of," said Virginia, scornfully.

"Really," began Bevra, visibly confused; "I don't think
this is the time or the place to discuss Virginia's affairs,
father. What must our friends think . . ."

"I assure you, Princess," interrupted Count Quinnox,
raising his hand and smiling; "we are all profoundly interested in Princess Virginia's affairs. As a matter of
fact, we have seen this complication coming and I rather
fancy we have discussed it from all angles—ah—behind
closed doors, so to speak. I submit it would not be fair
to leave such good friends and such loyal ones out in
the cold. If I may be pardoned for my impertinence,
permit me to remind you that you would not hesitate
to discuss the problem in the presence of these old and
trusted servants. Pray do not forget that the Prime
Minister and I are among your oldest and most devoted
servants."

"Nicely put, Quinnox," cried the Duchess. "The War

Department having spoken with military candor and the usual lack of diplomacy, let us now have the crafty, ambiguous opinion of the Department of State."

The Prime Minister cleared his throat. "I fear, your grace," he said, with mock gravity, "that I should be guilty of the most heinous infraction of etiquette if I were to interfere in a matter which so obviously belongs to the Department of Foreign Relations."

"Evidently this is a matter that cannot be settled by diplomacy," said the sprightly old lady. "So let's see what the police can do about it. Do you know of any good reason, Baron Gourou, why Mr. Pendennis Yorke shouldn't be admitted to our constantly increasing colony of American husbands and wives?"

Even Prince Dantan smiled at this.

"I must refer you to Mr. Yorke's father-in-law, your grace," said the Baron. "He is better qualified to answer your question."

"Well, then, Dantan, what's wrong with the young man? You've been looking him up pretty thoroughly ever since he got into your family by accident. What's wrong with him?"

"Why—er—as a matter of fact, Duchess, there isn't anything wrong with him. That isn't the point, however. We—"

"Have you any one else in mind for Virginia?" interrupted the old lady, remorselessly. "I mean, any decent, clean-blooded chap whose children would be as perfect as yours? Have you got anybody in mind that can make Virginia as happy as you have been yourself with your own American? And what is more to the point, do you know of any one you'd rather see her married to than the man she is in love with?"

"But, Duchess," cried Beverly, plaintively, "how do we know that Pendennis Yorke is in love with Virginia?"

"I can answer that question," said Prince Robin. "He's heels over head in love with her. Told me so himself, weeks ago."

Virginia's eyes popped wide-open. "He did?"

"He certainly did. The day I met him."

"Oh!" gasped Virginia, faintly.

"And I can tell you something else," cried Bevra warmly. "If I weren't married to Robin, I'd fall in love with him myself."

"Bevvy!" cried her mother.

"That being the case," said the Duchess composedly; "I should say that the best thing that could happen would be for Virginia to marry him and take him off to the Wild West, if only for the sake of Robin's peace of mind."

"The Wild West," mused Baron Gourou, aloud. "It isn't a circumstance to the Wild East. I've read several novels of the Wild West lately and—but no matter. Yorke lent them to me. Ahem! I would recommend them to you, Prince Dantan. They are excellent reading."

"You haven't answered my question, Count Quinnox," said Virginia, abruptly. "Is there a train going up to Ganlook to-night?"

"No, Princess. There's one early in the morning. I—"

"See here, Virginia, I cannot permit you to go to Ganlook on this mad—" began Prince Dantan, sternly.

"One moment, father—please. You did not give your

permission for me to go to Russia with Michael Rodkin, and there is where I would be at this moment if it hadn't been for Pendennis Yorke."

"Don't speak of it, Virginia," cried her mother, blanching a little. "I turn cold all over when I think of what might have happened to you. We *do* owe Mr. Yorke a great deal—more than we can ever repay, as you have said, Dantan. The least we can do is to let Virginia go to Ganlook and—and do what she can to . . . She will be quite safe there, won't she, Count Quinnox? The fighting is over, isn't it?"

"As safe as anywhere on earth," said the Minister of War, and had as his reward a smile from Virginia so dazzling that for an appreciable moment his gallant old head swam.

"But, hang it all," blurted out the harassed father of Virginia, "he may have nothing worse than a cold in his head. A pretty fool you'd be making of yourself, Virginia, if you went up there to nurse him and had to sit around all day listening to him blow his nose."

He did not mean to be funny—indeed, he was most serious—and his royal dignity suffered considerably from the roar of laughter that went up from the table. He got quite red in the face as he essayed to join in the laugh at his expense. Whereupon the watchful Virginia, detecting the sign of distress, sprang up from her chair and rushed around to throw her arms about his neck. Putting her lips close to his ear, she whispered something that caused him, after a brief mental struggle, to pat her hand tenderly while he went on to say in the gruffest voice he could command:

"Now, now, my dear! It won't work this time. You've bamboozled me for twenty-odd years, but—eh?"

She was whispering again.

"That's all very well and very sweet of you, my dear, but—Beverly, I wish you had paid a little more attention to this child's bringing up. It is most unmannerly to whisper in—in company."

"Virginia Louise! Stop annoying your father," reprimanded her mother. "Come back here and sit down, young lady—this minute! Did you hear me? Don't you know any better than to whisper in company? Ah! Now see what you've done! You've got him blowing his own nose."

"I think," remarked the Duchess, as Virginia resumed her seat, "that this would be a good time to drink the health of Mr. Pendennis Yorke. By the way, before I forget it, does Mr. Yorke know that he is going to be married? That's important. The last I heard of him— up to this evening—he was on the point of being divorced."

"There isn't going to be any divorce," announced Virginia calmly.

"That's the first sensible thing you've said to-night, Virgie," cried her sister.

"We will assume, for sake of argument, that this man— I mean to say, Mr. Yorke—believes that he is going to be married," said Prince Dantan, patiently. "And we will take it for granted that there is to be no divorce. Will you be good enough, Virginia, to let us hear just what plans you and Mr. Yorke have made for the future?"

"We haven't really had time to discuss our plans," admitted Virginia. "We were too excited—and I was so frightfully tired and nervous—you see. Naturally, father, I shall leave it entirely to your judgment as to whether we are to be married all over again at Shenzarm Castle, with all the pomp and fuss of a state ceremony, or whether we shall just simply—"

"I should never consider you married at all unless the ceremony took place at the Castle," cried her mother, indignantly.

"That isn't what I am trying to get at," said Prince Dantan. "What I want to know is this: does Mr. Yorke expect to take you to America to live and do you, by any chance, realize what you are giving up if you become the wife of a man, no matter how worthy he may be, who—"

"I cannot answer any of those questions at present, father," interrupted Virginia; "because I don't know what Mr. Yorke's ideas are on the subject. But no matter where he lives, so shall I—no matter how. If it will set your mind at rest, however, I will say this much—and this is as far as we've really gone in discussing the future. Pendennis, first of all, proposes to ask you and mother for your consent to our marriage. He's terribly stubborn on that point. My own consent, it seems, isn't sufficient."

"Ahem! Well, at any rate, he's got a level head on his shoulders. And supposing we refuse to give our consent —what then?"

"What's the use, daddy, crossing a bridge before you

come to it? Besides, you will not refuse to give your consent. I told him not to worry about that."

"Bless my soul!"

"Don't you realize, Virginia dear, that it will mean your leaving us forever?" cried her mother. "You will go away from Dawsbergen and all that has been dear to you. You will be giving up your—" She hesitated.

"If you mean I will have to give up being a princess— why, that doesn't mean anything at all to me, mummy. I am rather fed up with being a princess anyway. I'd like to know what a royal princess gets out of life. I realize that Bevra and I are more fortunate than most princesses, because our parents really love us. That isn't true in most cases. Princesses are just things to be traded in between nations. Nobody ever stops to consider their happiness."

"How can you say such a thing?" cried her mother.

"She speaks the truth," said the Duchess, somewhat sententiously.

Here Robin spoke up, a faraway look in his eyes. "I remember very distinctly hearing that my wife's parents began making plans when she was two days old to marry her off to a boy who was then only three or four months old. I happen to have been that boy. Great Scott, you wouldn't call that giving Bevra a fair chance, would you, sir?"

"Are you all against me?" groaned Prince Dantan.

"Every last one of us," announced the Duchess.

"I do not know Mr. Yorke," lamented Princess Beverly. "I shall have to see him and talk with him and decide for myself whether I am willing to give Virginia's whole life into his keeping."

Prince Dantan raised his hand and spoke with the finality of an emperor issuing a decree.

"The wedding will take place at Shenzarm Castle in June, my friends—provided, of course, Mr. Yorke does us the honor to ask the hand of our daughter in marriage. I am satisfied—as you will be, my dear Beverly—that Virginia's happiness will be safe with him. Virginia is right. And so is Bevra, who last night declared truthfully if inelegantly that the prince—ah, I don't quite recall the expression she . . ."

"The prince business is on the blink is what she said in the bosom of the family," supplied Robin.

"That a child of mine should ever use—but never mind, it can't be helped. We arrived at our conclusion last evening after discussing the matter with Prince Robin and Bevra. Nothing remains to be said at present except to call attention to the significant fact that no voice has been raised among you, my old and trusted friends, against Pendennis Yorke. If there was the slightest doubt in the minds of any of you regarding him, I am sure you would have expressed it openly. However, I am bound to say that our combined protests would most likely have made no impression on this headstrong young half-breed who is named after one of the first states to renounce allegiance to the parent nation and to defy a far greater ruler than I. Please keep your seat, Virginia! Don't come around here and interrupt me by whispering nonsense—"

"I am not going to whisper it!" cried Virginia, joy-ously. "You are the most wonderful old darling in all this world!"

"Ahem! As I was saying—er—where was I? Oh, yes. Permit me, your grace, as Mr. Yorke's prospective father-in-law—in fact, as his present somewhat anomalous father-in-law—to be the one to propose the health of the latest American to come to the rescue of the rapidly deteriorating houses of Graustark and Dawsbergen—Pendennis Yorke, ladies and gentlemen."

A little later on, the Duchess, speaking with a solemn note in her voice, uttered these words:

"Civilization, my friends, goes forever toward the West. The strength of the world that used to be ours continues to slip away from us toward the setting sun. We call ourselves the east. And yet we look longingly toward the sun as it goes down, for off there lies a new world. The sun is always traveling away from us, and it is taking the thoughts of our young with it on its ceaseless journeys. In our mind's eye we see the sun coming to rest for the night—in the land called America. Always to the West of us! And here we have sat for centuries, gloating because we cannot conceive of ourselves as being anywhere except east of the setting sun! Simpletons!"

CHAPTER XVII

"I COULD HAVE TOLD YOU SO"

WHEN he left London in February, Pendennis Yorke promised himself that he would be back in England by the first of May. He was in a Ganlook hospital on that day and for many days thereafter. The month was more than half gone before the doctors would consent to his removal to Edelweiss Castle where his first weeks of convalescence were to be spent at the urgent demand of Prince Robin.

He had had a close call. There was a night when the doctors declared he could not live till morning. The sinister opinion, based perhaps on experience and observation, that "strong men are the weakest when it comes to a fight with pneumonia," was voiced with sickening frequency during the period when Death fondled its intended victim with icy fingers and waited for the surrender. But life was stronger than death in the fight that was waged over the prostrate form of Pendennis Yorke. Death drew back to wait for another day. Time was its ally.

Late one afternoon well toward the end of May, Yorke sat in a corner of the balcony overlooking the parade ground which faced the Castle. The day was warm and sunny; there was a drowsy whisper in the breeze, a lazy caress to the shade that fell upon him from the lofty Tower at his back. Down at the edge of the parade ground Captain Sambo was reconstructing the "house that Jack built" under the arbitrary supervision of young Prince Dantan, ably bothered by three-year-old Princess Yetive. Two nurses stood by, waiting to shoo the children off to supper and to bed.

Graustark's hospitality was being taxed in a most unusual manner in behalf of the rapidly recuperating American. Fresh air and sunshine were what he needed, and there was an abundance of both. But, it appears, he was so far behind in his work that he was obliged to spend several hours out of each glorious day "pegging away" at his typewriter in the close seclusion of a room that had been set apart for his use in the Tower. There is no recorded instance of a modern, clattering typewriter ever having made its appearance on the balcony up to the 23rd of May, just past. But now, in an obscure niche at the corner of the extensive, pillared gallery an outdoor "office" had been established by Prince Robin for the industrious Mr. Yorke, who, it appears, had regular hours and who was not to be disturbed by man, woman or child. This, maintained Mr. Yorke, was treating the poor working man in a most princely fashion; and here, under pressure, he was conscientiously making up for lost time.

On this particular afternoon, however, he dawdled. The faithful typewriter, perched somewhat rakishly on a jog in the stone balustrade, was idle for long stretches at a time. There were occasional fits of activity, but they were short, spasmodic and, sad to relate, wasted. His thoughts were following his eyes—and his eyes were following Virginia, who was playing tennis with Robin and Bevra and a young nobleman from Serros. The courts, over against the ramparts, were some distance from the Castle but in plain view from his position.

On the little lacquered table beside his chair—which, by the way, was not a chair conducive to hard labor, being one of those contraptions with an adjustable back —on this table, held down by an empty flagon was a cablegram from his Aunt Belle, in far off Montana. It was a hasty response to the long letter he had sent to her from the hospital, and this is what the dear old lady said to him through thousands of miles of sea and air:

"I knew Rosa would turn out to be a princess. It sounds like a fairy story, and I love fairy stories. Uncle George joins me in best love but says you ought to give up roving now and settle down on our ranch out here in the Wild West where everything is peaceful. The only danger we have out here on the plains now is being run over by automobiles or getting elected to Congress. Letter following. Lovingly, Aunt Belle."

He was waiting to show Virginia the cablegram. The smile that had welcomed this characteristic message from the beloved old lady still lurked in his eyes and upon his lips as he dreamily watched the graceful, spirited girl who had turned out to be a princess. He was pleasantly idle now because he could not write and watch for the frequent wave of the racket which indicated that her mind was not entirely on the game she was playing—and it would have been grossly impolite of him not to wave his hand in reply.

Give up roving? When Virginia wanted to see the

world and was willing to rove with him to the farthermost reaches of it? When she was willing to be poor with him and to live in queer places? And while they were both too young to settle down anywhere, least of all on a ranch out in— Ah, but there was something alluring about the prospect of loafing for a year or so with her in the tame, peaceful security of the Wild West! After that— the wide world again.

He had watched the roses come back to her cheeks and the glow into eyes that had been filled with anxious shadows for so many days. She had been wonderful, magnificent.

(Candor compels the chronicler to report that Virginia's devotion and her untiring energy during the month she spent in the hospital at Ganlook sometimes caused the doctors and the professional nurses to wish that she—but then that is always the way with jealous professional nurses.)

He, however, was convinced that his recovery was due entirely to her ministrations. The doctors had nothing to do with it—nothing at all. Nature had nothing to do with it, either. She did it all! And now he was as fit as a fiddle, able to ride horseback, play golf, romp with the "kiddies," eat three prodigious meals a day and still be hungry—and he was filling out his clothes again with alarming rapidity. He liked being doctored and nursed and scolded by princesses! He liked everything in life. There was nothing wrong with life, nothing wrong with the world. The only thing that ever could be said against the good old world was the way it allowed the human race to abuse it.

She was leaving the next day for Shenzarm Castle in Serros, accompanied by her sister, the children and a retinue of maids, nurses and guardsmen. He was to follow in three weeks. The wedding in the chapel at Shenzarm was to be a quiet affair. That is to say, it was going to be what royalty considered a quiet, unostentatious affair—with nobody present except the family and a few hundred of the nobility from both principalities!

His future mother-in-law had promised Yorke that it would be as simple as all that. She had taken a great fancy to him; a liking which was enhanced by the discovery that his mother was related—rather distantly, it is true—to Robert Buchanan Merriweather, of South Carolina, whose grand-daughter, Polly Louise Prichard, had married Braxton Calhoun, a cousin of her (Beverly's) own father. Prince Dantan, on hearing of this, quaintly informed Pendennis that the last glimmer of doubt as to his fitness to become the husband of Virginia had been completely wiped out by the important disclosure; anybody who was related to the Merriweathers and the Calhouns, no matter how circumstantially, ranked about as high in his wife's estimation as any nabob in Europe— much higher, in fact, than some of the minor sovereigns with whom she had come in contact.

Higbee was coming out from Paris to be his best man— good old Higbee who had "stood up" with him, so to speak, at his first marriage. Princess Beverly had remonstrated a little at first, being rather dubious as to Higbee's own conjugal integrity. Wasn't he a bigamist, ten times over, by his own confession?

"You are frightfully old-fashioned, mother," Virginia

had said. "I think it would be thrilling to have a nice bigamist like Mr. Higbee for Denny's best man. It isn't every bride who can say that her husband's best man· was a hero with ten or twelve wives to his credit and not a single honest-to-goodness divorce."

"He deserves a Distinguished Service Medal," was Robin's comment.

The tennis game was over. Pendennis scrambled his papers together, put the tankard on them as a weight, and hurried out to meet the returning players. Captain Sambo joined him on the parade ground. A squad of guardsmen trotted across the upper end of the plaza on their way to the barracks, the hoofs of the horses beating a thunderous roll on the graveled surface. Both men glanced at their watches. Six o'clock. Yorke sighed. That same squad of dragoons would be escorting the princess to the railway station in precisely fourteen hours.

Virginia, flushed, radiant and breathing rapidly from the exercise, thrust her arm through Yorke's as the two parties met.

"You must not walk so fast, Denny," she said. "It isn't good for your heart."

"His heart's all right," panted Robin. "I can see it in his eyes. Gosh, Denny, she's starting mothering you already. If you let her have her way, old top, you won't be over that attack of pneumonia for ten years. They're terrible if you let 'em get the jump on you."

"You hustle in and get out of that wet shirt, Robin," commanded his wife. "You're dripping! I don't want you coming down with pneumonia."

Pendennis and Virginia fell behind the others, sauntering slowly. They purposely took the longest way up to
the Castle, veering off in the direction of the formal
gardens which spread out from either end of the terrace.
Several gardeners, in green smocks, were just completing
the day's work among the vast pansy beds.

A shadow clouded Yorke's eyes. In speaking of to-
morrow's parting, she had wondered—and there was a
little catch in her voice—whether she would ever see these
beautiful gardens again.

"You are giving up a great deal for me, Virginia," he
said soberly. "All this"—with a gesture—"and everything that goes with it. You belong in this little separate
world."

"Last night I had a queer thought about all this,
Denny. It seemed somehow to solve the whole problem.
You are right when you say that I belong in a little
separate world. But have you ever stopped to think that
if I were to die to-night I should go out of this tight little
world into a limitless world? The thought that came to
me was this—I don't mind confessing I had been thinking of what I am about to give up, Denny dear, when I
go away with you—the thought was this, and it was really
such a sensible one. I shall have to go out of it one day
anyhow—all alone. It makes me shudder to think of
going out simply because I am dead. Why, therefore,
should I grumble about going out of it while I am alive?
And when I suddenly realized that I would not be all
alone, that I would not be going out into darkness when
I left it with you, I—why, I was so happy I—" She
pressed his arm very tightly to her side.

His hand closed over hers. "You darling! What profound logic." He laughed softly.

"And then I went farther. If I were not to go out of —of all this—until I died of old age, why, I shouldn't be able to ever come back again. While if I go out when I am still young and awfully alive I can come back whenever I feel like it—for a visit, of course—and—well, don't you see what I mean?"

"Perfectly! In plain words, you think it would be much nicer to go out with me alive than to go out dead all by yourself."

"Don't laugh, Denny—please. It may have sounded very silly and very funny to you—I suppose it did—but I am serious."

"I am sorry, dearest. I know how serious it all is to you. I laughed because I thought I was saying something funny—and it wasn't funny at all. You will have to get used to us Americans laughing at the things we think are witty, especially when we say them ourselves. I knew a chap in the Navy who had both his legs blown off by an explosion. Just before he passed out he whispered: 'I hope God gives me a strong pair of wings. I'll need 'em.' And we who stood around, being Americans, laughed because we believed we were gratifying a dying wish. He wanted us to laugh."

"How dreadful! But how brave he was!"

"On the contrary, dearest, he was *bragging*—if you see what I mean."

They were both silent for a moment, watching the men gathering up their implements.

"I've said it a dozen times to you, sweetheart," he

began, the cloud returning to his eyes, "and here I am saying it again. We will be poor, Virginia. That is what I meant when I said you were giving up a lot for me."

She smiled up into his eyes. "People who live in castles are not always rich, Denny. Kings and princes are sometimes paupers and live on the bounty of their subjects. Goodness!" she broke off to cry in her old sprightly manner: "If you could hear father complain about the high cost of bringing up daughters, you'd soon realize how poor the people are who live in Shenzarm Castle. By the way, just to show you how thrifty I propose to be after we are married, I shall make use of a horribly cheap old traveling bag on our wedding journey. We can save a little money in that way because the dear old thing already has my name painted on it—'Mrs. Pendennis Yorke, U.S.A.' I don't mind if you laugh now, Denny, because that *will* be funny, won't it?"

His hand tightened upon hers. "And I shall be thrifty too, Virginia," he said softly. "I shall make the same old dream last as long as I live."

A man and a boy crossed their path, pausing for a moment to bow very low.

"Hello!" exclaimed Pendennis, staring. "Is that you, Sharpe?"

Virginia answered for the man whose thin lips were shaping themselves into an amused smile.

"Yes, but not the Sharpe who used to dress you and give you your tub, Mr. Yorke," she cried, merrily. "Since you saw him last he has gone up in the world, haven't you, Mr. Hobbs?"

"Hobbs?"

"Yes, sir—Hobbs," spoke up the beaming ex-valet. "Sharpe by nature but not by name, if you see what I mean."

"Mr. Hobbs is now First Deputy Commander of the Tower and Chief of the Secret Service of Graustark," explained Virginia. "You didn't know that you were being brushed and combed and polished by the great Mr. Hobbs, did you, Denny?"

"Oh, your Highness, I—" began the embarrassed Mr. Hobbs. The boy beside him was grinning.

"And this is Mr. Hobbs' son—the gardener's boy," went on the Princess.

"I remember him perfectly," said Yorke. "The gardenia ambassador."

"The same, sir," said Mr. Hobbs. "You see, Mr. Yorke, I was for a great many years Prince Robin's man. Ahem! As a matter of fact, if I may be pardoned for saying it, I sort of brought him up, in a manner of speaking. Perhaps you may have heard of me. I was the man from Cook's in Edelweiss a number of years back. Prince Robin took me in as a sort of valet when he was only seven years old. He has seen fit to dismiss me from a number of situations in the course of twenty-five years, but he has always been kind enough to see that I stepped into another one almost—ahem—immediately."

"You are very modest, Mr. Hobbs," said Virginia. "He developed into a second Sherlock Holmes, Mr. Yorke—and now he is second only in importance to the great Baron Gourou."

Yorke advanced and held out his hand.

"Put it there, Sharpe," he said, warmly. "I've missed

you terribly. I knew you were on Gourou's staff, but I never suspected that you were Hobbs, the man who unearthed Graustark for Cook's. But where have you been for the past two months and what have you been doing as Sherlock the Second?"

"Well, sir," replied Hobbs, obsequiously, "at present I am 'aving a bit of a vacation, so to speak—sort of watching the flowers grow in the garden." Then suddenly he divested himself of the manner of a servant. He spoke crisply, rather tersely, as to an equal. "I daresay Princess Virginia has already given you the latest news concerning Prince Hubert."

Virginia started. "Oh, dear me—I forgot to mention it. How funny! It slipped my mind entirely. You see, Mr. Yorke, we are so accustomed to hearing of the horrible things that happen to princes and grand dukes and even emperors that nothing surprises us any more. How stupid of me! I should have known that you would be interested."

"You don't mean to say—" began Yorke, looking hard at Mr. Hobbs.

"It's a way these Axphainians have," said Hobbs, as a brief preface. "Whenever they set out to do a housecleaning job they do it pretty thoroughly. You may remember, Mr. Yorke, that I did not report as usual on the morning of the 24th of March. You haven't seen me from that day to this. I was detailed by Baron Gourou to trail Prince Hubert. If we could by any hook or crook ascertain that he was actually responsible for the death of that miserable rascal who shot at you from a window across the plaza, Prince Robin was determined to make him pay the full penalty. To shorten the story, I followed him to Serros—where, you may be pleased to know, he met with such a chilly reception that he left almost immediately for Vienna. From there he went to Constantinople and then to Bucharest. Night before last he was assassinated. Shot down as he was leaving his hotel. The assassins—there were four or five men in the group that fell upon him—escaped. It is known, however, that they had been trailing him for several days and that they were from Axphain. As I said before, when the Axphainians start to clean house they do it to the queen's taste—perhaps I should say to the prince's taste. It is not for me to say that the new Prince of Axphain ordered this final bit of house-cleaning, but the fact remains that the former royal house of Axphain has been completely cleaned out—wiped out, you might say."

"I am sure Gregory would not have sanctioned the murder of Prince Hubert," said Virginia.

"Even so, Princess, young Gregory will go down in history as the founder of an absolutely new royal house of Axphain. There is not a trace left of the old one. The new broom has swept exceedingly clean. In any case, no matter who was back of the assassination of Hubert, the world is better off for the unwasted bullets." Turning to Yorke, he said: "May I be permitted to offer my congratulations, Mr. Yorke? I have already had the pleasure of felicitating the Princess." His eyes twinkled. "And I must ask you both to forgive me if you hear that I am going about saying to every one, 'I told you so,' because, you see, I *could* have told you so at the very beginning."

Late that evening, two shadowy, indistinct figures emerged from the gloom at the end of the great balcony and slowly moved into the soft radiance shed by the lighted windows of the castle.

"I *must* go in now, Denny dearest."

"But I shan't see you again like this for ages, sweetheart. You are—"

"Three weeks! And I waited five years to see you again!"

He drew her close. He could feel the throb of her heart against his breast. Her face was upturned, an arm stole up about his neck and drew his head down. And somehow, for one blissful moment, all the lights in the world went out.

THE END

www.ingramcontent.com/pod-product-compliance
Lightning Source LLC
Chambersburg PA
CBHW022148010726
47493CB00002B/396